becoming
PHOEBE

becoming
PHOEBE

a novel

J. MICHAEL NEAL

MELANCHOLY
DONKEY PRESS

Becoming Phoebe: A Novel
Copyright © 2016 by J. Michael Neal. All rights reserved.

This is a work of fiction. The portrayal of the game of hockey is as accurate as the author could make it, but all names, characters, places, and incidents are either products of the author's imagination or used fictitiously. No reference to any real person is intended or should be inferred.

Library of Congress Control Number: 2015921314

Cover photo © GoodMood Photo
Cover design by Brad Norr Design
Page design by Ann Delgehausen, Trio Bookworks

ISBN (print): 978-0-9970258-0-4
ISBN (ebook): 978-0-9970258-1-1

a **Trio Bookworks** *collaboration* | triobookworks.com

PART
1

This is my earliest memory. Despite what it says on my driver's license, I think of that day as my birthday even though it's wrong.

I'm walking down the street. I have no idea where I came from or where I'm going. I have a full Hello Kitty backpack and skates hanging around my neck. In memory they are big and heavy, though they couldn't really have been.

Finally someone stops me. Keeps me from walking into the street, really. A man. He asks me my name.

"Phoebe."

He kneels down next to me. "Phoebe what?" For some reason I always picture him wearing a fedora, but I'm pretty sure that's wrong.

"What?" I repeat back to him.

"What's your last name?"

"Phoebe. Just Phoebe."

"Everyone has a last name." His voice is gentle.

"I don't." I'd had no opinion about whether I had a last name before he asked, but now I am convinced that I don't have one and never had.

The man looks thoughtful. "Where are you going, Phoebe?"

That one stumps me. "I don't know."

"Where's your mother?"

"I don't know." I feel that it is something I should know. The memory fills with distress.

His expression becomes concerned. "Where do you live?"

"Ohio."

He nods. "Yes, this is Ohio. Where in Ohio do you live? Here in Dayton?"

That's when the roof begins to cave in on me. "Ohio." I start to cry. The adult me has a nagging feeling that some additional, vital piece of information is eluding me.

The man takes my hand. "Come with me. We'll find some help." He stops asking questions I can't answer. "How old are you, Phoebe?" We start walking.

"Four."

"You're awfully big for a four-year-old."

"I'm a big girl."

"You are. Those are nice skates. Are you going to be a figure skater?"

"I'm going to be a hockey player."

"Girls don't play hockey."

I take a deep breath and muster every ounce of patience I can manage. "I will."

We arrive at a police station, and he takes me to the desk sergeant. Such is my introduction to the authorities of Dayton, Ohio.

I don't remember the name of that man. I'm not even sure that's how it really happened.

I've been living in my past. Aside from a broken computer, memories are all that I have of my childhood. I shouldn't be looking through them. I've long since learned the lessons there, and all that's left is pain. When I'm happy I hardly think about the past at all.

CHAPTER 1

January 17, 2010

I locked the door and sat down with my back against it. My hands had begun trembling on the walk from the bus station to the apartment I'd found online before leaving Dayton.

It wasn't really an apartment—just a room with access to a shared bath and kitchen. My new home was 120 square feet, inefficiently laid out, a half mile from campus. Under the window was a ledge almost large enough to be a desk with no drawers. The paint was peeling, the floor was uneven, and there was a single, tiny closet. Rent was $450 a month. It didn't matter. The lock on the door meant that it was mine in a way that no living space ever had been.

Most of my possessions were in a locker I'd rented at the station. All I had with me was a backpack with a change of underwear, two computers, three books, a stuffed cat, and a sleeping bag. And my hockey bag. The last was heavy, but I had no intention of letting it out of my sight.

I was there; nothing else mattered. I'd been admitted to the university for the fall, but I planned to register for independent studies in the morning. More pressing was figuring out how to talk my way onto the hockey team. No one here had ever seen me play, and I needed to find a way to change that.

Still shaking, I unrolled the sleeping bag and then dug out my jersey and shoulder pads to make a pillow. My mood had risen, but not to happiness. It was relief: the feeling that a great weight had lifted from me sometime during the twenty-six-hour trip from Dayton to Minneapolis.

December 2009

I'm walking home from practice when John pulls up beside me. He rolls down the window. "Want a ride?"

It's the first time I've seen him in five months, and I smile. I can't help it. "Sure. Where are we going?"

He unlocks the back door so I can toss my bag in before joining him in the front.

"Does it matter?"

"Not really. I have to go home eventually anyway."

"How are things going?" I know that if I look over, his eyes will be filled with concern. I don't look.

"It's the Christmas season. Shouldn't you be wearing something other than black?"

"Phoebe . . ."

"What do you want me to say, John?" I snap. "It's going exactly like you'd expect. You're gone, so now I have no friends in school instead of just one. There still isn't anyone on my team that likes me. And I still have to go home."

"You don't have to go back there much longer."

"Hell, no. The ball will still be dropping in Times Square when I walk out of there. I have no idea where I'll go, but legally I'll be eighteen and no longer a ward of the state of Ohio. I'm never going to set foot in that house again."

I say it with too much vehemence, which only prompts him to ask again. "Will you please tell me what happened? Why . . ."

"No. I can't."

"Can't—or won't?"

"Can't. I've tried to tell you. I just can't do it."

"Will it be different once you leave?"

I sigh. "I don't know."

"I guess we'll find out in June. Or are you staying here for the summer?"

"Neither."

"What does that mean?"

"Not June. January," I say. "That's when I'm getting out of here. As soon as first semester is over I have enough credits to graduate. Finals end on the fourteenth. There's a game the next night, and for some reason I've decided to stay for it. A bus leaves for Chicago at seven the next morning, and I'm going to be on it. It will take me about two days to get all the way to Minneapolis."

We're both quiet for a moment.

"I can't wait to get out of this town," I said.

"You should ask my mother if you can stay with her after the first. I'm sure she'll say yes."

"Where would I sleep? You don't have a spare bedroom, and I don't fit on a couch."

"You can sleep in my room. I'm fine with that. I'd like it, in fact."

"When are you going back to New York?"

"On the second. One of us will have to sleep on the floor for one night."

I think about it for a moment. "I can live with that. Thank you."

"So have you figured out where we're going?"

"I'd be fine just driving around the block for four weeks."

I skated seven to ten hours a day that first week in Minneapolis, finding rinks with public skating that I could get to by bus. Most of them didn't allow sticks, and at one gorgeous rink in an old railway depot downtown they didn't want anyone doing anything but skating around in lazy circles.

My favorite was a sheet laid down outdoors in a park about three blocks from my room. It was smaller than a hockey rink, the ice was rough and uneven, and when I showed up early in the mornings, I learned quickly just how much colder it gets in Minnesota than it does in southern Ohio. In the chill emptiness, it was just me and the sound of skates on ice. At night it was almost like I was back at the rink in Vicksburg.

For ten days I did nothing but skate and decompress. I felt as if an unrelenting pressure had disappeared. Skating on that tiny rink, I finally understood what relaxation is.

I needed all the serenity I could get, because I still faced the task of trying to make a hockey team that had never heard of me. My first weekend on campus the Gopher women's hockey team was in Illinois, and I had no way to follow them. The next week they were back at Ridder Arena, playing Friday evening and Saturday afternoon. The booster club was holding a reception for the team after the second game, and I was going to be there, talking their coach into giving me a chance.

By that Wednesday I was already terrified.

January 30, 2010

I started watching that first game the way I always do: transfixed by the action. As it progressed, I spent more time studying the home bench. There was none of the tension that had always pervaded my previous team. Players laughed, coaches quietly instructed, and no one threatened to brain her teammates with her stick. It was almost unsettling.

When the game was over, I rushed up to the club room to be a part of the reception. I was too nervous to eat, but I grabbed a sandwich anyway because I couldn't afford to pass up free food.

When the program started, each of the seniors got up, and a guy asked them some questions. Then it got thrown open to the floor. Most of the questions asked came from other players and were designed to elicit good-natured embarrassment. I just sat there, fascinated by the camaraderie.

I approached Greg Long, the head coach, as things were breaking up. "I'm Phoebe Rose. I don't know if you remember me."

"You would be hard to forget. What can I do for you?"

"I was hoping you might give me a tryout." I was looking at the floor.

"Our roster is pretty full for next year."

"Even if all I can do is practice . . ."

"I don't think we have room for someone else."

I wished I lived in a world where I had a devastating reply. In this one, all I could muster was, "Okay. If something changes, please let me know."

I shuffled out of the room.

October 2002

Mr. Wilson picks me up after hockey practice. I push my equipment bag onto the backseat and then join him in the front.

"You look excited," he says.

"First practice of the season," I reply as I buckle myself in. But he's right. I am extra excited this year.

He knows why. "So was it as much fun as you were hoping it would be?"

"Well, we didn't do any real checking. We have to spend a few weeks learning how." I'd been pretty disappointed when they told us that.

"Good. My football coaches spent a lot of time teaching us how to tackle without getting hurt."

"That's what they said."

"Or hurting the other team too badly," he adds as he pulls the car out.

"I suppose."

Mr. Wilson chuckles very briefly. "I said too badly. It's okay to hurt them a little bit."

"I hope so. They all think I'm a girl."

"You are a girl."

"Yeah, but they think I play like one. They don't think I'm tough."

He laughs hard enough that he starts coughing.

"Are you okay?" I asked.

"Not really."

He never tries to hide from me how sick he is. I bite my lip but go on the way I know he wants me to. "I don't understand why. I'm almost the biggest one there."

"When they look at you, they don't really see you. They see a girl, and they have all sorts of preconceived notions about how girls play hockey. Because they don't see you as an individual, they don't see the ways that you are different."

"That's silly."

"Maybe, but that's what people do."

"I don't," I insist.

"Yes, you do," he says with a smile. "You do it less than most other people, but you still do it. We all do. Pay attention when you deal with people, and you'll see it happen."

I know he's wrong, but I need to do what he said. If I don't observe, I won't convince him. "You don't think I play like a girl."

"No, you play like Phoebe Rose. I know better than to think that you are like anyone else."

"I'm different."

"Yes, you are."

"I'm going to be the first girl to play in the NHL."

"Wasn't there a woman who played a few years ago?"

"That was just an exhibition game. I'm going to do it for real. Besides, she was a goalie. They're different."

"All right, then. I'll look forward to watching you there."

"I still want to hurt someone. Not too bad, but so that they know that I can."

March 2010

At the start of the semester I had registered for several independent study classes, hoping to clear out some of my distribution requirements. And I went to every home game, sitting as close to the team bench as I could. I elbowed a couple of eleven-year-olds out of their usual seats right at the tunnel. I needed the visibility more than they did.

It was clear to me that I could have made some of the visiting teams, but my dreams hadn't taken me to Illinois. The Gophers were not only one of the best teams in the country; they also played a high-tempo, speed-based game. I relied on size and positioning, so trying to keep up was going to cause me trouble. But no one was as big as some of the boys I'd played against in high school, and anytime I could leverage my strength I'd win the physical battles.

I felt a kinship with them. I'd been a huge fan of the Golden Gophers since I was nine, but this was different. It was an illusion, but I'd started to think of the team as "we," and I knew the players had begun to recognize me.

That solidarity made the end of the season more painful. We went into the NCAA tournament as the number-one team in the country and lost in the semifinals. The games were in New Hampshire, so I didn't get to watch, but it hurt.

With the season over I finally started tallying up who would be on the roster the next year and realized that, with an incoming freshman named Kennedy Kane, they had six defensemen. I could only hope they'd want an extra.

Most days I skated at Mariucci Arena, where the men's team played, mostly because I had to walk past Ridder to get there. Ridder had a concrete porch, and I'd look through the railing, staring through the glass doors. One day a voice right next to me surprised me. Startled, I banged my chin on the railing.

"You're here a lot." Abby Forrest, a freshman forward, stood there.

"I guess."

"You want to be on the team pretty badly."

Some things are so self-evident that there's no point in replying.

"If you were that good, someone would have recruited you." She had a burning look in her eyes that I'd seen during games. I later learned that it's a permanent feature.

I looked back at the arena. "No one knew I existed."

"That seems hard to believe."

"It's true."

"I just hate to see you wasting your time like this."

I pushed away from the railing and started to walk away. "It's only a waste of time if none of you ever find out whether I am that good."

December 2008

We're skating back to the bench after a whistle, and Stewie comments, "When I tap my stick on the ice, I'm open. Pass me the puck."

"I know what it's supposed to mean," I snarl. "The problem is that most of the times you do it, you aren't open, or there's someone in the passing lane."

"I'm open. Chad passes all the time."

"And I end up defending a two-on-one going the other way," I respond crossly as I swing my legs over the boards.

"Pass it to me, and I'll score."

Something snaps inside me. "This is what I do. I spend every waking hour thinking about playing hockey." I'm yelling. "You say that it's pathetic and shows that I have no life—"

"That's right."

"—but I'm good at this. That's why I watch all that tape that you laugh at me for." I'm up in his grill. Erik the Boy Scout tries to get between us, and I push him away. Coach Dawes doesn't intervene at all. "If you really need to make fun of me, do it somewhere else, but not here. Once we're on the ice, I know what I'm talking about. I work too hard at this to listen to some dipshit more concerned about impressing his girlfriend than understanding what's happening. You tell me you're open when there's a backchecker right behind you—"

That's when a couple of guys grab each of us. Coach glues me to the bench for the rest of the game, which I suppose I deserve. I decide to apologize to Erik later, seeing as how he's the most decent person on the team.

But I'm right.

I tell myself that a lot.

May 2010

I don't believe in moments that change your life. It's not a moment; it's all the hours you put in to get there that change you. I remember the moments, though. I got the email telling me that I was getting my tryout, and everything suddenly felt different.

I sat in the library reading it over and over, arms wrapped around my drawn-up legs. That's when I realized that I hadn't believed it would really happen. I'd walled that fear off and didn't let it out until it couldn't hurt me.

When I recovered, I packed up my things and walked across the Washington Avenue Bridge. The release had turned into giddiness. I arrived at Ridder and found Abby already standing out front.

"I knew you'd come here," she said.

"I got it. I got my tryout." I pounded my fist on the railing.

"Congratulations." She seemed subdued.

"I guess I wasn't wasting my time after all."

"Sarah Taylor's concussion isn't getting better."

"What?"

"The doctors have told her that she's done playing. That's why you're getting a tryout. We're a defenseman short."

That should have sobered me up, but it didn't. "I'm sorry," I managed. "That's too bad."

She looked at me with that burning gaze. "I hope you're worth it." As if it was my fault that an All-American defenseman was going to lose her senior year to blinding headaches.

My excitement refused to collapse. "You'll see."

May 18, 2010

It was a strange tryout. There were ten of us there, but no coaches. The people I was really trying to impress weren't allowed to supervise practices outside of the season, and technically this was a practice.

We went through drills and then, once I'd demonstrated basic competence, moved on to breakout plays, and I defended against some odd-man rushes. We didn't actually scrimmage, but we came close.

My performance pleased me. If it wasn't enough, no one could say that I choked. This team ran their breakout unlike anything we even tried in Vicksburg. It demanded patience, baiting teams into overcommitting, and then explosive action when you found an opening.

I'd predicted the one problem: I was slow. The Gophers relied on defensemen carrying the puck up the ice a lot and activated them in the offensive zone. I was used to passing the puck up the boards and staying glued to the blue line on offense. As long as I was back there, I could use smart positioning and gap control to compensate on defense, but if I tried the kinds of things this team did, that would be tough.

There was plenty of good to go along with it. My passing was crisp and accurate, aided by the upper-body strength provided by my ridiculous physique. My biggest advantage was how quickly I made decisions. If your opponents are really good, you have to know what you're going to do with the puck before it gets to you. You can't stop to think about it; making a decision *right now* is as important as making the correct decision.

People call this "having hockey instincts," but it's not. It's reflexes, and you have to learn them. You need natural ability, but repeating plays over and over is the key. I have those abilities, including great peripheral vision, but living and breathing hockey meant that I had done my thinking over years, not the fractions of a second you get in a game.

I could sense the others joking and laughing with each other, but I was too focused to be jealous. There was one player who matched my intensity, a sophomore forward named Tammy Jones. Everyone else mixed encouragement with competition, but she seemed out to beat me.

On one breakout play, as I retrieved the puck along the end boards, she wickedly cross-checked me in the back. I passed to my defense partner on the half boards, and as I turned to go up the ice, I slashed at her skates with the heel of my stick, like I would in a real game. When the play came to an end, we skated to each other.

Until I looked into her eyes, I'd thought this was just a test to see if I'd defend myself.

"You're a nobody."

I put my stick to her chest and shoved. "Get used to me."

The pushing escalated until a couple of the others got between us. I let it go, and with a desultory punch Tammy backed down as well. No one approached me, but Abby stood back and looked at me with an unreadable expression. I just smiled.

January 2009

I'm standing, shivering, out near the team bus, and it's not even my team. The Vicksburg Panthers are playing in Cincinnati tonight, but I picked up a fighting major last week so I'm suspended for two games. The fortuitous timing led to a spur-of-the-moment decision to run away to Columbus to see the Gophers take on Ohio State.

I feel sick. I didn't even really enjoy watching the game, even though the Gophers won 9–2. That's how hard it was to get myself to do this.

Finally he emerges from the OSU Ice Arena, after half the team is on the bus. "Coach Long." I force myself to keep my head up.

He stops and looks at me. "Yes?"

"Hi. I, um, I filled out your recruiting questionnaire several months ago. I want to play for you."

"What's your name?"

"Phoebe. Phoebe Rose."

"I'm sorry. I get a lot of those. I don't remember yours. What team do you play for?"

"Vicksburg High. It's a boys' team."

"How about during the summer? What team do you play for?"

"Um, none. There aren't any leagues near me."

He frowns. "What camps do you go to?"

"The Lipsett Hockey Clinic."

"I'm not familiar with it."

"It's in Dayton." *Look up, dammit*, I thought. "It's all I can afford."

"Have you considered other programs?"

"I want to be a Gopher."

"Why?"

"One of my—I mean, someone very important to me went there. He taught me to be a Gopher fan."

"Well, we get a lot of people who want to play for us. We don't have time to look at everyone."

"Please. I just want a chance to show how good I am." I'm suddenly acutely embarrassed that my hockey bag is right behind me. Why in the world had I imagined getting a workout on the spot?

He pulls a pad out of his pocket. "What was your name?"

"Phoebe Rose."

He writes it down. "And what are your parents' names?"

I look down. Again. "I don't have any."

"No parents?"

"I'm an orphan. I have foster parents, but they don't count."

"I'll still need to talk to them."

"No." It comes out almost as a moan. "Please."

I can feel him trying to withdraw from the conversation. "I need to go. I'll look you up."

"Okay." I turn away and grab my bag. I need to find someplace to sleep. Someplace cheap. I am not going to let my disappointment keep me from watching tomorrow's game. I just won't.

May 22, 2010

"So why do you want to play for Minnesota?"

I was in Coach Long's office, which I took as a positive sign. "The challenge, sir." It came out easily; I'd rehearsed my lines this time. "I think I'm good enough to play for the best, even if it means fighting for playing time." I was hoping he didn't remember how I'd answered this question the last time he asked me.

"It's also a good fit academically, sir. Minnesota has a good computer science program, which is what I'm going to major in. And I really like the idea of beating Ohio State four times a year."

"Why is that?"

Because my last foster father was a Buckeye fan, but I didn't say that. "I had a . . . strange childhood, sir. By the end I wanted nothing more than to get out of Ohio. Beating OSU would be a little bit of payback for the last eighteen years."

His chair squeaked as he leaned back. "You mention your childhood. What was so strange about it?"

I hate these kinds of questions. He knew enough that he didn't need to ask, so how I responded was more important to him than what the answer actually was. "I'm an orphan, sir. I have no idea who my parents were. I was found wandering the streets of Dayton in 1996. We only assume that I'm eighteen now because I claimed to be four then. There's no way to tell."

Despite my rehearsal, I was rambling, saying things I didn't want to share. "I never got adopted. I lived with five different foster families in the last fourteen years. I don't know how familiar you are with what being a foster child is like, but it's . . . unsettling." Inside, I'd gone from terrified to whatever lies beyond that, but I didn't think it was showing. "I never put roots down anywhere. I never really had a home and never really had parents."

"Parents play an important role in this program," he interrupted. "I often use meeting them to help judge a player. I like to see a stable family."

I froze, with no idea what the right answer was. So I looked at the floor and let a bit of the truth escape. "Some of them were obstacles to be overcome, not sources of assistance. The last family didn't want me playing hockey at all."

"So you defied your parents?"

That pushed one of my buttons. "They weren't my parents." My head was up, and I glared at him. "I never had parents." Except once. "They were just adults who were allowed to tell me what I could and couldn't do."

"But you defied them?"

I squirmed and felt myself deflate. "Not quite. My caseworker at CPS made it so that they had to let me play."

"Clever."

"I've made it this far without parents, sir. I think I can keep going."

He chuckled, and I breathed. "So tell me about that night in Columbus last year."

I was back on firmer ground. "I hadn't heard back from you on my recruiting questionnaire. You didn't answer my emails. I played in a league that you'd never scout. Even if I could have afforded to go to a hockey camp where you'd be, I wouldn't have been allowed to go. So throwing myself in front of your bus seemed like the only way I could attract notice."

"It was certainly a different approach. I've felt like I've had a stalker the last few months."

"I'm not a stalker, sir. Now that I've had my tryout, I can take no for an answer."

He looked at me, drumming his fingers on the desk. "Who is Brian Taylor?"

"He's the coach at Centerville High."

"I thought you played for Vicksburg."

"I did, sir. But my own coach hated me. He didn't want a girl on his team, and my caseworker had to threaten a lawsuit to make him take me. Coach Taylor liked the way I played, and Centerville is a much better team. So I asked him if he would be willing to be a contact person for me. He said yes."

"Did he ever." He held up a folder full of papers. "These are all the emails he's sent me over the last year and a half. There have been phone calls, too."

Without thinking, I lifted my feet into my chair and buried my face in my knees.

He continued. "I've had coaches put this much effort into promoting one of their own players before. I've never seen an opposing coach do anything like this."

I didn't lift my head.

"Let's see. From February 20, last year: 'I am not familiar with the talent level of women's collegiate hockey, but it is hard for me to imagine that Phoebe would not be an asset to any program.' There was a shuffle of paper. "From June 4: 'Phoebe has a work ethic unlike any I have seen in my twenty years of coaching. I would be proud to have her on my team.' I really like this one, from last fall: 'I coach my own players to watch how she plays and to learn from her.' That's some pretty heady praise, don't you think?"

"I think Coach Taylor exaggerates," I mumbled.

"On the other hand, in the last two months I've tried communicating with your own coach. It's quite a contrast, you know. I don't think I've ever known a high school coach who said so many bad things about one of his own players.

"So who do I believe? The opposing coach who thinks you're fantastic, or the coach who got to see you every day and thinks you're terrible?"

I sat still, arms around my shins.

"Look up at me, Phoebe."

Reluctantly, I complied.

"Which one do I believe?"

"I don't know, sir."

"How do you produce such divergent reactions to yourself from different people?"

"I think it comes naturally, sir."

He gave me a funny look but just said, "I suppose it does." His tone was gentle.

I stared at him, unsure of what to say.

"Thank you for coming in, Phoebe. I need to think about this. I should be able to let you know within a couple of days."

"Thank you, sir."

"If I say yes, I won't have any scholarship money to give you. Will that be a problem?"

"No, sir. I made all my plans assuming that."

He stood up and said, "It was good to talk to you." I shook his hand and left.

The very first thing I did when I got back to my apartment was to handwrite a long thank-you letter to Coach Taylor. I walked to the post office that night to send it to Centerville High.

I got the phone call the morning after the interview. Given that only five people had my number, I had a good idea who was on the other end when it rang. I let it ring three times before tentatively answering.

"Phoebe, it's Coach Long. Congratulations."

My thoughts were nothing but white noise.

"Are you still there?"

"Yes, sir," I whispered. "Thank you."

"You're welcome. And someday you're going to have to tell me the real story about why you want to play here so badly."

"I'll try."

"There's no rush," he said soothingly. "Why don't you come down to the arena and meet your new teammates? I'm sure you can find the locker room."

I knew I wouldn't need to. Abby would be waiting at the door.

"Thank you, sir." My voice was getting stronger.

"Now just prove us right."

I spent half an hour trying to calm down; I didn't want to show up at Ridder shaking. It was difficult. Only concentrating on Mr. Wilson and how happy he would have been calmed me down at all. I finally gave up, left my room, and entered my second life.

February 2000

Mr. Wilson takes me to a Gopher game. I've never seen them play before, and he's never seen a real hockey game. We drive to Columbus to see them play Ohio State.

"We must be lucky for them," I say on the way back to the car. I'm wearing my Minnesota hockey sweatshirt—the one he gave me for my birthday.

Mr. Wilson laughs. "You must be the lucky one, Phoebe. I watched the Gophers lose a lot of football and basketball games when I was a student there." I hold his hand as we walk. "Did you know that there weren't any women's sports back then?"

"Why not?"

"People didn't realize that girls wanted to play sports."

"Why wouldn't girls want to play sports?"

He picks me up and hugs me. "I don't know, but until we fostered you, I didn't really understand it either."

I still don't get it, but I don't say anything. He seems very happy about it, so I am too.

"Thank you for bringing me, Phoebe," he says as we walk. "I enjoyed the game."

"They play hockey in Minnesota all the time. You must have seen it."

"They play it in other parts of the state. Not in Mankato."

"Mankato State has a team. Men's and women's both."

He laughs and sets me down. "A lot must have changed."

"Can we come again next year?" Hopefully he'll remember what icing is and I won't have to explain it again.

"Sure."

Someday he's going to have to drive to Columbus by himself so he can see me play for the Gophers.

CHAPTER 2

June 3, 2010

I **stood in front of the locker** with the nameplate "29 Rose" and looked at the equipment within. I felt the cotton of the white practice jersey, tracing my finger along the crooked M, then the nylon of the breezers. I rapped the hard plastic of the gold helmet. Then I reached the bottom and picked up the skates

I sat down and started the ritual inspection I did with every pair I wore. The stiff leather and plastic. The laces. The blades with their concave base leaving two sharp edges to connect with the ice.

I hadn't realized Abby was there until she spoke. "You're pretty thorough about that."

"I learned to do this buying used skates." I ran a finger along those edges and drew three drops of blood with little pressure. I smiled.

"You bought used skates?"

"This is the first pair of new skates I've had in eight years."

She sat down next to me. "Your parents didn't have much money?"

I shrugged. "Not relevant. I had to buy my own gear."

"You bought your own gear?"

"I had some small gifts, but it was mostly mine." I slipped off my shoes to put the socks and skates on.

"How?"

"I had some odd jobs, but mostly I picked up programming gigs on Craigslist. Ones where I could work entirely from home."

"Computer programming?"

"Uh huh." I pulled up the laces.

"You did that professionally?"

I began to feel uncomfortable as she pressed. "Yeah, I guess."

"You must be pretty smart."

"Yeah."

"Also pretty sure of yourself."

"Sometimes." I got to my feet.

"Where'd you play?"

"Vicksburg, Ohio." I started for the door, headed to the Ridder Arena ice for the first time.

"Is that near Columbus?"

I didn't look back. "When you get to Hell, it's the next left."

June 18, 2010

"You like touching things, don't you?" Abby and I were walking through campus between classes.

"Huh?" Mostly I'd been wishing people would stop staring at me. When you're six-foot-two, there's no way to hide, at least not if you're a girl.

"Touching things. You do it all the time. Right now you're rubbing your shirt."

"I've never really thought about it." Suddenly I was conscious of my hands and had no idea what to do with them.

"When you got your equipment, you felt everything."

"I was trying to make sure it was real." I put my hands behind my back, willing them to stay there.

"Why do you do that?"

I looked away. "I don't know."

I heard her swear under her breath. "Phoebe, I just want to help."

"I don't want help," I mumbled.

"Please just talk to me."

"About what?" I replied with more volume.

"About what's bothering you."

I realized that the floating feeling had taken over. I hadn't felt it in months, and suddenly I was drifting away from Northrop Mall. "Nothing's bothering me."

"I'm sorry. I said something I shouldn't have."

A sort of numb tingle crawled over my skin. "Abby, stop trying to fix me."

She grabbed my arm, forcing me to stop. "Hold it. I was pushing too hard. You're right. I'm sorry. I'd like to help with whatever it is that has you down, but take your time."

"That's the thing, Abby. There really isn't anything bothering me. I don't know why I'm feeling like this. Everything is going fine. Fantastic, really. I shouldn't be in a bad mood. I just am."

"Are you going to be okay?"

"Yeah. I've survived worse."

"Will you let me know when there is something I can do to help?"

"Just keep talking to me. Please."

"Even when you're grumpy?"

"Especially then."

July 5, 2010

Abby invited me up to her folks' place for the Fourth of July. She'd decided, with remarkable speed, that she intended to chaperone me into this new life.

"Tell me something about yourself," she said—demanded, really—while we were sitting under a tree at her parents' place, eating hot dogs her father had grilled.

"Like what?"

"I don't care."

"That's pretty open-ended." Actually, it felt more like a yawning chasm.

"So is life." She was pretending a nonchalance she can't ever make convincing.

I sat back against the tree trunk, smelling summer and feeling the warmth of the sun. I thought for a bit. "I've always wanted to play hockey. That's my very first memory—telling someone I wanted to play. Don't ask me how a four-year-old girl in Dayton, Ohio, decides she wants to play hockey. This was before the Blue Jackets came into existence. It was a hockey wasteland.

"I was the only girl on every team I ever played on, from Squirts all the way through high school. I only played against another girl six times—the same one on a boys' team in Cincinnati. So being on this team is a whole new experience for me." I stopped to ponder that. "And I always took hockey seriously, even when I was five. I guess that's because it kept me going through some hard times."

"Sounds like things were tough."

I sat there for a bit, plucking blades of grass. "Yeah, they were. I don't know how to talk about it."

"That's okay. I'm not going anywhere." Abby can manage to be soothing when she really tries.

"Maybe you aren't." I got to my feet. "I'm going to get another hot dog."

She was still sitting there when I got back. "I'm trying to imagine what it would be like not to have parents."

"That's okay. I spend a lot of time trying to imagine what it would be like to have them."

"Tell me something else."

I didn't take as long this time. "I had a friend in high school named John Frank. He's at Columbia now, trying to become an art critic. We spent a lot of time hating Vicksburg together. It isn't a great place for a girl who wants to play hockey or anyone who cares deeply about avant garde art."

"You make Vicksburg sound awful."

"I spent the last year and a half there literally counting the days until I could leave. I had this desk calendar, and I wrote the number of days left until January 1, 2010, next to each date. I crossed them off one by one, and I always knew how many were left."

"Why January 1?"

"Officially, that's my birthday. That was the day I legally turned eighteen and was no longer a ward of the state of Ohio, and they could no longer tell me where I had to live."

"Oh." She paused. "What do you mean that it's 'officially' your birthday?"

"No one knows when I was born. I'm probably eighteen or at least really close, but that's a guess. As far as anyone can establish, I sprang into existence out of nothing one day in August 1996, claiming that I was four. So the authorities just arbitrarily declared that January first is my birthday."

"That seems strange, not knowing anything. Don't most four-year-olds know their last name and where they live?"

"Yeah. That's one of my mysteries. I didn't know then, and I literally have no memories of anything before that day. The police thought I was a runaway and just didn't want to tell them, at least until they couldn't find anything."

"That all seems . . . I don't know what to say, really."

"Birthdays don't mean the same thing to me that they do to the rest of you. They seem kind of fake."

"Yeah, I can understand that. Thank you," she said in that abrupt way that brings something to a close.

"For what?"

"Telling me these things. I know you better than I did a half hour ago."

"Really?"

"Sure. I like the way you calmly analyze things, looking at them rationally."

"It isn't as calm as you think."

We sat there for a few minutes, silent.

"Your father grills a mean hot dog," I said.

"He makes good steak and chicken, too. Just don't ever let him try to cook a fish."

May 2009

I feel stupid standing there, holding my blue skirt and a blouse in front of me.

"Hmm." John was pretending to ponder. "Yes, I think that that's the way to go."

"Yeah, right. There is no way to go."

"You're being difficult."

I drop the clothes so I'm standing there in nothing but a bra and panties. "Look at me, John. I'm surprised that you aren't the one attracted to me."

I'd snuck out of the house with an armful of my clothes because I have a date. An honest-to-god date. A physics student at U of D had asked me out in a way that hadn't frightened me off. So now John is trying to help me get ready. My foster mother would have kittens if she knew that I was standing in a guy's bedroom basically naked. Telling her that the guy was gay wouldn't help.

"What's that mean?"

"Does this really look like the body of a girl?"

"Yes."

"You're lying. There are two tiny bulges on my chest and none between my legs. Those are the only clues." I held up my arms and flexed. "Look at the way I taper from my shoulders down to my waist. Look at the complete lack of curves around my hips. Notice the muscle definition in my thighs."

"You look fine."

"You're avoiding my actual comment."

"No, I'm not. Stop worrying about how you look. He's clearly okay with it."

"He probably hasn't looked closely enough," I mutter. "I just want to look normal." I sit down on the bed next to him. The frame creaks with my weight. "I know that's never going to happen. I train all the time. My thighs are huge because I make them that way. But I still want to."

"You look beautiful."

I jump back to my feet. "I don't want to look beautiful," I yell. "I want to look normal."

"There's nothing wrong with not looking normal."

"That's easy for you to say. You don't look normal because you choose not to. I'm six feet and a fucking inch tall and I weigh a hundred and ninety pounds. I don't look normal because I can't. I don't think you grasp the difference."

"I do, Phoebe. Really. I've had to make some adjustments, too."

"For God's sake," I pleaded, "could you yell back at me? You're making me feel guilty for venting."

"Sorry. I tend to forget."

I sat back down. "I don't know what I'm going to do next year without you."

"Hopefully get yourself in less trouble."

"There is that."

"You'll do fine."

"I'm not so sure."

He starts to respond, but there is a knock on his door. "John, may I come in?"

"Sure, Mom."

The door opens, and his mother pokes her head in. "Oh, hi Phoebe. John, can I get your help finishing dinner in about ten minutes?"

"I suppose that's my cue to go," I said.

"Don't mind me. He's eighteen now." She shrugs. "Besides, naked girls in his room just didn't turn out to be the problem I always imagined they would be when he was younger." She closes the door again.

"I need to be home soon anyway," I tell John. "He's picking me up at six thirty." I start to gather my clothes, settling on the blue skirt. I look for tights to go with it.

"Phoebe, I need to ask you something." John hesitates "Is Mr. Jenkins abusing you?"

I almost crack. "I'm not going to say anything one way or the other," I manage.

"Because I think that's what's happening and I want to help."

"You can't. You really can't. I have thirteen more months, and then I'm gone. I can make it."

"I won't tell anyone if you don't want me to."

"Heh. You'd be about as good at that as I was at not beating people up."

"I can keep a secret."

"No you can't, John. Not one like this." I find the right tights and pull them on.

"Has anyone ever told you how stubborn you are?"

"Just about everyone."

As I slip my shoes on, he stands up to hug me. "Good luck."

"Thanks. I'm sure I'll need it."

The date is a disaster, but that has nothing to do with my appearance.

August 8, 2010

I took regular classes over the summer, so I didn't need orientation to get me settled academically, but I was hoping it would get me socially acclimated. After being guided around campus and shown important things like the bookstore, we sat in a room in Coffman Union. Everyone had a partner; mine was an innocuous girl from Minnetonka. We were supposed to ask each other introductory questions and share what we learned with the group.

It didn't go well.

She read the questions off of a card. "What do your parents do?"

Any answer close to the truth would only lead to follow-up questions, so I made something up. "My father is an architect, and my mother is a nurse."

"What is your favorite band?"

I didn't want to try to explain what industrial music is like, so I lied again. "Coldplay."

"When are you happiest?"

Finally one where I could be honest. "When I'm playing hockey."

"What do you do in your free time?"

"I play hockey, and I program computers."

"It says three things," she insisted.

"I play hockey, program computers, and practice hockey."

She gave me a funny look. "I don't think that counts."

"It's the best answer you're going to get."

It was the most innocuous question you can imagine that broke me. "What's your favorite food?"

I had a stock answer for that. Saying that your favorite food is pizza is safe. This time, though, I thought about the jambalaya Mrs. Wilson used to fix for Christmas dinner. That's when the stress that had been building all afternoon let loose.

I just sat there for a couple of minutes. The girl reading the questions asked whether I was all right. I don't remember how I responded.

Finally, I mumbled, "I need to go." As I got up to escape, the person leading the exercise intercepted me. "Is something wrong?"

I nodded. "I'm sorry. I just need to go."

When I got into the hallway, I called Abby. "Are you doing anything?"

"Not really. What's up?"

"Can you meet me at Ridder? I need a hug."

"Of course. Are you sure you don't want me to meet you somewhere else?"

"I'm at Coffman. If that's closer for you."

"I'll meet you halfway, at the north end of the mall."

"Okay. Thank you."

"No problem."

I spent the rest of the day curled up on the couch in the players' lounge near our locker rooms. Teammates came and went, and I got to feel a part of something.

August 2010

Abby and I developed a ritual. Maybe once a week we went to McDonald's in the middle of the afternoon. I ordered fries and a chocolate shake. It was about the only time I ever ate anything that I wasn't supposed to. Abby's order varied; she didn't need to have the same thing every time the way I did.

The first time we went was after a couple of teammates said something—I don't even remember what—that triggered my flashbacks, and she pulled me out of the lounge. The McDonald's three blocks away was the closest place she could sit with me and get me to calm down. So it became a place we would talk. Once we settled in, she would say the words, "Tell me something about yourself."

"My first foster family was Mr. and Mrs. Raburn. I was with them a little less than a year, and I have only vague memories of them, but they're mostly positive. They had no idea what to do with a kid who wanted to play hockey, but they kept me in skates and took me to the rink. Not as often as I would have liked, but I'd have preferred to live there even when I was five, before . . ." I let that thought trail off, and she didn't press. "I remember Mr. Raburn and me reading before bed: *One Fish, Two Fish, Red Fish, Blue Fish.*

"I probably owe them a lot. I don't remember why CPS took me out of their home. I was really mad when it happened. I thought they were going to adopt me. I had really, truly convinced myself of it, so it made no sense when I was uprooted all of a sudden."

I paused to eat some fries. Abby must have realized I wasn't done talking, because she didn't say anything.

"I think that's when I started to become angry and suspicious. I caused all sorts of problems for my next set of foster parents. It was mutual, though. Mrs. Hayes was a horrible woman and deserved what she got. I tried to make her miserable."

"Were they all that bad?" she asked.

"No. Absolutely not." I was as vehement as I could be. "I lived with Mr. and Mrs. Wilson from when I was seven to when I was eleven. I remember them as being perfect. It doesn't matter whether they really were—that was the happiest period of my life."

I emptied the shake. "Mr. Wilson is the reason I came here. He was from Mankato and went to the U. He was a huge Gopher sports fan. He didn't know anything about hockey, but we watched them lose a lot of football and basketball games together."

"What happened?" she asked.

"He died. Cancer. So CPS sent me elsewhere." I pushed the last few fries around, letting them go cold. "I owe them everything. I wouldn't be here, or anywhere else good, without them."

"So they made you the person you are today."

I snorted. "I wish. I think it would have been awesome to have ended up as that person." I ate the last fry anyway. "Now *you* tell me something about yourself," I said.

"I was wondering when you'd get around to asking that."

"Sorry. I'm getting used to this sharing information thing."

"Hmm. I started hockey later than you did, when I was about six. Before that I wanted to be a figure skater. Dad talked me into hockey instead. I thought it was because he was embarrassed to have a figure skater in the family, but the real reason was so that he didn't have to do so much driving. He first tried to talk Derek into figure skating."

I tried to picture her brother as a figure skater. "Any regrets?"

"None."

I looked at our empty trays. "Shall we?"

Abby nodded. She completed the ritual with its closing words. "Thank you for telling me these things."

One night after all of the incoming freshmen were in town, the seven of us got together. Just ourselves. No one else allowed. We went to Traci's parents' house in two cars.

Other than being eighteen-year-old female hockey players we were diverse. Two defensemen and five forwards. Three Canadians, two Minnesotans, a Californian, and me. Three of them—Jenny French, Caitlyn Morris, and Amy Heckenthorpe—played for their country's national Under-18 team, and Caitlyn's father played seven games in the NHL. Morgan Gaines and I were roster afterthoughts. And then there was size. There were days when I weighed twice what Jenny did.

Caitlyn got on my nerves from the very beginning. It took a long time for the little things to become endearing. She never stops moving and almost never stops talking. It's like she's afraid that we'll all forget who she is if she's not in the middle of everything. That night she wiped the floor with the rest of us at every video game we tried. My excuse was that I'd only ever played video games about four times in my life.

"Everyone plays video games," was Amy's opinion.

"Yeah. Are you some kind of freak?" Caitlyn tossed in. That was absolutely the wrong thing to say, of course.

"No," I mumbled. "I just didn't have them."

"Why not?"

"Different reasons."

"Did your family not approve of them?" Morgan asked.

"My last foster parents thought they were frivolous and decadent. The ones before them had a system, but their son kept it in his room. I didn't like him, so I never used it."

"It must have been tough, growing up like that," Jenny said.

"Kind of, I guess. I got used to it. I didn't really have anything to compare it to."

The one I hit it off with the best was Kennedy Kane. That's if you can call two people sitting next to each other hardly saying a word "hitting it off." She was from rural Manitoba, which makes Dayton look like the middle of somewhere. We sat on the floor watching the others for a couple of hours.

We were quiet for different reasons. I was terrified of the chatting and laughing. She just never said much. From the very first, though, her presence calmed me. It was like being with Mr. Larson, the guy who ran the ice rink I spent so much time in when I was in high school. I felt okay not saying anything.

I had to admit, it was a fun evening. I liked Jenny more than I thought I would. Combine a California blonde with a big-time hockey family, and I was expecting the worst. Instead, she was considerate, and I think she realized how annoyed I was with Caitlyn and tried to distract her.

We spent the night there. It was my very first slumber party.

Official practices didn't start until the third week of September, but, really, we were underway by Labor Day. There were absurd restrictions about how many of us could be on the ice at the same time, but we found ways to work on things.

It was a humbling process that only began with my skating. I've always taken pride in my play. It's one of those things I just know I do right. This was the first time I'd ever had that confidence shaken. At Vicksburg we'd played teams that beat us almost every night, but I at least knew what I was doing. When the Gophers first started practicing (unofficially) that fall, my angles were terrible as I tried to learn how to play defense without checking. It puts a premium on speed, which I just didn't have. I struggled to learn when to step up in the offensive zone because my high school coach had nailed me to the blueline and told me to stay there.

It was a confusing, frustrating time. Abby had to talk me off the ledge several times. Kennedy did the same but without the talking.

For reasons I couldn't comprehend, Caitlyn picked on me every day, putting extra effort into beating me when I tried to defend her. It bewildered me, because it wasn't difficult for her. In transition, the speed mismatch overwhelmed me. When I could keep her from beating me to the outside, I was fine, but that was rare. I did better against her in a set offense, but that was relative.

For all of my deficiencies it became clear that I was going to win a regular spot in the lineup. I had quick hands, played smart positionally, and was an utter beast in front of the net. No one in the league was going to overpower me. But really, it was because I was one of only six defensemen—there were no extra players for those spots.

So I prepared for my first year playing in the maroon and gold.

November 2008

Centerville kicks our ass. We haven't beaten them since I joined this team. I hate losing. I also hate that I'm paying so much attention to my individual stats, but I can't help it. If I'm objective, my team is a lost cause. I don't mean because we lose. It's that so many of them don't seem to care that we keep losing.

Besides, my individual stats mean a lot. Coach Dawes would bench me if he could justify it. I'm the best player on this team, and I'm always one screw up away from sitting.

I shouldn't be the best player. I'm a girl. I may be a giant freak of a girl, but I'm a girl. Half of them should be better than I just on physical gifts, but they aren't. None of them put the work in. None of them give a shit.

We lose. But I'm not on the ice for a single goal against. I have an assist. I'm +1, and that's hard to do when you lose 7–1. So I'm filled with the selfish feeling that it isn't my fault. I played fine. That makes me a bad teammate. But it's a bad team.

I make sure I am the last player through the handshake line. I stop by Coach Taylor when I reach him, making sure no one else can listen in. "Coach, may I ask you a favor?"

I'm looking down at the ice, dammit. I told myself I wasn't going to do that. I was going to look him in the eyes.

"Of course."

Once I start, the words just come tumbling out. "I'm trying to get recruited for college. I know you've said good things about the way I play. I was wondering if I could list you as someone to contact. Someone instead of . . ."

He chuckles. "Well, you're probably going to have to tell them who your coach really is, but I'd be happy to help in any way I can."

At that I raise my face to him. He's smiling. "Don't let them get you down, Phoebe. Just between you and me, Jerry Dawes is a terrible coach. Don't believe the things he says about you."

"I don't."

"Good. Don't start."

I feel like the whipped puppy that suddenly gets loving attention.

September 26, 2010

After all of the practice, the season arrived. When we came out of the dressing room for the lineup introductions that night, I started to shake. I wasn't the only one who was nervous, and Coach Long made sure that everyone got a shift in the opening minutes. That was all it took for me to settle into the idea that this was a hockey game. On that two-hundred-by-eighty-five-foot surface, if nowhere else, there wasn't anything to be scared of.

It was just an exhibition game against a Canadian university team. We won, and I did fine. The glare of the lights didn't bother me.

CHAPTER 3

October 1, 2010

We played our first official game in upstate New York. On the bus ride from the hotel to the arena, Linda, the team captain, sat down next to me for the pep talk she gave to each of the freshmen.

"Nervous?"

"It's just a game, right?"

"Great." She clapped me on the shoulder and then headed off to find another rookie.

My confidence was justified once I got on the ice. In terms of my play it was an entirely unremarkable two games. No goals, no assists, and I was +1 thanks to a couple of teammates who made a nice play. When you're a defenseman, there are many worse things that can happen than for no one to notice you. It helped that we're just much better as a team.

It was off the ice that I had issues. I was grateful someone had decided that Kennedy and I should be roommates for the year. It made sense—not only did we get along, but we were also partners on defense.

I'd warned her about the downside of being my roommate. Kind of. I just said that I don't sleep well and might disturb her. She didn't press it. The two of us made quite a pair, both scared of our own shadows for completely different reasons.

The first night of the road trip went fine. I woke up about two thirty a.m. and left to study, but I did so quietly. I didn't really think of it as a curfew violation. I was in bed at ten, just like we were supposed to be. The coaches never told us when we were allowed to get up. It was my normal schedule. I just didn't sleep much.

Friday night didn't go as well. Kennedy shook me awake not long after midnight. "Phoebe, are you okay?"

I rolled onto my side, facing away from her. "I'll be okay."

"Were you having a bad dream?"

"Yeah." That's one way to put it. It was about him, of course.

"You were yelling."

I hoped that it was nothing coherent. "I'm sorry I woke you up."

"Jesus. That's okay. I was kind of worried."

I checked to make sure my eyes were dry before turning to look at her. "Thank you for waking me." She looked really indecisive about what to do. "You should go back to bed. I should be fine now."

"Okay," she replied uncertainly. I think she watched me for a bit before falling back asleep

I waited about fifteen minutes to make sure she was really out before getting up. I didn't want to go back to sleep.

October 5, 2010

Between us, Kennedy and I had one complete sense of self-confidence. As tentative and confused as I was off the ice, she was almost as bad on it. It was frustrating to watch her get the puck and then be unable to decide what to do with it. Time is the currency that a defenseman has to spend in order to play effectively, and she wasted a lot of it.

We played different games. Kennedy had all sorts of natural talent for the game, far more than I ever did. We're built completely differently; she's slender, and while she would be considered tall in most company, she's five inches shorter than I am. The two of us spent hours at the rink trying to unlock that talent.

We spent most of our time working on skills. We passed pucks back and forth endlessly. We were working on one-timing a slap shot when we had our first lengthy conversation after knowing each other for more than a month.

"Let it get closer into you," I told her as I fed her passes.

"It feels awkward when I do that."

"You'll get used to it. You'll also get a lot more on it and be more accurate, too."

I fired another puck. This time she fanned on it entirely.

"How did you learn how to do this?" she asked me.

"The same way you're doing right now. A man named Mr. Larson spent hours passing pucks for me. You're at least managing to stay on your feet."

"That's a pretty low bar."

She got good wood on the next one and almost put it in the net.

"Maybe," I answered, "but it took me several days before I stopped falling over."

"That must have been a sight."

"It's a good thing I don't bruise easily."

"You don't?"

"It just looks that way after a game." I was developing a reputation for taking abuse on the ice.

"Anyway, thanks for doing this."

"It's no problem. I enjoy being out here with you."

"Why?"

"I never did anything like this in high school. Not with teammates at any rate. Mr. Larson was a wonderful old man, but it's not the same."

"I find it hard to believe you didn't do extra practice."

"I did. Just not with my teammates."

"Why didn't you practice with them?"

"They hated me. Besides, most of them didn't do extra practice anyway."

"Why?"

"Why didn't they practice or why did they hate me?"

"Both, I guess."

"No one took it that seriously. Half of them would rather have been playing football. The other half knew that they were in no danger of getting cut because there wasn't anyone else who tried out. They didn't have to be any better."

"So why did they hate you?" She looked perplexed. It never would have occurred to Kennedy to hate anyone.

"I was a weird kid, but the biggest part was that our coach made no secret that he hated me. So they just followed him."

"So why did he hate you?"

The repetition of feeding pucks to her helped to soothe my agitation about discussing my past. She did the rest naturally. "He didn't want a girl on the team. My case worker had to threaten a lawsuit in order to get the district to tell him that he had to take me."

"And you wanted to play for that team?"

"Not really. I just wanted to play, and that was my only option."

"Couldn't you have transferred?"

That started to touch on things I didn't want to discuss, even with Kennedy. "Why don't we talk about you?"

"Like what?" she asked.

"I don't know. Anything, really."

"There isn't a lot interesting to say."

"Tell me about Dauphin."

"Not much to say. I like it there, but nothing ever happens. I think that's part of why I like it there."

"How did you get to play hockey?"

She laughed. "It's not as horribly backwards as people assume. There were local girls' teams. Hockey's like a religion up there. Telling a kid she couldn't play would be like denying them communion."

"Football is a religion in southern Ohio. It doesn't mean that girls play. We're just supposed to be cheerleaders."

"What else?" she asked.

"What does your family do?"

"My father sells insurance."

"Isn't everyone up there a farmer or something?"

"All of my cousins are. Does that count?"

"Close enough."

She held up her hands. "Okay. Enough. I have a paper I need to write."

"Tomorrow, then?"

"I'll see." She started to skate off. "Coming?"

"No. I'm going to stay out here awhile."

"You need a life, Phoebe. And I say that as someone who loves this sort of thing."

"You okay?" Abby sat down next to me as I checked my phone.

I shrugged, mildly annoyed that I was so easy to read.

"Have you heard from your friend?"

I looked up with a start. "How do you know what I'm thinking about?"

She put her arm around me, and I couldn't decide whether to resist or slide into it. "Because you told me all about him and then stopped talking about him completely. For the last two weeks you've been staring at your email inbox like you want to destroy it."

"You're right," I grumbled.

"Have you tried to contact him?"

I shoved my phone back in my pocket. "Several times a week. Occasionally I get some short response from him. I got one substantial message from him back in May. Other than that, I don't think he's used an adjective once."

"Some people just aren't good at long-distance friendships." Other people would say that to be reassuring. From Abby it was an accusation.

"We kept each other sane through high school. He's my friend. How do you just stop talking to someone who's a friend?"

"I don't know," she answered. "It just happens. You don't need me to tell you that life isn't fair."

"I don't want it to be fair," I said. "I just want to have someone I can count on."

"You do." She turned me so that we almost faced each other. "We won't desert you."

October 16, 2008

"Mrs. Jenkins was ecstatic when I said I was coming to the Homecoming Dance. It's like the first proper thing I've done in two years." I sip my drink.

"Somehow that doesn't surprise me."

"That she's pleased or that I've been so improper?"

"The latter. That woman could be unhappy while having an orgasm."

"I suspect that it's a hypothesis that's never been tested."

"Are you implying something about Mr. Jenkins's prowess?" He waggles his eyebrows.

I look around the gym, taking a long draught of my diet cola. Then I crunch a couple of ice cubes with my teeth.

"You okay, Phoebe?"

"Yeah, I guess."

He looks at me hard for a few seconds. Really hard. "Okay." I can't read his expressions. He's inscrutable.

I shift uncomfortably. "I hate this dress."

"You look fabulous in it."

"I look like a linebacker."

"Darling, you know hockey. I know fashion." He's doing his flaming homosexual imitation. Sometimes I think that's the real him, not the goth. "Trust me, green is your color."

"It's a stereotype. Red hair, green dress."

"It's a cliché because it works. I recommend tried-and-true strategies for those just getting started in the game of dressing up."

"Hopefully I'm also ending that game."

His voice returns to its usual register. "You need to loosen up. You're wound so tight I can hear you creak."

"If I had any idea how, I'd give it a try."

"Have you considered therapy?"

"No. I mean, yes, I've considered it. No, I'm not going to do it."

"Why not?"

"John, if I won't open up to you, what makes you think I'm going to be able to with a complete stranger picked pretty much at random?"

"Because they're trained professionals?"

"Yeah. No. Not going to happen."

He sighs.

"This music is starting to drive me crazy," I say.

"See, that's what I mean about loosening up. This music is fabulous. Completely devoid of all content, mind you, but that's why it fits the setting."

I watch the crowd dance. "It's annoying. You're right. It fits the setting. They both suck."

"Maybe, but no one can dance to the stuff you listen to."

"That's not true," I say defensively. "I listen to plenty of stuff you can dance to."

"Like what? Coil?"

"Savage Aural Hotbed."

"Okay. I'll give you that one," he concedes. "But that's about it."

"You can dance to punk."

"I'm loath to call that dancing." He practically sniffs his disdain.

"That's your problem."

He sticks his tongue out at me. "Oh, hey, look. There's Will Framingham."

"The relevance of this is?"

"You have a crush on him."

I almost choke on a pretzel. "I do not!"

"There's nothing wrong with that. If I were his type, you'd have to fight me for him."

"I'm still looking for the relevance. You can drool over him without telling me." I do not like where this conversation is headed.

"You sound awfully defensive for someone who doesn't have a crush."

"Fine. I do. So what?"

"Go ask him to dance."

"No. If I do, I'll just feel nauseous walking over there and humiliated when I walk back."

"I'll pout."

"You don't know how."

"Sure I do. Watch this." He sticks out his lower lip.

"Meh. I give that about a 6.5."

"What are you, the Russian judge?"

"I'm scared, so drop it."

"Phoebe. Just try."

"I can't even dance. And the person I'm getting that opinion from is you, so don't contradict me."

"That's not the point."

"Yes, it is."

He tries to look authoritative. "Okay, here's how this is going to work. I'm going to go talk to some of my other friends . . ."

"How do you plan to find a bunch of people wearing black in this lighting?"

"Gothdar. I'm going over there, and I'm not coming back until you've asked Will Framingham to dance with you."

"Isn't he supposed to ask me?"

"It's 2008. Break out of convention."

"I can come up with excuses all night."

"Yes, but I'm done responding to them. I'll see you after you dance with him."

With that, he walks away. I stand there clenching my fists. If anyone says anything to me, I'm going to yell at them. But of course, if people actually came up and talked to me, I wouldn't be this uptight in the first place.

I finally reach the point where I'm more miserable standing there than I would be going up to him. Normally, that would be my cue to leave the building, and I seriously consider it. Unfortunately, hope wins out over despair, and I cross the room, getting farther from the exits.

"Hi," I say when I get to him. "I, um, was wondering if, um, you wanted to dance." Of course I'm looking down at the floor. That makes me more upset, because one of the reasons I have a crush on Will Framingham is that, along with being a blond god, he's someone I don't have to look down at to meet his eyes.

"You? Seriously?" I cringe as he speaks. "Where's that little turd you came with? Oh, I'm sorry. Even he won't dance with you."

I feel humiliated walking back.

John is waiting for me. His face goes ashen when he gets a good look at me. "Oh, Christ, I'm sorry, Phoebe."

"Just take me home now. Please."

October 15, 2010

There are different kinds of rivalries in sports. There is the kind where the perennially bad team dreams of beating the really good team someday. Those were the only kind of rivalries we had at Vicksburg, and that good team doesn't think of you as a rival, just a speed bump.

There are rivalries built on mutual respect. At Minnesota, that's what we had with Wisconsin. We battled to be the best team in the Big Ten every year and the best team in the country most years. Those produce great games—hard, physical games where you beat the hell out of each other—but they don't produce lasting animosity.

Then there are the rivalries based on sheer hatred. Not only do the fans dislike the other team, but the players do, too. Those games get brutal, so I'm right in my element. Michigan State was one of those teams, and they came to Minneapolis for the first league series of my career.

There were a lot of reasons for the hatred, but one of them was named Mallory Jackson. She was an elite, Olympic-caliber defenseman. She was also a former Gopher who transferred to East Lansing after her freshman year. There was a lot of bad blood and speculation about why she left. I never cared. I'm a Gopher. If you walked out on us, even before I was there, that's all I need to know. I'm pretty simple that way.

She also played dirty. I was always a physical player and had the penalty minutes to prove it, but there were lines I didn't cross. Mallory Jackson had none. It all finally came to a head halfway through the third period of the first game of the series.

With just over eleven minutes to go, I was on the ice when she delivered a wicked elbow to Jenny away from the play. Neither ref was looking that way, though the crowd sure was.

The choice of target lit my fuse. Jenny is tiny—picking on her crossed the line from being tough to being a goon.

So I had to skate out there and get in Mallory's face. It doesn't really accomplish much, usually just a bit of pushing and shoving and yelling at each other. Which is what we proceeded to do. I don't really remember what I said, but it doesn't matter. It might as well be inarticulate grunting. There was some wrestling to it, too.

The linesmen were coming out to break it up when she took an actual swing at me. My eyes lit up. I'd never have suggested actually fighting, because I was still trying to learn the etiquette for women's hockey, but there was no way I was turning down an invitation, so I went at it.

I was disgusted by what followed. I started to drop my gloves, but she just waded in without bothering. She threw a punch at my still helmeted head, which struck me as a complete waste of time.

It turned out that I was strong enough to do damage anyway. My third punch would have landed right on her chin if it hadn't been protected. It snapped her head back, and she wobbled pretty badly. Her eyes were glassy, so I didn't put up a struggle when the linesman grabbed me from behind.

So it took all of three games at the collegiate level for me to get into a fight. Naturally, I got suspended, but she didn't play the next day, either. That was a good trade-off for us. She also missed the next two weeks with a mild concussion.

I didn't feel bad about that at all. Maybe I should have, if I were a better person. But I didn't. It's not because she started the actual fight. Once she delivered that elbow, she was fair game. "Don't fuck with my teammates" has always been my motto. If I could drop the gloves to defend my high school teammates, I sure as hell was going to do it, if only figuratively, for Jenny French.

It was a horrible weekend. We lost both games despite my keeping State's best player off the rink for the second. We weren't focused, and we didn't play team hockey. We got what we deserved.

After the Saturday game there was a reception for the booster club, like the one I attended shortly after arriving in Minneapolis, except that it was the freshmen who got up to answer questions. I was last, so I had a lot of time to get nervous.

Each rookie in turn went to the front, where one of the club members asked basic questions like what we were planning to major in, why we came to Minnesota, and what our favorite hockey experience had been. It was banal, but a good time was had by most. The team sat on the floor close together and lobbed silly questions at us.

Then it was my turn. I could feel sixty pairs of eyes focused on me. All of them had watched me during the game but this was different. After six articulate teammates preceded me, I bombed. I didn't make it through the first question.

The emcee asked me what it's like being a walk-on among all the highly recruited players. My mouth refused to work. I don't know how long I looked down at the floor. It couldn't have been more than a few seconds, but it seemed like forever. Then I looked pleadingly at Abby.

She rescued me. Seated in the front row she hardly had to get up to reach out and take my arm. She gently pulled me back into the crowd. As I huddled there, I felt hands touch me. I couldn't tell how many of my teammates reached out to me, but it was enough. My panic attack slowly subsided.

The assembled fans were confused. Most of them had read something bland about my background in one of the press releases featuring the new Gophers. They had no way to know that no one interviewed me because I couldn't face the idea of describing my life to a stranger, so it was based entirely on public information and a few things Coach Long told them. A marketing intern wrote as if she were talking to me.

When it was over, Kennedy took my hand and led me out the

back door of the club room and down to the lounge. We sat there for about an hour. Abby joined us once her parents had gone.

Around this time, Caitlyn started pestering me about my workout routine. It was funny because while she wasn't lazy (no one at that level is truly lazy), she wasn't one of the workout nuts. "C'mon. What do you do when you get up so early in the morning?" she asked as we were preparing for afternoon practice.

"Why does it matter?" I didn't want to talk about it. I had started to recognize that my obsession with pushing myself was more a neurosis than it was productive.

"I just want to know. I bet it's pretty impressive."

"She's just trying to earn her spot here," Tammy said from across the room.

"Beats buying a spot," Caitlyn shot back. She turned to me with a sloppy grin. "So what do you do before we all get here at six am?"

"You could just show up and find out what she does," Jenny broke in.

"It's easier to ask. So what is it, Phoebe?"

"Just some yoga and some running, really," I said before Jenny could try to deflect it again.

Amy snorted. "Some running. How many times do you go up those stairs?"

"I don't really count," I replied. Which was true. I just did it as long as I could before walking back to Ridder.

"What stairs?" Caitlyn asked

"One of the parking ramps on campus," Amy answered. "I'll show you which one later."

"Right," Caitlyn continued. "Then it's back here. I've watched her lift and skate. Kennedy, how long do you two stay on the ice?"

"Sorry. I'm not getting involved in this. If you want to turn it into a competition, you'll have to do it without my help."

"Who said anything about a competition?"

Jenny laughed. "She works harder than you do, Caitlyn."

Amy punched Caitlyn in the shoulder. "Looks like you're going to have to get out of bed earlier if you want to keep up."

"Ugh. No, thanks."

I pulled on my jersey and escaped to the ice.

October 1999

I'm bored. We're doing math. We're just not all on the same page. Literally. I skip ahead, trying to find something that wasn't so simple.

I sort of hear Ms. Williamson call my name. "What?"

There are some giggles. "I asked if you could solve problem 12."

I begin flipping back. "What page is it on?"

She walks over toward me. "Phoebe, why aren't you paying attention?"

"Because we did all this last year. I want to learn something new."

"Please just pay attention and follow what we're doing."

"It's boring. It's just addition again. Over and over."

"Practice is how you learn to get something right."

"I already get it right."

"Phoebe, please just pay attention."

Later, I ask Mr. Wilson why they make everything go so slow at this school. His answer has something to do with bureaucrats. When I ask him to explain, he says that a bureaucrat is someone who wants everything to run smoothly with no complaints, so they make sure that there are rules for everything that they can point to when someone doesn't like something.

"But I'm complaining," I say.

He says that is a different kind of complaint, and it didn't matter to the bureaucrats. He says that he needs to think about how to explain it better. Right now, he's teaching me how to make it look like I'm paying attention even if I'm not.

October 29, 2010

Kennedy and I skated as the third defensive pair, sheltered from playing against other teams' top lines, particularly at home, where we had the last change. We got about twelve minutes on the ice per game, so I had plenty of time to watch.

Our second line had Amy at center and Caitlyn on her left wing. The uncanny way that Amy and Caitlyn worked together amazed me. They'd played together on Canadian junior national teams, and they knew where the other was going to be and where she would pass the puck.

Amy was a natural center unlike any other I ever played with—a wizard on face-offs and as a passer. Caitlyn was a finisher, which means more than having a great shot. She could find that empty space where she could use it. The two of them ran a backdoor play several times a game, and I never figured out how Caitlyn could manage to get open at the side of the net so often.

There was a joy to everything Caitlyn did. She annoyed me every day, but it was hard to dislike her. There was never any malice in the way she got under my skin. She just couldn't help herself. That really ought to be her epitaph.

Kennedy and I floundered around. The game was so much faster than what I was used to. Those who would know say that a decent boys' high school team could beat any women's team in the world. If so, that only demonstrated how weak the Greater Montgomery County Conference was. My hands and a good feel for the game kept me in it, but that didn't change the fact that some glaciers skate faster than I did. I was impossible to push aside around the net, but everywhere else my immobility was a problem.

It made a huge difference to play in front of a good goalie. I played more confidently not worrying about Josh Lipke giving up a goal every time I made a mistake. I could see myself getting better, but I still wasn't good enough. I was still short of being the caliber of player who could help her team win championships.

So I worked to improve my skating mechanics. Seven years of mostly self-teaching had left them woefully deficient. The coaches didn't want to make too many changes during the season, but I was going to spend the next summer relearning how to skate.

When Wisconsin came to town in early November, I faced a challenge I'd never experienced. How is an athlete supposed to feel when she plays poorly and yet her team wins? It never came up at Vicksburg, since we won a total of twelve games in three and a half years. If I was bad, we lost.

That Friday, I was horrible against the best team in the country, and we won anyway. Their goalie couldn't have stopped a beach ball that night. We scored four times on seven shots to start the second period, and some of them were embarrassingly soft.

Meanwhile, I got turned in every conceivable direction, including straight down, trying to figure out where their forwards were going. Kennedy didn't fare any better, and in eleven minutes of ice time we were out there for three goals allowed.

We won, though, 8–6. I really did want to be a good team player, so the win meant I should have been happy. Except that I also needed to focus on ways to improve, and there was plenty that night to focus on. It's so much less confusing if you play well in a loss. Not better, mind you, but less confusing. You're supposed to feel bad. That's easy.

I had no such confusion the next night. Dallas, another defenseman, tweaked an ankle early in the first period, so Kennedy and I got thrown to the wolves for more shifts against a bunch of Badgers who clearly took losing the first game personally.

The polite, optimistic thing to call the game was a "learning experience." If you'd painted me fluorescent orange, I'd have been indistinguishable from a traffic cone. I made the right plays most of the time. I was just too slow. It's a sickening feeling to see an opposing wing coming at you and to know, absolutely know, that they're going to fly past you. By the second period I was defeated before I left the bench. It was the closest I ever came to having my confidence in my ability to play shattered.

Sports can be funny. The week before, we were swept by Michigan, who weren't nearly as good, but we should have won at least one of those games against the Wolverines, and I was ready to take my chances against them the next time we met. I wasn't alone in believing that they weren't really any better than we were.

But when they focused, the Badgers destroyed us. At least there was so much video of bad play that I didn't get singled out in practice the next week. The loss was a complete team effort. We just needed to figure out a way to make sure that by February, it was our effort that produced a loss rather than their effort that produced a win.

In the interim, I made plans to order a pair of jet rocket skates from the Acme Company.

January 2009

The odor of a hockey bench, particularly a boys' team bench, is unbelievable and not in a good way. Thirteen bodies plus a backup goalie, and we sweat like you wouldn't believe. Even keeping myself hydrated I can lose eight pounds over the course of a game.

If you're the Vicksburg Panthers, and you're trying to protect a one-goal lead in the third, it's all flop sweat. A sense of impending doom is palpable, and suddenly I'm getting double shifted. It's like someone read the stat sheets and saw that I have the best plus/minus on the team.

Before an offensive zone face-off, I try encouragement. "Jesus, Chad. It's the first year of varsity hockey for these clowns. We're going to win."

My defense partner shrugs.

"If Stewie wins the draw back to you," I continue, "slide it over. They've been sagging off me all night."

That produces a nod, but I'm not sure it really registered.

Stewie does win, and the puck comes back to Chad. He promptly fumbles it, and a St. Xavier forward grabs the turnover. It's not all Chad's fault; Eddie did nothing to slow down the wing coming out to him. That would be interference, but everybody does it. You have to.

I see it coming, and I'm bailing the zone before the St. Xavier forward has full control. That prevents a breakaway. The center is also coming, though.

The key to defending a two-on-one is that you absolutely, positively cannot let the puck carrier pass across to his teammate. You shut that down, let the goalie focus on just the one guy, and count on him to make the save.

I have no confidence in Josh making that save. Having a weak goalie preys on your mind. I can run the numbers. Even Josh is going to stop that puck most of the time, but in my gut, I know that I have to make the perfect play. On the ice, my gut takes over.

So I angle in on the wing player, filling as much of the passing lane as I can. I'm counting on the fact that it's his team's first year and he can't thread that needle. If no one has picked up the trailer, we're in trouble, but I can't help that. Not my problem.

It's astonishing how many thoughts can go through your head in four seconds.

I win my bet. The rookie lets me get close enough to poke the puck away from him. For good measure I ride him into the boards and drill him. It's extra satisfying since St. Xavier doesn't admit girls.

Crisis over. Only 6:22 left to go.

CHAPTER 4

Abby and I took the opportunity of a weekend off to drive up to her parents' place. Somehow she got to talking about her new boyfriend.

"So what do you think of him?" she prodded.

"I don't know."

"I know you have an opinion."

"I have an opinion," I agreed. "I'm just not sure I want to share it."

She dodged traffic on I-94 doing at least fifteen over the speed limit. "I want to hear it, even if you don't like him."

"I'm more worried about what happens if I say that I do like him and then he turns out to be a jerk."

She gave me a glare.

"Please watch the road, Abby."

"Oh, all right." She complied without slowing down her words. "If it would make you feel better, you can drive back."

"I don't have a license."

"You should go get one," she insisted.

"I mean I never learned how to drive."

"You're kidding."

"No. My last foster parents weren't going to let me drive their car. I only had one friend, and I never thought that an art snob could be that possessive of his automobile."

"We'll have to fix that."

"There's the 'fix' word again."

"I wasn't talking about you personally."

"Yes, you were," I insisted. "I don't need to know how to drive. I don't ever go anywhere that requires a car unless I'm going somewhere with you. I'm perfectly happy not knowing."

It was the third trip I'd made up to her parents' since the Fourth of July. Increasingly it was a place I felt safe. It was thirty-five minutes away from all of my anxieties.

Mr. Forrest was loud, boisterous, and profane. He intimidated me for a long time, but he was simultaneously so friendly and so careful not to push my boundaries that it didn't intrude on my feeling safe.

Mrs. Forrest was something entirely different—and the source of my security there. On Saturday night, the others went to a movie, and it was just the two of us.

"How are you adjusting to Minnesota?"

"It's already colder than it usually gets in Dayton." That evaded her real question, but she didn't try to rush an answer. I thought for a few minutes. "I don't know. I spent five years thinking that once I got here, I'd be happy. Instead, I'm just scared of everything."

"Mmmm."

"I guess I was scared of everything before, too. I just didn't think of it that way."

"You don't sound scared right now."

That stopped me, and we sat in silence for a bit. That's when I realized something. "I'm not scared of you." More silence. "I am of Abby."

That elicited a chuckle. "She has that effect on people."

"I'm trying to think of the last person I wasn't scared of."

"Don't. That's not worth pursuing."

"I suppose not. It just surprises me."

"Why?"

"I had a . . . really bad experience with a therapist a few years ago. Really bad."

"Being a therapist is my job, and I don't work at home."

"I know. Abby's trying to take over that role."

"I hope you have the sense to tell her to back off."

"I'm working on it."

"Phoebe, do you have anywhere to go for Christmas?"

I froze for an instant but managed to cover it up by drinking some cocoa. "No. I was just planning to stay on campus."

"That sounds awfully lonely."

"There are worse things."

"I'm sure that there are, but that's no reason to do it. Why don't you come up here?"

"May I think about it for awhile?"

"Of course."

I drained my mug. "I think I'm going to go to bed, if you don't mind."

"I'll wait up for them. Tom is probably taking them out for malts."

"Good night, Mrs. Forrest."

"And please, call me Jerilyn, like all of Abby's friends do."

Halfway through November, neither Kennedy nor I had scored a goal. I'd never planned on being a big scorer, but she had a higher pedigree than I did, and it frustrated her. She had scored a lot in juniors and expected to keep doing so. It got in the way of playing good hockey.

So I set out to kill off a dream—gently—starting with our series against Purdue. Halfway through the second period on Friday night I had a brilliant idea while standing on the bench after Kennedy played a particularly tentative shift. Without taking my eye off of the play, I said, "Ken, this team has a lot of defensemen who can score. In fact, I think it has entirely too many of them."

"What?"

"Seriously. We need more defensemen who don't score. I nominate the two of us to fill that role."

"Think about it. There are only so many goals and assists to go around. If we take them, then Kathy and Julie aren't getting them. They have a chance to be All-Americans, and they need every point they can get. It would be selfish of us to take them."

"You're nuts."

"Well, sure. That goes with being a genius. I think we should take a vow not to score. We'll keep it to ourselves. No one else needs to know."

Kennedy just looked at me, and I forced a smile.

Coach Long tapped us on the back. "I didn't hear anything about a vow, but you two are on next." So we had to start watching for our players coming off on a change.

I never know whether my so-called brilliant ideas are actually good ones, and this case was no exception. The next night Kennedy picked up a goal and three assists. I couldn't decide whether or not that meant it worked. She signed onto the oath afterward. We agreed that if we scored a goal over the weekend, on Monday we'd head over to Mariucci and run what we called Four Corners. That means wearing all your gear except skates, running down the stairs in one corner, back up, sprinting to the next corner, and repeating it all the way around the rink. It's forty-six steps down and the same back up, and you have to go all out, so even one is a haul. The coaching staff normally uses them as punishment for violations of team rules.

On a shift shortly after proposing our vow, I pushed a puck in the crease into Erika's pads so she could cover it up. Right at the whistle someone drilled me in the back with her stick and into the net. Welcome to Indiana. I caught myself on the crossbar so I didn't go down.

I pivoted around, smiling. "Please tell me you can hit harder than that. You cross-check like a girl." I was hoping, in vain it turned out, that the refs would reward my forbearance by giving us a power play.

Back in our hotel room that night, Kennedy looked me over. I was sitting on the bed, ice packs on both ankles, my right hand, and my right thigh, and one under my shirt, in the small of my back.

"They worked you over pretty good."

"Yep."

"So why are you smiling?"

"It means they don't like me."

"That's a good thing?" she asked.

"It's only fair. I don't like them."

"One game and you don't like them? They weren't even that dirty, at least to the rest of us."

"I didn't like them before warm-ups." I grinned at her. "I already don't like Northwestern, and we don't play them until next week."

"Why?"

"It's the only way the game makes sense to me. It's us against them, and I take it personally. The rest of you have friends on other teams that you made when you were at camps or at tournaments. I don't. I've never socialized with any of them, and I can't really imagine doing so."

"Okay, tell me this. If you dislike them so much, why not retaliate?"

"They can't hurt me, so why should I retaliate?"

"Can't hurt you?" She was stuck in disbelief. "What's the ice for then?"

"Mostly to keep the swelling down."

"I know that."

"I didn't say that they can't cause me physical pain. Just that they can't hurt me."

"Aren't those the same thing?"

"Not for me." I paused, trying to figure out how to explain it. "You've seen me hurting. There's nothing some other hockey team can possibly do to me that could be that bad."

"So why the fight, then, if they can't hurt you? Why all those roughing penalties against Michigan?"

"That's different. Those all started when they went after someone else."

"So you think the rest of us need protecting?"

"I know the rest of you need protecting."

"That's kind of . . ." She searched for a word.

"Patronizing? Probably. It's still the only way the game makes sense to me."

"Maybe we don't need you to protect us," she insisted.

"Maybe you don't, but we aren't going to find out. That's my job. If I could go to war for three years with a bunch of assholes who hated me, I can do it for four here."

It was only later, thinking about it while listening to Kennedy snoring gently, that I grappled with the idea that the only way the game makes sense to me is as some sort of primal us versus them. That certainly hadn't been the case in Vicksburg. There hadn't been an "us" to fight against "them."

That had changed.

December has always been my least favorite month. My childhood was filled with bad Christmas experiences. Most of my foster parents treated it as a time to emphasize the child they wished they had rather than the one they did have. None of us got what we wanted.

So I was uneasy approaching Abby after practice one day in early December. I tried to stall her until no one else was around. She figured out what I was trying to do and led me out into the streets. We talked as we walked through Dinkytown.

I stammered when I started. "Abby. Your mom. She invited me to spend Christmas with you."

"Okay. So what's the problem?"

I wasn't sure how to respond to that. "Well, I wanted to make sure that it was okay with you. I don't want to impose. It's your family, and, you know, Christmas is a family thing. I don't want to impose," I said again.

She had to reach up, but she put an arm around my shoulders. "Of course you can come. I was worried about what you were going to do over the holidays."

I looked at the ground. Around us, people were getting off the bus. I used their presence as an excuse to avoid responding immediately. I thought about my conversation with her mother and tried to draw strength from it. I was still looking straight down, though. "I'm scared of you."

"How can you be scared of me? We're teammates."

"You can hurt me." I turned and started walking away quickly.

She grabbed at me and caught a corner of my coat. "What do you mean? I wouldn't hurt you."

I tried to dislodge her hand. "I don't want to talk about it."

All she did was tighten her grip. "No, we're going to talk about this."

"I don't want to."

She didn't let go. I realized that people around us were starting to stare, and I stopped fighting her. "I don't care," she insisted. "We're going to talk about this. You live around here, right? We'll go to your place and work this out."

A flash of humiliation ran through me at the idea of showing her where I lived. "How about we get something to eat at the McDonald's?"

"No, let's go to your place."

She started pulling me up Fifteenth Avenue. I trotted after her, trying to recover full control of my coat sleeve. It sounds comical, and it's even more so given how I tower over Abby. Dominance is entirely psychological, and I was not in the driver's seat.

"Wow. These are a bunch of dumps. Please don't tell me you live there."

"No." I pointed at the one across the street. "It's that one."

Abby pulled me across Seventh Street. I fumbled for my keys as I was herded to my house. When I opened the door and let her shove me in, she said, "This doesn't look like apartments."

I made for the stairs. "It's not. Quite. I have a room upstairs."

I didn't know how I'd lost control of the situation so completely. If I had stood up to her, or even just answered her questions in the first place, I'd have been spared the look on her face when I opened the door to my twelve-foot-by-ten-foot room.

"You live here?"

I said something to the effect that it's what I could afford.

"I've lived in a dorm room smaller than this, but I have a home. My parents keep stuff for me."

I started to flinch but managed to turn it into a shrug. She stood against the door, and I couldn't help but think she was deliberately blocking my escape route. "Now we're going to talk about this. You're scared of me?" She sounded incredulous.

I nodded.

"Why? How can you be scared of me? I've seen you play."

"That's different," I mumbled.

"It can't be that different."

I sat down on my futon. "You're playing hockey with people you've known from elite teams and development camps for years." I wanted to yell, but my voice stayed flat and my eyes stared at the floor. "You have this great family and just casually mention that they keep all of the stuff you can't fit in your apartment. Abby, this is everything I own. It all fits in this room."

She seemed to become aware of her posture and stepped away from the door. "I'm sorry."

"It's okay," I mumbled. "All I want is to be one of you. I'm just not sure how."

"Shit." She dropped down beside me. "Phoebe, you are one of us."

"I guess."

Her voice dropped to a whisper. "How can you doubt that?" She reached out and pulled me into her embrace. "Of course you can join us for Christmas."

December 1999

Mrs. Wilson sets a plate of pancakes in front of me. "What do you want for Christmas, Phoebe?" she asks me.

I pour out a bit of syrup. "I don't know."

"Don't you want more syrup than that?"

"It's not good for you. I want to eat healthy."

There is a tinge of horror in the look she gives me. "Child, you're seven . . ."

"Almost eight," I interject.

"Almost eight. It's good that you care about what you eat, but you should also just enjoy things."

"Good luck with that," Mr. Wilson says from behind his newspaper.

"I want to be big and strong."

"You already are big and strong, girl."

"Then I want to be bigger and stronger." I took a bite of the pancakes.

She almost continues but then gives up. "So what do you want for Christmas?"

I swallow. "I don't really need anything."

"Christmas doesn't have to be about what you need. What is it that you want?"

"I don't know," I repeat around a mouthful of pancake.

"Phoebe, we don't know you well enough yet to know what we should get you."

The newspaper rustles as Mr. Wilson sets it aside. "Doris, she wants a family."

"I know that, but—"

"She wants one so badly that she doesn't want to think about your question." My mouth is dry, and I set down my fork. "It's our job to help her figure out what else she wants."

Mr. Wilson lowers the paper and looks at me, his face serious. "Phoebe, Doris and I are going to do our best to be that family."

"Will you adopt me?"

They share a glance. "Howard . . ." she starts to say.

"I promised her we'd be honest." He returns to me. "No, Phoebe, we won't. We can't."

I pull my legs up into my chair and hug them. "Why not?"

They stare at each other for a longer stretch. "Honesty," Mr. Wilson mumbles to himself, "is hard." Mrs. Wilson turns away.

Finally, Mr. Wilson says, "Phoebe, they won't let us adopt you, because we're black and you're white."

"Why not?" I feel tears on my face.

Mr. Wilson looks over my shoulder. I suddenly feel Mrs. Wilson wrap her arms around me from behind. "There are some well-meaning people who think that African American children should be raised by African American parents and white children by white parents."

"What difference does it make?"

"It doesn't," Mr. Wilson answers heatedly. "But some well-meaning damned fools think it does. And so we can't adopt you."

He stands up from the table and stalks out of the kitchen.

"That doesn't make any sense."

Mrs. Wilson hangs onto me. "I know it doesn't. If things change, we'll adopt you. Until then, you can stay here. We'll be your family in everything but name."

I try to relax in her arms. She has to make my pancakes over again, because the first ones get cold. I put a lot of syrup on them.

December 14, 2010

Christmas break meant no games and no practices. The NCAA mandated we take a month off. That didn't prevent us from getting together informally.

So eight of us were on the ice, mostly just goofing around. There was a serious edge to some of it, though. It wasn't an official practice, and no coaches were around, so Tammy felt uninhibited.

"You don't have to take her shit," Caitlyn said when we were alone along the boards.

"It doesn't bother me."

She tilted her head looking at me. It reminded me of a sparrow. "Yes, it does."

"Not much."

"Keep going."

"It doesn't matter," I insisted. "I can handle it."

"She's a bully. Just stand up to her."

"Just leave me alone."

"Okay." She smiled. "Do you mind if I tell her to go fuck herself then?"

She didn't wait for an answer.

When we jumped back in and Tammy started up, Caitlyn indeed told her to go fuck herself. That's when it got nasty.

"Can't defend yourself?" Tammy said as she skated right up to me.

"Jesus, what is your problem?" Caitlyn demanded before I could respond.

"She didn't earn her way here the way the rest of us did. She just shows up and makes the team." She didn't take her gaze off of me. "And she doesn't have the heart to prove me wrong."

"Just stop," I said desperately.

"Make me."

I could see Caitlyn's eyes pleading for me to do something, but I skated away.

We sat down to dinner on Christmas Eve, and Tom said grace. There was a lot of food on the table, but three teenage hockey players can take care of that. Abby and Derek started talking. I silently tucked into the ham and the potatoes. My nerves hadn't stolen my appetite.

"What was Christmas like for you, Phoebe?" Jerilyn asked.

I shrugged. "It depended on which foster family I was in."

"What was it like, to switch families like that?" Derek interjected.

My face froze. "It was kind of tough."

"Were there any that you really liked?"

I watched myself push food around my plate. The silence lengthened until Jerilyn said, "It's okay, Phoebe. You don't need to say anything."

"Yes," I whispered. "Yes, there was. One."

Suddenly I was crying. I pushed my chair back and rushed for the room Abby and I were sharing. I curled up on my bed and wept, facing the wall.

A little while later someone sat down on the bed. "It will be okay, Phoebe," Jerilyn said.

"I'm sorry I ruined dinner."

"You didn't ruin anything." She put her hand on my shoulder. "You're safe here, Phoebe. Not just some of the time and not just from some things. Always."

I listened but didn't say anything. She just sat there for awhile, gently stroking my hair. I finally rolled over. "Thank you, Jerilyn."

There were tears in her eyes. "There's food downstairs for you when you want some. Do you want me to leave you alone?"

"Please."

"Then we'll all be in the living room if you want to talk or just want to be with us. And we're sorry that we upset you."

"It's okay."

"Thank you. Stay up here as long as you want." She patted my shoulder and left the room.

December 1997

We're walking around the mall. Mrs. Hayes has some shopping to do, and then I stand in line so that I can sit in Santa's lap and tell him what I want for Christmas. I try to tell her that the whole thing is bullshit. I know that Santa is a fake. If there really was some guy who gives toys away for free, the world would be a better place.

She insists. It's a part of Christmas, she tells me. She accuses me of trying to spoil the season. I stand in line under protest.

When I get up there, I tell Santa that for Christmas I want real parents that don't lie to me about some fraud in a red suit. Quietly. I don't want Mrs. Hayes getting mad at me. Santa thinks that she is my real mother and that I should be nice to her. I tell him I'm an orphan and don't have any real parents.

Mrs. Hayes gets antsy. "Just tell him what you want." Loud enough for her to hear, I say that I want a pony. I get up and walk back over to her. I don't bother smiling.

I think I made Santa cry.

CHAPTER 5

I **often lingered on the ice** after practices, but this time it wasn't my choice. After everyone else had filed into the locker room, Linda stood on the bench, running me through extra drills. It got ridiculous when she told me to put away the nets, something the rink crew usually does, but when the team captain tells a freshman to do something, she does it. The bench always beckons if you don't.

When I finally got back to the dressing room, there was a loud chorus of "Surprise!"

They had hung a banner that read, "Happy Birthday, Phoebe," on the wall. It was crude, but it was one of those rare moments when it really is the thought that counts.

Kathy brought out a cake with four artistic disasters that were supposed to be frosting roses. "You didn't let Caitlyn bake this, did you?" I remember asking before I ate any of it.

After a few minutes, it became overwhelming. "Excuse me," I said. I went into the equipment room and sat in the corner. I slowed my breathing, trying to relax.

I don't know how long I abandoned my own birthday party, but Abby came looking for me. "Are you okay?"

"I don't know. No one has ever . . ."

"Don't tell me," she interrupted. "Come back out and tell everyone. They're all worried that we did something to upset you."

I nodded and let her help me to my feet. I was still wearing my practice uniform, including skates. When I reentered the dressing room, I could see the concern on all of the faces.

I stammered trying to talk but eventually managed, "Thank you. No one has ever done anything like this for me. I haven't had a real birthday party since I was thirteen."

They sang "Happy Birthday," Caitlyn adding some vulgar lyrics. Then I went around the room hugging everyone. When I was done, I felt the urge to flee again. I fought it. "I'm sorry," I said. "This is just . . . too much to take. I'm happy, though." I sat in front of my locker, hugging my knees. It's kind of an awkward position when you're wearing skates, but I managed.

When the cake was gone, we did the large group hug thing. "Thank you. Very much," I said. "But I'm exhausted. I need to go home and be by myself for awhile."

Everyone seemed to understand. I got undressed, showered, and changed. Kennedy was waiting for me. "Can I walk with you?"

I thought about it for a moment. "Sure. I can handle one person."

We didn't say anything the whole way, but I felt her presence. We embraced at the door to the house. Then I let myself in and sat on my futon, just letting the feelings wash over me.

A few days later Abby and I went to McDonald's. "You seem nervous," she said as we picked up our orders.

I took my seat in the booth we always use. "I . . . you'll see."

"Tell me something about yourself."

I'd been working myself up to this since Christmas. I checked to be sure no one was close enough to listen, but I dropped my voice anyway. "I haven't talked about my last foster family yet. I have said things about those times, but not them.

"I don't ever use their name. Maybe I will someday, but not today. I'm also not going to mention the worst part of it. Most of my childhood was miserable, but the three years I lived there were something else. Horrifying, I guess. You'll have to take my word for it on that right now."

"Okay."

My world narrowed until I didn't hear anything but my own voice and didn't see anything but Abby's face. Everything else disappeared.

"He's the minister of an evangelical church in Vicksburg. They made me be a part of the church youth group on Sundays and Tuesday evenings. They told me on numerous occasions that John was going to Hell and that I shouldn't hang out with him."

"Lovely."

"You and Jenny are reeducating me about what religious people can be like. He was the exact opposite. Bigoted. Authoritarian. And violent. He beat me with his belt over the slightest infraction of his rules. And he had lots of rules. I think he got off on the beatings."

Words were pouring out. I had to stop to catch my breath.

"He would have been bad regardless, but the state of Ohio telling him that he had to let me play hockey made him angry beyond words. He doesn't believe in girls' sports at all and certainly not playing with boys. And he really didn't like CPS imposing rules on how he could treat me.

"I had to be at home whenever I didn't have something specific scheduled. School. Hockey practice. Church. That was about it. Well, that was the rule. It was the one I broke most frequently. I did it mostly to go to the rink, but there was also the time I ran away to Columbus for two days. I know everyone loves that story, but they have no idea how angry he was when I got back.

"I just took the beatings for that. It was worth it. I didn't even argue with him. There were others where I did. The ones where he had some ambiguous rule or decided on a sudden reinterpretation. We screamed at each other about those. He always got his way in the end.

"I hate him. I hate him with an intensity I can't really describe. It isn't just that I would kill him if I had the chance. It's that I want to do it as slowly as possible. I lived with him for one thousand one hundred and thirty-seven days. That's how long I want it to take. No more and no less."

I looked down at my untouched, cold fries and melted milkshake. I was embarrassed to realize that I had been close to shouting by the end. I didn't really want to broadcast my torture fantasies to the world.

"And you haven't gotten to the worst part?"

"No."

"I don't want to think about it. I will, but I don't want to."

Her expression mixed all sorts of things. Anger. Sadness. Probably some disbelief. Definitely bewilderment. I have no idea what, exactly, to call what I was feeling, but I was shaking pretty hard.

She sat there for a few minutes, absorbing it. Finally, I couldn't take it any longer. "Abby, please. I want to leave."

"Of course." She started to pick up her tray.

"No. We have to end it the way we always do. You have to say it."

"I'm not sure I want to."

"Please. It's important to me." I was starting to cry. "The ritual is important to me. That's what makes it safe."

"But I'm not sure . . ."

"Abby, it's more important today than it ever has been. Please say it. That's how I'll know it's over."

She swallowed. "Thank . . . thank you for telling me these things, Phoebe."

"Thank you," I whispered. I got up. Before I could grab my tray, Abby hugged me. I'm afraid I tried to crush her returning it, but she didn't complain.

"Let's go," I said at last.

January 2008

Mr. Galvin walks into the gym carrying four basketballs. "Guess what we're going to play today." Several students obligingly say the obvious. "Right. So break up into boys and girls and we'll pick teams."

As we break up, he adds, almost as an afterthought, "Phoebe, why don't you join the boys?"

There is quiet laughter around me, and I turn scarlet. "But . . ."

"You're too big to play with the other girls. It wouldn't be fair. Besides, you play with the boys all the time. You should be used to it."

So I play with them. I don't like basketball, and this doesn't help. But the worst is when I get back to the locker room. Mandy Williams tries to close the door on me. "You're not allowed in here. You're a boy."

They all laugh. It continues in that vein, including shrieks when I take off my shorts. Health class is almost unbearable. We are, of course, in the middle of sex ed. Ms. Gershwin has no idea what is going on or why she is being asked questions about cross-dressers.

January 3, 2011

The click of skates hitting the ice and the scraping sound as you come to a stop or turn was soothing to me. When I was by myself, my consciousness would drift away on those sounds. I'd learned that this is meditation. I've been doing it for my whole life without realizing it. Clicks and scrapes. Clicks and scrapes.

But I wasn't on my own today.

"You're like two different people."

"How so?" Kennedy and I were out on the ice by ourselves, just working on things. Those times together helped us solidify as a defensive pair. Coach Long played hunches with the other four defensemen but left us alone. I'd taken almost 90 percent of my shifts with Kennedy, and it felt comfortable.

"As soon as you're on the ice, all of your nervousness goes away. You're confident. You're fearless. Even when you get beat, you're convinced that it's not going to happen again."

"That means you're only paying attention half the time," I said.

"Okay, not always. But a lot. It's those times you don't blow up that I watch you."

"It's not that I don't think I'm going to get beat. It's that if I don't make a mistake and I get beat, it's because the other girl is better than I am." I leaned on my stick as I talked. "I've worked as hard, but I'm not the best. A lot of players in this league are better than I am. I know they're going to beat me sometimes. If Coach puts me on the ice, it means he thinks that's what's most likely to lead to a win. So I accept that it's going to happen. That doesn't mean that I don't get mad at myself when I screw up."

"I wish I knew how you do it." She skated lazy circles in front of me.

"Hockey has always been a refuge for me. The rink is the one place where I'm not scared, no matter what happens."

"You're tough."

"I guess. In some ways."

"Can you teach me to be that tough?"

I went cold and my voice flat. "You don't want to be this tough."

"Why?"

"I lived with five different families growing up. I didn't have parents, really, except for a little while. You know all those mornings when you didn't want to go to practice and your parents made you get up and drove you to the rink?"

She nodded.

"Mine didn't do that. I had to want to go to practice every time, because no one was going to make me if I didn't. I had to get to the rink on a bicycle, because no one was going to drive me. I'm tough on the ice because hockey was the only thing I had. Losing it was unthinkable. I'm this tough because everything else hurt so badly that hockey was always better than the alternatives."

"I . . ."

I bulldozed past her. "And there's the other thing. We have completely different ambitions when it comes to hockey. What you want more than anything else is to become good enough to play on the Canadian national team. My goal was never to be the best player I can be. The goal, the thing that got me through each day, was to make this team. To be a Gopher. As far as I'm concerned, I've already achieved everything I've ever wanted from the game. To be here. With you."

"So why do you keep working so hard?"

"Habits. I've been doing this so long that I'm pretty much on autopilot. It's easier to keep doing it than to stop."

"So you keep getting up at four a.m. because it's easier?"

"You know why I get up at four a.m.—nightmares," I said, more sharply than I'd intended.

She turned red. "Oh, I'm sorry. Yeah."

"It's okay." I swiped at a nearby puck. "Let's keep working."

She skated to a position so we could coordinate behind the net. "So why here? Why was this the place you wanted to come?"

"Why did you want to come here?"

"I knew some of the girls coming here because we were in Canadian development camps together. That wasn't true for you though. So why?"

"I don't know. Maybe my obsession to get out of Ohio and on a college team needed a focus. Minnesota was as good as any other."

"Nice try," she said. "I don't believe you."

I wondered why I didn't want to talk about the Wilsons, why I didn't want to talk about anything happy. Instead, I held it tight, a secret shared only with Abby. It made no sense, but I did it anyway.

"I had to pick one. So here I am."

She looked at me skeptically. "So when did you decide on Minnesota?"

I wanted to change the subject but couldn't think quickly enough. "When I was about eight, I think."

"Wow. That sounds like some of the local girls, who grew up rooting for Minnesota and always dreamed of playing here."

"It was probably just like that."

She gave me a little smile. "Tell me someday." She skated out to center ice. I passed her a puck, and she raced to the other end, pretending she was on a breakaway.

We all have dreams.

I spent months looking forward to our trip to Columbus. I wanted to beat Ohio State as much as I wanted anything. As the date drew nearer, I started to get nervous. I don't think anyone but Abby noticed as dread replaced anticipation. By the time we were on the flight there I was a wreck.

My head was never in the game. Coach Long thought he was doing me an honor by putting me in the starting lineup in my home state. He thought it would pump me up. After all, I'd told him how much I wanted this.

Twenty-one seconds later, we were behind 1–0. It wasn't entirely my fault, just mostly.

I played my way out of the rotation by the end of the second period. Thank God we won the game. It wasn't a lack of talent, just a lack of mental toughness, I told myself. No excuses.

He was in the stands, sitting at the end of the bleachers about ten rows up. He was easy to spot, given how empty the arena was in Columbus. I saw him during warm-ups. I almost crumbled right there.

Coach Long told me after the game that I wouldn't dress the next night. I couldn't blame him. I didn't want me to dress, either.

It worked out. I sat in the press box during play, which made it easy not to look into the stands. Without me in the lineup, we ran them out of the building, 8–1. I was still on edge the whole time, but it qualified as a good night.

Afterward, Kennedy, Amy, and I were loading all of the bags into the bus. It was just the three of us out there. The other two were joking around. I even managed a smile, reflecting on how things had changed since the last time I'd been in the same spot.

I shrieked when I saw him walk up. Or so I've been told. All I remember is a hot, white energy that overwhelmed my senses.

"Stay away from me." I gripped Kennedy's shoulders so hard she showed me the bruises later. I struggled to keep her between us. My memory goes from being a film to a series of discrete snapshots.

He says something. The next thing I remember is Coach Gill holding me. There is a commotion somewhere behind me.

After that, we are on the bus. Dana, our trainer, is right in front of me, but I can see the coaches behind her. "Are you okay?" she asks.

God help me, I nod. My default setting is to deny pain.

"Who was that?"

I'm not up to avoiding that question. "My last foster father."

"What happened?"

That's what brought me back to life. That's the instant my memory snaps entirely back into focus. "I don't want to talk about it."

She decided that whatever it was, it was beyond her ability to solve right there. "Okay." She put her arms around me.

My awareness skips forward again. I'm sitting in a booth in the hotel restaurant where we get our postgame meal. I have a vague recollection of insisting that I wanted to go down with the team rather than stay in my room. Linda is next to me, and an untouched plate of food is in front of me. Her hand is on my shoulder.

Then I'm in a hotel room. Maybe it's mine. Maybe it's not. Kennedy isn't there. Coach Gill is. She puts me to bed. I don't sleep well, even for me. I think she watched me all night.

December 2007

I feel numb. The floating has never been like this before. I feel nothing. My body lies in my bed where it hides under the covers. I leave all of the pain, all of my feelings with it. The rest of me is nowhere. He can't touch me when I'm nowhere because I don't feel anything. I can remember what happened, but it can't hurt me.

Mr. Jenkins found out that I screwed Josh Lipke. I figured he'd be mad. I didn't figure . . . this.

I can't believe I trusted Josh. I just wanted to be friends. I guess he told everyone, not just the team.

Mr. Jenkins is waiting for me when I get home from practice. He sends me straight to my room. I do homework for a couple of hours. I can hear him yelling about me during dinner.

He doesn't knock when he comes in about eight p.m. He has his belt out, but there's something different in his face, something that scares me. I leave my body when I see it. My flesh obeys him remotely. I don't even watch as he thrashes it. He calls me a slut over and over, says I humiliated him.

He loses control when he realizes my mouth isn't saying any-thing, not expressing any pain or anger. I barely register that the blows have stopped when he shoves my face down into the bed and pushes himself into me.

That's when I leave completely, into a place of no time and no sensation.

By Monday I was feeling almost normal, whatever that meant. The other girls had long since figured out how much physical contact means to me. They had taken every opportunity to put an arm around me or squeeze my shoulder or just touch me. Coach Long was less comforting. He told me I needed to see a counselor if I was going to continue to play, which I agreed to only reluctantly.

I was more agitated when I left his office than I had been going in. Abby was waiting for me. I knew what she was planning to ask me. I nodded and then said quietly, "Somewhere private. Really, really private." We both knew what was coming.

"No one is using the video room. I told no one to disturb us."

When we got there, she took one of the chairs, but I sat on the floor, wedged into a corner. I was hugging my knees.

Abby knew the rules now. "Tell me something about yourself."

"He raped me." My voice was emotionless. "That's the worst part. The part I couldn't tell you. Not once. Nine times. I'd been there a little over a year the first time. Then it was about six months before it happened again. They grew more frequent." I started rock-ing back and forth. My eyes were fixed on the floor.

"The last time was the September before I left. I don't know what changed, but there weren't any more. Maybe it was that I had my plans finalized for getting out in January. I never told him, but maybe he saw something different about me.

"For a couple of weeks after each one, he'd get into these moods where he would go on about what a sinner he was. About how his behavior was foul and how Satan was stalking him. He never apolo-gized or anything. He just worried about himself and what it all meant for him.

"When I told you that I think he got off on beating me, I was lying. I know he did. He always beat me before he raped me. There was something in his eyes those times. After the first couple, I always knew what was going to happen as soon as he came into my room."

I was still talking in a flat monotone.

"Usually there was something that set him off. Sometimes it was something sexual. The first time was when he found out that I'd fucked my goalie, not that he cared who it was. The second was after the school counselor told him that I'd told her about the rape."

Abby inhaled sharply but didn't say anything.

"Another was when he found out that I'd disabled the parental filtering software he'd installed on my computer. I was using it to go to rape survivor websites. His software filtered those out. I got careless and forgot to clear my cache one night. It probably would have been safer for me to look at porn."

I went silent for an extended time.

"What I don't understand is why I let it happen. I was bigger than he was from the day I moved in. I could have pushed him off. I could have done all sorts of things. I got into plenty of fights at school, and I just dismantled people. I got into two full-out fights during games and several others that could have been called that way.

"I was angry all the time. Except when he raped me. When it was just a beating I defied him. A lot of times I defied him by submitting even before he ordered me to. That's a strange sort of defiance, but that's what it was. It was my choice to surrender.

"But when he came in with that look, I just collapsed inside. There was no fight in me. No anger. Just fear. I can't even tell you what it was that scared me. It was just this vast, amorphous weight. I can carry so many things, but not that.

"I died inside each time. Not a little piece of me. Everything. The only thing that put me back together was getting to the rink. I usually waited about an hour before sneaking out. The guy who ran the rink, Mr. Larson, gave me the keys. So I'd get there in the middle of the night. I had a ritual. Very specific patterns of ways I'd skate. Drills. I'd shoot pucks into an empty net. There were specific sequences in which I had to score and miss, or I had to start all over.

"By morning I'd put my mask back on. I could face the world. Not happily, but I could do it. John always knew that something had happened, but I never told him what."

For the first time I looked up at her. "I've never told this to anyone, Abby. Not since I told just a small part of it to the school counselor. I never told John. You're the only one who knows. I'm not ready to tell anyone else yet."

She nodded.

"He had that look in his eyes. That's what set me off on Saturday. He was going to beat me. He was going to rape me. And I was going to let him. That's what went through my mind. That's why I collapsed."

I curled up and finally started to cry. I felt her sit down next to me. She had to rearrange me a bit to have room, but she pulled my head down into her lap. And I cried.

"Thank you for telling me these things, Phoebe."

It didn't stop the tears. Not this time. But it did make things a tiny bit better.

"Mr. Jenkins. That's his name. Christopher George Jenkins."

December 2007

In the morning I'm in my body again. I can't go to school. I can only get out of bed because it's the only way to get away from him. I don't want to talk to anyone. I don't want to see anyone. I don't want to move. I don't even really want to think. Add it all up, and I don't really want to be.

I get on my bicycle, but I turn left on Fremont instead of right. I take the route to the rink. When I get there, some adult team is practicing. I slink in. No one sees me. I sit behind the boards, under the bleachers. I curl up, chin on my knees, but I don't lie down. I just lean against the wall, letting it take my weight. Every so often someone crashes into the boards next to me. Those jolts are my only movement. I feel them. There's no separation.

Sometime later that morning Mr. Larson finds me. He says my name and then starts to say something else before he gets a good look at me. He watches me for a couple of moments and walks away. He comes back with a pair of skates. He crouches down and sets them next to me. "These should fit, when you're ready."

I look at them for awhile. I have no idea how long. Finally I pick them up and take them to the gate before putting them on. The rink is deserted. I start skating. Aimlessly at first. Then I do Herbies—skating goal line to blue line and back, goal line to red line and back. Over and over. Trying to turn the hurt into pain.

I have no idea how long I skate. I go all the way to exhaustion and beyond. At some point I start crying and then screaming something with every stop. I skate until I collapse. I crash into the boards after trying to stop on the goal line.

Mr. Larson comes out while I lie there sobbing. He sits next to me for a bit and then helps me to my feet. "You don't need to tell me, but I'll listen if you want."

I shake my head.

"Go take a shower."

"I don't have anything to change into." It was the first time I've spoken coherently in almost a day.

"That's okay," he replies. "Just shower. Hot shower. It will do you good."

The water hits my face and runs down my body. It sluices away sweat. Maybe it takes something else with it. I don't know. I guess it must, because I think I can face the world. I don't want to, but I think I can.

CHAPTER 6

Kennedy hadn't left my side since we'd loaded the bus in Minneapolis. I wasn't sure whether to be grateful or annoyed. Round about Eau Claire, I took out my earphones and spoke up.

"I'll be okay," I said irritably.

"Hmm?"

"You don't need to hover over me. I'll be okay."

"I'm just worried about you." She seemed remarkably nonchalant for someone so worried. She hadn't even looked up from her book.

"I don't need you to protect me."

"If it were one of us, you'd have punched someone by now."

"I don't see what that has to do with anything."

"You express concern for others your way, and I'll do it my way."

"I want to be left alone right now," I grumbled.

"I was just reading a book until you started talking."

"You know what I mean."

"Not really, but you're going to find that I can be unreasonably stubborn when I put my mind to it." She finally looked at me and smiled.

"Why don't . . ."

"Nope."

"You didn't even let me finish."

"No point in it, really. Just go back to listening to your music."

Which is what I did. I fumed most of the way to Tomah. That's about where being grateful took over. I was never by myself that entire weekend. If it wasn't Kennedy, it was Abby, or Caitlyn, or Jenny, or at least one of about six others.

As for the hockey, that weekend marked a turning point for us. We'd won a bunch of games since the last time we'd played Wisconsin, but, other than taking two from Michigan the week before going to Columbus, we hadn't played anyone very good.

None of that is to say that we won in Madison. We played better. Not good enough, but better. We actually took fewer points than we had back in November, managing just a tie and a 3–2 loss. We were a better team, though. The shot totals didn't reflect it, but we played them evenly for the last fifty minutes of both games. All we needed was for the league to let us ignore the first ten.

Kennedy and I had improved a lot as a pairing. I'd sensed it when we'd played Michigan, but Madison made it clear. She'd gained confidence, and I had figured out the angles I needed to take to keep from getting torched all the time. We weren't on the ice for any even-strength goals against that weekend, although we demonstrated why we didn't get a lot of penalty kill time. I even got an assist, though that was more a matter of making a routine pass to Caitlyn and then standing around while she and Amy worked magic. Hockey assists are funny things; they're awarded to the last two players on the scoring team to touch the puck before the goal scorer, without any real regard for whether the play was instrumental in scoring. Many times, players more important to the goal don't get an assist because they didn't touch the puck.

We were too good a team to talk about moral victories, even against Wisconsin. We needed to beat them, but I felt a lot better about our chances of doing that than I had forty-eight hours earlier.

We'd climbed into second place. The Badgers weren't losing to anybody, so there wasn't much hope of catching them, but we'd avenged the two losses in Ann Arbor and were eagerly anticipating giving some payback to Michigan State, too.

In the meantime we had to stay focused because we couldn't afford to lose any games to teams in the bottom half of the league.

The idea that there were teams much worse than mine was still new and exciting to me. It was in one of those games, against Indiana, that I passed a milestone. Early in the second period I had the puck at the right point. As I wound up for a shot, the Indiana wing went down to block it. That's gutsy, because I sometimes cranked a shot into their feet to discourage others from doing so in the future.

This time I stepped to my left to get around her. Once I'd done so, my original shooting lane had closed up. I had a few different options. If I were Kathy, I could have started skating it in deep, looking for an opening or to force a reaction from the defense. Since I lacked those kinds of skills, I could drop it down to the wing on the right side, or I could push it across to my defense partner. Unfortunately, Kennedy was covered at the other point, and Caitlyn had gone to the net when she saw me wind up.

With those options gone, I should have dumped it into the corner and let the forwards get it back. Instead, I tried to feed Amy on the goalie's right since it looked like Caitlyn would be open for a backdoor pass. It was a dumb play, but sometimes Fortune smiles on the stupid. It was, of course, blocked by the defenseman I tried to get the puck through. But rather than behaving nicely for her so she could start a breakout the other way, the puck glanced off of her stick and on net. It went through the goalie's legs before she could react to the change of direction.

So there it was. My first goal as a Gopher. I raised my stick and let everyone congratulate me. The post-goal ritual then involves skating down the length of our bench touching gloves with all of my teammates. By then I was as mad at myself as I was happy.

When I got back to the bench after skating past Erika, Coach Long clapped me on the shoulder. On the other hand, Kennedy recognized when my body language meant that I was frustrated.

"What's wrong?" she asked incredulously.

"That was dumb. I did the stupidest thing possible, and I get rewarded with a goal."

"Phoebe, relax. You just scored your first goal. Enjoy it."

As I glared at her, she tried to suppress a smile.

"Okay, I should know better than to tell you to relax, but you should see your face right now."

I gritted my teeth.

"But I am disappointed that you broke our pact by scoring, even if it was accidentally."

I lost it and yelled at the ceiling. That's when Kennedy had to grab the boards to keep herself from collapsing, she was giggling so hard.

I still have that puck.

November 2007

It's my first high school game. It's supposed to be different from all of the games you've played before. Partly it's that the competition level has gone up, but it's also that you're representing something that you're loyal to. Be true to your school. That's the theory.

If Vicksburg High burned down, I'd be thrilled. If I could pick some of its denizens to be trapped inside, I might be willing to believe in God.

Yet there I am, wearing the green jersey with the word "Vicksburg" in diagonal lettering down the front. I'm on the third defensive pairing with Colin Mitchell, a junior who hardly puts any effort into the game. Watching my teammates, it's easy to see how Coach Dawes couldn't justify leaving me off the team.

I do my best to have a good attitude. I shout encouragement from the bench. I make sure to pass the puck to anyone who is open, even the two forwards who refuse to talk to me.

It doesn't help. We're dreadful, not helped by the fact that we are playing Centerville. By the standards of the Montgomery County Conference, they're the elite. They skate around us, through us, and over us. If they wanted to beat us by fifteen goals, they probably could. They take it easy, and the final score is 9–1.

I'm on the ice for three of the goals we allowed. On the second one, I get caught out of position chasing the puck along the boards when I should be covering the front of the net. The problem is that everyone is out of position, and I'm not sure when I should rotate. When I get back to the bench, I try to ask Coach Dawes what I should have done. He just glares at me. I'm going to be skating suicide drills again on Monday.

The only thing really surprising happens after the final buzzer. The last person in the handshake line is Brian Taylor, the Centerville coach. When I reach him, he grabs my shoulder to stop me from just skating past him. "I like the way you played, Rose."

I freeze. "I was –3 in seven minutes. I was terrible." It comes out as a mumble.

"The last three were a lot better than the first four. You're going to be good—just keep working."

He lets me go, and I make my way to the small room that's been set aside for me to dress and undress so that I don't cause whatever mayhem would result if my teammates saw me naked. At least there's a shower I can use. I know there are going to be road games when I'll have to ride the bus home still sweaty.

January 2011

One morning I found Caitlyn already at the rink when I got there at five a.m. "Okay if I skate with you?"

"I guess."

We ran through some basic drills. As usual, she put in extraordinary effort to beat me, even in the ones that weren't really a competition.

"Why do you take this so seriously?" I asked her.

"You're asking someone else why they take this so seriously?"

"Well, I just mean, why are you so determined to beat me? You do it all the time in practice. You make a big deal out of it, but beating me isn't hard. You're a lot better than I am."

"I don't know. I've never thought about it. I guess I've never played against anyone like you. I'm not sure there is anyone like you."

"Thanks," I said, with a distinct lack of enthusiasm.

"Is something wrong? I meant that as a compliment."

"It's okay."

"No, I . . ." She bit back what she'd been about to say and really looked at me. "Something awful happened to you. Well, duh. We knew that in Columbus."

I looked down at my skates.

"I always manage to say the wrong thing, don't I? Phoebe, please look at me."

Reluctantly, I did so.

"I talk too much, and I ask the wrong questions, and it annoys you or hurts you, and that's why you don't like me, isn't it?"

"I don't dislike you," I said defensively.

"I'm sorry. I don't mean to, but I don't know when to shut up. Like right now."

"It's okay."

She took a deep breath, and her words came marginally slower. "Can we start over? I mean, really start over, like from before the season?"

"I'm not very good at starting over."

"I'll try not to say the wrong things. I promise. Please? I want to be friends. I admire you. That's probably why I try so hard against you . . . and I'm babbling again."

"You admire me?"

"Oh, yeah. I think about how fucked up my family is, and then I see you and think about how much worse it could have been and try to imagine what it would have been like. And how you're mysterious and don't tell everyone everything."

"It isn't romantic."

Her face fell. "I did it again. I didn't mean that. Please don't think that I meant that."

"It's okay."

"I'm going to shut up. Really. Please tell me to shut up whenever you want to. I'll try."

She did, and we skated for another fifteen minutes before the rest of the team began to arrive. I did my best to let her start over.

August 1999

Mr. Wilson lifts the cover off of his computer. "Look at this."

I'm fascinated by the fan, and I giggle. "Does it need to cool off?"

"Exactly," he replies, just as if I had been serious.

"Oh."

"It gets very hot inside a computer. You know how you get all hot when you run around a lot?"

"Uh huh."

"Well, all of the electrons in a computer run around a lot, really fast, and they get hot, too. The fan keeps the parts from melting together."

"What's an electron?"

"It's a tiny little particle, too small for you to see. It travels around inside the computer, carrying messages from one place to another."

"Like one of those people on a bicycle?"

"Just like that. That's how a computer works."

"Neat."

"Would you like to learn how to build a computer?"

"Yeah!"

"Then on Saturday, we'll go shopping for the parts we'll need, okay?"

I nod and hug him.

February 2011

I've always hated shopping for clothes. I loved them as much as any other teenage girl, but going into a store drove home both how little I had to spend on them and my freakish dimensions. I was shopping in the adult sections by the time I was thirteen.

Nothing had changed with my move to Minnesota. I had exactly one outfit that was borderline appropriate for those times on road trips when we were supposed to dress nicely. So late in the season I started to panic about the senior banquet. I complained to Abby that I had nothing to wear to it, and then I had to explain that it wasn't a euphemism for having nothing that I was excited about.

So we headed to the mall. This was something I hadn't enjoyed since I was twelve. I wanted to like clothes shopping, but it inevitably brought up pain and embarrassment.

At least Abby seemed to be having a good time until she noticed the look on my face. "You're not even trying," she accused me.

"There's nothing here that fits."

"You haven't even tried anything on."

"There's never anything that fits."

"So where do you get your clothes?"

The desire to do this alone almost hurt.

Abby suddenly recognized my distress. "What's wrong? Is it money? Mom said that she's paying for something for each of us."

That added a new source of discomfort, and I shook my head and said softly, "We need to go to the men's department. I'll get some slacks and a dress shirt."

That's what we did. She talked me into a blue shirt—rather than white—to go with black pants. After we found something for her in a different store, she pulled me into the food court. "Do you want to tell me about it?"

I fidgeted for a bit before saying, "Other than church, I haven't worn a dress since homecoming my junior year. Anything my shoulders fit into hangs like a circus tent around my hips. Otherwise I have to find specialty stores."

"It's okay. You look good in those pants."

"I don't care whether I look good in them," I said bitterly. "I want to be able to wear dresses sometimes."

"Then next year," she replied, taking hold of my hands, "we'll get started earlier and get you a dress."

At that point I thought we were done, until she reminded me of the obvious.

"Are you sure?"

"Trust me. You need shoes."

"Well, yes, I need them," I protested. "I just don't want them."

"We're getting you some shoes."

"We'll need to go to one of the men's stores for those, too," I said glumly.

October 2004

I carefully check all of the seams on the set of shoulder pads. I'm not sure why. I've outgrown the ones I have, and this is the only pair in the store that comes close to fitting me. I'm buying them no matter what.

I'm not entirely happy, but they stubbornly remain my only choice. I certainly can't afford to buy new ones, so whatever shows up used is what I get. This is the only used sporting goods store that has hockey equipment at all. With a sigh, I stand up and take them to the counter. "These."

Mr. Horton doesn't even bother to look at the tag. "With the ones you're trading in, that will be ten dollars."

I pause, working up the courage to ask a question that's bothered me for awhile. "How can it be only ten dollars? That means you're giving me as much credit for the old ones as they cost when I bought them."

He smiles. "They're in better shape than they were when I sold them to you, too. You take care of things."

"That doesn't make sense," I mutter. "How do you make money?"

There's a sad look in his eyes. "You love the game." He speaks very softly. "You love the game like no one I have ever known, in any sport. It would be a crime if you couldn't play. If the kids in Highland Park got to play and you didn't because you couldn't afford it, it would break my heart."

I squirm as he continues. "So when you come in and spend an hour and a half looking at skates, finding the ones least likely to fall apart on you, I charge you as much as I think you can afford. I'm not going to let you get out of here with a penny if I can help it, but you also aren't leaving without the gear you need."

"I don't want charity." I try to look defiant.

"The correct response, Phoebe, is 'Thank you.'"

I stare at him, trying to hold on to my resolve. "I want to repay you for everything."

"I insist that you do. Do you want to know how?"

"Work for you?"

He shakes his head. "No. You're never going to pay me an extra dime. What you are going to do is someday, when you can afford it, you are going to do for someone else what I am doing for you. You are going to make sure that they can pursue their dreams. And you are going to tell them the same thing I am telling you, that they also need to do that for someone. If you do that, then you will have paid back everything you owe me with interest. Understand?"

I nod, not quite able to come up with words.

Mr. Horton pushes away from the counter, smiling. "Say, 'Thank you,' Phoebe."

"Thank you, Phoebe." I grin.

Our last road trip of the regular season was against Michigan State, and it was a frustrating weekend in East Lansing. I'm not sure whether that was because I was on my best behavior or despite it. Coach Long warned me before we got on the plane that he wasn't going to tolerate my getting into any fights. I'd made it too clear that I didn't like Mallory Jackson, and he decided he didn't trust my judgment.

It wasn't just me, though. State got inside all of our heads, and we didn't play our best hockey.

On Friday night Julie, one of our All-America candidates on defense, had perhaps the worst game of her career. She committed some awful turnovers and then, in the second period, came off the bench on a change and charged into the offensive zone just as the Spartans jumped on a loose puck and went the other way right past her. They scored on the breakaway to tie the game at 3.

Julie looked crushed on the bench. The coaches tried to comfort her, and she ignored them. In another of my brilliant ideas, I sat down next to her. "Everyone else is scared to sit here because they're afraid that they're going to say the wrong thing and make you mad."

"And you think you can say the right thing?" she snarled back.

I looked away from her. "No, but I never know the right thing to say, so I'm not scared about it."

"What's your point?"

"Just that I think we have a better chance to win if you're mad at me instead of at yourself."

I offered a weak smile into the glare she gave me. I had no idea if that was the right thing to say or not. Either way we lost 5–3, dropping us into a second-place tie with Michigan.

The next night we beat State for the first time that season. Going 1–3 against them was a disappointment. We took it as a statement about our mental toughness.

I had a tolerable weekend. I had an assist and was +1. More importantly for my continued place on the team, I avoided any serious altercations. I did pick up one roughing minor in a scrum around the net, but Coach must have agreed with me that it wasn't my fault because he didn't bench me.

My personal highlight was watching Mallory make two trips to the box for taking hacks at me.

November 2007

Mr. Jenkins waits until we're in the house before he begins the tirade he's held back since we were in the doctor's office.

"You're not a girl!"

I'm still in shock. "I feel like one."

"But you're not. You're some sort of . . . of . . ."

"I'm a freak."

"That's right. You're a freak."

I curl up on my bed and let him rant. It doesn't matter what he says. It's what the doctor told us that's so awful. Mr. Jenkins is right. I'm not a girl. I look like one, if you ignore my build. But I'm not. Genetically I'm a boy. Biologically, I don't really have the parts of either.

I turn to face the wall before I start crying. What am I?

In hockey the clock only runs during play. Unlike football, you can't hold a committee meeting while it ticks down. If you want to waste time to protect a lead or kill a penalty, you have to be more creative about it.

The best option is just to keep the puck at the other end of the ice, but against a good team this isn't so easy. The next best option is to tie the puck up along the boards. Nothing bad can happen when it's pinned to the wall. The trick is that you have to keep the other team from pulling it out without freezing it so completely that the ref blows the whistle.

To do it right, you need to be physically strong, and you need good hands so that you can corral the puck when it makes a bid for freedom. And you need stamina, because it's grueling, tiring work.

In other words, I was good at it.

Which brings us to the beginning of the worst hockey week I ever had. For two periods against Wisconsin in the Big Ten championship game, we played our best game of the season, without question. This wasn't a repeat of the games in Madison. We came out flying. Jenny scored twice in the first period, and we controlled play, no matter what the shot totals say.

When Tammy made it 3–0 halfway through the second, I felt really confident. That got shaken when the Badgers scored twice in less than a minute, one of them on a power play. We got the two-goal lead back right at the end of the period on a pretty play by Kris, Jenny, and Tammy. I wasn't as confident as I had been earlier, though.

We were exhausted. Amy looked like she'd died every time she came off the ice after a shift. The lack of a reliable third line was the main culprit, though playing six freshmen unused to the long season didn't help. Wisconsin rolled three lines, sometimes four, relentlessly, and they were one of the few teams that could match us in size and strength. They just wore down the top two lines.

The coaches changed the game plan for the third to entirely defense. We played some trap, which we rarely did, and just tried to dump the puck back into their zone. It wasn't our style, so we weren't good at it, but we really didn't have a choice. We didn't have the energy left to play both offense and defense.

It worked for about ten minutes. I got a regular shift and did my thing along the boards. Other teams would have gotten frustrated down by two with ten minutes to go and having trouble getting the puck into the scoring areas. Wisconsin wasn't other teams.

When things fell apart, they did so quickly and completely. Once again they scored twice in two minutes and were running all over us. It made me sick that I was on the ice for both of them. I lost control of Kelly James in front of the net, allowing her to keep a rebound alive long enough for it to get jammed in. Then I got beaten in one of those battles along the boards.

Erika stopped everything she had a chance on and carried us to overtime, but the extra period was an eight-minute formality. We had nothing left and couldn't even muster a shot on a power play. When they finally ended it, no one was surprised, least of all us.

It was disheartening. We'd played as well as we possibly could, and it wasn't enough. They weren't just better than we were; they were so much better that they could take the best punch we could deliver and return it. Hockey is a game of funny bounces, and it isn't hard to imagine a scenario in which we had won, but by the end they were skating, and we were gasping for air.

The NCAA tournament started the next week. I wanted to get one more shot at them. That team was a whirlwind, and the eastern schools had no idea what was about to hit them.

After the game, Abby and I sat in her apartment. "It's not your fault," she insisted.

"Yes, it is." My voice was dull.

"No, it isn't. We all collapsed."

"Winning those kinds of battles is my whole game. The rest of you score. You make pretty passes. You do things. If I can't keep people tied up, I can't do anything for this team."

"Stop it, Phoebe. Most of us didn't do any better. The first line did all the scoring. I had the same –2 you did. They just weren't in the third period."

"But mine were in the third. That shouldn't happen."

She paced around the living room. "They're the best team in the country for a reason. They just beat us."

"You sound like you're trying to convince yourself."

"Of course I'm trying to convince myself. We have six days to get ready to play Cornell."

"May I at least blame myself and be miserable for tonight?"

"No. We're putting an end to this right now."

Tammy came out of the kitchen. I minimized the amount of time I spent there, since she was Abby's roommate. "Suck it up." That was easy for her to say. She'd had a goal and two assists in the losing effort.

The two of them were close friends, which was part of the reason I stayed away. It put Abby in an awkward spot when Tammy got started on me. I stood up. "If you won't let me sulk here, I'm going to go home."

Abby grabbed me and gave me a hug. "Don't be too hard on yourself. We'll get them in two weeks."

I had to walk past the arena to get home. Kennedy was standing there. "Come on in. We're throwing a pity party, and you're welcome here."

"How did you . . . Abby called you, didn't she?"

"Yep. She threatened to kill me if I let you get by."

"Then I'd better come in." I walked up the steps.

"Yeah. I don't think she was kidding."

"Abby is never kidding when she threatens to kill someone."

I spent the rest of the night watching movies with Kennedy, Caitlyn, and Jenny.

September 2008

My computer teacher asks me to stay after class the second day of the semester. "Phoebe, why are you taking this course?"

"I want to have some computer classes on my transcript. And I think it will be an easy A."

"It would be an easy A if I let you take it, yes."

"What do you mean?"

"My job is to challenge students and make sure that they are learning. You won't learn anything in this class. You know it all already."

"Are you kicking me out?"

"In a manner of speaking, yes. You can sit in this room during third period so long as you are learning. I'm going to drop you out of the class and reregister you as doing an independent study. I'm going to give you some serious projects, not the basic stuff I'll be teaching the other students. They're going to be the kind of things you can expect to do if you go into programming professionally. Next semester, it will be just one project."

The excitement must show in my face.

"I take it that you like this idea?"

"Yes, sir."

"Great. Since I will be teaching a class, you're going to have to do most of the work on your own. I assume that you are capable of not letting the regular class disturb you and focusing on something else?"

"Yes, sir. Most of my teachers complain about it."

"Well, you'll find that it can be a very useful skill in a lot of IT work. I'll provide you with whatever materials and books you need. I'll make some time for you when the class is working on writing programs, and I'll always be available after school if you need more help."

"Thank you, sir. In a couple of weeks I'll need to be at hockey practice right after school. Could I meet you during lunch hour?"

"I'm sure that we'll be able to make time somewhere."

The back end of that week involved a flight to New York that we shouldn't have bothered getting on. There just isn't any polite way to say it. We quit. We started horrifically and then decided that it wasn't worth the effort to fight back. Every single one of us. Cornell scored on their first shot, twenty-four seconds into the game. Two and a half minutes later they scored on their third shot. By the end of the first period it was 4–0. There wasn't any reason to play the last two periods because the game was already over.

We turned pucks over in our own end. I did, leading to the third goal. Erika should have picked up an assist on their first goal. We didn't forecheck with any effort. We didn't backcheck with any effort. We didn't fight for pucks with any effort.

We never recovered from losing to Wisconsin the previous week. Mentally we were still in a place where we gave everything we had and it wasn't good enough. Finding out that we had to travel didn't help, though we shouldn't have let that defeat us. The first round of the NCAA tournament is played at the rink of the higher-seeded team and there was only one team in the country we thought was better than we were, but we kicked away our chance to prove it. But no matter how badly we thought we should have played at home, we needed to, as Tammy put it, suck it up.

It hurt. It should hurt forever. Every time in our lives we face something important, we should look back and remember what that game felt like and make sure we don't quit again.

The season was over. It was time to put the uniforms away and figure out what we needed to do to be better next season. There were only five seniors on that team, and I was going to miss them. They did all kinds of little things to make me feel welcome and deserved better than to end their careers on that kind of game.

There was reason for optimism. All of the teams who could claim to be better than us were losing a lot more than we were. Wisconsin graduated two players who each had more goals than our entire senior class. The same was true across the country.

Mallory Jackson was coming back, but I was tired of losing to her.

January 2003

"You aren't supposed to go out, Mr. Wilson."

"This is important," he answers in a voice that is little more than a husk of its former self.

So I go with him. We slowly walk downtown. He quizzes me on math along the way, but he pauses in the middle of questions because talking causes him pain. He takes me into the Fifth Third bank branch on Jasper. "Now you just let me do the talking, okay?" I nod.

We don't go up to the teller, like Mrs. Wilson does. Instead we sit at a desk with a nice man in a tie. He has a sign that says his name is Gary Davis.

"I need to set up a savings account for my girl," Mr. Wilson tells him. He coughs into his handkerchief. I don't think the man notices the blood in it; he's too busy wondering how I'm Mr. Wilson's girl.

When they finish, Mr. Davis gives Mr. Wilson a bunch of papers. As we leave, Mr. Wilson hands one of them to me. "You see those numbers?" He points to two long numbers at the bottom. "Those are the routing number and the account number. You need to memorize those, so that you'll never forget them, just like you did with the Social Security number last week."

I nod. I'm good at memorizing numbers.

"You now have a bank account of your own. There's some money in it, and Mrs. Wilson will put some more in when she can. She'll make sure that it stays open. Don't tell anyone that you have it, understand?"

"That's against the rules, isn't it?"

He looks sad. "I'm sorry, Phoebe. I've taught you how to follow the rules, but I'm not going to have time to teach you when to break them. This is one of those times. Don't tell anyone."

I nod solemnly. "I won't."

"It's more than just the money we put in. You can use it, too. You'll figure out ways to put money into it that you don't want anyone to know that you have. Maybe your next foster family will be better than we are, but in case they aren't, you won't be entirely dependent on them."

"Thank you, Mr. Wilson."

"You're very welcome, Phoebe."

CHAPTER 7

The off-season was a time to reflect, with no practices and no games to play. I didn't have a summer team to play for; that would have cost money. For the same reason, I wasn't a part of the intense sessions at a private facility in the northern suburbs with high-tech machines to help you improve your skills, like skating. Some of the others informed me that Tammy noted my absence.

Instead, I slowly relaxed into a real life. It wasn't like the previous summer, with the terrors of finding my way in a new place. It might have qualified as the first thing approaching a normal life I'd had in eight years.

Kennedy and I spent time exploring the Cities. We left all of the native Minnesotans behind, got off campus, and wandered. We found a nice spot in south Minneapolis around Lake Calhoun that we returned to regularly and just sat looking out over the water, talking.

"Wait. So you don't know who your real parents are?"

There was a cool breeze coming off the lake. Kennedy was sitting on the grass watching the world go by. I was on my back, looking up at the sky, enjoying the sun.

"No. No one has any idea who they are."

She was still trying to put all of it together. "But they had your name. Couldn't they find someone named Rose who had had a daughter named Phoebe?"

"My original last name wasn't Rose. I didn't know what it was when they found me. Just Phoebe."

"So how did you get the name Rose?"

"I picked it, with the help of my case worker."

"And you picked Rose."

"My first choice was Gretzky. Fortunately, Ms. Louder had enough sense to make me pick something else."

She laughed at that. "How old were you?"

"About four."

"I think you picked well. I like your name. It's a lot better than mine."

"What's wrong with Kennedy?"

"Nothing by itself. It's the whole thing: Kennedy Kane. I should be dating a superhero."

"Hmm?"

"The alliteration. Like Lois Lane or Pepper Potts."

"Ah. I get it now."

"I love my parents, but they blew that one."

"You can always change it."

"Meh. Not worth the hassle."

"So what do you plan to do when you graduate?"

"I'm transferring to the School of Veterinary Medicine next year. I want to be a vet. I've always been good with animals. They seem to like me."

"Everybody likes you. Why should they be different?"

She blushed a little. "I try to be nice."

"No, you don't. It doesn't take any effort at all for you. It's just who you are."

She just smiled, proving my point.

"Why be sorry? I think it's great. I don't understand it at all, mind you. I'd have as much trouble trying to be that nice as Caitlyn does trying to sit still."

"You do fine in your own way," she assured me.

"I'm nice to people who deserve it. You manage to be nice to everyone who doesn't deserve it, too."

"Is that a compliment?"

"It's more a description, but, yeah, I think it's a good thing. If everyone was like you, the world would be a better place."

"Thank you."

We were quiet for awhile. "What are you looking at?" she finally asked.

"The clouds. Just watching them float on past."

"I like to do that sometimes. I think about what shapes they look like."

"Like a Rorschach test, but fluffier."

"That's a good way to put it."

I didn't voice my suspicion that we see entirely different things when we look at the clouds.

I spent more time with Caitlyn. I don't know how to explain it, but she grew on me. To the world, she was hyperactive and cheerful, but in private she could be moody. Occasionally, the spring would wind down, and she would sit on the couch and do nothing. When I finally got to see that side of her, she seemed more sympathetic.

Most of the time, though, it was nonstop motion and chatter, and I slowly learned how to treat it as background noise when necessary. Somehow she got me to play video games with her.

"Come on, Phoebe, you're not even trying."

"Yes, I am." I set the controller down as my character died another gruesome death.

"No, you're not. I've beaten you ten times in a row."

"I'm trying, Caitlyn. I'm just not very good."

"That's because you don't even practice." She growled her frustration. "You don't want to get better. That counts as not trying."

I leaned back on the couch in the apartment she shared with Amy Heckenthorpe, which we generally shortened to "Heck." "All right, I'm not trying very hard."

"Why?" It was practically a wail. "Don't you want to beat me?"

I shrugged. "It's not that important."

"So why do you play, then?"

"I play because you ask me to and you like it."

"That's it?"

"Isn't that enough?"

She was in full outrage. I enjoyed watching it. "Don't you hate losing all the time? You sure do on the ice."

"That's different."

She nodded. "I'll accept that. I still wish you'd try harder when we play. It would make beating you more fun."

"If you really want the competition, why don't you play Morgan more often?"

She gave me a funny look before resetting the game. "Give it another shot."

So I picked the controller up again and lost another eight games.

One of the ways that Caitlyn endeared herself to me is that she really did try to work on the things that I found irritating. She even practiced not talking. It didn't necessarily go well.

"Oh, hey, the pairs for *Dancing with the Stars* were announced." We were reading in the lounge. Other girls wandered through from time to time, but they knew they weren't supposed to interrupt the silence.

I clicked off the stopwatch I had going. "Seven minutes and forty-three seconds. Not bad."

"That's it? That had to be at least fifteen minutes."

"Sorry. It was 1:58 when we stopped talking about summer vacations, and it's 2:06 now."

"How long did we say we were going to do this?"

"Until 3:30."

"I don't think I can make it."

"You'd rather do my laundry next week?"

We lapsed back into silence.

"I need a snack."

"Four minutes and twenty-two seconds."

"Aaaaaaaarrrrrrggggggghhhh."

January 18, 2008

As I get a pen out of my desk, I notice that my keepsakes envelope isn't there. I search all the drawers. It isn't anywhere else in my room, either.

She helped me clean my room yesterday. She was trying to show me how it should be done, because I can't do anything right.

I go down to the kitchen and ask her if she's seen it. She says no, but also that I need to leave my past behind. She's worried that I'm letting nostalgia interfere with moving forward.

I'm pretty sure the bitch took my things. I spend an hour looking through the garbage. Then I spend three hours searching the rest of the house. It isn't anywhere.

It's gone. It had everything I had left from the Wilsons in it. The note I got from him the first Christmas after he died. The pictures from the time they took me to Disney World. It's all gone. All I have left is the computer. Thank God I never told her why it's important to me.

If looks could maim, she'd be on her way to the hospital in a picnic basket.

"Tell me something about yourself."

I had the bag of fries in front of me, but I knew they'd go cold. I was looking at the table. Abby recognized the signs that I was going to tell something uncomfortable and kept quiet.

"This is probably the last thing that really scares me," I finally said. "There's other stuff that hurts, but not that scares me. This is different because it's actually about me rather than something someone did to me."

I paused again.

"I don't just have a man's physique. By some definitions, I am a man. I have a 46XY chromosome, which is the genetic marker for being male. I also have a condition called Androgen Insensitivity Syndrome. My body doesn't process testosterone properly.

"It means that, externally at least, I developed the breasts and genitals of a female. Inside, it's a completely different story. I don't have ovaries or any of the other reproductive organs of a woman. My vagina ends in a blank wall. There's nothing beyond it."

Abby's eyes had gone wide.

"Instead, I have a pair of testicles in there. They're completely internal. I didn't even know that I had them until I was sixteen. Until then, I thought that I was perfectly normal in at least this one way. I was wrong.

"I can't have kids, either as a man or as a woman. The parts just aren't there. But learning that didn't really bother me that much. I had a lot more important things to worry about. I got my diagnosis about two weeks before . . ." I faltered at continuing. "I'm pretty sure it was the thing that pushed him over the edge."

She was straining to keep herself from saying anything.

"Most girls who have AIS in this form find out about it when they never have their first period. For me it got lost in the shuffle of living with different foster families during puberty. I sure as hell wasn't going to tell anyone about not getting my period. So no one else ever realized that I hadn't gotten it.

"I found out I had AIS because of my strength coach back in Vicksburg. He was a Russian immigrant named Mr. Radic. He's the kind of guy you start out thinking is a mean old bastard and only realize six months later, if you're paying attention, that he really cares about you.

"Mr. Radic constantly preached about avoiding steroids. He took one look at me and immediately thought I was taking them. He made me get tested. When we got the results, my testosterone levels were off the charts, beyond what you'd get from a drug regime. Those testicles produce as much of it as if I were a guy, but it never binds to anything, just floats around in my body, doing nothing. Mr. Radic made me go to a doctor.

"That's how I learned that my body is even stranger than I thought. One of the reasons I'd walk through a minefield if Coach Long asked me to is that he never even blinked when I gave him the paperwork about it. I had to, because I fail every drug test I take."

I moved my shake from my right to my left, which is the signal that I'm opening up the floor for questions.

"He's never breathed a word to anyone as far as I know," Abby said. "And they let you play? Obviously."

"Yeah. If I were good enough to play in the Olympics, there's a chance I wouldn't be allowed to. They've been fighting to prevent a South African woman with AIS from running track."

"So how are you allowed to play? Does the NCAA have different rules?"

"The NCAA doesn't have any rules at all. You can get a waiver for it, though, if you have a medical diagnosis of a natural hormonal imbalance."

"Wow. That's all . . . unexpected. You're talking about something I didn't even know existed. Does it have side effects?"

"Bad ones? Yeah. I'm going to have to have the testes removed at some point. If I don't, they're very likely to become cancerous as I age. After that, I'll have to take synthetic estrogen since my body won't be making any. I haven't yet because I have no idea whether the NCAA would change its mind if I were actually taking hormones. I'll need to start taking them sometime after I graduate."

"So this is why you're so big?"

"I have no idea. Most women with AIS are hyperfeminine, but not all. People with AIS have different symptoms, different bodies. There's no way to know whether anything I develop is related to it."

"I'm going to need some time to process this."

I obviously looked hurt.

"No, I don't mean that—oh, hell, I don't know what I mean. But it's not going to change anything between us. That's solid."

Between summer and fall terms I stayed with Abby's parents for two weeks. It was the first time I'd been off campus for more than four days since I'd arrived twenty months earlier. Abby wasn't there. She spent the two weeks in Italy with some high school friends. It had taken me forever to convince her that I wasn't jealous, a task not made easier by the fact that it wasn't entirely true.

At first I was uncomfortable with the idea of being at her parents' place without her. I wasn't sure what my relationship to her family was independent of her, so it was with some trepidation that I accepted their invitation.

I shouldn't have worried, because I felt right at home. Her brother and I spent a lot of time at a rink skating together. Abby is built like her father: squat, compact, and solid. Derek takes after their mother. He had more skill than Abby, but his slight frame prevented him from even hoping to play Division I hockey. He ended up having a decent career at the small college level and had the sense not to try to extend it further than that. As he put it during our sessions, the fact that a girl could push him around the rink disabused him of the idea that he had a long-term future in the game.

As much as I liked Derek and Tom, though, it was Abby's mother who made me feel welcome. I often imagined that if she had been the mental health counselor at Vicksburg High School, things would have turned out differently. Instead, she never let me forget that she was not my therapist.

So it was with her cautions in mind that I asked her for advice. I started with something simple that I couldn't see blowing up on me. She was an early riser, so I'd only been awake for a couple of hours when she came downstairs.

"Do you know anything about meditation?"

She laughed. "Could you let me have some coffee first?"

Once she had caffeine, we sat down in the living room. She guided me through relaxation, and I succeeded in achieving a nice hypnotic trance. I think I was hoping that she would ask me questions once I was under.

She didn't take the bait. Her voice remained calm, but her words remained entirely neutral and uninquisitive. I remained in a trance for about forty-five minutes, but she didn't ask anything until she was sure I was out of it.

"Do you really need my help, Phoebe?"

I rolled my shoulders as the feeling of deep relaxation left me. "Yes," I said emphatically.

"Why?" She said it in a tone of voice most people don't have, one that had no hint of contradiction, just inquisitiveness. "I've watched you. Did you teach yourself meditation?"

"Yes."

"You figured it out very nicely. I'm not sure you need my assistance."

"I don't usually go under that easily."

The corners of her mouth quirked up. "Then I'm glad I could help." She took a sip of her second cup of coffee.

"Thank you."

"You're welcome. You were hoping for something else, weren't you?"

"Yes," I admitted.

"Phoebe, I want to set some ground rules. They mostly concern my behavior, but you should know what they are. I want to help. I will always be there when you want help, but you are going to have to ask for it. You are going to have to decide whether you trust me enough to ask something."

I looked at the floor. "Why?"

"Because that's not my role."

"What is your role?" I asked before she could continue.

"The two of us are going to have to work that out. But I am not your therapist. I am not your mother. I am not your lover. And I am not, yet at least, your friend."

"You aren't my friend?"

"No. Abby is your friend, and keep in mind that that means you shouldn't let her boss you around."

I giggled a little, an indication that I was still relaxed. "Don't worry. I've figured out how to wind her up."

She smiled. "Good. Someone needs to. But that makes me the mother of your friend, and that's a relationship with plenty of complications of its own. Until we sort those out, you are going to have to be the one who defines what we share. There aren't any short cuts."

"If I really want help on something I can't bring up, is it okay if I get Abby so wound up that she asks you about it?"

She smothered a laugh. "No. Thank you for warning me, but I'll tell her the same thing. If she wants to know something about you, she'll have to ask you."

October 2006

CPS dropped me off at my new foster family this afternoon. I'm slightly taller than Mr. Jenkins even though I'm only fifteen. I don't think he likes that, but I'm not sure that he likes anything about me.

It takes him two hours to tell me all of his rules. It takes me a minute and a half to tell him mine. I'm playing hockey. Mrs. Hawley got it declared to be therapy for me. I have no idea how she managed that, but it shuts up his arguments quickly.

My room is larger than I know what to do with. I get my computer set up on the desk. The poor thing is hopelessly outdated, but it's mine. I had to leave the one I was using with the Kilpatricks; they didn't let me keep it like Mrs. Wilson did after Mr. Wilson died. I almost disassembled all of the improvements I made on it but for some reason decided not to be petty.

Three years and three months. That's how long I have to be here.

Abby finally knew pretty much everything awful about my childhood, but none of the others really did. Even Kennedy didn't know about my past in much detail.

That started to change in June of my freshman year. Kennedy was the only one in the players' lounge when I came in one day.

"Are you okay, Phoebe?"

"No." I sat down on the floor, leaning against the TV stand. I tucked my knees under my chin. I was crying.

"What's wrong?"

"It's dead. I can't fix it."

"What's dead?" There was alarm in her voice.

"My first computer." I saw confusion in her face. "Mr. Wilson and I built it."

That clearly didn't help her grasp why I was so broken up.

I tried to explain but broke down in sobs instead. Fortunately, Abby had seen me going in and was attracted by the noise. I heard her ask what was going on, though I had buried my face.

"Something about a computer dying." Kennedy's voice came from right in front of me. "Who's Mr. Wilson?"

"Oh, shit. He's the only foster father she had that she actually liked." I felt her hands on my shoulders. "Come on, Phoebe. Let's sit on the couch."

I let her pull me to my feet and lead me there. I cried on her shoulder. "They built a computer together when she was like seven. She's kept it running for twelve years."

I felt Kennedy sit on the other side of me and put her hand on my leg. When I looked up next, there were about seven or eight others in the room, watching. Abby pulled me against her. "Phoebe, I don't think you've ever told people about Mr. Wilson."

I was caught in indecision for a bit, but once I started, the words came pouring out. "That computer was the only thing of his I had." I told them about arriving at the Wilsons' house, how they were my third family. I told them about the computer and the way he helped me with my homework and how he assigned me homework even if my teacher didn't. I told them about how he always took me seriously and how he let me teach him about hockey. I told them about how he was the last person who made sure that I had proper equipment and who drove me to practices.

And I told them about how much he loved the University of Minnesota and that he was the reason I'd been determined to come here. Even Abby had never heard that part of the story.

When I was done and fell silent, Abby pushed me up, and everyone gathered in a huddle. They all hugged me in turn. Abby and Kennedy walked me back to my room, and they watched as I carefully slotted all of the pieces back in their places and screwed the cover back onto the case. Abby said that she'd take it up to her parents' place that weekend, and we could figure out what to do with it later.

Kennedy pulled me back over to the athletic complex. "I'm not letting you stay in that room by yourself." I spent the rest of the afternoon and evening sitting on the couch. I don't think I said anything the whole time, but as the girls came and went, I slowly pulled myself together.

Right after Labor Day a sense of excitement started building. Our first official practice wasn't until the twenty-first, but we all knew it was coming. A placid summer gave way to the anticipation of a season that would allow us to complete those things we'd made a mess of in the spring. No one, we were determined, was going to stop us from winning a championship. The only ones who could do that were ourselves.

CHAPTER 8

Before every season, a team has to integrate its new rookies. Serious hazing is mostly a thing of the past, but there is still a pecking order. Establishing that hierarchy while also making them feel like a part of the whole can resemble one of those awful corporate team-building exercises, except that there is a lot more buy-in from the participants. It's hard to explain to someone who has never been a part of it.

My second year they came up with a new way to haze the freshmen. By "they" I mean that year's captains. I wished someone had warned me about it, because the first I knew was when they started showing up while I was meditating. Curious, I asked Katarina Janacek what she was doing on the front lawn of the Bierman Building at four a.m.

"Kathy and Jackie said that we need to train with you if we want to learn to be champions." She sounded so earnest. "They said we were supposed to meet you here."

"Oh, they did, did they?"

She nodded. The joke was on me, then. So much for my nice, peaceful morning.

Pretty soon all five of them were there, decidedly less perky than usual. "Do any of you do yoga?" They all shook their heads. "Well, you will today." I started them slow. It was after the yoga that I tried to kill them. The two-mile warm-up jog ended at the big parking ramp on Washington. Seven stories. Seven flights of stairs. I usually spent about a half hour running up and taking the elevator back down to the basement, but I added an extra fifteen minutes just to be mean.

That's when they started asking if we were done. I laughed and took them to Ridder. We skated agility relays and did some passing. I heard one of them ask the building manager if I really did this every day. He said yes, but only for a couple of hours now that the semester had started.

About 7:15 I told them they were lucky that I had an 8:05 class, so no trip to the weight room. They groaned their thanks.

I rode Amy Cross especially hard, and I confess to enjoying it. She's almost my height, but the similarities end there. She's graceful, slender, blonde, all limbs, and beautiful. She can skate, and she was planning to take my playing time. I couldn't dislike her for that. She was not only nice but also better than I was.

That's the way it works in sports. But I wasn't going to make it easy for her.

That afternoon when I got back to the rink, I glared at Kathy. She put on her best poker face. "Something wrong?"

"You enjoyed telling them to get out of bed that early, didn't you?"

"Oh, come on." She lost control of her smile. "You can't tell me you didn't have fun running them ragged."

"If you were so confident I'd have a good time, why didn't you warn me?"

"You'd have found some way to get out of it and missed the fun."

I sighed. "Yes, it was entertaining. Once. I really do prefer my mornings peaceful, though."

"It won't happen again until next year. I promise. Unless they decided they enjoyed it."

That fall I became the team's unofficial math tutor. The most common major among the players was a business degree, which required a semester of calculus and one of stats. I kept my opinion on the rigor of the business school's stats class to myself. Most of the time.

Being a teacher was hard and taught patience to all of us. I learned a lot about how other people see math. It had come so easily for me that I had never really appreciated that it's not always easy for others. The idea of a limit, that one can get infinitely close to something without ever getting there, seems obvious to me. I hadn't appreciated that that's not true for everyone else.

The tutoring experience was good for me. If these hadn't been people who were already friends, I'd have been pretty contemptuous watching them struggle. I'd have assumed that this inability to get stuff easily was a defect. It made me sensitive to the level of condescension my fellow techies often display. I realized that I didn't want to be like that. Why should everyone be able to write a Perl script?

So I sat down and tried to teach my friends math. I got better at it. Slowly.

Once the season started, I was only a hockey "player" in the loosest possible sense of the word. The problem with being the seventh-best defenseman in a six-player rotation is that you spend a lot of time watching the game from the stands.

The year before, Morgan had T-shirts made that read, "Watching hockey since October 1, 2010," for herself, Katie, and Gloria. In the locker room before the first game of the season she gave me mine, except it had that day's date. I wore it with pride. The rules were that it got taken away in a special ceremony if we arrived at the arena and found that one of us was dressing for the game. You only got it back when you were scratched again, the date crossed out and updated with a Sharpie.

The phrase "healthy scratch" bothered me less than I had thought it would. The three of us discussed whether it's harder for Morgan, who has never dressed regularly, or Katie and me, who played regularly for a year before losing our spots. The consensus was that Morgan had it easier, but I think that had more to do with her upbeat personality than her role.

It was easier to take since I couldn't argue with Coach's decision. I wasn't sure that either Kennedy or Amy Cross was better than

I was right then, but they both had a lot more potential to improve than I did.

You can tell a successful sports team in part by watching the scrubs. No one is really happy when they don't dress or only get three shifts a game on the fourth line. On a team of twenty-four players, at least twelve of them are convinced that they could be an All-American if they played on the first line. On a good team, everyone accepts their role and maintains a good attitude even if they grind through practice every day only to watch the games in street clothes. I was never able to figure out if the team was good because everyone remained positive or whether it was the other way around. But I knew it didn't really matter.

My first stint as a healthy scratch lasted exactly two games. Frustrated at being shut out 17-0 over two games that weekend, a St. Cloud State forward slashed Julie on the wrist and broke a couple of small bones. She was out for six weeks. The fun part was that we made the trip to Madison the second week of the season.

The first adjustment I had to make had nothing to do with playing. Roommates got shuffled with graduations and new freshmen. I'd have preferred to stick with Kennedy, but we were told we had to change.

I'd developed a greater appreciation for Caitlyn as we spent time together, but I wasn't sure that I wanted to be roommates and have no escape route. Nevertheless, that was the assignment I was handed.

If you observe Caitlyn casually, it's easy to conclude that she doesn't pay the slightest attention to the world around her or anyone in it. That's only sometimes true. At other times, she surprises you with her awareness and concern.

The series at Wisconsin was early afternoon games on Saturday and Sunday. We bussed to Madison on Friday and killed time that evening. When we were back in our room, Caitlyn sat on her bed, looking at me with a quirky smile. "You don't need to warn me about how you sleep. I knew the stories before I volunteered to room with you."

"Stories? Volunteered?"

"Crap. That came out wrong. Not really stories. You scared Kennedy a few times last year, and she talked to some of us. So everyone knows that you have nightmares."

"Everyone?"

"Yeah. Sorry. She kind of freaked out in Columbus."

I supposed that I couldn't blame her. "So you volunteered?"

"Several of us did. We all vetoed Abby straight off."

"Really?"

"Yeah. No one should have to put up with her that many hours of the day."

Her facial expression almost made me giggle. "Probably for the best. I'm glad it's one of you guys"—meaning someone from my class.

"That's what we thought. Jenny and Morgan wanted to do it, but I talked them out of it."

"How?" What I really wanted to ask was why.

"Because I can sleep through a war."

"Thank you." I had no idea what else to say.

"You're welcome. I'm looking forward to it."

"Really? Why?"

"Because if I miss curfew, I know you'll try to cover for me."

"I will?"

"Duh. Of course."

"Don't be too confident about that." We both knew that she was right and that I was bluffing.

"I live on the edge."

I slept fine that night; the nightmares came the next afternoon. I skated to the bench after my fourth shift, swearing. I probably would have snapped my stick in the tunnel if Coach hadn't put one hand on it to prevent exactly that. He wouldn't let me punch the wall, either. I sat there trying to figure out some way to vent my frustration.

Ten minutes into the game and Wisconsin was already ahead 2-0. It was my fault. I was not just on the ice for both of them but directly involved. Gigi Reynolds turned me into a pretzel on the first one. She broke into the zone; I bit on her deke and then flailed wildly at her as she sailed by. I couldn't even get a stick on her to take a penalty. On the second, I left my position to chase the puck along the boards. Angie Payne promptly passed it back to where I should have been. Kennedy couldn't get there in time to bail me out, and the red light came on again.

Kennedy sat down next to me. "What would be the proper, crazy thing to say right now?"

"Don't worry about it."

"No, I want to learn how to do this."

"Only someone truly insane would tell me not to worry about it because we'll get it back."

She made a face. "Anyone could come up with that. I want something truly unexpected and out of left field."

"This isn't going to work."

"Why not? It always works when you do it."

I grabbed a water bottle and squeezed a stream into my mouth, mostly so that I was doing something with my hands. "I'm better at it than you are."

"I want you to teach me." She said it with her best look of wide-eyed innocence.

"Well, the first thing to do is stop asking how. If you can't do it with absolute certitude, then don't bother."

"So I should just go, 'Tell me the right zany thing to say, dammit.' Is that better?"

"Closer, but zany and anger don't mix well for this purpose."

"I suppose. Anger really only begets anger, and you seem to have enough of it for both of us right now."

"You should try writing an advice column," I suggested.

"Do you think I should go for ditzy and clueless to deliver my lines?"

"It doesn't really fit you. Ditzy is more Caitlyn's thing."

"Hey, I heard that!" drifted down the bench.

"Okay, then what do you suggest?"

"I think your best approach is . . . how the hell did you get me talking about this?"

"Oh, so I am learning. Thanks."

We ended the first period down 3–0. We outplayed them the rest of the way and almost tied it up at the end. Losing close games to the Badgers was getting old.

Fortunately, in our league you played the same team twice in a weekend, and we took advantage. We got out on top in the second game and didn't blow the lead this time.

It was a huge win for us. Psychology in sports is a funny thing. None of us would have said it, but before that game, in our hearts, we thought they were better than we were. The previous year that had been true; the only time we beat them it was because they played poorly.

That shouldn't have carried over that next season, but it did. We were still convinced that we would come out, play our best, and lose.

The credit goes to our coaching staff and our captains that after the first ten minutes of the Saturday game, we played our hearts out despite that fear. There's a doctoral thesis on leadership in there somewhere.

The researcher can interview me because I watched almost the whole thing. I only played seven minutes. That was okay, because they were seven boring, uneventful minutes. We didn't score, but they didn't score either, and that was all I wanted. I figured that it was tough for us to lose if we never gave up a goal. We had a lot of players who could win games, so I'd done my job.

Kennedy and I weren't a pair any longer. Rather than having a top four with the two of us as the third pair, it was now a top five and I was the sixth on the depth chart.

I wasn't able to fool myself into thinking that I was better than the defensemen who were getting my playing time. I wasn't. I could play my best and still lose the battle for playing time.

March 2003

It's raining. It's a cold, gray drizzle, not even a storm. That's fitting. My world goes out with a whimper, not a bang.

Protective Services comes to get me a few hours later. I say good-bye to Mrs. Wilson. She cries, and I wish that I could, too. Why can't I cry? Even when she said again that she wished she could adopt me, I didn't cry.

I didn't cry at Mr. Wilson's funeral, either. It's like there's this big dam and all the tears are stuck behind it. No way to get them out.

Mrs. Wilson understands, I think. She doesn't say anything, but it's in there, in her eyes. She knows I want to cry. No one else does. I hear someone say that I'm ungrateful, sitting there in the front row, unmoved. I don't look to see who said it.

I'm never going to see those people again. I'm never going to see Mr. Wilson again. I'll probably never see Mrs. Wilson, either.

Should I feel grateful that I had a family for four years? Maybe. Instead, I'm angry that that's all I got. It's no one's fault, I guess. That makes me even angrier.

So I'm angry, but showing it would be pointless.

Now I get to not show anger at Mr. and Mrs. Kirkpatrick and some kid they've told me is now my older brother. Which is bullshit. They say you don't get to pick your relatives, but if I'm not going to have one family, I should at least be able to make people audition to be admitted.

Now I'm crying. At least I have my own bedroom.

My arms and legs can't move. He's behind me. On top of me. In me. I'm crying. Screaming for him to stop, like I never have before. It goes on and . . .

I sat bolt upright. I didn't realize at first that it was dark. It took some indeterminate amount of time to remember that I was in Iowa City, not Vicksburg. To remember that I'm free.

Before I could do that, I felt another touch. Something soft. Something that gripped me around my shoulders instead of behind them. Something that pressed against me instead of into me. Something that smelled of roses.

Awareness slowly returned. She gently rocked me. She started making noises. I suppose she was talking, but I really have no idea. But it was slow. Even.

Safe.

My shaking slowed until I started to cry. It started with a great, heaving breath. She gathered me in. I shriveled up. My big, slow, freakish body collapsed until she could encompass it all. I turned and cried on her shoulder. She smelled like white roses.

She put her arms around me. Everywhere our bodies were in contact felt . . . not peaceful, but soothed. She didn't offer salvation, but it was respite.

She gently pulled me back down, still making soft sounds. She began singing something. A lullaby, I think, but that didn't matter. She pressed against me.

Sobs descended into oblivion. Sleep without dreams. Sleep that was just sleep.

CHAPTER 9

When I woke up, Caitlyn still had me in a tight embrace. I lay there for awhile just enjoying the sensation. It gave me a new appreciation for how important physical contact with other people is to me. I surrendered to the powerful urge to remain motionless.

The other thing I noticed was her breathing. Almost without realizing, I used it as a focus and slipped into a trance. I floated, but her embrace was a tether back to my body. I'd read that meditation involves contradiction, and this was it. I'd never been as free to float through space as I was with an anchor. At last I returned to my body. It was only seven thirty, but it felt decadently late as I managed to free myself from her clutches. She mumbled something but didn't wake.

I sat on the bed cross-legged and watched her sleep. Black hair obscured her face, but I was struck by her beauty anyway. I used the time trying to think through exactly how I felt.

Just after nine she took a deep breath and rolled onto her back, eyes opening. I'm usually groggy when I first wake up and take a couple minutes to really remember where I am. Caitlyn was alert immediately and smiled up at me.

"Thank you," I said.

"You're welcome."

"Why'd you do that?"

"It seemed like the right thing to do."

"Is this why you wanted to be my roommate?" I'd worried at that question for an hour.

"Does it matter to you?"

I thought about that, and all I'd concluded was that I liked looking at her. "I guess not," I finally answered.

"Then I don't want to answer that question."

I pondered what that meant, the first of many failed attempts to think like Caitlyn.

"I don't know about you," she announced, "but I need some breakfast." With that she hopped out of bed. I watched her get dressed.

That weekend in Iowa produced another road split, less satisfying than the one in Madison. The Iowa Hawkeyes always gave us more trouble than their place in the standings indicated they should, always bringing their A game against us. I have no idea what their problem was on other weekends because they gave us fits.

On Saturday, I was the message sent to Amy Cross. She was so gifted that she thought she could make any play. Sometimes, you need to just chip the puck out of your zone and make the other team reset. After she forced a couple too many breakout passes that became bad turnovers, I started getting some of her shifts.

I did my best with the opportunity. I even scored a goal in the losing cause, a slap shot from the point that managed to miss everything except the net.

It didn't do me any good, because Crosser got the message and cut down on the defensive zone errors. I'd have done better in that end, but she also went on an offensive tear that made my defensive prowess irrelevant. Even I had to admit that some of her moves were beautiful.

So my minutes vanished as quickly as they had appeared. It wasn't that I was playing badly, just that I couldn't play well enough. As Julie's hand mended, my return to the press box became imminent.

I had no idea what to make of Caitlyn. We didn't talk about that night. She seemed moodier than usual, but maybe I was just more sensitive to it. At the same time, her habit of trying to beat me at everything became so pronounced that everyone noticed. When we went up against each other in practice, the chatter would start up. She rarely gets angry, but that did it. Unfortunately for me that didn't cause her to lose focus. I got torched in every way imaginable. Given the direction my career was headed at that point, it didn't do my mood any good.

January 2009

Hockey is a crazy game.

We're playing St. Loyola, and I get into a fight. A real drop-the-gloves-and-throw-punches fight. It lasts maybe ten seconds before the linesmen pull us apart, but we get our licks in. I'm probably going to have a black eye, but you should see the other guy. I'm also suspended for two games.

The perverse thing isn't that I got into a fight. I don't need hockey for that. What's fucked up is that it started when the other guy slashed at Josh after the whistle. Josh. Anywhere else and I'd probably help. But on the ice my job is to protect him, even if he is an asshole.

What's even more twisted is that I respect the other guy for punching me. He didn't back away because I'm a girl. We just dropped 'em and went at it like two hockey players.

So I end up liking the guy I'm punching and loathing the guy I'm defending.

I can live with crazy. What makes me angry is my team. I thought the rule was that the player who stands up for their teammates wins their respect. They bang their sticks on the boards as you're escorted off the ice as a tribute.

Nothing. Not a fucking thing. So I go sit by myself in the little space they give me to get dressed in. It doesn't have a shower, and I can't go into the real dressing room, but I don't want to watch from the stands. It's a good thing I brought a book.

The bus ride home is silent. We lost, of course, and they all leave me alone. I no longer know whether I'm upset by that. I think they're glad I won't be playing next week.

So: crazy. The craziest thing is that I'd do it again. Absolutely. Without hesitation.

So is the game crazy, or is it just me?

We started a tradition of Talking Tuesdays, where a group of us would gather in the lounge and tell stories about our childhood. No one said so, but it started after I talked about Mr. Wilson and was intended to help me open up to everyone.

My state of confused frustration was probably why I shared one of the more sordid elements of my past. After listening to Erika explain the history of why she has to tap the skates of the defenseman with the lowest number on the ice with her stick before every defensive zone face-off, I talked about getting into fights.

"I picked up two fighting majors in high school, but I don't mean on the ice."

"Did you win?" That was Caitlyn.

"Shut up," Abby said.

I looked at the floor. "It's a good thing Coach Long didn't call the administration at Vicksburg High for a character recommendation when deciding whether to let me on the team. I got suspended twice for fighting in school. Not hockey. Real fights."

I paused. I think I'd started out trying to impress Caitlyn with something, but I no longer had any idea what it was. "One day, I went hunting for someone. Some guys had been harassing my friend John, shortly after he came out. They were calling him all sorts of names, making his life miserable."

I could feel my anger building. "The teachers didn't do anything. I guess because it was just verbal. I didn't find out about it until the next day, from gossip going around. John didn't say a thing about it to me. He knew how I'd react."

Everyone else had fallen silent, and whatever jokiness there had been was gone. "The ringleader was a guy named Todd Harris. I went looking for him. I found him between fifth and sixth periods.

"I was smart enough not to just wade in and get arrested on a battery charge, because I wanted to do real harm to him. So I made sure to start an argument first, a loud one that could escalate nicely. I waited until he called me a queer lover."

My shoulders had tightened up. "Then I punched him. It's funny. The slur that gave me the best cover was the one that I wear proudly.

"It was better than a hockey fight. It helped being on a regular floor rather than ice. And it turns out Todd Harris was a wimp . He never landed a thing on me. In fact, he mostly just covered himself up. It wasn't really fair to keep hitting him, but I didn't care. It wasn't like he'd been fair.

"I broke the bone above his eye. All in all, it was very satisfying. And definitely worth being suspended for a week.

"The hard part was talking to John the next time I saw him. He's a pacifist. I mean on a deeply philosophical level. I knew that he'd be mad at me for getting into a fight because of him. I don't think I'd ever seen him really angry before. He never lost his temper with the people who gave him shit. Just me."

Someone put her arm around me. I wasn't paying enough attention to see who it was. I just sat there for a bit.

"You must have had a lot of anger built up," Abby finally said.

"That was part of it," I agreed. "But I only had one real friend, and I wasn't going to let the assholes make his life miserable. I put Todd Harris in the hospital. I still think it was the right thing to do."

There was silence as they digested that. I decided that I'd said enough. If I'd continued, I'd have gotten even angrier. John's old email address was dead, and he never sent me a new one.

We played at home the next three weeks and rolled over our opponents. The team was doing well even as I sat more and I avoided wondering whether there was any causation there. I had my T-shirt back, at least.

Our next road trip was to Boston over Thanksgiving weekend. I spent a lot of time wondering what would happen once Caitlyn and I were alone in our room. I'd been trying to convince myself that there was no reason to expect that anything would happen. But that night four weeks earlier had meant so much to me that I couldn't help myself.

I was overthinking it. I put on my pajamas and got into bed as Caitlyn undressed. Then she got into my bed with me as if it was something she'd done forever. No questions. No comments. Just, bang, there she was.

I tensed up in surprise at first and then some more in panic as I worried that she would interpret it as an indication that I didn't want her there. At last I whispered, "Thank you."

She giggled. "What did you think was going to happen? I liked it, and I know for a fact that you did."

"I just . . ." My voice trailed off.

"You were scared. You've been nervous since dinner. That's why I didn't ask or say anything."

"But what if . . ."

"You didn't."

"But I might have."

"No you wouldn't."

She rolled onto her side, facing me, and put her head on my shoulder. She was asleep before I could come up with anything else to say. So I lay there for awhile, just thinking and listening to her breathe. Unlike Kennedy, she doesn't snore. For some reason, I kept focusing on the scent of her hair, trying to figure out what shampoo she used.

Eventually I fell asleep, too. The next thing I knew, I could see the dawn creeping around the shades. We were both still in the same position. My arm had fallen asleep, but I didn't really care. I didn't want to move at all for fear of disturbing her, which didn't make sense. It was a running joke on the team that she could sleep through Armageddon.

I lay awake for several hours, enjoying her presence, before I moved. She mumbled something as I extracted myself from the bed. I watched her roll over onto her other side. I kept looking at her as I got dressed, but she didn't move again.

I had a lot to think about as I ate my two bowls of Cheerios and an English muffin. Rather, I had one thing to think about over and over. It was more pleasant than most of my obsessions.

The next afternoon we had free time. Caitlyn and I used it to wander around Boston. She was sightseeing, and I was tagging along.

"Don't you enjoy seeing all of these famous places?" she asked me as we toured historical landmarks.

"Not really. I can read about them if I need to." I dug into a cup of fried clams I'd picked up at a market along the way. "The seafood is pretty good, though."

"Reading about them isn't the same as actually seeing them."

"True. I'm less likely to get rained on when I'm reading."

"Why'd you come with me, then? Heck would have been excited."

"I couldn't care less about the sights," I answered. "I just like the idea of spending time with you."

"Oooh, I like that answer. You're off the hook."

As we walked I finally asked, "Caitlyn, what are we doing?"

"I thought that was obvious. We're sleeping together."

"Well, yes, but are we doing anything more than just literally sleeping together?"

"Not so far." She laughed.

"I'm serious, Caitlyn."

"So am I." She helped herself to one of my clams. "What's wrong with just letting things happen and enjoying it?"

"That's how bad surprises happen. I like to know the situation."

"You analyze everything to death. You do all of that relaxation work, and you're still uptight about everything."

"I have reasons," I said as a defensive tone crept into my voice.

"I know you do. That's part of why we're going to do things my way. It'll give you a chance to just go with something."

I wasn't so sure that was a great idea. "Don't I get a say in this?"

"Of course. I'm not going to try and stop you from overanalyzing it, but I'm not going to help." Before I could say anything else, she continued, "I've been thinking a lot about that story about the fight you got into."

"You're changing the subject."

"Sort of. But thinking about that story helped me understand you better. I mean, we've all known that you're like a mother bear guarding her cubs out on the ice. I don't think we realized how much it's true everywhere else. That was the point of the story, right?"

"I have no idea what the point was," I said glumly. "It just started coming out."

"Well, I think that was what you were trying to tell us."

"I'm not really like that anymore. I'm not carrying around as much anger."

"I think you're still exactly like that."

"Okay." It wasn't worth arguing about.

"But then I kept thinking. I can do that, you know."

"I do wonder sometimes."

She reached up and smacked the back of my head. "No, really. I think the other thing you were trying to tell us is that you want other people to defend you like that."

"I can take care of myself."

"I do wonder sometimes."

"No, really."

"Touché. But I don't mean in a fight. I mean in other ways."

"Like what?" I asked.

"Like someone who will be there when you have nightmares."

"That's a major commitment."

She snorted.

"So is this something more than just sleeping together?" I asked.

"I guess. I want to protect you."

"But no analysis?"

"Nope. None. Zero."

It seemed like a good idea at the time.

The next weekend was our annual trip to East Lansing. Coach Long didn't have to worry about me getting into any fights since I wasn't dressing. That made things easier for both of us, because I spent most of both games really wanting to punch Mallory Jackson.

It was a road trip to a conference opponent, so we split, though the scoreboard on Friday night lied. We lost 1–0 because a goalie with a career save percentage under .900 stopped 45 of 46 shots, at least 15 of which were from six feet or less. Sometimes those nights happen, and you just tip your helmet to her, but we dominated the game everywhere outside her crease. You just have to move on, which we did by winning 7–2 on Saturday.

That morning Caitlyn caught me messing up the second bed in our room. She giggled.

"I don't want anyone realizing that we're only using one of them," I said crossly.

"Why are you worried about it?"

"There are rules about teammates sleeping together."

"No, there aren't."

"Maybe not explicitly," I conceded, "but they're implied."

"Where?"

"It's bad for team morale. Things can get complicated."

She came over and put her arms around my waist from behind. "Why are you trying to talk yourself out of this?"

"It's still true."

"So do you want to stop?"

"No." It came out vehemently.

"So you want to violate team rules every night?"

I hesitated. "Yes."

"I think it's just because you'd be embarrassed if anyone found out."

"No, it's not."

"It's okay. I would be, too. I think making it look like both beds were slept in is a pretty good idea."

"You'd feel embarrassed if anyone finds out? Why?"

"I'm not gay," she said. "It would be hard to explain."

"I suppose. Thank you."

"For what?"

"Sleeping with me anyway."

Her arms tightened. "Phoebe, stop thinking that I'm doing you a favor. I like it, too."

"Why?"

"It makes me feel wanted. I know you're not going anywhere, and I know I can count on you. You're solid. It's nothing like what you went through, but my parents' divorce was ugly. The custody fight was more like they wanted to beat each other than anything else. You're not going to do that to me."

"I'd be there for you even if you didn't sleep with me."

"It feels more real to me this way."

That made sense to me. "Can I still say thank you?"

"Oh, all right. If you insist. However, if you want to keep it a secret, you should probably stop acting like a giddy schoolgirl at dinner."

"I did not!" I insisted. I thought for a moment. "Is that what a giddy schoolgirl sounds like? I'm sorry. Last night was the first time I've really gotten to look forward to it."

"Don't apologize. No one's going to guess. They'll notice and try to figure out why you're talking nonstop." She giggled again. "They won't get it right, though."

"Are you sure?"

"No, but life's full of risks."

"You make that sound easy to accept."

"You'll get there, Phoebe. I promise."

Two weeks later, with both finals and the first half of the season over, Caitlyn dragged me to a movie. I couldn't have told you what movie it was. It's not just that it was sappy and had horrible dialogue. I spent the whole time wondering if we were on a date.

When it was over, we took a bus back to campus. It was empty except for us and one guy sitting in the back corner.

"Do you have nightmares at home, too?"

"No," I answered.

"Did you know that when you avoid a question, or want to fib, you drop your right shoulder?"

"No, I don't."

"Uh huh. We've all noticed. So do you have nightmares at home, too?"

I just stared at the seat in front of me without saying anything.

"I'm going to take that as a yes."

I squirmed but didn't deny it.

"I have a roommate, so we'll have to go to your place."

"Wait, didn't we skip a couple of steps here?"

"I challenge you to say you don't want me coming over. It has to be convincing."

"I . . . well, kind of."

Her voice switched to actual concern seamlessly. "What's the problem?"

"Well, my apartment . . ."

"Do you have porn magazines strewn all over or something?"

"No!"

"I bet it's not dirty dishes, either. You don't want me coming over because you live in a shitty little dump because it's what you can afford and you're going to be embarrassed to have me see it for the first time despite knowing you for more than a year and a half."

"Um . . ."

"Yeah. The thing is, I don't care. Knowing you, it meets the hygienic standards of a hospital. Beyond that, it's probably really small. But we're not going to try to play volleyball in there, so why does that matter?"

"And the radiator makes this banging noise whenever it comes on."

She looked at me kind of disgusted at how weak my arguments were becoming. "Are you worried that that's going to keep me awake?"

"No, I guess not."

"Do you want to just give in now?"

I thought about it for a second—at most. "I'll give in. Thank you."

She snorted.

"You said I could thank you," I protested.

We got off the bus and walked to my house. "Yeah, this is a dump," she said when she realized we were walking up onto a porch that sloped about fifteen degrees.

"Wait until you get a look at the bathrooms."

"You do have your own bathroom, right?"

"Nope. Reconsidering?"

"No. That's what I had in the dorm. I just didn't realize that I'd see it again."

"Welcome to life on the cheap."

We went up the stairs to my door. Before I could unlock it, she gripped my arm and looked into my eyes. "Phoebe, don't let it bother you. You got screwed by life. That's all it means."

I fished out my key. "I'm getting better at believing that."

"Good." The door swung open. "Okay, this is smaller than our hotel rooms. It's even smaller than my dorm room."

"If you're trying to make me feel better about this, you're not doing very well."

She stuck her tongue out at me.

Once again, it took her less than three minutes to fall asleep once we were in bed. That's what I was the most jealous about.

That Christmas wasn't nearly as stressful as my first with the Forrests had been. It was quiet and peaceful, with no breakdowns.

Abby and I began a tradition of staying up on Christmas Eve and talking deep into the night. I hadn't realized it the previous year, but she can barely sleep on Christmas Eve. Her mother says she's been like that since she was three.

That first time I sat in their living room with her because I felt guilty. "I'm sorry I haven't spent much time with you lately."

"Don't worry about it. I know you don't like Tammy."

"It's not that. Really."

"Well, I wouldn't blame you if it was. There are times I want to strangle her."

"You don't need to take responsibility because she's your friend. I mostly just ignore her now."

"That doesn't excuse the things she says."

"No," I agreed, "it doesn't. But it does mean that you don't need to let me come between you. I assume she has enough virtues to make her a good friend."

She snorted. "Cute. I like the way you phrased that."

"I'm serious. I respect you too much to think that you'd like her if what she shows me was her best side."

"There are still times her mouth should be boarded up."

"It's okay. You know, you might be able to get to sleep if you'd stop drinking so much coffee."

She smiled. "No, I wouldn't. Not tonight. I don't want to miss Santa coming down the chimney."

"This is so unlike you."

"I know." She laughed. "Don't tell anyone."

"Why would I bother? None of them would believe me."

I got back to the subject. "I feel bad because you spent all that time helping me adjust, and once I felt comfortable, I started hanging out with other people."

"That means those conversations were successful. You certainly seem to have found a spot. Your whole class is fun to watch together. Even you and Caitlyn seem to have found a way to get along."

I almost choked on my cocoa. Fortunately, Abby was looking at the stockings. "Yeah. My first impressions of her were wrong."

"If you say so."

"You don't like her?"

"I wouldn't say that. I just think she's flaky."

"She can be flaky, but there's more to her than that."

"I'm sure there is. She would just have to stop moving long enough for anyone to notice."

I wanted to point out that Caitlyn barely moves at all when she sleeps but thought better of it. "Merry Christmas, Abby, but I think I'm going to turn in."

"I'll keep an eye out and make sure Santa leaves you some good stuff."

She came through for me, but Santa had nothing to do with it. Her parents shocked me the next morning by giving me a note promising to pay for whatever training program the team used the next summer.

December 2003

I open the package with a distinct lack of enthusiasm. Much to my surprise, it isn't a doll. It's a kit to get started on scrapbooking. I paste the appropriate fake smile on my face before looking up at Mrs. Kilpatrick. "Thank you."

"You're very welcome, dear. I hope you spend many safe, happy hours using it." Emphasis on "safe."

Across the room, Tim lets out a whoop as he unwraps a box containing some video games he wanted. I think they all involve shooting things, but I don't look closely.

I take stock of all of the gifts I'd received. One scrapbooking kit. Two pretty dresses. A couple of books about cute, precocious girls that don't cause any problems. Some makeup. And there is a small envelope that I've been saving for last. It came from CPS, and the handwriting on it came perilously close to making me cry when I first saw it.

I open it as carefully as possible so as not to damage the writing. Inside is an astonishingly large gift certificate for sporting goods, enough to keep me in equipment for a year. There is also a handwritten note from Mr. Wilson that I quickly stuff into my pocket, hoping that I won't have to share it.

Mrs. Kilpatrick looks suitably appalled. I smile happily at her, secure in the knowledge that she is too much of a coward to keep me from using the gift certificate, no matter how much she wishes I wouldn't. If I can weather the scowls and indignation, everything should be fine.

When I get back to my room I read the note. It's vague, of course, since he wrote it almost a year ago. It has the email address of someone who would be happy to take me to Columbus if my current foster family doesn't want to.

I fold it up very carefully and put it in my desk.

CHAPTER 10

The first Saturday of January marked a turning point for us. The day after a lackluster tie against Wisconsin, Kennedy slipped a harmless-looking wrist shot past Wisconsin's goalie in the first. That was the only goal we could manage, and we made it stand up. We gave the puck no choice but to let us win.

From the opening face-off we controlled everything. We dictated the pace. We won the physical battles. Wisconsin's speed was swallowed up by our gap control and backchecking forwards.

Halfway through the third period, they surrendered. I can pinpoint the moment. Twice on one shift, Jenny went to the boards and pulled the puck away from Badgers forty pounds bigger than she was. For all her gifts, that shouldn't happen. We broke their will.

We played defensive hockey in the third, but it bore no resemblance to what we'd done in the previous year's Big Ten final. We didn't just drop into a shell. It was an aggressive form of defense. We controlled the puck, and when we lost it, our forecheckers made them work for every inch of the ice. The defensemen stood them up at the blue line. Everyone blocked shots. Not much got through to Erika, and she smothered what did.

It was a thing of beauty, the best any team I'd ever been a part of had played for an entire game. I wanted to be out there so badly that I could taste it, but I was stuck watching from the stands.

When we played the way we did that night, no one in the country was going to beat us. No one. We just needed to harness it once the calendar turned to March.

That night was really the culmination of something that started back in October when we won in Madison. Never again while I was there did we take the ice with that sinking feeling that we were going to lose. There were nights that maybe we should have, and there were plenty of nights when we played poorly, but we never started out beaten.

Over the next several weeks some things got better, and some things didn't. I was learning that life is like that.

I dealt with my lack of playing time by falling back on one of my old habits: watching video of our games. I started breaking things down, at first trying to figure out how to improve my game. When I hit the wall of my physical abilities, I started watching others.

"I figured out what Crosser's problem is," I told Abby as we walked down the mall toward Coffman Union.

"Oh?"

"She can't anticipate plays. As soon as she sees a hole or some-one open, she's on it, but she doesn't see any of it before it happens. It's why she's late on breakout passes and why she gets her shots blocked so often."

Around the game, this is called "hockey IQ." It's a terrible name for it, but I had it, and apparently my rival didn't. That she got play-ing time and I sat in the stands is an indication that, as valuable as it may be, it's possible to compensate for its absence.

"Congratulations. Did you tell the coaches?"

"No. For exactly the same reason you were going to laugh at me when I said yes."

"Why is that?"

"Because they figured it out months ago. I'm not trying to say that I invented the wheel or anything, just that I figured it out."

"So what are you going to do about it?" she asked.

"I don't know. Maybe help her out with some drills, if I can fig-ure something out."

"Do you think that the coaches are maybe onto this already?"

"Of course I have, but at least let me try to do something

anyway," I pleaded. "I'm not doing much to help this team right now. Give me something."

"You do a lot to—"

"Don't give me that being a good teammate crap. You would be going berserk if it were you getting scratched. I'm a paragon of patience compared to what you'd be like."

She wanted to deny it but had the decency not to.

"The last couple of weekends haven't been that bad," I continued. "She's been playing better, and I don't mind being scratched when she is. But I want to find some way to help."

"You'll have a chance."

"I guess. I'm just frustrated. I wouldn't trade this for anything. I really wouldn't. I'm just having to make some adjustments." I could rationalize with the best of them.

"We all do."

"That's easy for you to say. Your adjustments consist of figuring out how to play on a line with two future Olympians. Scoring goals must be hard to get used to." I was a bit more agitated than I really wanted to be.

"Phoebe . . ."

"I know. I'm sorry." I kicked at a pebble. "It goes beyond hockey. I'm just finding that maybe I do like people after all, and it's harder to deal with than I ever would have thought it would be."

"Huh?"

"I like Amy. She's a good kid. She's got a lot to learn, but don't we all."

"She's a teenager."

"Until three weeks ago I was a teenager," I pointed out.

"Only chronologically. You were never a teenager."

"What does that mean?"

She stopped and faced me with her concerned expression. It differs from her angry expression only in that she looks like she plans to eviscerate someone else. "It means that teenagers have a set of formative experiences they go through, except that you didn't have them."

"Did you learn this in class?" I asked.

She plowed on. "When the rest of us explored our boundaries, we got to do it without stuff blowing up in our faces. Most of us didn't know it at the time, but being a teenager is about getting to make adult decisions without facing adult consequences. Someone gave you a seat right at the no-limit table."

"OK . . . So what do I do?"

"I don't have a clue. Life probably won't let you put the training wheels on now. I'm going to do the best I can to support you, though."

"Thanks, Abby."

With twenty-twenty hindsight I wish I'd mentioned right then that I'd been sleeping with Caitlyn. Things might have gone differently.

Just as Abby promised, something broke my way: she sprained her knee. I told her that it was a nice gesture, but I wasn't that desperate to get back in the lineup. She didn't laugh.

I hadn't played forward in an organized game since they first divided us into positions when I was seven. It wasn't just that defense was the position I knew tactically and that all of my reactions were built for it. It's who I was. Glory is for other people. I protect my goalie. My email address was defenseman.phoebe@gmail.com.

With Abby out, the coaches decided to try me at right wing. I had good hands, and Coach Long decided that what the third line needed was a big body to stand in front of the net and cause mayhem. If she knocked in a few rebounds, even better. I fit the bill.

It hurt Katie that I got picked. If you aren't dressing, you don't *want* one of your teammates to get injured, but one of the things that keeps you going is the thought that, if it happens, you might get to play. I'd waited for one of the defensemen to get hurt, giving me my opening. Katie had done the same thing with the forwards, but when it happened, I got the call.

I can't say that she never grumbled about not playing. We all did, even Morgan, who had walked on knowing she'd be the last girl on the depth chart. But Katie never expressed resentment about not replacing Abby in the lineup. I can't promise that I'd have been as gracious if the roles had been reversed.

It took me exactly 37:04 of game time as a forward to pick up a goal. I was innocently standing in front of the net, taking up space and keeping their goalie from seeing anything. Kennedy took a shot from the blue line that hit my shin and ricocheted in. She did all the work.

Playing forward the way I did doesn't take a huge amount of skill, but it does take a willingness to get beaten up. As a defenseman, I'd done more than my fair share of the beating, so it was only fair that I got subjected to it. Goalies also don't like being screened and are happy to hack at your calves trying to get you to stop.

But if there's one thing I knew how to do, it was to take abuse. And at that moment, my goals per game as a forward were higher than Jenny's. That was plenty of incentive to come back for more.

What was totally unfair was Kennedy accusing me of cheating. I argued that goals as a forward shouldn't count against our vow. I also pointed out that I bailed her out. If I don't get in the way, she's the one that ends up with a goal. She claimed the shot was going wide, but that was weak. All we know is that she took it, and it went in. She owed me.

I needed all the jocularity and positive reinforcement I could get because the next week we were going on the road to Ohio State.

In the interim we had four days of practice. On Tuesday, after we finished, Kennedy approached me as we left the locker room. "You okay?"

"Yeah, I guess."

"You sure?"

"Yes." I got a little irritated.

"You just don't seem to have the same . . . I don't know. I was going to say intensity, but that's not it. You just haven't seemed like yourself recently."

I stopped to think about it for a moment. I'd noticed the same thing, and I couldn't describe it, either. "I don't know. I think it might be that I'm happy more often than I've been in a long time. I think that's affecting my drive on the ice."

"Is that such a bad trade-off?"

"I'm afraid I'm starting to think that it isn't."

"Why afraid?"

I shrugged. "It's affecting my hockey."

She came to a stop and grabbed my shoulder so that I had to look at her. "None of us think that hockey is more important than you being happy."

"I know you mean it. It's me. Hockey has meant so much to me, and it bugs me that I'm slacking."

"You're only slacking relative to the ridiculous things you've been doing. You're still working hard."

"I can only compare it to myself. That's all I know. There have been days lately when I don't get up to do my workouts."

"Hopefully that means you're actually sleeping."

"Well, yeah." On the nights Caitlyn came over that was exactly what it meant.

"Then it's another good thing."

"Fine. I just wish it would leave my hockey alone. If I'm going to be happy, I want to enjoy it."

October 2000

"What did you do at school today?" Mr. Wilson asks me.

I swallow a mouthful of meatloaf before answering. Mrs. Wilson gives me a look if I talk with my mouth full. "I taught some kids about computers." This school is different from the one I went to last year.

"You taught them?" He acts surprised.

"Uh huh. I taught them the things you taught me."

"Like what?"

"Like how computers only think in ones and zeros, and how they do exactly what you tell them so you have to be very careful in telling them what to do, and what all the parts are, like the processor and stuff. And they asked questions."

"What kind of questions?"

"Mostly about games," I say disdainfully.

"There's nothing wrong with games, honey," Mrs. Wilson says.

Mr. Wilson and I look at each other.

"I like making a computer do things," I say.

"Why?" he asks.

"Because they do what they're told." He laughs, and Mrs. Wilson scolds him.

"You need to learn how to talk to people, too," she says tartly. "Not just machines."

I sigh. "I know. It's not as much fun, though."

Mr. Wilson is trying to look serious.

"I like this school," I say.

"Why do you like it so much?"

"Because they want me to ask questions, just like you do."

"Like I do?"

"Uh huh. I said that you told me the most important question is, 'Why?' They said that you were a wise man."

"Don't let it go to your head, Howard," Mrs. Wilson says. Mr. Wilson ignores her.

"They also let me go as fast as I want in math. Mr. Kent gave me a book about rolling dice."

"Probability?" he asks.

"Uh huh. Probability and luck."

"Oh? So you can tell me how lucky you are?"

I giggle. "I'm very lucky."

Coach Long tapped me on the shoulder. "You good to go?"

I nodded. "Yes, Coach." I'm pretty sure it came out more confident than I felt. I would rather have been anywhere than Columbus, Ohio, right then.

Katie went out for warm-ups to be ready anyway, just in case he decided I wasn't in a state to play. That was sensible. When we got out there, my eyes were drawn up into the bleachers. He was sitting by himself to Erika's right. It took everything I had to pretend that he wasn't there and go through the drills.

Everyone sensed that there was something wrong, but not that there was more to it than just being there again. By the time we made it back to the dressing room I was absolutely determined to make a go of it. Katie tapped my shin pad with her stick as she went to change back into street clothes.

I didn't play badly. I wasn't great, mind you. All kinds of things that I usually do without thinking required concentration. I was able to keep my focus on not making mistakes and making sure I was in the right place pretty close to the right time. It mostly worked.

It helped that we scored twice in the first two minutes of the game and never let them get started. When it was 4-0 with about five minutes left in the second, Coach shifted me back to defense. Kennedy and I took regular shifts together from there to the end. I felt more comfortable and was finally able to just settle in.

Once we got back to our room, it turned out that not everyone thought it was just being in Columbus that had made me nervous. Caitlyn, at least, figured it out. "That guy was here, wasn't he?"

After a brief hesitation I admitted that he had been.

She embraced me. "I'm proud of you. I'm not sure why you didn't tell anyone. I can make some guesses, though. You made it. God, you're tense." She pulled me tighter. "Just let it go."

I took a deep, ragged breath.

"What do you want me to do?" she asked.

"I want to sit down. And I want you to keep talking to me. I don't care what you say—I just want to hear your voice."

So we sat on the bed, Caitlyn behind me. I had no idea what she talked about. I just listened to the sounds, and I relaxed. Muscle by muscle, limb by limb the tension drained out of me. "Thank you," I said when it was done.

"What did you do? I felt you ease up a little bit at a time."

"I just listened to you without paying any attention to the words and just emptied my brain of the fear."

"You make it sound simple."

"The idea is simple. Doing it can be hard."

"So what do you do now?"

"Hopefully stay like this for awhile."

"Like this?"

"Hypnotized. When it all comes together, it's pleasant. I feel like I'm floating."

"You're hypnotized? So you'll do whatever I tell you to?"

"You don't need hypnosis for that, Caitlyn."

"I . . . oh." She was quiet. "Thank you, I think."

"You're welcome. And thank you. You're the only person I've ever tried this with."

"This may be the first time anyone has told me that I'm helping them relax."

"You're good at it. This is a place where I can really, truly relax. You protect me from the things that frighten me and the things that anger me."

"Does Abby do that, too?"

"Yes, but it's different. That's analytical. With you I can just feel things. I can recognize that it makes me angry that he's never been to a hockey game before, except when we were here last year. He never came to see me play when I lived with him. He cares nothing for the game. All he's trying to do is intimidate me."

"You don't sound angry about it. Almost more sad."

"That's what you do for me. While you're holding onto me, the anger doesn't control me. I can see it there. I can examine it, but it's all from a distance. I can observe it, but I don't have to let it touch me. During the game, I had to either ignore it or try to harness it. To turn the fear into something else. I had to fight it."

"Now you really sound sad."

"I don't think it's sadness. I'm tired, Caitlyn. I just realized that. I haven't been able to put a name to it. I'm very, very tired."

"Tired of what?"

"Everything. That's not quite right. I'm not sure how to put it. Maybe it's that I'm tired of motivating myself. I don't ever do anything for positive reasons. It's always because I'm scared of what will happen if I stop. I don't do anything because it's fun. I can't have fun while my fears are chasing me."

"Even hockey?"

"Especially hockey. It should be fun. I watch the rest of you, and you're having a great time. I'm just hiding. Kennedy thinks I'm some sort of role model. Playing the way I do would just suck the life out of her."

"You're tensing up again."

"I know. It's gone. That feeling is gone. Talk to me."

"You are a role model. You are for me. You are for Kennedy. For all of us. You don't look like you're running from anything. You're overcoming fear. And if you can, we can."

I hadn't meant to focus on what she was saying, but I did.

"You challenge us. Somewhere inside, we're all afraid that we're going to reach a point where we aren't good enough. Jenny's terrified of it. She goes into every game thinking that this is the one that's going to expose her. We've all found ways to cope with it. She uses that fear for motivation."

I was starting to get that relaxed feeling back. I should have stopped listening to what Caitlyn was saying and just drifted, but I wanted to listen to this.

"But you're not scared of that. Somehow you've accepted it. You're content with being what you are even if you aren't satisfied with it. Does that makes sense? We watch you, trying to figure out how you do it.

"None of us should want to be just like you, but we all have ways we want to be more like you. The only person you aren't a good role model for is yourself. And maybe Tammy."

I exhaled slowly.

"You're relaxed again. I think it's time to go to bed."

"Yes it is," I said.

I think it only took me about ten minutes to fall asleep. Caitlyn was way ahead of me.

The next weekend back at Ridder had its own sort of dread. Nothing like Columbus, but I was uneasy anyway. Caitlyn's mother had flown in from Vancouver to watch the series.

I'd met her briefly the previous year, but it hadn't registered that much. It was different the second time for obvious reasons.

Ms. Morris reminded me of a sparrow. She was a tiny little thing and constantly in motion. She's half-Chinese, and by trade she's an artist.

"Phoebe, this is my mother."

"Hi, Ms. Morris."

"Oh, please, call me Anne. Nothing formal." The way she crowded up to me made me nervous. "Caitlyn talks about you all the time. You have such an interesting background."

Caitlyn tried to interrupt quickly. "Mom—"

"I don't like to talk about it very much, Ms. . . . . Anne."

"Oh, I'm a good listener, don't worry."

I started to get agitated. "Really, I'd rather not."

Caitlyn stepped in, but Kathy is the one who really rescued me. She took my arm. "Phoebe, we've got something to go over in the video room."

I looked at her gratefully and let her pull me away. "We can talk later," Ms. Morris threw in as we left.

When the door was closed, I started shaking. Kathy embraced me. "Come on, let's go downstairs where no one will find us."

Once we sat down in the lounge, I said, "Thanks."

"Just sit here for awhile."

Eventually Caitlyn came in, rolling her eyes. "I'm sorry I told her about you."

"It's okay. She's your mother. Of course you tell her stuff."

It was time for dinner. I ate with Kathy and Abby. Caitlyn had to deal with her mother by herself.

We played Iowa that weekend to end the regular season. Mathematically we still had a chance to finish in first place. All we had to do was to sweep and hope that Wisconsin lost a game to Ohio State. The Buckeyes came through for us.

Unfortunately, we didn't do what we needed to do. We were horrible in the first game, showing all of our warts. Our breakouts were terrible, and they kept us bottled up in our own end for long stretches.

We were lethargic through the first half of Saturday's game, too. We were ahead 1-0 thanks to luck and Iowa for once looking sluggish. In the middle of the second, someone flipped a switch. Kathy skated the entire length of the ice with the puck, around every player wearing black, including the goalie. One short pass later, Jenny put the puck into an empty net. We never looked back. The final was 5-1.

For the second year in a row we finished second in the conference behind Wisconsin. Given the number of sloppy games we played, we really had no one to blame but ourselves. There were four weeks of playoffs ahead in which to make up for it.

I finally asked Caitlyn something that had been bothering me for awhile. We were sitting on my futon getting ready for bed. "Doesn't Amy wonder where you are all these nights?"

"No. She knows exactly where I am."

"You told her?" I was aghast.

"I kind of had to." She seemed nonchalant about it.

"What do you mean?"

"As you were trying to point out, she's my roommate. It would be hard for her not to notice that something was up."

"Yeah, but . . ."

She took my hands. "You worry too much. She's fine with it, and she won't tell anyone."

"Still."

"What's your alternative? Should I have lied to her?" She waited expectantly.

"No," I said grudgingly.

"Should I not spend nights here?"

"No."

"Do you have any other ideas?"

"No."

"So there. I told her. It's an option you should really consider with Abby."

I fidgeted. "I know."

She put her arms around me. "I understand that it's hard for you. Trying to get anything out of you is a challenge."

"I'm sorry."

"Don't apologize. Not for this."

"He raped me." I wasn't sure why it came out right then, but I sagged into her embrace.

There was only a brief pause. "I know. I figured it out. I've just been waiting for you to tell me."

"Abby's the only other person I've told. Ever." I omitted the school counselor.

Caitlyn didn't say anything for awhile. I clung to her, trying not to float away. I cried silently. "Please say something. Anything."

"I'm glad I can be the person you share things with. It means a lot to me that you trust me like that. Next year we're going to get you out of this dump. You, me, Heck, maybe someone else are going to share a place. Girls we trust and who won't care that you and I share a room. We'll be together every night. Won't that be nice?"

"Yeah." I was starting to relax. "Thank you."

"You're welcome, Phoebe."

The first round of the Big Ten playoffs was a cakewalk. That left us heading back to Madison to play Michigan in the semifinals on Friday for the right to play in the final on Saturday. The team doctor cleared Abby to play, which meant that I got pushed down to the fourth line, and I figured I'd be on the bench the whole game.

I was wrong. We blew them out of the building, and I got regular shifts for the second half of the game. Michigan didn't play badly, but we found that same place we were in during the second game against Wisconsin in January. The way we played, the Wolverines never had a chance. It was like trying to stop a train.

The only disappointment that weekend was that we didn't beat Wisconsin in the final, but that's only because we didn't play Wisconsin. They played poorly and lost to Michigan State in their semi, so we got to end the Spartans' season, which was a nice consolation prize.

They played us a lot tougher than Michigan did. In ten games against them over the previous two years I'd never seen them play as disciplined. The trap they used to smother Wisconsin was a new wrinkle, and they played it well. Erika came up huge about six times to preserve the shutout. It was really a 1-0 game, though with six seconds left Kathy added the only empty net goal off of a rebound I've ever seen.

We were on a roll. It's hard to describe the feeling you get when everything is just right. It's not just a sports thing; I've had days like that programming, where code flows out your fingertips. But a sport strips away all of the things that hide performance and puts it right up on the scoreboard. When everything goes well, it's exhilarating in a way that almost nothing else can be.

The next night the NCAA tournament seedings were announced. There were only eight teams in the country left playing, and any loss ended your season. I liked our chances to be the last ones standing. Wisconsin's aura of invincibility was gone after losing twice in three weeks to teams that didn't make the tournament, and we were convinced no one else could match up with us.

We drew Michigan State for our quarterfinal performance. If you'd told me that a month earlier, I'd have been nervous. Things had changed. After the Big Ten championship game, their psychological hold on us was gone. Now they had to come to Ridder, and they looked more like a speed bump than an obstacle.

The bad part was admitting to myself that I couldn't wait for the season to be over. I wanted to win the title and then take off my skates. As the team took off, I was asking myself why I was even there.

It was fatigue. I felt sluggish, and I was having trouble getting up in the morning. I let the comfort of Caitlyn's embrace bewitch me, and that had implications I didn't want to think about. I didn't want to push myself anymore. I started feeling comfortable, and, hockey-wise, that was a bad place to be.

State spent all week saying that the rematch was going to be different. They were going to be aggressive, take the game to us, generate chances and capitalize on them. It was the first trip to the NCAA tournament for any of their players, except Mallory, who did it as a Gopher. They vowed not to let the opportunity go to waste.

We beat them 9–1.

They never had a chance. Everything we tried worked. They didn't even get the puck into our zone with possession until the game was eight minutes old and we were ahead by two. Their only shot in the first ten minutes was a dump in from the red line.

Hell, even I scored a goal.

It wasn't about them. It was about us. It was nice to end their season, but it didn't really matter. It would have been impossible to convince anyone in our locker room that we weren't the best team in the country. It didn't matter who we played, just how we played. It wasn't our job to match up with anyone; it was their job to keep up with us.

The contrast to the previous year was complete. We had played beaten against Cornell from the opening face-off. This time we came out of the tunnel before the game as if we were being launched from a cannon. It's fifty-four feet from the locker room door to the edge of the ice surface. It took me four seconds to get there, which is pretty good when you're running in skates and have to make a ninety-degree turn. As long as I was in uniform, I was fine.

Whatever it was, we had it, and we only needed to keep it for eight more days.

It disturbed me that I wasn't as excited as that sounds. By the time Caitlyn and I made it back to my room all of the exuberance had worn off. For me at least. She was bouncing off the ceiling.

It took her a bit, but she noticed. "What's wrong?"

"I don't know. Somewhere between everything and nothing. Or maybe either everything or nothing but nowhere in between." I sat down on the futon.

"That doesn't make any sense."

"I know. But that's how I feel."

"Why can't you be happy? There are only four teams left playing, we're one of them, and none of them is going to beat us."

"I don't know why I'm not happy," I said in a flat voice. "You're right: I should be. If I could figure out how, I would be."

"This should be fun."

"Yes, it should. But I'm really starting to understand that hockey has never been fun for me. Not since I was twelve. I thought it was the losing that kept it from being fun. Or the fact that I hated my teammates. I thought that once those weren't true anymore, then I would start having fun."

"How am I supposed to be happy if you're miserable?"

"Does it help if I say that it makes me happier watching you be happy?"

"Maybe." She sounded dubious.

"Well, it does. I think I get more enjoyment out of watching you while we win than I do from winning itself. I almost think I was happier up in the press box."

"You were climbing the walls in frustration."

"Yeah, but look at me now. Maybe if I didn't expect to play . . . I don't know."

She sat down in my lap. There was concern and misery in her eyes. I mentally kicked myself for killing the excitement she'd had.

"Phoebe, promise me that you will try to enjoy the next week. From now until three days after we win it all. I'm not demanding excitement. I can supply all of that, but I can't supply all the happiness. You have to bring some of it yourself. That's ten days. Be happy for ten days. Then we can figure all of this out."

"I'll try. Honest."

"I want to dance with you. Right now."

"I can't dance. You know that."

"You don't need to be good." She stood up and started pulling on my arm.

"There's no room in here."

"You're making excuses. We can go outside if you'd prefer."

"No, we'll try it right here." I got up. What commenced was mostly her dancing around me to music in her own head. I did feel a bit better, though.

"I think I can do ten days," I said when she was done.

"I'm going to hold you to that."

We won. That doesn't make it sound very dramatic, but the games weren't either. We beat Boston College in the semis in a game that wasn't as close as the 4-1 final score. Unlike the Big Ten tournament, we did get Wisconsin in the final, but their old magic was gone. They kept it close until the third period, when we scored three times and won 4–2.

We won. There's a video of the highlights, and you can see that I'm the last one off the bench. Caitlyn was first, of course. Erika didn't throw her helmet in the air like everyone else, because she saw that freight train coming.

I really was happy, not just pretending. I didn't express it on the outside, but I was. I even played ten minutes. The only sad part is that it was Abby's spot I took. She retweaked her knee against BC and had to sit it out.

I'd say that I would have traded places with her if I could, but I'd be lying, and Abby would smack me. I know because she told me that when we learned of the decision. We're all competitive, and a part of me is glad that someone was hurt so that I got to play. That's an ugly thing to say, but it's true, and I think Katie and Morgan would have agreed if they had been able to dress.

I didn't celebrate the way the others did. I just didn't know how. I kept reassuring everyone that I was happy, but I'm not entirely sure they all believed me.

Abby and Caitlyn did. I know that, and it was enough for me. Learning to show my feelings was an ongoing process. I smiled most of the time, and I hugged everyone enthusiastically. That was progress, right?

Inside, I was shouting, "We're the National Fucking Champions." I decided that it meant that I got to decide what an appropriate celebration was.

CHAPTER 11

The night after winning was crazy. There were excited young women running around the halls of the Holiday Inn all night. Some guest called the front desk to complain, which was pointless.

I just sat on a bed in the room Kennedy and Morgan shared, watching girls come and go.

"You're awfully quiet," Katie said as she plopped herself down next to me.

"I am," I replied amiably.

"Anything wrong?"

"Nope. Just quiet."

We sat there next to each other for a bit, not saying anything.

I broke the silence, finally. "I'm going to miss you next year."

"I'll miss being around."

"Thank you."

"For what?" she asked.

"Well, a lot of things, really."

"You sure you're okay?"

"Yes. Definitely. I'm just . . . it's complicated. I'm happy about winning. I just think this is the first time I've ever been glad that hockey season is over. So there's a sense of relief, too."

"Is it about playing time?"

"No. At least, I don't think so. I'm just really tired."

"Are you sure that's about hockey?"

"Yes. At least it's a part of it. I've been asking myself why I play this game."

"Any answers to that one?"

"I'm still working on it." I was starting to feel melancholy. "Let's change the subject. Isn't winning great?"

"It is," she said, laughing. "And I'm sure you'll come up with an answer. Now come on." She grabbed my hand and pulled me out of the room. "We have some real celebration to do."

The next day I got an unexpected email.

> To: defenseman.phoebe@gmail.com
> From: fran2712@columbia.edu
> Subject: Congratulations
>
> I apologize for never writing. You've tried to keep in touch and I've failed at my end. I can't really explain why. Maybe it's just that New York is such a different world than Vicksburg was that I can't figure out how to communicate. That's a bad sign for someone who wants to be a writer. I won't promise to try to do better because I don't know that I'll keep it.
>
> I do think about you regularly. I hope that you are happy in Minneapolis. You said that you are at one point. I know that I'm a lot better off here than I was in Ohio.
>
> Obviously this note was prompted by Sunday's game. I watched it online, which did some serious damage to my cred as an aloof, elitist art snob. It was probably the first hockey game I've ever watched start to finish, except those two you dragged me to back in high school, so I won't pretend that I understood what was going on at all.
>
> There was a good close-up of you pushing with someone from Wisconsin along the edge of the rink. I remember that facial expression and could have told that player she'd have been better off getting out of your way. I thought it was horribly unfair that they gave you a penalty for it. You didn't seem to like it much, either.

I don't know that it really matches your hair, but maroon is definitely your color.
Love, John

I deleted it unanswered.

The next weekend Abby and I went up to her parents' place. The high had finally started wearing off, and it gave me a chance to talk with her mother.

On Saturday morning, Jerilyn watched as I ate a bowl of Cheerios. "Are you okay? You're awfully subdued for someone who just won a national championship."

I contemplated methods of drinking the milk left in the bowl. "I don't know. In some ways I think I'm doing fine. In others . . . probably not."

"What's going well?"

I took a deep breath. "Please don't tell Abby any of this."

"There's a reason I waited until she was off shopping with her father."

I played with the milk and then drank a spoonful before answering. "This is pretty serious."

"Is it a good thing?"

"Maybe. I think so. At least kind of. It's got some bad stuff, too, I think." I watched my spoon make swirls in the milk. "I'm sorry. I don't seem to be giving a straight answer to anything this morning."

"If there aren't any to give, then I'm glad you're talking about it."

"I do seem to be getting better at that, at least." I closed my eyes. "Caitlyn and I are sleeping together."

She didn't say anything, so I opened my eyes to look at her face. "Is it helping you?"

"Yes. I'm sleeping. I mean, that's all we're doing. Just sleeping. And talking a lot. Not just her, either. She actually lets me get a word in sometimes. And I just enjoy it. I wake up in the middle of the night and feel her there, and I can go back to sleep."

"Then I'm glad for you. And no, I won't tell Abby."

"Thank you. But I think it's also a problem. I feel too comfortable. I don't want to get out of bed. I'm having trouble getting myself to the rink some days."

She laughed. "That's normal. All of us are like that. What's been unusual is the level at which you've pushed yourself before now, not that it's harder now."

"I don't like it."

"No, you probably don't. It's something new for you. But I don't think that it's necessarily a bad thing, either. You need to find a new equilibrium. I don't know where that's going to be, but you're changing. There is no way you could have begun to heal yourself without changing."

"I know. I just wish I wasn't so confused."

"You should get used to it," she counseled. "Through no fault of your own, you've lived a starkly black and white life. It was confusing, but figuring out the right thing to do wasn't very complicated."

"I guess so," I admitted.

"Now, while I won't tell anyone, you should probably at least consider telling the others. Abby for certain. I can help you if you'd like."

"I'll think about it."

December 2006

I'm skating in the empty rink in Vicksburg. Then the guy who runs the place skates up to me. I'd seen him around but never talked to him. "You're here a lot," he says.

He's an older man, probably in his sixties. He's never seemed that friendly before and doesn't really now, either. Not unfriendly, but quiet and standoffish.

"I need to keep in practice." I'm breathing hard after the drills I've skated.

"Don't you play with a team?"

I make a face. "I go to Vicksburg High, but they won't let me on the team."

"Why not?"

"They don't want a girl on the team."

He looks startled. "You're a girl?"

I feel myself cringe. "Yeah."

"I'm sorry," he says. "I should have thought more before I said that."

"It's okay." I look at the ice. "Lots of people make that mistake."

"No, it's not okay. I should have noticed. It's just that lots of boys wear their hair long these days."

All I do is shrug.

"I'm Peter Larson."

"Phoebe Rose."

"It's good to meet you, Phoebe. I have to lock up now to go home." That's when I realize that open skating was supposed to have ended an hour ago. Mr. Jenkins is going to be mad when I get home so late. "But you're welcome at this rink any time I'm here."

With that he skates away. I don't know why, but I like him immediately.

It turned out that asking Jerilyn not to say anything was pointless. Someone figured out what was going on, and Caitlyn and I found ourselves called to a players-only team meeting.

I just sat curled up on a chair, listening. Caitlyn wasn't going down without a fight.

"It's not good for team unity," Abby argued.

"We just won a national title," Caitlyn shot back. "We seemed pretty unified."

"That was before."

"Before what? It's been five months, and it didn't cause any issues."

"No one knew," Abby said quietly. "If it was so innocuous, why didn't you tell anyone?"

"Maybe because we knew you would react like this."

No one backed her up. That I stayed quiet disappointed me. This "team meeting" was very exclusive. There was no one from our class, just upperclassmen grilling us.

"Maybe because you knew it was wrong." Tammy's entrance to the conversation made me cringe. "Phoebe hasn't been working out nearly as hard."

That really got Caitlyn wound up. "She still works harder than the rest of us do. And do you know why she's not out there at four a.m. running around Minneapolis?" She was yelling. "Take a guess."

"Why?" Tammy's opinions carried extra weight since we all knew she was going to be the captain next year.

"Because she's actually sleeping eight hours a night. She's actually spending as much time in bed as the rest of you do."

Abby looked at me. "You of all people should know that this won't work out."

I sat bolt upright as the blood drained from my face. "Abby, please."

She seemed to realize just how far she'd trespassed.

"What's that supposed to mean?" Caitlyn demanded.

"Nothing." My gaze remained fixed on Abby, who turned crimson.

"No, there's something—"

"Drop it."

Tammy took charge at that point. "This isn't getting us anywhere. Everybody go home. Let's all think about this. We're going to come to a consensus before anyone takes this to the coaches. It's a girls' thing. Is that clear?"

Everyone gave their assent.

"I'm going to talk to people individually before we all get together again. If I hear that there has been any arguing between any of you before then, I'm going to be royally pissed. Is that also clear?"

There was more agreement.

"All right then. Get out of here."

When we got back to my place, Caitlyn sat next to me while I lay down.

"I'm sorry for abandoning you in there," I said.

She ruffled my hair. "It's okay. That was an ambush."

"I should have said something. You don't have to do this. We can back out."

"Why? Why would we?"

"You've got too much at stake here. I don't want to ruin things for you."

"Like what?"

"You're going to be on Olympic teams. I don't want this to blow up and cause you problems with that."

"I have principles, too. What they're doing isn't right."

"I don't know. I think they have a point. It isn't good for team cohesion."

"The only reason it would be bad for team cohesion is if they don't take the time to understand."

"How can they understand if we don't actually explain it? Why didn't you tell them that we don't have sex?"

"Because they don't need to know that. That's personal, just between the two of us."

She lay down next to me and spooned. "And what was that bit at the end? Abby talking about what you should know?"

"I don't really want to answer that question."

It meant a lot to me that she just bit her lip and didn't ask why.

"But I'm going to answer it anyway. Caitlyn, you aren't the first teammate I've ever slept with."

She turned over to look at me. "This isn't a happy story, is it?"

"No. I told you my foster father raped me, but there was more to it than that." And so, slowly, I told her the whole sordid tale of sleeping with Josh Lipke. And that led to telling about the school psychologist. I spent hours telling her stories about my childhood. It came out very different than when I'd told Abby. There was a lot more emotion in it. It came out easier.

"Christ. No wonder you have nightmares."

"Only Abby knows any of that."

"And she brought that up in a team meeting?" She was angry again.

"I don't think she meant to. She was mortified when I called her on it."

"I don't care. That was vile."

"Please let it go."

She took a deep breath. "Okay. But only because you asked."

"I don't want to talk anymore. I just want to lie here."

She kissed my forehead. "I don't blame you."

We curled up together. Caitlyn drifted off to sleep long before I did. I just listened to her breathing.

Word got around to the whole team quickly. The next time she saw me, Kennedy greeted me with, "Well, no wonder you've been happier lately." She was grinning. The sun was shining. Even the birds were singing.

So it was fitting that I felt gloomy. "I take it you've heard."

"Indeed I have."

"I'm sorry," I said.

"For what?"

"For creating this whole mess. For keeping it secret."

"No apology needed. I think it's great."

"I don't know." I was looking at the sidewalk. "There isn't any explicit rule, 'Don't sleep with your teammates,' but it seems to be pretty much assumed."

"Maybe. But you guys are different."

"I don't want to have different rules for me."

"Tough. There are different rules for you. The rules were written for people with very different circumstances than yours."

"I just want to fit in."

She came to a halt. "You're fitting in just fine. And sleeping with Caitlyn can only help that."

"Yeah, well not everyone seems to think that."

She put her hands on my shoulders to look at me. "None of them have ever roomed with you. That's just me and Caitlyn, plus Traci and Morgan a couple of times each."

"What difference does that make?"

"They've never really seen what happens to you. What you're fighting. We've described it, but that's not the same as really seeing it. Caitlyn said that to me after the first time you had a nightmare rooming with her. That she hadn't really understood it."

"I can take care of myself."

"Awhile back you told me that the rest of us shouldn't have to protect ourselves on the ice. That it was your job to do that. This is the same thing. You shouldn't have to take care of this by yourself. That's our job."

"I don't want to be a burden."

"You aren't a burden." She was as intense as I'd ever seen her. "I don't say these things just out of the goodness of my heart, as big as that may be. You do the same thing for me in all things where you can. How many hours did you spend feeding me pucks so I could really learn how to one-time a slap shot? How many truly crazy things did you come up with to say on the bench when my confidence was flagging? How many ice packs have you worn over the last two seasons trying to keep me from having to wear any of them?"

I mumbled some sort of response.

"You were right," she declared. "I don't want to be as tough as you are. But you know what? I don't want you to be as tough as you are, either. Sometimes it hurts just to watch you. Not just the times you're in obvious pain. No, it's worse when you pretend that you aren't. That's when I have no idea what to do."

"I'm sorry. I don't know how to stop doing it."

"I know. That's why I'm happy to see you and Caitlyn together. It's how you can learn, and maybe teach her a few things, too. So the others can stuff it. The rest of our class thinks so, too. No one told us about that meeting, so we held one of our own yesterday. We've got you on this. All of us."

I didn't know what to say beyond, "Thank you."

"You're welcome. But don't think this means that I'm not disappointed that you've scored seven goals since we made an agreement not to."

"Four of those were while I was playing wing." There wasn't a lot of energy in my denial. My mood doesn't recover that quickly, no matter how it's prodded.

"It's pretty sad watching you try to weasel out of a deal."

"Okay. You're right. I'll try harder next year."

"You'd better. There are three openings in the lineup on the blueline for next year. You're going to get the playing time."

"We'll see."

Life went on. That meant that Caitlyn and I kept going as we had been, sleeping together most nights and spending even more of our days together as a form of defiance. We had our occasional disputes, too.

"Have you figured out what you're going to major in yet?" I asked her one day.

We were in Coffman. We desperately needed a place with privacy and enough room to sit together.

"Probably marketing or MIS." I failed to keep my opinion out of my expression. "What? I know you don't like them."

"No. I don't. If you want to learn IT, the business school is a terrible place to do it."

"I'm not an idiot, Phoebe. I may not be a genius like you, but I'm not dumb."

"No, you aren't," I said heatedly, "and that's my problem with it. You're damned smart, and I hate to see you in a major that isn't going to challenge you."

"Then why do you treat me like a moron sometimes?"

I wondered briefly how we had gotten onto this track. "Because you act like one sometimes. Which wouldn't bother me except that you aren't a moron. Erika isn't the highest wattage bulb in the closet, but she does all right."

"So why do you end up yelling at her when you're trying to tutor her?"

It knocked me onto the defensive. "Not that often, and she knows that I'm not really yelling at her. I'm yelling at me because I lose track of the fact that a lot of things don't come as easily for her, and so I do a poor job of teaching."

"It's still a crappy way to treat her."

"Yes, it is, and if she ever wants to get mad at me for it, she's entitled. Just like you're entitled to get mad at me when I treat you like a moron. There are plenty of times I treat people shitty. But that doesn't mean I think you're an idiot."

"Is that supposed to make me feel better?"

"I don't know. I thought it would have, but my judgment on these kinds of things is pretty suspect."

"Why would that make me feel better?"

I sighed. "Because it means I don't think you're an idiot and because it means that you can chalk this up to my being poorly socialized."

"You really don't understand how people think, do you?"

"Not a fucking clue. I thought I'd made that pretty clear over the last two years."

"Start by apologizing for making me feel like an idiot. Make it sound convincing."

"I'm sorry. I don't know if that sounds sincere, but I am. I don't like hurting your feelings. Most of the time I don't even realize I'm doing it."

"Good enough. Next, accept my apology. I shouldn't have jumped on you. I keep forgetting that you usually mean exactly what you say, at least when you're not talking about yourself. If you had meant that I'm an idiot, you either would have said that or said nothing. You wouldn't have said that you think the business school is terrible. I'm sorry."

"That's okay. I just want things to get straightened out."

"Phoebe, just accept the apology."

"Isn't that what I just did?"

"No. If I apologize, it's because I think I did something wrong. Accepting the apology is as much about letting me know that you recognize that as it is about saying it's okay. Probably more."

"I accept your apology."

"With that out of the way, we can start doing what you always want to do and analyze everything to death."

"Um, I lost track of where we were."

"Oh, good. I wanted to change the subject anyway."

"To what?"

"Your clothes."

"What about them?"

"Now, Phoebe, it isn't that I think you have terrible taste, but you often dress like someone with terrible taste."

"The last few minutes have been nothing but trying to set up that line, weren't they?"

"Pretty much," she agreed.

Abby and I hadn't been talking much. She was angry that I hadn't told her about Caitlyn and finding out that I had told her mother didn't help. She was one of the ones pushing for there to be some sort of prohibition on us continuing. On one level I agreed with her that we had violated unspoken team rules. At the same time it hurt that she stood against me.

Despite that, she was the one I went to when it was finally time. She made it clear that we were having a special session of our Tuesday talk and that everyone should be there. The two of us got there before anyone else. As the others came in I was sitting in a chair. Abby stood behind me, arms wrapped around my chest. Whether that was to support me or to keep me from running away, I don't know. Probably both.

"Phoebe has something she wants to tell us," she announced once the whole team was there.

Want didn't have much to do with it. I needed to. I told them about the rapes. I stared into Caitlyn's eyes the whole time. I wished she were the one holding onto me, but it worked. I didn't float away. It was important to me that I stayed there and felt the pain.

It was different than telling either Abby or Caitlyn had been. This was going public no matter how close to all of them I was. For those moments it felt as if I had broken the power he had over me. It mostly didn't last, but maybe a little of it stayed with me.

It was short. I didn't give any details. When I finished, they came up one by one and hugged me. As she did, Tammy whispered in my ear, "I'm sorry." She didn't say for what, and it didn't change our relationship, but it made an impression.

September 1999

"It's not fair."

"Why not?" Mr. Wilson asks me patiently.

"Mrs. Hayes would have let me go."

"I'm not Mrs. Hayes, now am I?"

"You don't like me." This is the point at which Mrs. Hayes would have started to fold.

Instead, Mr. Wilson just looks at me with an expression that makes me squirm. Then he starts to leave, stopping at the door to my room. "I want you to stay in here until you are ready to apologize to me." His voice is perfectly even. "And I want you to know why you need to apologize."

With that, he closes the door quietly. I sit on my bed, fuming. I try to read, but I'm too angry.

I lie there for four hours, wasting a Saturday afternoon. That's how long it is before I start thinking. I begin with the realization that the Wilsons aren't like the Hayes. It only takes me a half hour to reach that conclusion.

I slip out of my room quietly and go to the door of his den. It's open, and I can hear a football game on the television. I knock anyway.

"Come in," he calls.

I walk over to him, hands clenched in front of me. "I'm sorry, Mr. Wilson."

He mutes the TV. "What are you sorry for, Phoebe?"

"For being mean to you." There is an empty feeling in my stomach.

"How were you mean to me?"

I shift awkwardly from one foot to the other under his gaze.

"By saying that you don't like me."

He nods. "Good. Now sit here beside me." He pats the empty sofa cushion, and I sit down. "Phoebe, you tried to make me feel guilty in order to get what you wanted."

The words hang there for a moment as he doesn't follow them up. Finally, I say, "Yes."

"Did that work with Mrs. Hayes?"

"Yes." I'm the one feeling guilty.

"It won't work with me or Mrs. Wilson. I'm going to do what I think is right for you, and I won't feel guilty about it. Understand?"

"Yes."

"Good. Now, you can always disagree with me. I will never tell you to keep your thoughts to yourself, at least when it's just the two of us. Understand?"

"Yes."

"Now slide over here and watch the game with me."

He turns the sound back on as I lean against his side. I don't even pay attention to what teams are playing. Football is a dumb game, but he likes it.

What had been pitched as a consensus decision about Caitlyn and me had turned into Tammy's alone, and how much I had at stake hit home in early May. Each off-season the various national teams hold camps to evaluate prospective members. Caitlyn was scheduled to travel to Toronto for a month starting the third week of May. I regarded the prospect of not seeing her for that long with dread. We avoided talking about it, which really meant that I clammed up whenever she asked how I was going to deal with it. Instead, we talked about it obliquely.

"I don't know how you do it."

Caitlyn didn't break her focus on the video game she was playing. We were taking advantage of Amy being out of town to spend time at their apartment. "Do what?"

"Play for the Canadian national team."

"Sorry. I'm not going to play for the US team. I'm Canadian."

I dog-eared the page of my book and let it close. "No, I mean I don't understand how you can play for any national team."

"Why not?"

"It's not a team. You get together for ten days to practice and then play five or six games. Then you're done and go home."

She set the controller down. "It's still a team."

I shook my head. "It's a group of hockey players. That's different. A team means people I can count on. It's more than just hockey."

Her game continued to make beeping noises, then started playing music.

She thought about it for a minute. "I guess I can see that."

"It also means that opponents are opponents. To take the extreme case, there's no way I could play on the US team with Mallory. She's not a teammate."

She laughed. "I can definitely see that. I'm surprised Tammy hasn't gotten into a fight with her by now."

"Agreed. So I don't see how you do it."

"Love of country. Plus the drive to play on the highest stage possible. Isn't that what sports is about? Playing against the best?"

I stopped for a moment. "No. I mean, I'd always thought that it was, but no, it really isn't. Not for me. Who I'm playing with is far more important to me than who I'm playing against."

"If you had gone to Michigan State, you'd be saying the same thing about Mallory."

"I wouldn't have gone to Michigan State." It was too close to Ohio.

"True, but you know what I mean."

"Yeah, I do," I said. "Yes, I would say that about my teammates no matter where I went. At least, I would if they had treated me as well as everyone has here."

"So how do you limit it just to us?"

"Because I didn't go anywhere else. I went here." I grimaced as the game's music started its third lap around the same tune.

"That seems pretty arbitrary."

"Sure, it's arbitrary, but you do the same thing. I don't get the love of country thing."

"You don't love the US?"

"No. I don't understand how one loves a country."

It was her turn to think. "I was raised in Canada. I just . . . I don't know how to put it."

"That something you can't explain is something I don't get. I don't hate America, either. To me, 'country' is just an abstract concept. It has no meaning in itself. It's just a way of differentiating groups of territories, or groups of ideals, or people, or a government, or what have you."

"Phoebe, you're starting to drift off into your philosophy talk again."

"Sorry."

"I don't know. I just love Canada." She sounded defensive.

"There's nothing wrong with that. I'm not saying that I'm opposed to loving a country. I'm just saying that I can't. It doesn't make sense to me."

She frowned.

"I'll try it this way. I can love people. I can love groups of people, but they have to be groups small enough that I know everyone in them. But that's it. I can't love people I don't know, or groups that are made up mostly of them."

"I don't know. I'll have to think about it."

"If I smell smoke, I'll call the fire department."

She hit me with a sofa cushion. And, believe it or not, that led to us having sex for the first time.

It wasn't magical. In fact, it was almost more painful than anything else. Caitlyn had no idea what my triggers were, and we spent as much time bringing me back from a state of panic as we did actually having sex.

But it was good. "Cathartic" is the right word to use. We fell asleep afterward, bodies entwined. When I woke up, I felt different, closer to her. I rolled over so I faced her and traced lines on her body with my fingertip. I traced them on my own body and then between us, binding us together. I tied her wrists together with invisible cords and then tied them to mine. She muttered in her sleep as I worked, her incoherence allowing me to imagine whatever words I wished.

I didn't tell her about it. It was my secret ritual, ensuring that she'd always come back. So I suppose it was magical after all.

CHAPTER 12

The next day I went with Caitlyn to the airport. The security checkpoint was the only thing that kept me from getting on the plane with her.

"It's just a month," she told me as she tried to get into the line.

Instead, I held onto her. Ensuring that she'd come back didn't make her departure any easier.

"I'm scared."

"Of what?"

"Not having you around. Not sleeping."

"You'll be okay. Phoebe, I need you here."

"What?"

"I need to know that you are here," she repeated. "This is it. This is the first step to my making the Olympics in two years. This is when I get to impress the coaches. I need to do well."

"You did a pretty good job of ripping up half of Team Canada when we beat Cornell."

"You know what I mean."

"Not really," I responded. "This is out of my league. I didn't play on the Under-18 team like you did. I've had enough trouble just staying in our lineup."

"I still need you here."

"Why?"

"Because I know you'll be here. Whether I wow them or completely fuck it up, you aren't going to change. On June 20, I'm going to be coming the other way through this airport, and you aren't going to judge me. You don't care whether I succeed or fail."

"That's not true. I care a lot."

"Maybe, but you don't show it much."

"I'm sorry."

"It's refreshing," she said. "I'm surrounded by people who judge me by how well I play. Then I come over to your place, and there's none of that. Even on game nights. There's no worrying about whether I played well. It's just you and me and nothing else matters."

"No one on the team judges you that way."

She laughed. "I have no idea how you've maintained such a positive opinion of people. The team splits about fifty-fifty on that."

"They don't treat me that way."

She paused. "That's expectations. If I play badly, I've let them down."

"And if I play badly?"

"You don't have to be great every single night. I do. Jenny does. That's life at the top of the depth chart, and I already regret bringing this up because now you're going to be self-conscious about it."

I took a deep breath and let the implications about my abilities slide by. "So what do you need me to do?"

"Just be here. Take my phone calls and understand that I'm going to be on edge every time I call."

"You?"

"Yeah, me. I want this so bad. I know you don't get it, but just accept that this is a training camp that leads to what I've dreamed about ever since I put on skates."

"I think I can understand that. Maybe not the team, but the desire."

"God, I'm nervous."

"You're going to do great."

"Yeah." She was trying to muster some enthusiasm.

"And if you don't, I'll be right here. I can't say I don't care, because

I do. But it won't change anything either way. Trust me, what I really want is for you to come back."

Her arms tightened. "Thank you."

"Good luck, Caitlyn."

She disengaged and picked up her carry-on. "They're not gonna see what hit 'em."

"Nope." I let her go, and she was off, and I had to figure out what I was going to do for thirty-five days without her.

Caitlyn's absence crystalized something growing within me that I hadn't been aware of while she was present: I was thinking about quitting the team. If hockey wasn't fun, I didn't want to play it any longer.

I had a meeting with Coach Long and let my unhappiness spill out. He looked at me when I was done. "So what are we going to do about it?"

"I'm thinking of quitting," I replied.

"Does it change anything if I tell you that I have half of a scholarship for you next year?"

I looked at my hands. "Maybe. I don't know."

"How about if I say that I'm thinking of making you a forward next year? Full time."

That stopped me cold. I'd played wing for a third of the season, but I hadn't stopped thinking of myself as a defenseman. "But we'll need defensemen," I finally said. It was true, because we'd graduated three of them, including two All-Americans.

"We have a good class coming in. I liked the way you played up there. You added an element on offense that we didn't have. You'll be good at it."

"I've always played defense."

He leaned forward. "It will also be a clean break for you. Maybe you'll enjoy playing forward. Besides, I'd rather have you as a wing than not have you at all."

"I'll think about it," I said weakly.

"Do that. Take a couple of months, and then let me know."

I left his office as confused as when I'd entered it.

It was a meeting of three, but only two of us were in the room. Tammy had Caitlyn on speakerphone. I was seething about the fact that we were doing this while she was out of town. It was clear that Caitlyn was boiling over, but our objections had been overruled.

"Here's what we decided. What the two of you do in private is your own business. But it stays in private. In public you're just two more teammates. No displays. No talking about it. It's a nonevent."

"In other words," Caitlyn said through the slight static, "we should do exactly what we were doing for six months until you brought it up."

"Obviously you need to do a better job of it."

"Uh huh. And how exactly did we violate this rule?"

"I can't tell you."

I had my suspicions but didn't address them explicitly. "Can we get an apartment together? To cut down on comings and goings that might get noticed?" At least I was talking this time.

The expression on Tammy's face confirmed that my guess was correct. So, the who might not have been solved, but the how had been. I didn't care about the who. I had my suspicions about that, but no intention of pursuing it. My relations with Abby were fraught enough at the moment.

"Yes," she answered. "That's probably a good idea."

"We'll make sure never to invite anyone over," Caitlyn muttered, barely audible on the iffy connection.

I winced. I just wanted this over with. "And we are roommates on the road, just like last year."

Tammy hesitated and then nodded. For Caitlyn's benefit, she added a verbal assent.

"All right. I'll commit to that, and I'll convince Caitlyn to do so as well."

"Hey—"

"I'll talk to you later, sweetie." I used my sappiest voice just to see what sort of reaction I'd get from Tammy. Her glare suggested that I probably shouldn't have. "We'll be fine."

There was some additional posturing and grumbling between them, but the conversation was basically over. A few formalities later I was out the door and walking home. Caitlyn called me twice in those twenty minutes, but I let it go to voice mail both times.

I called her back as soon as I had the door closed. "Phoebe," she exclaimed as soon as she answered, "this isn't fair."

"'Fair' has nothing to do with it. Everything was good before anyone found out, and it will be again."

"I don't want to have to be all secretive."

"I agree. I don't really want to either, but—"

"Then why are you going along with it?"

"—we don't really have to be. We just have to be selective."

"How so?"

"Did you listen to Kennedy and Jenny when we talked about this?" I asked. "They're okay with all of it. We have a set of friends we can act natural with. We just have to play act for the rest of them. I can do that and you can, too."

"It's still not fair."

I disagreed, but I knew that my reasoning wouldn't go any-where. "It's also only for one year. After that, those guys will have graduated, and we can renegotiate." The thought slithered through my mind that the real reason it wouldn't matter at that point was that we'd never be on the team together again, unless she somehow failed to make the Olympic roster. But that thought was scary, so I pushed it away.

"I still don't like it."

"I appreciate that you don't. But we can still do it. Think of it this way. How often do you get a chance to be the responsible adult in a situation?"

"I don't like being a responsible adult." I knew from her tone that I'd won.

"That's usually why you have me, but we're both going to have to step up this time."

She surrendered. "Okay, okay. I get it."

"Thank you."

"Now we have to find an apartment."

"I'm already working on that," I assured her.

"It pisses me off that we can't even ask Heck if she would live with us, but I'll deal with it."

"See," I said, "you can do this."

"Pfui."

"How's it going up there?"

"I'm in Toronto. That's south of you."

"Irrelevant. Your sparsely populated tundra of a country is always referred to as 'up there.'"

"It's going pretty well. I'm holding my own."

"I'm expecting more than that."

"I'm lulling them into a false sense of security. How are you doing?"

"Meh. I'm lonely and still unmotivated."

"How are we going to change that?"

"I don't know. I'm still thinking about quitting."

"You're not going to. We both know that."

"I guess one of us does."

"When do workouts start?" she asked, meaning my trips to the specialized training center the Forrests had paid for and that I was feeling guilty for wanting to skip.

"Next Monday."

"What time?"

"Nine in the morning."

"I'll call you to make sure you get going."

"Aren't you going to be busy?" I asked.

"I'll figure something out."

"Thank you."

"You're welcome."

"I should let you get going," I said.

"Phoebe, just don't be miserable, okay?"

"I'll try."

"Promise?"

"Promise."

"Okay. Time for me to go demonstrate how to play NHL 2012 to these people."

"Go get 'em, Tiger."

"Love you, Phoebe."

"I love you, too."

The phone disconnected. I stared at it for awhile before figuring out something to do.

The next day I tracked Abby down. We hadn't spoken in almost two weeks. I cornered her coming off the ice at Ridder. "Caitlyn has been teaching me how to apologize," I said. "Do you mind if I practice?"

"Why didn't you just tell me?"

"Some combination of being stupid and just never telling anyone anything I don't have to."

"Well, it was dumb." We moved into the locker room, the only people there.

"Yes," I agreed, "it was. I'm sorry. I'm sorry I didn't tell you."

"The whole thing was a bad idea."

"Well, I won't say I'm sorry about sleeping with Caitlyn, because I'm not."

"That's okay." She worked her skates off. "I don't blame you for that."

"What does that mean?" I asked suspiciously.

"Caitlyn took advantage of you."

"She what?" I was incredulous.

"You were vulnerable, and she took advantage of you."

"You don't have any fucking idea what happened."

I stalked out of the room.

When the month was up, it was hard to keep myself from going to the airport to pick up Caitlyn. This despite the fact that I didn't own a car and we would have just taken a taxi back to campus.

Instead I waited anxiously in the players' lounge, figuring that she'd show up. Kennedy was there, sitting next to me on the couch. Others drifted in and out, but mostly it was just the two of us. We didn't say anything, but she was definitely with me as opposed to just hanging around.

Of course, my anxieties were getting the better of me. About twenty minutes after Caitlyn's scheduled arrival, my phone rang. I didn't look at the incoming number before I answered.

"Hello?"

"Phoebe! Where are you?"

"I'm at Ridder."

"Is that where you want to meet?"

"I . . . sure. Wherever is good for you."

"I'll meet you there, but I want to get some dinner. The stuff on the plane was disgusting."

"Okay. That sounds good."

"I'll see you then. Bye!" She disconnected.

Kennedy was looking at me when I put my phone away. "That was her?" There wasn't anyone else there at that moment.

"Yeah." I couldn't control the excitement in my voice.

"Good. No offense, but you've been kind of a pill to deal with while she was gone. You stopped talking to me."

"I did?" I thought about it. "Yeah, I guess."

"I've been worried about you."

"I've been worried about me. I've been thinking about quitting the team."

That got a reaction. "You're kidding."

"No. I'm sure you've watched me the last few months."

"You can't quit. What the hell am I going to do?"

I smiled. "Don't worry. I'll still harass you."

"You're just afraid that you'll keep scoring goals."

We kicked that subject around for a half hour before Caitlyn walked in. She gave me a big kiss in defiance of the new rules.

Kennedy looked at both of us. "Okay, I'm leaving. You two obviously don't need me."

"Don't bother," Caitlyn responded. "We're not staying. I don't know where the hell I'm going to take her dressed like that, but it's definitely somewhere else."

"Do I get to help decide?" I asked.

"Not a chance. Girls that play for their national teams get to make the decisions."

I stood up. "Sorry, Kennedy. I'm being summoned."

"Oh, that's no problem. Get out of here before I get embarrassed again."

Caitlyn spent much of that summer dragging me around. Most importantly, three days a week she got me out of bed and into Traci's car to go to hockey training. Once there, I learned more than I ever had before. It was the first time I'd ever worked with instructors who were devoted solely to teaching me basic skills and techniques without spending time on game situations.

Naturally, most of the work was on my skating. A lot of the time we weren't even on the ice. Instead I used a skating treadmill. For awhile I was in a kind of ugly limbo in which I couldn't skate the way I had been, but the new approach was still so rudimentary that I was actually slower. Fortunately, I had four months to work on it. I never did get fast, but I did achieve adequacy for the duties of playing forward.

The other thing we focused on was working in front of the net as an offensive player. I was surprised at just how different it is from defending. I worked on keeping my stick free and trying to deflect shots on net.

I still wasn't convinced it was going to work. I had more ground to cover in transition on both offense and defense. I was suddenly supposed to catch up to opposing players carrying the puck up the ice instead of not letting them get behind me in the first place. It required speed.

Nevertheless, I warmed to the idea of making a permanent

change. Coach Long was right; it allowed me to drop a lot of mental baggage and start, if not all over, at least somewhat fresher.

Somewhere along the way, I stopped being miserable thinking about playing and started being miserable at the idea of not playing. So it made no sense to me that Caitlyn had to badger me into going. She insisted that everyone feels this way about doing drills and that it was a sign that I was becoming normal. It took awhile to really accept that.

November 1997

Mrs. Hayes is waiting impatiently for me to leave the ice after practice, so I make sure that I'm the last person off. Even after Mr. Johnson retreats through the doors, I skate another lap. Part of it is that I don't want to go home, but I also do it to annoy her.

When I finally step off, Mr. Johnson is talking to her. "There she is." He puts his hand on top of my head as I lift my face shield. "She's the most dedicated player out there."

"It's just a phase, I'm sure," my foster mother replies. I roll my eyes, but no one notices.

"Well, the exercise is good for her."

"I'm sure it is." She holds out her hand for me. "Come on, Phoebe. Get your skates off so I can take you home."

Neither of us says anything else until we're in the van. "We're going to see Grandma tomorrow."

I look out the window. "She's not my grandmother."

She sighs, and I don't need to turn around to know the exact expression on her face. "You should try to think of us as family."

"Then you should adopt me." Pushing her buttons is so easy, but I also mean it.

"We can't, honey."

"Why not?" If I keep her feeling guilty, there is no chance she'll make me stop learning hockey.

"You're too young. You wouldn't understand."

I understand perfectly well: I'm not my foster parents' idea of a perfect little darling. "It's because you don't like me, isn't it?"

"No," she insists frantically. "We love you. It's just that . . . you wouldn't understand."

Mission accomplished, I lapse into silence. For a few minutes, so does Mrs. Hayes.

"Will you be nice to Grandma?" she finally asks as we pull into the driveway.

"I'll try." The van hardly comes to a stop before I jump out and grab my hockey bag from the backseat. "Do I have to pretend to like the food?"

"Yes." This time I know her exasperation is because she agrees with me.

The whole process ended exactly where everyone predicted. I went back to Coach Long's office in early August.

"Coach?"

"Yes, Phoebe?"

"I've made up my mind. I'm going to play."

"Good." Other than a slight smile, his face didn't move.

"You never really believed I wouldn't, did you?"

"No, I didn't."

"Neither did anyone else."

"It's too much of who you are. But it's important that you made the decision on your own."

I snorted. "Too many people decided to help me make it to say that."

"I'm not surprised by that, either. Anything else I can help you with?"

"No, sir."

"Get lost then. I have work to do."

"Yes, sir."

A few days later, as I tried to get to sleep and assumed that Caitlyn already had, she asked me, "When did you know you were gay?"

"Huh?" I grunted, feigning being sleepier than I was.

"I mean, did you know before we started sleeping together? Or was it after?"

"Do you deliberately ask these kinds of questions when you know I'll bang my chin on your head if I avoid them?"

She giggled. "No, but I'll keep that idea in mind for the future."

"I don't know," I finally answered. "I'm not even sure I am gay."

She twisted herself so that she could look at my face. "What do you mean?"

"I mean that my sexuality is so screwed up at this point that beyond being Caitlyn-sexual, I really have no idea what I am."

"Really? You're usually sure about yourself."

"It's not something I like to think about. I guess I must be bi, but it doesn't really matter."

"How can it not matter?"

"Because I can't imagine wanting to have sex with anyone, present company excluded."

She hugged me. "I'm sorry."

We lay there for a few minutes before she spoke again. "I'm not gay."

"Okay," I replied.

"I love *you*," she continued. "I mean, I love everyone, but you're the only woman I can imagine doing this with."

"I guess that makes me special."

"Of course you're special." She kissed me and then, being Caitlyn, fell asleep, leaving me to wonder what it all meant.

Shortly before that, Abby had knocked on the door to my room one afternoon. "I'm sorry," she said before I could overcome my surprise.

"For what, exactly?" I asked.

"For saying that Caitlyn took advantage of you."

I mustered everything Caitlyn had been teaching me and stopped at, "Apology accepted."

A certain amount of tension went out of her when I said that. "Thank you."

"Come on in." I closed the door behind her and sat on the futon. She took the chair at my desk-ledge. "Abby, before I say anything else, can we at least agree to start talking to each other again? I miss spending time with you away from the rink. So even if we have to just avoid talking about this subject going forward, can we do that?"

She nodded. "Yeah, I'd like that."

"Okay." I took a deep breath and plunged into the questions I'd rehearsed. "Are you apologizing because you said that Caitlyn took advantage of me, or because you've changed your mind and don't think that she did?"

She grimaced. "I was hoping you wouldn't ask anything like that."

I waited a moment to see if she'd say anything else. "I'd still like to hear your answer."

Abby is too honest to lie about something like that. "I'm sorry I said it. I didn't mean to cause such a rift. I still think it's true, though."

"That's what I thought. Do you know what makes me the angriest about that?" I suspected she did but continued before she had a chance to answer. "It isn't that you're slandering Caitlyn, though that does make me mad. It's that you're assuming that I don't make choices."

Watching her, I could tell I was wasting my time. She wasn't so honest that she didn't say the right thing. "You're right. I'm sorry I didn't give you credit."

I sighed and pretended she wasn't a horrible liar. "Please remember that. I'm not the same person I was two years ago. I appreciate the way you sheltered me. It made an enormous difference, and I don't think I could have made the adjustments without it. But I don't need that anymore. I think you enjoyed playing that role, but you need to let go."

"You talked about this with my mother, didn't you?"

"Yeah, I did," I admitted.

She sat there. At last she said, "I guess I'm okay with that.

"My talking with your mother?"

"Yeah. It's just kind of strange knowing that my mother will talk about me like that with a friend."

I smiled. "I'm not going to apologize for that. She's been as important to me as you have."

"No, no," she broke in. "I'm not asking you to apologize for it. Her either. It took me awhile to realize it, but I don't have a problem with the way you two have connected. It's just kind of weird. It's like I've suddenly developed a younger sister."

I thought about that for a bit. "I suppose. It's kind of hard for me to tell."

"Trust me. It's like having a brother, but different."

"Can you try treating me like an adult?"

She nodded. "I'll try."

That night I talked to Caitlyn before she fell asleep. "You were right. She's decided to absolve me of all blame and put it all on you."

"Told you." She was angry.

"I'm sorry."

"Don't apologize for her. You're not responsible for her pigheadedness."

"I'm still sorry."

Her voice softened. "It's okay. Actually, it's probably better this way. She's important to you. I know that. She shouldn't blame either of us, because we didn't do anything wrong. But if she feels like she has to, it might as well just be me. She's never liked me anyway."

"Thank you."

She giggled. "It's pretty easy for me to be magnanimous. I'm the one lying in bed with you."

I snuggled against her.

"I don't promise to be polite to her, though."

"Um." I was unsure where this was going.

"I won't ask you to take my side when we argue. And we will argue, because I'm not willing to hold my tongue. Just don't take her side. I'm okay with public neutrality on your part."

"Are you sure?"

"Yes."

"That's—"

"This isn't your fault, and it isn't fair to you. So just avoid it."

"I told Abby that I don't need a protector anymore."

"If I were trying to act as your protector, I'd just suck it up and not tell her what I think. Phoebe, don't get in the middle of whatever happens. Just tell me in private how awesome I am."

"I can do that."

Some things, at least, got back to normal. My early mornings returned to their proper purpose, although Caitlyn disagreed. "Where are you going?" Caitlyn asked sleepily one day.

"Working out."

She managed to raise her head enough to see the clock. "Phoebe, it's quarter to five in the morning."

"I know."

She dropped her face into the pillow. "I'm starting to wish you'd given up on playing. At least I'd get some sleep."

"It's going to take you three seconds to get back to sleep once I'm out the door." I didn't get a response, suggesting that it hadn't taken that long.

As for me, I don't know what happened, but that drive was back. And this time, I was enjoying it.

PART

2

March 24, 2015

We started out on campus with the other seniors. The atmosphere was like a wake for someone who lived a long, fulfilling life with lots of great stories to tell. It wasn't really sad, but there was a hint of it behind the laughs.

Jenny, Caitlyn, and I abandoned the other six long before it was over. We all graduated at the same time, but our strongest bonds were elsewhere. Heck, Traci, Morgan, and Kennedy had been at the championship game and followed the caravan back to Minneapolis. They met us for a late dinner.

After that we went out to a bar to shoot pool. I lost everything I'd won playing poker on road trips. Kennedy cornered me at one point. "You're awfully quiet."

"I think the euphoria is wearing off," I replied.

"So what are you thinking about?"

"The future, mostly."

She ruffled my hair. "In a good way or a bad way?"

"Bad, I suppose, but I'm still euphoric enough that it's not bothering me too much."

"You'll figure it out."

"Actually my immediate concerns have nothing to do with leaving here or losing Caitlyn. In six weeks I'm scheduled to have potentially life-altering surgery, and then there's the trial this summer."

"I forgot about surgery." She made a face.

I shrugged. "It's not like I talk about my AIS much. The surgery itself is simple, and I'm not going to miss what they're taking out. If anything, it'll reduce the amount of ambiguity. Maybe. So I'm not sure what's bothering me about it."

"Oh, for God's sake, Kennedy," Morgan called out as she lined up a shot. "Make her drink."

Kennedy looked at me, and I complied by draining the half shot of whiskey I had left. Morgan had declared that being a downer was a drinking offense. It was only fair that she got to set the rules, since she and Heck were picking up the tab for us poor students.

"Why do you drink that stuff?" Kennedy told me.

"It puts hair on your chest. Since my body failed my genes' instructions on that, I have to find other methods."

She laughed harder than the line merited. "That's better. Black humor is tolerated."

It wasn't that black. Unlike some of my psychological issues my body image really had gotten better since I'd arrived in Minneapolis. Not perfect, but it had come a long way.

"However," I announced as our server passed by, "I need a Knob Creek because I do want to talk about the trial briefly, and that's likely to turn into a major infraction."

Morgan emitted a loud sigh but didn't say anything. Everyone immediately turned their attention to me, though most of them tried to conceal it.

"All right," Kennedy said evenly. "Did you know that I've been subpoenaed to testify?"

"No, but it doesn't surprise me."

"The DA wants me to talk about the nightmares and that night in Columbus by the team bus."

"I'm sorry."

"Don't be. I want to be there when they send the son of a bitch away." My friends have all adopted my convention of never using his name. It's one of the little, never-spoken-of things that makes me feel so comfortable with them.

"Thanks. I'm still not sure I want to go through with it, but I appreciate it."

The waitress delivered my bourbon. The real answer to Kennedy's earlier question is that on the rare occasions I want to get drunk I'm not interested in screwing around. Drinking straight whiskey also helps my tough-guy image. Normally I don't drink anything but what's on the rail, but Morgan had also made it clear that she wasn't going to be seen paying for a cheapskate.

"I know. If you back out, we'll all understand."

"I'm not going to back out. I'm going to hate it. It's going to make me a wreck. But I'm not quitting on this." I threw back the whole shot, which I admit is a bad way to treat top-shelf liquor. I do like the flavor.

Morgan came up, having lost her match to Caitlyn. "I hadn't even ruled yet. Nothing wrong with that. Hell, I approve."

"That's okay." I put my arm around her. "I needed it."

"Do you want me to change the rules?" she asked.

"No, I'm good. It doesn't matter much, though. I plan to get completely trashed and pretend that the future doesn't exist."

"Good. We're all going to join you. Kennedy is the only one whose attitude I'm worried about." She gave my one-time defense partner a stern glare.

"I'm in, I'm in," Kennedy protested.

"Have you ever been drunk before?" I asked her.

"Once."

"Really? When? You never have when we've all gone out."

"It was back in high school. I did something stupid and said I'd never get drunk again."

"Are you sure you want to now?"

"Oh, come on." Morgan punched my arm. "Are you going to fall for this sob story?"

"It's okay," Kennedy said, looking at me. "I trust the rest of you will keep me from doing anything that dumb."

"Famous last words," I warned.

"I'll take my chances."

Caitlyn squeezed her way in between Morgan and me. "Hands off my date," she said.

"Aren't you supposed to be playing Traci now?"

"I forfeit. Kennedy, you're up."

"But—"

"Don't make me deliberately sink the eight ball."

Kennedy rolled her eyes. "Oh, all right."

Caitlyn pushed back against me, and I wrapped my arms around her.

Morgan started to ask something. I knew the subject from her expression and preempted her. "Remember, for tonight the future doesn't exist."

"True enough," she replied smoothly.

I spent the evening going through all of the premium whiskeys the establishment carried. I lost almost every game I played, but I didn't mind because Caitlyn and I spent a lot of time snuggling and making snide comments to the others.

We played until they kicked us out. After that we went back to the place Jenny, Morgan, and Kennedy shared, and we raided their liquor cabinet. That's what led to a really silly stunt. Kennedy's faith in us to keep her from doing something dumb proved misplaced.

No of us can remember being the one to come up with the idea. Half of us can barely remember it at all. Traci insists that I'm to blame, but I don't trust her memory. Regardless, we all agreed that we should become blood sisters, pledged to each other forever. It was like a bad *Leave It to Beaver* episode with girls, except that no one showed up to stop us.

So we actually did it. Fortunately, no one hurt themselves badly slicing open their palm. I couldn't possibly repeat the oath we took even if I wanted to. I just know that we took it and that we all took it seriously even after we sobered up.

CHAPTER 13

We opened the 2012-13 season by beating Indiana 8-0, but the real event was raising the championship banner before the game. As I watched it ascend into the rafters, satisfaction, pride, and something approaching giddiness replaced the frustration of the previous year. I even enjoyed the crowd. Most of the time, I would rather have played in front of a bunch of empty seats, but for that one night, I fed off of the fans' excitement.

I wondered whether I really deserved to win a title. We didn't win it because of me; if Coach had moved someone else up to the third line when Abby got injured, it wouldn't have changed the outcome. There were many better players in the league who never did win one.

So was it luck that I got a national championship ring? Did I earn it? There was a lot of luck that Mr. Wilson had gone to a school that wins hockey championships with a team that coincidentally developed an unexpected hole in its lineup at the same time I arrived on campus. But I earned it, too, to the extent that a nonstar earns much of anything in sports.

I think about the idea of luck a lot. It's pervasive in sports, but it's also amorphous and athletes tend to deny that it exists except in passing. It's uncomfortable to acknowledge its role in success, but it's there. Take the two goals Kris scored in the final. They were the same play—one she tried regularly—and most of the time she shot it wide. On that afternoon, she was two for two with it. Is that luck?

Was she just particularly good? Is there any way to tell the difference between those two things?

I asked Caitlyn about it. She told me I needed to stop taking philosophy classes because they were messing with my head.

I had fun learning to play wing that fall, successfully fighting to stay on the third line. Despite my enjoyment, as a team we weren't as good as we'd been the year before. Erika had become the best goalie in the world before graduating, and my fun was mitigated by the yawning void caused by losing two All-American defensemen.

It wasn't just inexperience that killed us; immaturity played a big role, too. On the Monday after a brutal 4–0 loss to Iowa, Tammy cornered our new goalie, a quiet kid named Alice, in the locker room. Kennedy and I were the only others there to witness the encounter. It was brief. Alice was putting on her skates when Tammy walked up, pointed at her, and snarled, "You can't play like that. This team needs you to be better. If you would have stopped more pucks, we could have won that game."

That was it. She walked out, heading for the ice, and Alice blinked a couple of times, a blank look on her face. By itself, the expression was unreadable, but the way she stopped lacing her skates was telling.

Kennedy and I looked at each other. "Who do you want to talk to?" she asked quietly.

I sighed, and pointed toward the rink. I didn't really want to deal with Tammy, but it was the better alternative. Goalies are mysterious, magical creatures that none of the rest of us will ever figure out, and I didn't think trying to reinflate Alice's confidence would play to my strengths. "Thanks," Kennedy muttered as I followed the team captain.

I found her skating lazily near the bench. "What are you doing?" I asked her.

She didn't really look at me. "Toughening her up. She needs it."

"Really? By telling her that Saturday night was her fault?"

"She can't give up four goals to a team like that. It's not good enough."

I managed to keep my voice down, hoping none of this carried back into the locker room. "For Christ's sake, we got shut out. No goalie could have helped us win."

"I'm motivating her for the future."

"Like that? That's your idea of leadership?"

"It works." She turned to regard me fully. "What's your idea?"

"Maybe try to be nice to your teammates rather than intimidate them?"

"We all know how nice you are with your teammates. I'll pass."

I stared at her as she pivoted and skated away.

"My father used to take me to Canucks games."

There were five of us in the lounge that Tuesday to swap stories. Kennedy told us about a cat she'd had when she was a kid. Kat explained why she hates traditional Slovak costumes. Then it was Caitlyn's turn.

"It was our night out together. We'd have dinner somewhere downtown and then go to the arena. One time, when I was fourteen, he managed to get us admitted down to the players' area after the game, and we met the team. He called in some sort of old connection. It was neat. I talked with Brendan Morrison and Anson Carter for a bit. They gave me autographs. I got to brag about it with my teammates. Those trips were something I missed after my parents divorced."

That left just me. I fidgeted momentarily as I had changed my mind about what I wanted to say. I didn't want to follow Caitlyn's short bit with something depressing, and I went with something happier.

"My senior year, before I left, we had the best team I'd ever played on. The atmosphere wasn't nearly as toxic. I couldn't see that then, but I do now. It helped to have fewer people who were around when I forced my way onto the team.

"We almost had a winning record, and one night I scored a hat trick against St. Xavier. They were really bad, even relative to the rest of that league. It was only their second year playing varsity hockey, but it was still a surprise. It must have been a really slow week in girls' basketball, because a local paper named me Female Athlete of the Week. It was one of the few times I got teased by the guys in a good way, and for a moment I felt good about it all.

"It probably seems strange that it's taken me this long to mention this." I looked at Abby as I said, "I've never told Abby about it."

"I guess I'm starting to remember a few more of the good times. There weren't many, but I've probably given the impression that there weren't any of them, and that's really not true."

As we walked home, Caitlyn was fidgeting in the way that means she's disturbed about something. "What's wrong?"

She kicked at something imaginary. "My story was bullshit. We went to Canucks games together, but that's it. It sure as hell wasn't a good time. He'd spend the whole game comparing the way I played to what we were watching. He always talked about how he had connections that were going to get us down to the locker rooms, but it never happened. I did meet Brendan Morrison, but it was at a hockey camp."

I sucked in my breath. "Why?"

"Why what?"

"Make things up. I don't get it."

"Oh, come on. You all think I embellish everything." I was startled by the amount of bitterness in her voice.

"Not like this. It's always seemed innocent. Fun exaggeration."

"What's the problem?" she said.

"Where would you like me to start?"

"Wherever you want."

"Can we wait until we get home?" I said, trying to defuse a fight I hadn't anticipated.

We walked the rest of the way in silence. When we got there, I wrapped my arms around her before I started. "Is there anything in particular wrong? Today, I mean?"

"Why does there have to be something wrong?" She tried unsuccessfully to push me away.

"No, Caitlyn. I don't know for sure that you need a hug, but I do." She complied, but obviously only to appease me. "There doesn't have to be anything wrong. I'm just wondering if there is."

"No. Nothing."

"Okay. Then I'll start with my worry about me. I don't mind embellishing in those sessions. I don't, but that's for my own reasons. Until today, I've enjoyed watching you do it and trying to figure out what's true and what isn't. Today was different. And now I just want reassurance that you haven't been embellishing about other things, just to me. Like when you talked about your own fears." She jerked. "You have been?"

"No. Not on that." Now her embrace was real. "But I could have. It just never occurred to me, not until right now, how you would take it if I did. That was stupid. And I probably have, though not on anything that important."

"Okay. Please promise me that you won't."

"I promise. I won't lie about stuff like that."

"Thank you. Is it okay to tell you that I'm worried about you right now? You've been acting strangely today."

"My father is coming next week, for the Michigan State series."

"That's what's bothering you?"

"Yeah. I don't want him here. I just want to be left to play in peace."

"I understand that."

She gave a short, harsh laugh. "I bet you do. What a fine pair we make."

"We do all right, all things considered."

"I'm glad one of us thinks so."

"I'm not used to being the optimist, Caitlyn. You're going to have to help me here."

"Well, if I were you, this is when I'd suggest taking a nap."

Which is what we pretended to do. I'm not sure either of us actually slept.

My relationship with Abby was strange. We talked about everything except the elephant in the room. For a time I managed to talk myself into thinking it was a good thing, that it meant that I had a normal relationship with someone that wasn't dominated by always talking about serious problems.

"Phoebe," she asked me early that November, "I have a favor to ask."

"I figured you might since you offered to buy lunch."

She gave me her look that means that she recognizes that an attempt at humor has been made. I smiled sweetly at her.

"I have to write a paper for my Interpersonal Relationships class examining a relationship that I have. I was wondering if you would mind if I used the two of us."

I looked at my sandwich. "Can I think about it?"

"I realize that it's a lot to ask, but ours is easily the most fascinating relationship I have."

I was silent for a moment. "You still think of me as a project, don't you?"

"No," she insisted. "It's not like that."

"I don't appreciate being your lab rat."

"It's not like that," she insisted.

"So what do you mean about me being fascinating?"

"It's just that . . ." She closed her mouth, and I could see her jaw clench with frustration.

"It's just that you're trying to be my therapist, and you want to turn in your clinical notes."

"No, it isn't," she yelled at me. Then she lowered her voice, embarrassed by the attention she'd drawn. "I'm sorry I brought it up."

I started to say something sharp but checked myself. Instead I drew a deep breath and tried to relax my muscles beginning with my face. I didn't stop looking at Abby as I did it, and I could see her recognize what I was doing and shut up.

We sat there in silence for almost five minutes before I could calmly say, "Do you trust your teacher?"

"I do," she answered in the same way. "If I didn't I would never have asked."

"Then go ahead and use us for your paper."

"I don't want to do it if it bothers you."

"It doesn't bother me."

"Really?" she said in a tone that indicated skepticism.

"Okay, it bothers me a little. You can do it on one condition. I don't want it to be a part of any class discussions, just something that only you and your professor see."

"I'll clear that with him before I write it. And I don't see you as a research project."

"Yes, you do," I said, making sure to smile as I did so. "At least a part of you does. That's how a part of you sees everyone. You can't help it."

As usual when presented with something she doesn't like about herself, Abby neither confirmed nor denied it.

"It's stupid of me to get upset about it," I continued. "I know it's actually benefitted me a lot over the last three years."

"I'm sorry I treat you like that."

"No, you're not. You're sorry you can't hide it better." She started to take umbrage, so I rushed on. "I'm joking."

"I like helping you," she said defensively.

"I know. Thank you."

And we both pretended that we'd talked about what was actually bothering us.

Moving to forward gave Mallory Jackson more opportunities to get payback for that first fight. If she could have confined herself to just making me look silly, she'd have been in good shape. Instead she took dumb penalties hacking at me, and in the three years we played against each other, she drew thirty-eight penalty minutes targeting me: nine minors, two majors, and a misconduct.

Hockey coaches go to a lot of effort during a game to match lines against the other team, getting certain players on the ice against specific opposing players. Usually one of the objectives is to keep a fringe player like myself out of the game when an elite player like Mallory is in it. By that third year, it had gone the opposite way; Coach Long took advantage of every opportunity to have me out there against her.

Meanwhile, I had some of my best games against State, and that series in November was one of the high points of my whole career. In two nights I had two goals and three assists, and I drew four penalties leading to two power play goals by my teammates—much of it coming at Mallory's expense. She was -2 while I was on the ice, and I scored one of my goals while she tried to chop my feet out from under me.

Caitlyn's father came down for a couple of series each year, so I'd met him before, but not while knowing Caitlyn's real feelings. It would be an exaggeration to say that I wanted to be on my best behavior, but I tried.

Really, I tried just to sit back and watch. After the first game, he was waiting in the arena concourse, where players met up with their parents. I stood with Tom and Jerilyn, drinking a bottle of water. To a casual observer, Caitlyn probably seemed like her normal self, but she kept playing with her hair, a giveaway that she's nervous.

Mr. Morris was the embodiment of good cheer. Players like talking to someone who has played in the NHL, even if it was only for seven games over two seasons. He told way more than seven games' worth of stories. His daughter told her tall tales in exactly the same way.

He was charming a knot of people, arm around Caitlyn's shoulders. "Aren't you going to join them?" Tom asked me.

"No."

Both of them looked at me sharply. "Something wrong?" Jerilyn asked.

"I just don't want to talk to him."

That's when she started watching closely. "Caitlyn looks uncomfortable," she ventured after a few minutes.

"She is."

"I thought they got along great."

"That's what she wants everyone to think. I really shouldn't be talking about it."

"About what?" Abby came up behind us.

Even as I said, "Nothing," I felt my head duck. "Nothing I should be talking about."

So Abby started watching, too. She's sharp enough to pick up on the cues once she knows to look for them. I'd wrecked Caitlyn's pretenses.

And then he came over. Caitlyn half-heartedly tried to redirect him, to no avail.

"You must be Phoebe. Caitlyn's told me a lot about you." He held out his hand as his voice boomed. I hesitated before shaking it.

"Good to see you again, sir." I could hear the lack of affect in my voice, but he seemed to miss it.

"That was a good game you had tonight."

I shrugged. "Better than I usually manage. My season totals are a good weekend for Caitlyn."

"She should learn from the way you stand tough in front of the net."

All of a sudden I realized just how much I hated him despite not actually knowing him. Caitlyn tried to intervene. I have no idea what she said, but I know she was attempting to derail me.

"The last thing your daughter needs to do is try to imitate a converted defenseman who can't skate. Maybe you should just appreciate the game she plays." Either Abby or her mother, I'm not sure which, was pulling on my sleeve. I just glared.

Then I saw the pleading look on Caitlyn's face. Someone said something while I looked at her. I put the cap back on my water and reached out with my right arm to pull her close. "I'm sorry," I whispered. With that, I turned toward the stairs down to the dressing rooms.

When I got there, I kicked at a trash can, but at least had the presence of mind to make sure it was empty first.

Later, at home, Caitlyn cried. She didn't get mad at me. I couldn't even tell if she wanted to.

The next morning I made breakfast: waffles, fruit, and bacon. Caitlyn appeared to be doing a lot better. Still quieter than normal, but not radiating distress.

"I'm sorry," I said. "I should have been ready with a neutral answer."

"It's okay." She forced herself to sound chipper. "Really. I figured something out last night. I wanted you to do that. I don't think I'd ever have told you about him if I didn't."

"Now I'm really confused."

"Do you have any idea how long I've wanted to tell my father that he's full of shit?"

"I'm going to guess that the answer is more than five years."

"That's a rhetorical question, Phoebe."

"I know. They're the easiest kind to answer."

"Whatever. But, yeah, a long time. I don't think it was conscious on my part, but I wanted something like that to happen."

I hoped that this wasn't just after-the-fact rationalization, but even I knew better than to ask that. "I'm glad that it's worked out, but I'm still sorry. Based upon the information I had, I should have kept my mouth shut."

She thought about that for a moment, giving me a chance to eat a few bites.

"I guess it's my fault. If I'd known what I was doing I'd have told you."

"That probably would have helped," I agreed.

"All of that leads up to a request. I'm supposed to have lunch with him today. Would you please come along?"

"I . . ." I really wanted to say no, but I also had no intention of letting her down.

"I want you to say what you really think."

"Then I'm going to start by saying that I really think it would be better if you told him what you really think."

I'd never seen her look bashful before. "You're right. I'm hoping that if you get it started, I'll join in."

"I'll come, but I really want you to start it. I'll support you, but this should be your conversation."

She nodded.

Lunch turned out to be short and explosive. Despite my good intentions, I'm the one who blew it up. I should have asked Caitlyn beforehand whether he knew we were sleeping together. When I let that slip, all of the latent hostilities came out in a hurry. He had something else to belittle Caitlyn about, except that she had moved past caring—on the surface at least.

We left half of our food on our plates when we walked out. I called him a bigot as we left. He didn't show up at the game, so he missed the first two-game sweep of Michigan State that we were ever a part of.

We finished the first half of the season with a 13-5-2 record. We were in third place, behind Wisconsin and Michigan. Most teams would have been pleased with that record, but we held ourselves to higher standards.

My new sense of fun wasn't limited to hockey. I had started to enjoy lots of things that most people think of as normal. One of them was movies. When I'm by myself, I like dark stories. Not necessarily horror but always something dark and disturbing and about the evil in men's souls. Black, absurdist comedy. Dark dramas. Gothic. Whatever.

It's different when I have company. Lightness is the order of the day. Maybe it's Caitlyn's influence, since she hates scary or creepy movies.

Abby, her mother, and I started another Christmas tradition. On the twenty-third, we watch a marathon of Christmas movies. And no *A Christmas Carol* here, either, unless it has Muppets in it. Just fluff. The whole thing lasts about twelve hours. Derek and Tom make themselves scarce, mostly off the premises.

Our attention isn't exactly focused on the screen. Rather, we talk a lot and miss a lot of stuff. During *The Bishop's Wife* Abby asked me, "So did you open presents Christmas Eve or Christmas morning?"

"Both. It seemed like it changed every time I changed homes, but I prefer Christmas morning, because that's what the Wilsons did."

"What was your favorite Christmas dinner?"

"The answer to any question that starts off, 'What was your favorite . . .' is always going to be what the Wilsons did."

"So what did Mrs. Wilson make for Christmas dinner? Ham, turkey, or goose?"

I shook my head. "Jambalaya."

"That's different."

"Maybe, but it was fantastic."

"Did you leave out cookies and milk for Santa?"

"Cookies and beer, actually. I think Mrs. Wilson ate the cookies and Mr. Wilson drank the beer."

"So you didn't believe in Santa by then?"

"I'm not sure I ever believed in him. I don't remember ever doing so. By the time there's a Christmas in my memories I thought the whole thing was a fraud."

"Fraud? That's pretty harsh." Jerilyn was just listening as Abby asked questions.

I shrugged. "I didn't like Christmas. I never got what I really wanted, and I knew that I wasn't going to get it. I thought my very short wish list was perfectly reasonable, and that made celebrating seem kind of hollow."

"Even with the Wilsons?"

"Especially with the Wilsons. Knowing that they couldn't adopt me made it hurt more. They never tried to convince me that I should really be happy when something upset me. I enjoyed the rituals when we did them, like lighting candles in the windows and decorating the tree, but I liked them entirely separately from the holiday itself. I just liked doing anything with them."

"They sound wonderful."

"I probably overromanticize it. I don't really trust the emotions I attach to some of my memories. They get scrambled by everything around them."

"They still sound wonderful."

"They were. I mean, that's how I remember them, and that's really all that matters. And I think it's true."

We lapsed into an argument about what to watch next. Abby lobbied for *Die Hard*. I wasn't prepared to admit that that's a Christmas movie.

The next night Abby and I sat down for our second annual Christmas Eve talk. Not long after everyone else was in bed the festering wounds were opened up.

"For God's sake, Abby, Caitlyn is your left wing. Would you please start talking to her again?"

"I don't think she wants me to," Abby replied.

"That's because whenever you try, it's with veiled hostility."

"I don't really have anything positive to say to her. She's a reckless flake."

"Bullshit, Abby. You tolerated her just fine when you thought she was just a reckless flake. What you don't like is that she and I are romantically involved." Abby had no way to know that this was the first time I'd described Caitlyn and my relationship as romantic. It was in its own way an important moment.

"I think it's inappropriate for two teammates to be romantically involved. You put yourselves ahead of the team."

"Yes, we did, and I'd do it again." She glared at me, a look that a year earlier would have intimidated me. "We had a deal that Caitlyn and I have honored. We leave our relationship in our apartment. We don't do anything to draw attention to it, verbally or physically, even when we're with only teammates who are okay with it."

"That's all because of you. If it were up to her, it would be different."

"You have no idea whether that's true or not." It was true, but that was beside the point. "We're complying, and it pisses me off that there are a bunch of you who at a minimum aren't living up to the spirit of the deal. You are treating one of your teammates with a lack of respect. Tammy can't stop getting in her little digs. Dallas avoids the subject directly but manages to criticize everything we do. Kris at least manages to mostly conceal her feelings, even if she disapproves."

"I told you it would be divisive," Abby retorted, sipping coffee.

"Oh, come on. It's a symptom. It's not the real problem."

"And what is the real problem?"

"The senior class is displaying an appalling lack of leadership. You're just using this as an excuse."

"All of us?"

I thought for a moment. "Yes, even you. You've got a lot of great qualities, but you're a shitty leader."

"Gee, thanks."

"Please, Abby. I'm engaged in your favorite pastime of bluntly stating the perfectly obvious. You said as much yourself when you weren't elected as one of the captains."

"That doesn't mean I want myself quoted back at me," she said sullenly.

"Fine. I won't. You aren't the big problem anyway, because even if you should be handling it better, you actually believe that Caitlyn and I sleeping together is the real problem."

"What's that supposed to mean?"

"Honestly, you think that's what's really bothering Tammy and Dallas? That Caitlyn and I aren't just the scapegoats for animosities that were under the surface for a couple of years?"

That's when Abby's objectivity deserted her. "Yes, I think that's the real problem. I know Tammy doesn't like you, but she wouldn't let that interfere with the team."

I had no idea what to say to that, so it lingered in the air while I figured out a way to change the subject.

That left Abby an opening to charge ahead. "I don't know what you were thinking."

It took a conscious effort not to lose my temper. "I'm thinking that I sleep better and am generally happier, at least when I'm not getting grilled about my dating choices."

"It doesn't make sense."

I stood up. "I'm going to get more hot chocolate. I don't want us to yell at each other, so let's both try to calm down."

When I returned a few minutes later, she'd composed herself. "I want to understand. So tell me, and I promise not to interrupt."

I squelched a brief temptation to needle her. "I'll do my best, but I'm not sure I can explain it. Not entirely, because I don't fully understand it, either. Caitlyn does things for me that you don't. That you can't. That's not intended as a knock on you. So you don't need to be jealous," I said, inadvertently letting slip my worries about Abby's motives.

"I'm not jealous." The edge had returned to her voice.

I couldn't see a way to walk that back gracefully, so I ignored it. "With you it's always rational. You listen to facts and offer advice. It's . . . I don't want to make it seem like you ignore emotional stuff because you don't, but there's always this balance, and you try to figure things out.

"Caitlyn doesn't do any of that." I left that hanging deliberately, and she snorted with derision. "I don't think she tries to understand, really. She's just there. Always. And the physical aspect of her presence is . . . You commented not long after we met on how important touch is to me. Well, she provides that. She holds me to the earth and makes me want to be here."

"You make it sound like it's something mystical," she said skeptically.

"It *is* something mystical. Or at least spiritual."

"I'm surprised to hear that from you."

"I thought you weren't going to interrupt. But you can't be any more surprised than I've been. It's something I never would have thought about until it happened. All of the work I'd done with yoga and meditation suddenly made sense in a way it never had before.

"You guys—the whole team—are like a family. I don't think I realized that until now, but you are. And I love all of you. But Caitlyn is my center."

She thought about it for a few minutes. "I guess I just don't understand."

"Well, I tried," I said glumly.

CHAPTER 14

May 2015

Spring sun shone down on the plaza in front of Northrop Auditorium. It was filled by the University of Minnesota's newest graduates and their families and friends.

"Congratulations, Phoebe," my mother said as she smiled up at me. Thinking of her as Mom felt far more comfortable than "Jerilyn" had ever been.

"Thank you."

"I hope that you take pride in this."

"I will, I'm sure, but right now I'm mostly scared."

"I know. Tom and I will be going down to Dayton with you. He promised not to start a fight this time."

"Thank you." I was deeply grateful. "It's not just that, though. I'm not ready to be done here. I don't want to be out on my own."

"You're more ready than you think you are, honey."

We started walking north, her to her car and me to a private celebration with the team.

"It doesn't feel that way."

"There's a big world out there. You need to explore it."

"That's what scares me. I don't want to explore."

"I know I sound trite, but it's time for you to spread your wings."

"I guess."

"Really. You've grown in five years. There's nothing left for you to do here."

"If I really have to leave, I wish I'd applied to a master's program in Toronto."

"I know it seems that way, but that's not what she wanted."

"I'm going to be alone again."

"No, you won't. We'll always be there for you."

"You'll be here, not there. And I don't know anyone in California."

"It's hard, I know, but you'll be okay."

The sound of running footsteps gave me a second's warning to brace myself.

"We're graduates!" Before I could fully turn around, she launched herself into my chest.

"I'm not wearing a helmet," I chided, though my heart wasn't in it.

"That's okay. I know you'll stay on your feet." She let go, at least for a moment.

"You're out of breath."

"Hey, I had to run all the way from the West Bank to catch up to you."

"You must be out of training." I turned back to Mom. "Thank you. For coming and everything else."

"You're welcome, Phoebe. Call me when you have more information about the trial."

"I will."

She headed for the parking structure, leaving me alone with Caitlyn.

"Let's go celebrate."

"Sure thing."

I just had no idea what there was to celebrate.

June 2015

Surgery was painless and left just a tiny scar; the trial was not. It wasn't my finest hour, and I don't talk about it. Suffice it to say that the jury believed him and not me. They deliberated forty-five minutes to decide that.

I spent those three weeks surrounded by teammates and family, and I saw many ghosts from my past. There are two of them I like to remember.

The first was Mr. Larson. The DA called him as a witness. He described finding me at the rink that morning. He helped the case more than I did. I talked to him in the corridor when he was done.

"I never did like that man," he told me.

"Thank you."

"It's good. You're in a better place now."

"Well, it's not quite heaven," I replied.

The corners of his mouth turned up, and only his eyes gave away his amusement.

"That was the most I think I've ever heard you talk," I continued.

"You remind me of my daughter," he said. It was the first I'd ever heard of her. "She wanted to be a figure skater, and you don't look anything like her. But your voice. I can never hear just one of you, always both. It healed my heart to listen to you."

"What happened?"

"Cancer. Years before you arrived. It hurt that I couldn't say more. I never knew how to help Becca, either."

"Thank you," I whispered.

"You have something special, you and the dark-haired girl?"

I nodded.

"Once I wouldn't have understood, but with love, who it is doesn't really matter, does it?"

"No, sir."

"Hold onto it tightly. It can take so long to find another person like that."

I shouldn't have been surprised when Mrs. Wilson walked into the courtroom the first day of the trial, but somehow it hadn't occurred to me. She sat in the back and watched. At the first recess, I got up and embraced her.

"My, you got so big," she said. "Let me look at you."

I could hear Abby ask quietly, "Who is that?" and the glee in Caitlyn's voice that she could answer.

"I'm sorry I didn't write," I said, feeling guilty.

"Honey, you were surviving. Don't ever apologize for doing what you need to do to survive."

I nodded, feeling unsettled by finding myself seven or eight inches taller than she was. I guided her over to our group. "I want to introduce you to some people. This is Tom and Jerilyn Forrest, and Abby. They've kind of adopted me." I stumbled over the word "adopted." "And my teammates Kennedy, Svetlana, and Caitlyn."

We had lunch together, and Mrs. Wilson filled them in on some of my childhood that I'd never gotten around to mentioning. When it broke up, I could feel Abby bristling, waiting to ask the obvious question until she could corner me with no one else around.

"Why didn't you tell me?" she finally exploded.

"Tell you what?" I replied, making her say it.

"That she's black. I never knew."

"No, you just assumed," I said, more crossly than I should have. "You assumed that the Wilsons were white because I'm white."

"But why didn't you tell me?"

"What difference would it have made? We've never had a conversation where I thought it would be relevant." That was a lie. "I never thought that mentioning it would lead to anything that I wanted to talk about."

She glared at me. "You should have told me."

"Yeah," I sighed, "I probably should have at some point. It just never seemed right. I'm sorry."

She embraced me. "You need to stop just surviving."

After the trial, Caitlyn and I had one week together before her departure for Toronto in July. On the last night she fell into one of her dark moods. She sat on the couch, clutching a couple of her stuffed animals and wearing her bunny slippers. I had my arm around her shoulders, holding on.

"I'm making a mistake, aren't I?" she asked me.

My breath whistled through my teeth as I kept myself from saying the wrong thing. "Don't make decisions when you're like this."

"I don't understand why you don't hate me."

I closed my eyes, trying not to feel the pain. "I can't hate you."

"You want to, don't you?"

"Caitlyn, stop. Please."

"You should. I don't deserve you." There was real venom in her voice, and she seemed to shrink into herself.

I embraced her. She sat passively, neither returning it nor resisting. "It doesn't matter. You have me anyway."

"I don't want you," she said dully. "Haven't I made that clear?"

Stung, I let go of her. "You don't mean that. Not really."

"Yes, I do. I don't want you."

"This is your depression talking. You're trying to hurt me and push me away so that you can feel even more miserable." I stood up. "I'm going to leave before you really succeed at it."

She looked up at me with rage and sadness in her eyes. I continued before she could say anything.

"I hate it that this is how we're going to spend our last night. But you will not push me away for good. I'm too stubborn, and no matter what you do, I'll be waiting."

I slept on the couch. I curled up, miserable and lonely. I could hear Caitlyn crying in our room. It took effort to visualize the cords that bound us together.

CHAPTER 15

Something wonderful happened shortly after New Year's: I started getting regular time on the power play. Having more players than the other team is a lot of fun. You score more, and it means that your coaches think you can help the team score more.

Our second power play unit had been struggling, none of the freshmen defensemen really clicking, so they threw me out as a fourth forward. I played from the low slot in, spending a lot of time in front of the net or fighting for pucks along the end boards, but there were also moments when I'd drift out to the face-off circle, hunting for empty space and a clear shooting lane.

It was less enjoyable by the second game. I found that spot, about eight feet out from the net, with the penalty killers so scrambled they had no idea I was there. Then the puck didn't arrive; Tammy swung it behind the net, where Kris got tied up, losing possession.

It happened again a period later, except that it was Dallas who didn't pass to me. When the shift ended, I skated back to the bench steaming but also determined not to say anything about it. I'd gotten past having shouting matches during a game.

There was a huge divide between the senior class and the juniors, with the underclassmen looking on confused. Caitlyn and I were the locus of the issues, but they really went beyond that. Tammy had disliked me from the very beginning, bringing a couple of the others along with her, and she hadn't treated Jenny well, either. It was workable until she became the captain.

It wasn't conscious on their part, but the three seniors on the power play unit were reluctant to pass me the puck. As much as I didn't like her, Tammy had never been as bad as my teammates in Vicksburg. Until this point, she had never let her antagonism come out during games.

Jenny vented her frustration as we left Ridder after that game. "You don't have to take Tammy's crap," she told me.

"Yeah, actually, I do," I replied. "I've been a team's excuse for underperforming before, and I'm not going to make this any worse than it already is. I am really, truly enjoying playing hockey for the first time in a decade. There is no verbal sniping that Tammy can do, no passes Dallas fails to make, nothing that's going to change that."

"Are you sure?"

"Positive." It was mostly the truth. "I appreciate the concern."

Jenny merely shifted her concern. "So what are we going to do?"

"About what?"

"About the divisions. About the fact that we aren't acting like a team."

"I can tell you what I plan to do about it: absolutely nothing."

She stopped walking and looked up at me. "Nothing?"

"Nothing. I think the two of us agree on the source of the problem, but I'm not going to start fighting with the captains. And my advice is that what 'we' are going to do about it is to suck it up and do what we're told."

"I can't believe you're taking this so calmly."

"Don't get me wrong," I assured her. "I'm plenty angry. We had a deal. Caitlyn and I have kept up our end. Tammy and Dallas are the ones who keep poking. But I'll get over it."

"It just seems awfully—"

"There's another reason I don't plan to do anything. I don't know if you noticed, but Coach never expressed an opinion one way or the other on Caitlyn's and my relationship. I can't imagine that he's thrilled with it. Making waves now invites him to step in, and I'd rather avoid that."

"That's it?"

"Long-term, though, there is something else we do."

"What's that?" she asked.

"Not let it happen again. Next summer, the seniors need to sit down and figure out what went wrong and how to prevent it. And when you come back from the Olympics the year after next, you're going to be captain, and you're going to do the same thing."

"And so we just give up on this year?"

"Oh hell no. We're going to score a ton of goals, even if Heck has two wingers who won't talk to each other off the ice. If the defense comes together, we're going to be tough to beat come March."

"That's it?"

"I'll give it to you in four words: shut up and play."

"You make it sound so easy."

No matter how easy I made it sound, we were struggling. At the same time, I was loving every game. At even strength, I skated on a line with two girls who could fly, covering up for my weakness. We weren't expected to score a lot, but we got regular playing time with the goal of frustrating the other team with forechecking and a lot of energy. We played hard every shift, and the fans loved us out of all proportion to how valuable we really were.

I wondered how it would have gone if I had ended up at a place like Iowa, always in the middle of the pack. I'd have played more, but I was better served being a fringe player for two years. That gave me a chance to work through a lot of things I otherwise might have ignored.

I also liked being in the Cities. I could get lost there and be as anonymous as a six-foot-two woman can be. I could sit somewhere and watch the world go by and actually see a significant part of it without being asked if I played basketball. I was definitely happier, and I enjoyed it while I could.

Still, there comes a point in the middle of a season where it all seems to run together. It doesn't happen at the same time every year, but it happens. It usually occurs when you play a string of weak opponents. We started the second half against Indiana. The next week we hosted Ohio State, and then it was a trip to Purdue.

It's worse if you're the Boilermakers and you played in Madison the prior week followed by us and then Michigan coming to town. We found it traumatic my freshman season, when we played our best and couldn't beat Wisconsin. A team like Purdue faces that eight weekends a year. I have nothing but respect for a group of coaches and players that can do that and stick together.

It's hard getting motivated every night during the doldrums of a season, even if I was enjoying the game. This isn't an individual phenomenon. Entire teams come down with it together. Each player has ups and downs, but we feed off of each other so much that it's tough to sag too much on your own.

Those are the nights when upsets happen. Like that January 18. We didn't do anything right. As slovenly a game as we played, we almost tied it up once we pulled the goalie for an extra attacker. Jenny hit the post on a shot that beat their goalie cleanly, and then Tammy missed the wide open net on the carom.

It was our weakest performance in more than a year. Traci was the only one who looked good. In the second, she set me up with a gorgeous pass that I proceeded to shoot wide by four feet. Kat tanked one, too, so Traci finally just went to the net herself and scored. That closed the gap to 4–3, but we didn't score again.

We knew that the tone for an entire week of practices was going to be set the next night. If we came back strong and angry, the loss would just be chalked up as one of those things that happens and then forgotten. If we fell on our faces again, it was going to be a long, grueling week.

After looking flat in a 4–4 tie, we skated a lot of grinders the next week. The standings started to look grim.

"I have a question. There's something I don't understand," Caitlyn said one evening while we were eating dinner. "I assume since you've never talked about it that it's kind of sensitive."

"Okay," I said cautiously.

"From everything you've said about the Wilsons, it sounds like they loved you. So why didn't they adopt you?"

I tensed up.

"Feebs . . ."

I shook my head. "I won't lie to you. I'm just trying to figure out if I want to tell the truth."

Her fork clattered down as she stood up. She moved behind me and put her arms around my shoulders. "You don't have to tell me."

I thought for a couple minutes, the two of us motionless. "I will, but you have to promise not to tell anyone, not even Abby." I paused. "Especially not Abby. I lied to her when she asked. Told her it was because Mr. Wilson had cancer."

"That wasn't it? It's what I would have guessed."

"No. It was already established that they couldn't before he got sick."

"They couldn't?"

"No. Or at least someone was making it really hard. I don't know which."

"Why?"

I took a deep breath before plunging in. "Because of something I've never described about them. They were African American."

"Oh."

We were both silent for awhile. Finally, I continued. "Legally that shouldn't make a difference. There's a law that says it shouldn't be used to make decisions, but a lot of adoption agencies make it difficult. As I said, I don't know any of the discussions they had. They just told me that it wasn't possible."

"Why didn't you tell anyone they were black?"

I could feel tears leaking out. "Because it shouldn't have mattered. Getting adopted was the most important thing in the world to me, and someone didn't let it happen because of something that didn't matter."

"I know, but still—"

"And I don't bring it up to anyone because if I do, we'll inevitably start talking about race, and I don't want to talk about it."

She withdrew slightly and sounded offended. "I'm sorry."

"You don't need to be sorry," I said, crossly. "But one thing I learned living there is that there's nothing stupider than a bunch of white people sitting around and discussing race among themselves. And so I don't want to do it, and that means not bringing it up."

She sat back down, looking at her plate. "I didn't mean to make you angry."

"I'm not angry," I snapped. "At least, I'm not angry at you. I'm angry at the world. And I'm angry at myself."

"Why at yourself?"

"Because being African American was a part of who they were. It was important to them. And here I am, telling friends and lovers about them except not mentioning it. I feel like I've betrayed them." I went back to eating morosely.

After a few minutes, Caitlyn said, "If I promise not to ask any questions, not say anything, will you tell me about them? The stuff that you think is important?"

I thought about it while pushing steamed peas around my plate. "I'll try," I said at last. "Mr. Wilson grew up in Mankato because his grandfather and great-grandfather worked for the Pullman Company. That's where they settled when they weren't working the trains. There weren't many other African Americans in town, so he was used to being the odd one. He said that was why he appreciated me so much.

"He joined the air force out of high school, as an airplane mechanic. He was in Vietnam but said that he never got anywhere near any fighting. Mrs. Wilson was from Alabama. They met while he was stationed down there.

"After the air force he came back to Minnesota. That's when he went to the U. He majored in engineering—mechanical or aeronautical, I'm not sure which—and then ended up in Dayton working on planes again.

"He loved the blues. We'd listen together. If he hadn't died, I'd have completely different musical tastes than I do now. I started listening to industrial music because it was as different from Howlin' Wolf as I could imagine."

I stopped, and silence descended once more. "I don't know if any of that explains why being African American was important to them. Probably not. It made more sense in my head."

"It's okay," she answered. "You use the past tense whenever you talk about them. Is Mrs. Wilson dead, too?"

I buried my head in my hands. "I don't know," I mumbled. "Once things got really bad, especially after my last foster mother threw away my keepsakes envelope, I didn't want to think about the Wilsons. If I did, it would just have left me weak as I tried to face each day. Some people draw strength from the past, but it didn't work that way for me, or at least I didn't think it would. So I never tried to communicate with her.

"Once I got up here, I still didn't. I should have. I should have written her, told her I was okay. You know, every two months, she put money in that bank account I had, right up until the June after I left Vicksburg. So she must have still been alive."

I started bawling. "Why didn't I ever write her?"

Caitlyn wrapped herself around me again, pulling me back. "We'll do it tomorrow. I promise."

We did. I got the letter back a month later, marked "No such addressee."

There's quick, and there's fast, and they're two different things. Between them, being quick is more important. Most of the girls on our team were both. I was not fast, but I was quick.

Fast is about skating. If you're fast, you can get up and down the ice in a short time. Quickness is about reaction times and getting your body to move. It's also mental. The fastest reaction in the world won't help if you don't know what you're going to do.

My game minimized the importance of speed but emphasized being quick. I joke that my job was to stand in front of the net and let my teammates bounce pucks off of me and in. That actually happened a couple of times, but what I really tried to do was to react to shots from the outside and get the shaft of my stick on them so they changed direction.

If the goalie made a save but didn't hold onto the puck, I went hunting for rebounds. It's fair game to start whacking away, and if she did cover it up, I tried to dig it out. When I played defense, I took great offense at opponents who did this and protected my goalie. Proving that ethics can be flexible, I was an enthusiastic convert to doing it myself. Until the ref blew the whistle, I tried to pry that puck loose. Of course, I never, ever kept working after the whistle. That would have been illegal, and the defense might lose their temper. Most of my goals were described as scoring ugly or picking up the garbage. Whatever. Nature has a need for scavengers, too, and Phil Esposito made it to the Hall of Fame doing it.

I'd had an off weekend in Columbus the previous November. It was only partly the usual issues, as I also had the flu. I played, and I wasn't horrible, but I wasn't very good, either. I just didn't have enough energy.

I made up for it the last weekend in January. I bullied Ohio State's small defensemen from my first shift to my last. I got called for three penalties, none of which I thought I deserved, but that happens to big players sometimes. Some tiny girl goes flying, and it's assumed you did something wrong.

I also had the first multigoal game of my career, and I missed a hat trick by about six inches. On the first, I dug the puck loose in the corner and skated it out. I pushed an overmatched defenseman out of the way and arrived at the side of the net with the puck. I didn't really shoot it so much as just jam it in. It took a couple of tries, but the red light went on. It went on the score sheet as: Rose (6) (Unassisted) – 12:34. It looks like I had a breakaway.

The second was a deflection. Crosser took a shot from the point. It was going wide, but I saw it clearly the whole way and caught it with the heel of my stick. It came back in and right under the goalie's arm.

Caitlyn doused me in ginger ale in the shower. I had to bend down to let her. She said we'd be of age by the time I actually got the hat trick and she'd use champagne then.

In life there's always a price for success, and I had to run three laps around Mariucci the next Monday. I'd mellowed over the previous months. There were still plenty of days I was out of bed at four thirty, but my personal workouts became much saner. As I'd suspected, it didn't really hurt my conditioning that much. I still worked plenty hard, though, and I wasn't looking forward to the punishment for success. It was never mentioned between us, but it would have felt wrong if I'd compensated by cutting somewhere else. These really were extra drills. A deal's a deal.

So I got to work. Kennedy, damn her, did nothing but supervise. She'd picked up two assists against the Buckeyes but no goals, so I was running by myself.

For a lap to count you had to go all out, so by the end of the second one I was gasping for air. I stood there with my hands on my knees, and Kennedy decided she wanted to chat.

"Boy, that looks tough."

"This is nothing," I wheezed, trying to play the tough guy.

"Really? What's something?"

I somehow managed complete sentences. "I spent the last year and a half of high school taking classes at the University of Dayton first thing in the morning." I paused to suck in some air.

"That doesn't sound so bad."

"Yeah, well, let me get enough breath to finish the story."

"Oh, all right."

"I got there and back by bicycle. Monday, Wednesday, and Friday at first, then every day. It was seventeen miles each way. I made that commute, rain or shine." I stood up straight, almost caught up on breathing. "Getting there was fine. Coming back was more of a challenge. I had seventy-two minutes between the end of class at U of D and when I had to be at Vicksburg High."

"That sounds tolerable."

I coughed. "You have no idea how exciting commuting by bicycle can be until you've done it when it's fifteen degrees out."

"Now you're getting to the fun part."

Actually what I was doing was stalling to recover better before running my last lap. "I had some spectacular wipeouts during the winter."

"Any lasting damage?"

"That's why God invented knee and elbow pads."

"I like your attitude."

"It was worth it," I said. "Man, it was worth it to get away from high school, if only for an hour each day."

"I imagine." It was the first time she'd sounded sympathetic.

I decided I was ready to get this over with. "So I'm plenty prepared to finish this."

I was always deeply ambivalent about playing Michigan. They were a dirty team, bad sports, whined about calls, and their coach was a lousy dresser. Games against them were physical, penalty-filled affairs, nothing aesthetically pleasing about them. Still, skating against a bunch of thugs did allow me to contribute what I thought was the most indispensable element to my game: protection.

It was worse when we played in Ann Arbor. Refs were scared to call penalties on them, so the games tended to get out of hand. It was a recipe for me to get into trouble. In our Friday game at Yost Arena, we got out to an early lead and extended it in the second. That was a dangerous thing to do against the Wolverines. Once they lost interest in trying to win the game, the nastiness really began.

There were a number of incidents, but on one shift early in the third period Kelly Shuster twice tried to take out Tammy's knees. Once she stuck out her leg on a trip, and the other she just went in low. It was particularly gutless since one of those knees had been surgically rebuilt three years before.

If they'd called the penalties, maybe nothing else would have happened. I don't care how intimidated you are by a coach, you have to make those calls, or someone is going to do what I did. If the person who got paid to protect the players didn't do his job, then I had to.

I got my chance the next night. I came out on a change while Kelly was on the ice and Michigan was breaking out of their end. She got control in the neutral zone. I already had her lined up.

I was really good at checking in high school. I had the size for it, I really learned the technique, and I enjoyed it. A lot. Those skills were three years out of date, but it's like riding a bicycle: you might look sloppy doing it, but you don't really forget.

This one was a beauty. She had her head down, assuming that I cared that what I was about to do is illegal in women's hockey. I didn't leave my feet to make the hit, and I never touched her head, two big no-nos. I did manage to really drive my shoulder into her chest and up.

She bounced when she landed. I got my stick on the puck, prompting the whistle. I didn't even look at the officials, just skated right to the box. Max, the really nice old man who worked the door to the visitor's penalty box there, opened it up and greeted me for the third time on the weekend.

I didn't get a chance to chat with him: the refs gave me five minutes for elbowing and kicked me out of the game. It was a terrible call, because my form was perfect, with the elbows down. It should have been two minutes for bodychecking, maybe a five-minute charging major. At least I didn't get a match penalty for intent to injure, which would have meant an automatic one-game suspension.

So I got to hit the showers before anyone else had used any of the hot water. I also got to listen to another one of Coach Long's lectures about keeping your composure. It was a stock speech, and his heart wasn't really into it, probably because he'd have done the same thing.

Shuster had a bruised sternum and at first was questionable for the next week. I hoped it hurt like hell.

"I have a question for you," I asked Abby as we crossed the Washington Avenue bridge on our way to practice one day. She was coming from class and I from a trip to the library I'd planned for the sole purpose of getting her alone. "Whatever happened to that project you did last semester? The one where you analyzed our relationship?"

"Oh that," she said in a tone that had me dreading what came next. "I didn't do it. I used someone else."

"Really? But . . ." I stopped as I dealt with being hurt that she hadn't followed through with something I hadn't been enthusiastic about in the first place.

"It just didn't seem like a good idea right then, given the way we were mad at each other. I didn't really want to analyze our relationship."

That at least got us to what I'd wanted to talk about. "So are we doing better now? I mean, it feels like we are, but we haven't really talked about it since Christmas."

"By 'it,' I assume you mean you and Caitlyn?"

"I guess." I'd actually meant the team more broadly, but chickened out on saying that.

"We're good."

"And you and Caitlyn?"

"None of this would have happened if it weren't for her."

I came to a stop. "What?"

"She should have stayed in her own bed."

"No, she shouldn't have. One minute, I was having a screaming nightmare, and the next she was protecting me from it. That's what she does." I was almost shouting.

"We'd have found another way."

I started walking again and lowered my voice. "I'm pretty happy with the way we did find. And I don't really appreciate being told that I didn't make any of the decisions."

I started to get really angry as I watched those words go through her head without being absorbed at all.

"You left us in an impossible position."

"How so?"

"I mean, what would have happened if we had said you had to stop? How does that play out?"

"Easy. I'd have quit the team."

She waved her hand. "You were never serious about that."

"I was more serious than you think. And if you'd pushed on that, I'd have been more so."

"Why didn't you talk to me more?" she demanded.

"Given the context of this discussion, you need to ask that?"

"So who did you talk to?"

"Are you sure that that's your business?"

I could tell that it stung, but she didn't have a response.

"Caitlyn came through for me. She didn't ask questions. She didn't pressure me into staying on. She just made sure I didn't pack it in before I'd really made a decision."

"You should have come to me."

"Abby, I'm not the same person I was two years ago. I'm not as dependent on you as I was. I'm not as dependent on anyone, even Caitlyn, as I was last year."

"So you don't need me?"

"I didn't say that," I said heatedly. "I don't need you for everything the way I used to. And if I'd come to you with this, you'd have just made me feel like a quitter."

Her eyes went wide. "No, I wouldn't have."

"You wouldn't have meant to, but you would have."

"How can you think that?"

"Because," I almost screamed, "I already felt like a quitter."

"So? I wouldn't have said that."

"You don't need to say it. You'd have been so disappointed you couldn't have hidden it."

"I would have been disappointed, but I wouldn't have called you a quitter."

I was near tears. "Don't you get it, Abby?"

"Get what?"

"You're like my big sister. Or at least you're like what I think a big sister is supposed to be. I don't know because I've never had one before."

"I . . ." Her voice trailed off, and she looked confused.

"I didn't want to disappoint you, so I couldn't come talk to you about it. That's part of why I need Caitlyn, because you aren't just a friend anymore."

It would be nice to think that such an admission would have patched things up between us, but life doesn't work that way. "I have a brother," she said. "I don't need another sibling. I just wanted a friend."

That wasn't the best practice of my career.

The amount of fun I had playing declined as the team's on-ice frustrations caught up with me. It was a different regular season, but the result was the same: we finished behind Wisconsin. Beating out Michigan for second was a sorry consolation prize not made better by backing into it. We found a way to tie Iowa on the last night of the season and only came in second because Michigan lost to Michigan State. So we finished one point ahead of them in the standings.

It wasn't that we were terrible down the stretch—just mediocre, like the rest of our season. Iowa was inspired, fighting to stay ahead of Michigan State for home ice in the first round. They just managed it by tying us and got to host the Spartans instead of traveling to East Lansing for the third year in a row.

The flight back to the Cities was mostly silent. We needed our confidence back, and I was hoping we'd find it pulled over on the shoulder of I-35, but no such luck.

My scoring touch, such as it was, was hiding out with our confidence. I couldn't get anything to go in. I also tried to deal with the fact that this concerned me. I'd gone much, much longer stretches without a goal. It had been eight games. I only had three goals in sixty-three games over my first two years. Being a forward really was different, and I got overconfident during that hot streak the month before.

Our expectations of ourselves can change any time we aren't looking at them very closely.

The season came to a disappointing end two weeks later. We beat

Michigan in the Big Ten semifinal, but by that time we'd lost enough games that the only way for us to make the NCAA tournament was to beat Wisconsin in the final.

It was a very different game from two years before. It was more like the very first time we played them. We were sloppy, disjointed, and lethargic. For two periods, they played down to our level before coming out in the third and blowing the doors off the building.

When I went from Vicksburg to Minneapolis, I thought that playing on a better team would mean that the season would end happily. It doesn't work that way. All it does is raise the bar on what constitutes a good year. In the end, the odds are good that you're going to be crying when it's over no matter how good you are.

I couldn't help but feel that perhaps having fun that year was the problem. I didn't think that it led to any less effort to win, but maybe it led to a focus on my individual play rather than the team. Maybe everyone in the locker room did the same thing for their own reasons, and we never came together to find that extra level needed to win.

That's my take, and I say that without anger or regrets. I had to go through that year. I had to focus on having fun, even if that meant pursuing an individual goal. I couldn't have kept playing any other way. So I'm not in a position to criticize anyone else for what happened, even Tammy. As a team, we were what we were.

Abby is less forgiving—of herself and everyone else. Except me. She gives me a pass on it. I've never known whether to appreciate that or to be irritated that she doesn't hold me to the same level of responsibility as everyone else. For all of her denial, we were starting to be a family, and I was definitely the little sister.

I promised myself that it wasn't going to happen again. Whatever it took, I was going to figure out how to go from having fun to being team first. I would never have the chance to play competitive hockey with Abby again, and it hurt that it had been an unsatisfying conclusion to her career. I wasn't going to let my senior season play out the same way. We might not win, and given the firepower we were losing, there was a very good chance that we wouldn't, but that was not going to be because we didn't play the right way.

Unfortunately, I was going to have to do it without Caitlyn.

Watching the seniors clean out their lockers got more painful every year, as players I had spent more and more time with departed. I may have had differences with that season's group, but they'd been a huge part of my life for three years. Laughs. Tears. And then there was Abby. The person who did the most to help me fit in right away. The first person who figured out how to get me to talk. The person who brought me into her family. She still lacked a sense of humor, and her moralizing streak could get really irritating, but she was family. They all were, but none so close as she was.

On top of that, there was the fact I'd played my last game with Caitlyn and Jenny. I was coming back the next year for my last season. They would spend the summer trying to make the Olympic team. If successful, they would take the year off from school to chase that dream. When they came back, I'd be gone.

I made it through the gathering we had that felt like a funeral, but by the time Caitlyn and I got home, I was in a foul, foul mood. She noticed, and she knew exactly what was causing it.

"Life moves on," she told me as we settled on the couch.

"I don't want it to move on. I finally got it to where I like it. I should get to enjoy it for longer than this."

"I know."

"If I only get one more season, I want to do it with you."

She pulled my head down into her lap. Caitlyn recognizes when I'm in the throes of full-blown self-pity and there's nothing she can say that won't get rejected. So she just stroked my hair.

"I don't want things to change."

We remained like that for awhile.

"It's pathetic that I can't face this, isn't it?"

"It's unfair that you have to. If I could figure out how to keep anything from changing, how to make it so that you and I and

Kennedy and Jenny and Heck could just keep playing here forever, I'd give that to you. I think that's what we'll get in heaven."

"Thanks," I said, unable to keep the bitterness out of my voice.

"I'm sorry you don't believe in it."

"Can we at least skip the games against Michigan?"

"Sure."

I lay there for a bit longer, not saying anything. I think she fell asleep, because she started when I finally lifted my head. "Let's go to bed."

"Yes, let's. It's much more comfortable."

As we undressed, I asked, "Do you want to know one of the really perverse things?"

"Not really, but I'll listen."

I hoped she would, because I'd recognized the same things in her when she was depressed. "I know that I'm going to get over this. I'll keep going. I'll be happy. And right now, I don't want it to be that way. Right now, not only am I miserable—I want to stay miserable. I think that somehow, if I don't, it will be a lie. I never feel like I understand the world like I do when I want to blow the whole thing up. That's the only time that things make sense."

She grabbed me by the shoulders. "I'm sorry, Phoebe. If I can do anything to help you understand the world in a different way, I want to."

Then she kissed the tip of my nose. She had to stand on her toes and pull my head down to do it, but she did. Something popped in me as she did, and I almost giggled.

CHAPTER 16

"Do you have any friends out there?"

After one semester in California, Abby had turned our Christmas Eve conversation back toward its original purpose of worrying about me.

"Define 'friend.'"

"You're being evasive."

"No, not really," I admitted. "I've got people I'm friendly with but no one I'd say I can count on. No one I trust."

She regarded me silently.

"What do you want me to say, Abby?"

"I don't know."

"I'm trying. Really. Besides, things are going pretty well. I enjoy my classes."

"I don't doubt that. I just don't believe you when you say that that's enough."

"Why not?" I insisted.

"You're a social creature. You've said it yourself. It wasn't the game that motivated you. It was the team."

"Okay."

"So you need to get out and do something about that."

"Look," I said heatedly, "I'm not sure what else you want me to do."

"You can do better," Abby insisted.

"You mean I deserve better. You aren't any more confident than I am that I can do better."

"That's not true."

"Okay, you're right. You and Caitlyn both have this boundless optimism when it comes to my latent social skills."

She grimaced and covered it by drinking coffee. "I don't think you're trying very hard."

"That's because you know me too well. I'm not trying all that hard. But I'm okay. Not great. Okay. That's good enough."

"No, it's not."

"You don't acknowledge that the concept of 'good enough' even exists."

She wanted to argue with me some more, but my expression must have dissuaded her. "That's sad."

"That's life. I'm not sure what we all expected would happen when I moved out all by myself."

"Maybe you should have come to Boston."

I refrained from pointing out that she was one of the ones who had encouraged me to go to Stanford. "Maybe. I don't think it's fair that Heck and Caitlyn are both in Toronto, Traci and Morgan are both still in the Cities with Kennedy as long as she's in school, and Jenny's with you and others in Boston while I'm the one with no teammates within eight hundred miles. But it's where I chose to go."

"Are you following through on not playing?" she asked.

"Yes. I don't have any equipment, and I don't even know where any rinks are."

"I don't know whether to feel admiration or pity for going cold turkey."

"Probably some of both," I said. "I miss it a lot, but I don't have any sense that trying to continue would solve that. It's like people who are nostalgic for high school. You just have to let it go. You don't get out there much, either."

"About once a month. Just pickup games. I'm too busy with school."

"If it's any consolation, it's not like I have more spare time than you do. So I don't have a lot of opportunities to be really miserable."

"How are you sleeping?"

I didn't bother fighting my reaction. "Poorly."

She sipped her coffee. "I understand all of the reasons why I'm going to get the reaction that's coming, and I won't push it, but have you considered trying therapy again?"

I got a crawling sensation just thinking about it. "No."

"Fair enough."

"If it makes you feel better," I continued, "I got some books, and I've been reading about it."

"Is it helping?"

I shrugged. "I'm learning a lot of the terminology, so I can at least bullshit people better."

"Great."

April 2016

Caitlyn visited during the spring of my first year in Palo Alto. Before she arrived I told myself we were just friends and not to let things slide beyond that. My resolve lasted all the way until I saw her coming through baggage claim. We slept together for two very comfortable weeks.

As we stood outside the security checkpoint the day she left, she said, unprompted, "You're surrounded by better people out here than you imagine. Try to get to know them."

"Most people are probably better than I imagine. I suspect that Vicksburg isn't really hell on earth, either. That's unlikely to change how I feel about it."

"Please try," she said.

I closed my eyes as she vanished through the security checkpoint, letting myself see the cords stretched between us.

I only felt a little empty as I took the train back to Palo Alto.

We kept in touch over the phone. It was mostly chitchat, but when she went more than a few weeks the next fall without mentioning her job, I felt compelled to ask.

"It's okay. It's a job."

"Does it keep you fed and clothed?"

"Yeah."

"Then it's a decent job. Just go to it every day, and wait for the opportunities to get on the ice."

"Thanks for the advice." Her sarcasm had no bite to it.

"It's what I'm here for."

"You're right, though. It doesn't suck. It's just tedious."

"What exactly are you doing?"

"I'm supposedly helping to design an ad campaign, but I mostly end up filing paperwork."

"When does your season start?" I asked.

"Next month. I'm surprised you don't know that."

"Honestly, the only time I talk hockey is when I'm on the phone with you or Jenny. I don't even discuss it with Abby anymore."

"You weren't kidding when you said you were quitting."

"It's easier to pretend it doesn't exist."

"So how are you doing?" she asked.

"Same as always. I just keep trundling along."

"You ducked your head, didn't you?"

"Only a little. I miss you. Other than that, things really are going okay."

"I wish I could get out there. I just don't have the time."

I knew better than to ask if I could visit her in Toronto. The unspoken rule was that she came to me, but not the other way around. "I understand. Just keep plugging away, like I do."

"You have a longer attention span than me."

"Tough. Just do it."

"Okay, I need to go if you're going to start doing advertising slogans."

"Sorry to encroach on your professional expertise."

"It's okay, but I do have to go."

"Bye, Kitten."

April 2017

One afternoon the next spring I came home from school to see someone sitting in the hallway outside my door. My wariness turned to shock when I realized who it was.

"Caitlyn?"

She raised her head. "Hi, Phoebe. Can I stay with you awhile?" Her voice sounded empty.

"I . . . sure. What's wrong?" I unlocked the door, then embraced her as soon as she got to her feet.

"Everything."

"It can't be everything. You were just named Most Outstanding Player at the world championships."

"Everything that doesn't involve hockey."

I stood there for a moment with the door open. "Hold on. Let me sit down." I dropped my bag on the floor and myself on the bed. Caitlyn looked subdued. "Okay. Start at the beginning, which was you after the championships, on your way back to a place to live and a job, neither of which were great but were both at least tolerable."

"I got fired a couple of months ago." She was standing, not quite in front of me, and looking out the window.

"A couple of months ago?"

"I didn't tell anyone because I was embarrassed. I thought I could just get something else and it would be fine. It didn't work out."

"Did you really try?"

"I was busy. It just didn't seem so important."

"Not important?" I took a deep breath to keep myself from yelling.

"I don't have a place to live, and I have $43.52 to my name."

"Where's your gear?"

She grimaced. "And I have $3,000 worth of hockey equipment sitting in a bus station locker in the city."

I sat there, at a complete loss for something to say.

She looked at me, and I couldn't read her expression. "Can I stay here?"

"Of course." That much came out without hesitation. "Do you have any plans?"

"Well, I'm supposed to be in camp in three weeks. After that, no."

"Come here and sit down." She collapsed next to me, and I pulled her close. "We'll fix this."

The next morning I got a call from Amy Heckenthorpe. "Have you heard from Caitlyn? She's gone missing. No one has seen her since she left the Toronto airport."

I swore. "I should have thought of that."

"What? Have you?"

"Yes. She's with me. Not right at this instant, but she's staying with me."

"Oh, thank God. I was hoping she'd talked to you."

"Yeah. She's—well, I won't say she's fine, but she's in one piece."

"What's wrong?"

I hesitated. "I'd like to talk to her before I say anything about what's going on. I don't know what she wants to keep private. I'll have her call you tomorrow. In the meantime, physically she's fine and isn't in any danger unless I decide to strangle her."

"That sounds like Caitlyn. Thanks. I'll let the authorities know that we've found her."

I knew Abby would grill me and was surprised only that it took her two weeks. "Phoebe, she just showed up on your doorstep and invited herself in."

I had to hold my phone away from my ear because of the volume she was projecting through it. "Pretty much, yes."

"And you're letting her stay with you."

"At the moment she's up in Regina, but that's correct."

"She's taking advantage of you."

"That's certainly a valid way to look at it."

"Why are you letting her?"

"Because I said I would."

"You told her you would do this?"

"Basically."

"Basically? Why are you responding so passively to every question I ask?"

"Mostly to see just how wound up I can get you. But yes, that's what I told her. I didn't realize it would play out this way, but I did tell her she could come here any time she wanted."

"Why?"

"Because I meant it, and that's not just a passive nonresponse."

"Why?"

"I like having her here. My problem isn't when she comes," I pointed out. "It's when she leaves."

"Yes, but you know that's going to happen. In the meantime you're enabling her."

"She doesn't need enabling to be irresponsible. She's damned good at it on her own."

"But you're helping."

"Would you rather she were living on the streets? That was the alternative."

"She could move back in with her mother like most failed twenty-somethings."

"No, she couldn't. Physically she could do it, but I'll bet you a semester's tuition she'd rather be sleeping on the streets."

"She isn't going to learn anything, and she's going to end up right back in the same place." She was shouting again.

"Which is exactly where I want her."

"She's going to end up on the streets at some point if she doesn't learn."

"No, she won't."

"Yes, she will. She'll keep doing it over and over again."

"And I'll take her in every time."

"Why?"

"You keep asking that same question. It's what I want to do. I will outstubborn you on this."

She said something inarticulate. "You're being stupid."

"It's been known to happen."

"You aren't going to change your mind."

"No, I'm not." Instead, I changed the subject. "So who is this Scott fellow I've heard mentioned?"

"He's someone I met."

"I assumed you'd met somehow since you've been talking about him."

"We're kind of dating. It's not serious."

"I'm not going to let you off that easily." I kept myself from laughing only because that would really have caused her to blow up.

"Yes, you are, because I need to go."

"You're embarrassed about something."

"Look, I'll call you in a few days."

"I'm going to pick the questioning up right here when you do."

"I'll be warned. And for God's sake think about what you're doing."

"I already have, Abby. I love you."

"Love you, too."

My professional career got underway two months later, when an entrepreneur arrived in my office at the university. "Are you Phoebe Rose?"

I swiveled my chair and found myself looking at a man barely taller than I was seated. "Yes."

"Hi, I'm Dennis Graham." He held out his hand, and I shook it. "I'm looking for someone who can help me with some programming work. Professor Najayaran recommended you."

I blinked. "What sort of programming?"

"Robotic manufacturing. Specifically dealing with quality control."

"What sort of manufacturing?"

"That's the thing. I'm working on processes that would be applicable across many industries with enough modification."

"So this isn't a manufacturing company itself."

"Right. It's pretty much a pure tech start-up."

"I'd be happy to take a look. What kind of time investment are we talking about?"

"Not much to begin with. I have a couple of specific problems that are beyond my expertise. I'm primarily a hardware guy. If those work out, there would almost certainly be more work, probably leading to a full-time opening." His arms were in constant motion as he talked.

"Why are you asking a graduate student instead of an actual professional?"

"You work cheaper than they do."

"That's confidence-inspiring."

"I also prefer to build a relationship from the ground up. If I went to a professional right now, I'd be hiring a consultant rather than an actual employee. The need just isn't great enough right now to justify hiring someone directly yet for anything other than piece-work. With a graduate student, I know what you're doing with the rest of your time."

His eyes wandered my body, but that didn't bother me as much as it used to. Two national championships can mend one's body image issues. "So, control."

"To put it bluntly, yes."

"You want a lab monkey who will work for nothing but a few bananas and some stock options and with whom you don't need to share any of the credit if it works."

He was unfazed by my sarcasm. "That's a good summary."

"I'll think about it. Send me the info."

"Okay, but time is a factor here."

"I have lots of experience in making quick decisions."

"Great, I look forward to working with you."

Caitlyn stayed for three blissful months, except for the trip to Saskatchewan for her national team commitment. I finally found a rink nearby that she used to train daily. I cooked dinner every night with real ingredients from a real cookbook. Caitlyn made me shop for new clothes, which I only enjoy with someone to help me.

We lived our different schedules. I was usually gone by the time she got out of bed on weekdays. Weekends were different. Usually I lay in bed for a couple of hours just being close to her.

One Saturday I tried to return to being productive after dinner, but she was having none of it. After fiddling with my stereo and complaining about my lack of a video game system, she came up behind me and rested her chin on my shoulder. "None of that makes any sense."

"It's a language specifically for industrial robots."

I kept trying to write, but it was distracting when she started kissing my neck.

"Why are you still working on this? It's Saturday night."

"Because I'm not done."

"You realize that Dennis is only paying you to be part-time, right?"

"It's a tech start-up, Kitten. 'Part-time' means I don't have to work ninety hours a week."

"So why do you do it anyway?"

"I do not."

"Uh huh. I've been keeping track."

"Some of that is school work."

"Oh, fine. So I'm going to have to go out on my own?"

I grumbled something about getting more done before she showed up.

"But this is California. You don't stay in on a Saturday night."

"This is Palo Alto, not LA. Trust me, lots of people stay in on Saturday nights."

"I'm going to pout."

"Please, not that. Okay, I'll go."

"Yay!"

I even had a good time.

I knew it couldn't last. If nothing else, there was another Olympic year coming up. Officially she was just on the list of players who would be invited to the final tryouts for Team Canada, but she was a lock to be selected if she kept her head screwed on.

It was more than that. She actually followed through on looking for a job and finally found one back in Canada in July. It was a temporary position, but it would carry her until the Olympic team went full-time and paid a stipend.

So on a Sunday morning I propped my elbow on my pillow, head resting on my fist. I lay there for about fifteen minutes, just watching her sleep. Caitlyn stirred briefly under her ridiculous pile of blankets and then settled on her back. I suddenly felt the need to get up, to burn off agitation over her impending departure.

"Where are you going?" Her murmur barely carried the five feet between us.

"Running."

"Morning people." She rolled over to face where I'd been, eyes never opening. "Leaving me alone by myself."

"I'll make breakfast when I get back. Omelettes and pancakes."

"Oh, sure. Try to make it up with food."

"It works." I pulled on my tights and leaned over to kiss her brow.

"Fuck you."

"Later. I need to run first." She smiled and was asleep again before I'd left the room.

Four days later I had both of my hands on Caitlyn's shoulders as we stood at the bus station. "Tell me again what you're doing."

She gave me the look a six-year-old does when asked to repeat instructions, complete with rolling her eyes. "I'm going up to Montreal. I'm going to stay with Erika. I've got a job lined up with an advertising agency there to do graphics work. I should consider myself lucky just to have it.

"I'm going to go to work every day. If I don't like it, I'm just going to suck it up until I already have a different job. I'm not going to just quit. I'm going to take a part of every paycheck and put it in a separate bank account so I don't spend it."

"Good. What are you going to do if there are problems?"

"I'm going to tell Erika and not just keep it hidden. If things get really bad, I'm going to call you before I do anything stupid."

I looked at her. Miss Perky Hyperactive was back. What I couldn't tell was whether there was any real resolve behind it. "Are you sure you're ready for this?"

"Yes. I've got it. I'm all set."

I pulled her into an embrace. "And you're still always welcome here, Kitten."

CHAPTER 17

May 2013

Caitlyn and I did a lot of our talking at night, lying in bed together, which is when the subject of my personal biology finally came up. "Do you plan to have children?"

I let that hang for a moment, wishing she hadn't asked. "I can't." I was glad that I was facing away from her.

"What do you mean you can't?"

"I lack the necessary parts for having them."

"Like what?"

"All of them. Internally, I have no girl parts."

"A birth defect?"

"Sort of. Technically, I'm not even female at all."

I felt her sit up. "You're a guy?"

"Not really. I have the genes of a boy, the appearance of a girl, and the insides of neither."

"So no kids."

"No kids."

"That must be really tough."

"I'm not sure I would have wanted them anyway."

She fell silent, and I looked over and saw her chewing her lower lip.

"What's wrong?" I asked.

"This is pretty serious," she said quietly.

"Well, yeah." I couldn't think of how else to respond.

"When were you planning on telling me?"

"What? I don't know. Whenever it came up."

"So you might never have told me?"

"I'm sure I would have at some point." I sat up and really looked at her. "I have to have surgery for it someday."

"We've been together for a year and a half, and you've been hiding this?"

"I was not hiding it," I said sharply. "It just didn't seem important."

"How can it not be important?" I could see tears forming.

"I don't like talking about it. Hell, I don't like thinking about it. So I didn't. Don't be angry."

"I'm not angry," she whispered. "I'm hurt. When did you tell Abby?"

"How do you know I told her?"

"Because you tell her everything. Every time I learn something about you, she already knew."

"That's how we spent my first year here. She helped me face a lot of things."

"I want to help you, too."

"You do. You know that."

"So why can't you tell me the things that hurt to say?"

"It's not that I can't," I said, feeling frustrated. "It's that I don't need to say them again. Getting them out was the important part."

"But I need to hear them," she cried. "I want to know who you are, and I want to be the most important person in your life."

"It's not a competition." That got a poor reaction, but I plunged on before Caitlyn could say anything. "It's different with Abby."

"Why? Because she's easier to talk to or something?"

"No. Well, she is about some things but very definitely not about others."

"So what is it?"

"It's just a different relationship. I think of her as a sister, really. I don't worry about you sharing things with Jess."

"Well, yeah. I mean, she really is my sister."

"I want a family. I've tried pretending that I don't, but it's a lie. I know it sounds strange, but that's how it feels with the Forrests. I don't know if it's the same thing the rest of you experience, but it's what I imagine."

"Yeah, that is strange," she replied.

"Consider where I'm coming from."

"I'm trying," she said, taking a deep breath. "It still bothers me."

"If it makes you feel better, I not only haven't told her that stuff, I couldn't."

She inched closer, and I shifted so that she could sit behind me. "Probably a good call."

My laugh had a touch of bitterness. "I really should have talked to you first. The reason I know I can't tell Abby is because I tried."

She put her arms around me and rested her forehead between my shoulder blades. "It didn't go well?" I could feel her breathing, and I started to relax.

"She blew me off. Told me we should just be friends."

She started to chuckle and cut it off. "Sorry. That wasn't funny."

"I tried to make it funny."

"Well, you didn't succeed."

"I'm sorry I didn't tell you. It just didn't occur to me that it was important."

"I forgive you. But please think about other things you haven't mentioned and whether you should."

"I'll try. I really will. I'm just not sure what is and isn't important. I've spent my whole life not telling people about myself and not asking about them."

"Okay. If you really try, I'll try not to get upset."

"Thank you."

"And tomorrow I'm going to ask you a whole bunch of questions about whatever this thing you have is."

"Fire away. I don't think it will hurt me to talk about it."

Few people realized that the perpetual motion machine that drove Caitlyn wasn't really perpetual. Her depression didn't strike frequently, but every once in awhile she would just come to a complete stop.

She was good at hiding these episodes from teammates, but living together meant that her attempts at subterfuge were futile with me. I hadn't said anything because Caitlyn clearly didn't want me to know. Maybe I should have spoken up, but keeping secrets was so ingrained in me that I just accepted her reticence without challenge.

That summer, her depression became more frequent and more intense. One afternoon, I came home from the lab and found her sitting on the couch almost motionless. She wasn't watching TV or reading. She just sat there limply. Despite the lack of outside distractions she clearly hadn't heard me come in.

I stood in the doorway between the kitchen and the living room. After five minutes I finally decided I couldn't ignore this. "You okay?"

She jumped, obviously startled. "Yeah. I'm fine." Her tone of voice was as forced as the smile she offered me as she grabbed the empty glass on the coffee table. "I just need to get more water." She got up and went to the kitchen. Her posture gave away that she wasn't fine. She looked different by the time she returned, but it still wasn't normal. I waited until she'd set the glass down before reaching out and pulling her to me. "What's wrong?"

"Nothing." She pushed against me, trying to escape. "I'm fine."

"No, you aren't." I held onto her, carefully, like holding a kitten that might hurt itself trying to get away. "This is the third time this month I've found you like this."

She kept squirming. "It's nothing."

"It's okay, Caitlyn," I said. "You don't have to pretend. Not here. Not with me."

"I'm not pretending." Her struggles grew weaker.

"Okay," I said. "Then I'll talk about me. Don't stop me if you've heard this before because I'm telling it again anyway." I swayed gently. "I get depressed sometimes. Serious depression. I just feel like I'm floating away. Out the window and up into the sky. It can last several days at a time. Sometimes I wonder if that happens to everyone and we all just hide it from each other."

"It's not like that," she whispered, finally going still. I fell silent, waiting for her to continue. "I don't float away. I just shut down. I think about all of the things I could be doing but don't want to. Everything feels so heavy that I can't move. I can't even reach for the remote. Today I couldn't lift my head even though my neck hurt from the position." Her arms reached around me to return the embrace.

"It's okay. I can imagine it."

"I shouldn't hide it from everyone. That's what you're going to tell me, isn't it?" she asked.

"Hell, no. Don't hide it from me, because it's my job to help you. Other than that, conceal it from anyone you want to. I know you like the image of being Miss Perky Hyperactive, and I don't see any reason to spoil it if you don't want to. But in here, you can turn it off."

"I'll try. I think I can handle it if you don't think of me that way."

I chuckled. "Too late. I do think of you that way. You're my favorite perpetual motion machine. No matter how many times you run out of energy, that's how I'm always going to think of you."

"Good." She buried her face in my shoulder.

"Does my presence help?" I asked.

"Yes. It doesn't make it go away, but it's not as bad."

"Then I need to do some reading, but I can do it while we snuggle. Would you rather sit out here or in bed?"

"In bed, I think. Hopefully I'll fall asleep and be better when I wake up."

"Okay." I kissed the top of her head. "Let me grab my books, and I'll join you in there."

As it happened, she stayed with me while I got the books and a carafe of juice, clutching the back of my T-shirt. And she did fall asleep, arms wrapped around my thigh and mumbling things I didn't listen to.

No matter how intensely I tried to keep from thinking about it, the date when Caitlyn would leave for five months to play in the

Olympics approached relentlessly. After being in denial I finally talked to her about it one night late in August. "I'm going to miss you."

"Phoebe, I don't leave for another month."

"I know, but I'm already thinking about it."

"Well, you shouldn't."

"I'm trying to figure out what I'm going to miss the most."

"Phoebe . . ."

"I think it's your breathing."

"Really?"

"Not just meditating. In the early morning, I'm usually awake, and I just listen to you. I have to be quiet, because it isn't very loud, even if I'm right next to you. So I lie there quietly and listen." I smiled sheepishly. "Sorry it isn't something more . . . I don't know . . . sexier. Or livelier. Or something."

"No, I think that's pretty sexy. I like it."

"Have you ever just listened to a kitten purr?"

"I've mostly just watched them run around chasing stuff."

"You should try it some time. That's what your breathing reminds me of."

"No one has ever said anything like that to me."

"Most people don't pay attention to the important things."

"That's true. I'm as guilty as anyone. I get distracted and start chasing stuff around."

"Mmmm. That makes you my kitten, I guess."

Caitlyn insisted that it was an obvious choice and that I shouldn't have been surprised. Nevertheless, when the captains for my senior season were announced and I was one of the assistants, I was shocked.

The day of our first official practice, I examined my jersey and touched the new addition. That *A* sewn onto the left shoulder meant more to me than I could put into words. My teammates had elected Heck, Traci, and me. I hadn't doubted my place, but to have something tangible, something that I could feel with my fingers, took my breath away.

Most of the girls had been a captain on their high school or junior teams. For me, it was a new experience. I sat there, soaking in what it meant, as players filtered in.

Kennedy sat down next to me. "Thank you," I said quietly.

"You earned it."

"You guys still had to think that I'll do a good job of it."

"Just do what you always do. Heck can do all the talking. I'm sure that's why she got the C. All you have to do is be yourself, and we'll follow."

"You have a better idea of who I am than I do."

"It's good enough."

I was ready. It was going to be my last season of competitive hockey. There was going to be no Caitlyn or Abby to pull me along. Instead, I was going to have to do the pulling. Sitting there clutching the symbol of that change, I realized that I intended to run over anything in the way.

We said our good-byes at the apartment. We'd developed rituals for her departures. We reassured each other that I'd be fine. She told me how much she needed me to be there for her return. This time it had the added edge of marking a real ending.

"I have too many responsibilities to miss you this year." I was trying to convince myself.

"You'll be great at it," she assured me.

"How about you?" I took her hands and ran my fingers up her arms. She didn't know I was recharging the bindings.

"What about me?"

"Isn't this where I'm supposed to give some sort of speech about coming home with your stick or on it?"

"Please don't."

"Then I'll settle for saying that you shouldn't let the fact that you look better in silver than in gold affect your play."

"I'll just let you wear the gold medal, then. It would look fabulous."

I hugged her. "Thank you."

"Nervous?" I asked between spoonfuls of granola and fruit.

All I got was a shrug and, "Is hockey," which was what I deserved for answering that question the same way before my first game. I was sitting in the stands at Indiana, with one of the new freshmen, a Russian girl named Svetlana. Even in the two weeks of practice before the season it was obvious she was the most talented player on the team. She was nearly as large as I was, nearly as fast as Caitlyn, and she did everything with an elegance neither of us could manage. (Three years later, it surprised no one when she was named the best player in the NCAA.)

In other ways, though, she reminded me of me when I'd first arrived. She was quiet and either aloof or just awkward. She understood English just fine but had trouble expressing herself.

All of that made me the obvious mentor for her, so of course I was uncomfortable with the idea. Like a cat making a beeline for the person with the worst allergies, it took her three days to attach herself to me. When I expressed my frustration, Heck laughed and exercised her captain's prerogative to assign it as my permanent duty, suggesting that I learn Russian.

So there I sat, trying to exorcise my nervousness about having a leadership role. "This is where I scored my first goal," I said. "This end. Lucky bounce on a shot from the blue line. It was dumb."

Another shrug. "Then not dumb."

"I wanted my first goal to be prettier than that. A one-timer that goes through cleanly."

"Goal is goal."

"That's easy for you to say. You scored, what, six times in last year's U18 Worlds? I scored three times total in my first two seasons." I realized I was babbling and stood up to return to the dressing room.

"You think too much," she said. "Just let hockey happen."

"Oh God, please don't say that where anyone else can hear you."

Midway through the second period the next Saturday, against Michigan, I lost the puck in my skates along the boards. With my head down trying to find it, I never saw Kelly Shuster coming. She slammed into me, making only a marginal effort to make it look accidental.

Pain exploded as I hit the boards awkwardly, catching my elbow on the dasher. Pain like nothing before. Raw physical pain.

The whistle blew before I could find the courage to stand up. Kennedy helped Dana, our trainer, across the ice to me, and they helped lift me. Bent over and holding my elbow, I slowly made my way to the bench. Payback is a bitch. Shuster got two minutes for boarding, and I got six months of rehab.

Dana pointed me straight to the dressing room. When she moved my arm, I gasped. After that, she cut my jersey off and then gently lifted the pads away. I looked down, and even from the bad angle I could see the big lump in the front of my shoulder.

She ran some tests, most of them moderately painful, and then decided to go ahead and try to reduce the dislocation. In lay terms that means she pulled on my arm and twisted so that the top of my arm bone slipped back over the lip of the cup it's supposed to rest in and slid back into place. It was about as much fun as it sounds.

That night I found the outer limits of my pain tolerance. I didn't sleep because I couldn't find a position that wasn't excruciating.

The bad news came with an MRI the next morning: I had not only a dislocated shoulder but also a torn labrum and small fracture of the humerus. Right then we knew that my season was done. The good news was that doing it that early meant the NCAA would give me my last year of eligibility back. If I was diligent in rehab, I'd play again.

With Caitlyn.

CHAPTER 18

October 2017

Given what had transpired the last time, I viewed the approach of the 2018 Olympics with great trepidation. "How are you holding up?" I asked Caitlyn in early October.

"Great," she said enthusiastically. "Nothing but hockey and interviews and promotional appearances, so you'd hate a lot of it, but I'm having a blast."

"And you're handling the stress?"

"There's no stress. Really."

"It'll come," I told her.

"I don't know. This group is really loose. We're going to win, and it's all going to be okay."

I couldn't hide my skepticism. "Okay. But if it goes bad, remember the things I've taught you."

"Sure, sure." She paused so briefly other people might not have noticed the hesitation. "I met this great guy a couple of weeks ago at a function. His name is Brent, and he's in finance here in Montreal. We've gone out three times in the last week. He's a lot of fun."

"I'm glad for you."

"I know. Things are really working out for me. So how are things going for you?"

"Pretty much the same, really. Classes. Work. Not much else." My tone was flat, and Caitlyn missed it. Normally, she's vigilant about how I'm taking something, but here her enthusiasm overran her awareness.

"Are you seeing anyone?"

"You know the answer to that already," I replied crossly.

"Find someone."

I had one of those moments where I want to reach through the phone and shake her. "Can we just drop this?"

"Okay, but I'm going to keep thinking about it."

"You do that."

"So when do you want to meet Brent?"

Only seven years' experience of Caitlyn kept me from shock. "Is it at that stage after a week?"

"I think so."

I couldn't end the conversation quickly enough.

"The burgers here are fabulous," Dennis said.

"I'm just going to have a salad." A week later, the conversation with Caitlyn was still affecting my appetite.

"I don't know why I bother looking at this," he said as he flipped through his menu. "I know everything on it anyway."

"So why are we here?"

He looked up. "You've worked for me for six months, and we've barely talked. I like to get to know my employees."

"So what do you want to talk about?"

"You. Maybe me if we have to."

"All right." He looked at me expectantly, so I continued. "It's tech. I can't be the first uncommunicative misanthrope you've ever hired."

"So what's it like to play hockey?"

"Fast. I told you I have practice at making quick decisions."

"So do you play at all out here?"

"No."

"Why not?"

"I'm too busy."

"Were your teams good?"

"I'm sure you've already looked it up."

He flapped his arms in frustration. "Can we at least pretend that I'm trying to learn something about you? It seems more social."

"Okay. Over five years, we had a record of 150-37-10, and we won the national championship twice. How's that?" My salad arrived, and I started eating.

"You were pretty good."

"I was mostly along for the ride. I had a lot of very good teammates."

"How do you juggle that with the kind of coursework you were doing?"

"By having no life. They were the only two things I did for five years. It renders me an uninteresting conversational partner."

"So I take it there's no reason to ask about your hobbies?"

"Smart man."

"So what else is there? Where did you grow up?"

"If you've researched me enough to know about my hockey experience, you also know where I grew up and why I don't want to talk about it."

"There's not much left to talk about."

"I told you. I'm not interesting."

"That only leaves me to talk about. So what do you want to know?"

I didn't look up from my food. "Are my meager paychecks likely to start bouncing?"

"No. Why?"

"That's the only part I'm curious about."

"C'mon. I'm a fascinating man."

I set down my fork. "Let me see how much I can get right. You're from Buffalo. Your parents were middle-class, and I imagine that your father owned an auto repair business, but that's just a guess. You became fascinated by computers when your junior high school got some, probably Commodore 64s. You were a complete nerd as a teenager, but you were the one with some social skills. You went to MIT and decided to get a business minor to go with a computer science major. I don't know if they had a specific program in entrepreneurship back then, but that's effectively what you did. You worked for someone along Route 128 for a couple of years before deciding you wanted to be your own boss and moving to California. You spent fifteen years as a consultant so you could take orders from a lot of different people instead of just one, until you had an idea for a new generation of industrial robots and started a real company.

"You're garrulous and like people. You're particularly good at getting them to like you. You have the soul of a carnival huckster buried beneath a huge amount of technical knowledge. You're basically a decent guy, but you have the ability to turn your conscience off when you need to and never regret it. You used to be bothered by your height but are over it, except for a curious inversion that causes you to leer at me regularly. I haven't figured out yet whether going bald is causing you any distress.

"How'd I do?"

"My father's a dentist, but other than that you're a lot closer than I really want to admit. Sorry about the leering."

"I work with tech nerds. I'm used to it."

"Most people wouldn't dare say that about their boss."

I shrugged. "I paid my college expenses by being willing to fall down and let a six-ounce disk of frozen vulcanized rubber hit me in the face while going eighty-five miles an hour. It changes your perspective on fear. If you fire me, you fire me."

"Good Lord, no. It was refreshing."

"So there we are. Anything you want to add?"

"Tons, but I think I'll wait until some other time."

"I won't sleep with you on the first date."

"Right now I'm too scared of you to even think about it."

"Practice getting hit by a hockey puck. You'll get over it."

"How do you figure all that out?"

"Female intuition."

The real key is doing your research, changing your quotes enough that they aren't recognized, and deliberately getting enough wrong to avoid suspicion.

I sat on the sofa in my parents' living room almost unable to move. "I really shouldn't eat like I used to," I said in something close to a moan.

"None of us should," Abby agreed from the recliner in a similar tone.

"C'mon, guys, it's Thanksgiving." Dad seemed far too energetic given that he'd gorged himself right along with the rest of us.

"We know that," Abby responded.

"That means it's time for football." He eagerly turned on the TV.

Abby gave me a look full of suffering. I almost laughed at her. Instead I just settled in next to Dad, with no intention of paying any more attention to the game than I absolutely had to.

Somewhere in the middle of the second period Dad shook me gently. "You asleep?"

I lifted my head from his shoulder. "No. Just thinking."

"About what?"

"Memories."

"Good or bad?" Abby asked.

"Good. Mr. Wilson loved football. He was a lineman in high school. On Saturdays in the fall I usually had practice or a game in the morning. He would always come and watch. He didn't know anything about hockey before I moved in, but he really watched. When it was over, we'd go to McDonald's for lunch, and he'd ask me all of these questions about what we'd done. He probably never did really care about hockey, but he really wanted to know what I was doing."

Dad ruffled my hair, but no one said anything.

"After that we'd come home and sit in his den, just like this. He'd have the games on, and I'd just lean against him. Sometimes I wish I'd asked him questions about football like he did about hockey, but it didn't really matter. I was there, and he was there. He always watched the Minnesota game if it was on. When they lost, I'd always say, 'They'll get 'em next week, right Mr. Wilson?' I said it even if I knew it was the last game of the season."

I fell silent. Dad went back to watching the game. Abby watched the clock. Her limit for sitting around doing nothing had been exceeded by halftime, but she wasn't about to admit that she didn't like just sitting there with us. I enjoyed watching her fidget.

My phone rang, and I idly wished I'd turned it off, but I picked it up to see who was calling. I wasn't too surprised to see that it was Caitlyn, so I answered it. "Hi, Kitten."

"Hi, Bear." She sounded excited, even for her. "Where are you?"

"Mom and Dad's. It's a holiday down here, you know."

"I remember that, silly. That's why I called with good news."

I'd like to report that I had a deep sense of foreboding, but there was nothing of the sort.

"What is it?"

"I'm engaged."

CHAPTER 19

Morgan wouldn't give me my T-shirt back. She changed the rules on the fly to say that you only got them if you were a healthy scratch. We played that season with such a short roster—thanks to the Olympics—that it only took one injury for everyone else to dress, so no one wore one. That meant Morgan was in the lineup every night. She didn't get many shifts, but she did score her only career goal against Indiana. We were already up 6–1 in the third period, but all of us were thrilled to see it.

I found it harder to deal with being injured than missing games because I wasn't good enough to be in the lineup. I'd come to grips with the latter, and when I was a healthy scratch, I had to stay sharp because someone else could get hurt any time. It didn't help that I couldn't sleep from the pain.

I spent five months watching the team without any possibility of playing. As boring as practice can be, watching practice was worse. I was there every day, doing whatever I could.

I couldn't remember a time I'd gone more than a couple of days without skating. I looked ahead and saw at least two months before the doctors would let me on the ice. The team started a pool to pick the day I had to be committed. I wanted December 12, but they wouldn't let me enter.

As for the team, the fact that losing my talents made a meaningful difference summed up our prospects. Heck was our only forward from our top two lines the year before. She and Kat made up the bulk of our offense. I could see the pieces that were going to get better: Alice had become a strong goalie, and the defense had really solidified. We had all come together, but there was no way we could score enough goals. We lost a bunch of 2–1 games.

No one should cry for the 2013–14 Minnesota Golden Gophers. We were still on the fringe of being one of the ten best teams in the country. That just wasn't what we were used to.

I had surgery the first week of November. Nothing arthroscopic—they cut me wide open and left a big scar down the front of my shoulder. They filed down the rough spots on the bone, stapled my labrum to my scapula where it belonged, and tightened up the stretched ligaments.

In other words, just about the time my shoulder had stopped throbbing in pain all the time, they sliced it up all over. I was not a fun person to be around. My teammates had enough sense to tease me a lot, which helped.

Finals ended the second week of December, and the team played its last game until the new year. So Kennedy, Heck, and I drove up to Duluth one weekend for the Minnesota-Duluth Bulldogs exhibition against Team Canada. We were all interested in watching the hockey, but for me it was mostly a chance to see Caitlyn.

Olympic teams are astonishing to watch. With that much talent and several months of training together they dominate any college team they play. The Canadians won 5–1, and Team USA was going to do the same thing to us in early January.

Team rules said that I couldn't actually stay the night with Caitlyn, but we did have a good chance to talk and snuggle after the game. It was a little awkward, since she usually sits on the side of my injured shoulder. We made it work.

"How are you doing?" she asked.

"As well as can be expected. I'm not sleeping well, but that's probably more my shoulder than being alone." I left unsaid that I hadn't slept all that well in the three weeks before I got hurt, either.

"You look worn out," she said.

"It's turning into something of a lost year. I'm mostly just bored."

"I know what you mean. I love the hockey, but living out of hotel rooms is wearing on me."

"How's it going? I see you're playing on the third line."

"I am a lot, but it's all still in flux. There are just so many good players, we're juggling the lines constantly." She let her head fall back and looked at the ceiling. "I'm glad you came up. I'm not lonely, but something is missing."

"Are you having your funks?"

I felt her flinch. "Not really. Just one or two."

"You don't need to pretend." I pulled her closer with my left arm.

"I'm not pretending," she insisted. "I'm fine."

I couldn't think of any way that I wanted to express my skepticism, so I just said, "I'm waiting for you."

We sat there for awhile, talking without saying much. Mostly we were just there together.

"I should probably get going. You must have a curfew or something," I said finally. Sadly.

That perked her up. "That's what you think. I cleared out for Riley's boyfriend last month, so she's crashing with someone else tonight. If you're ready to go to bed, we can just go back to the room."

"Oh." I lit up. "Let me just tell Kennedy that I'm staying here instead of the Motel 6."

"Pffft. I told her on Tuesday. I just wanted to surprise you."

"I don't usually like surprises."

"That's okay. I like them enough for both of us."

So we went to bed and tentatively played out a familiar ritual. For all her free-spirited nature Caitlyn was always sensitive to when I needed to do things by a rigid routine. Nothing brought out that side of me like sex.

I enjoyed sex with her, and in this case in particular I definitely wanted it, but I'm incapable of asking for it. Caitlyn had learned to understand the signals I gave and made sure to ask me explicitly if she had them right.

Once we were in bed she took charge and followed our script. She rolled over so that she straddled my hips, taking extra care because of the wounded arm that crossed my chest. She told me what she was going to do, and at the start I just lay there and let her do it. Eventually, I would unfreeze and begin to respond.

From there we could laugh, giggle, and do all of the other things that lovers do. We could be spontaneous and try new things. But up to that point it was deadly serious, and Caitlyn had to do the exact same things every time, or I would get lost in the fear.

I felt better when we were finished. My worries about her continued to nag at me as she cuddled up into my side, but they weren't overwhelming. I could relax and listen to her breathe.

On December 27, as I was getting ready to go back to Minneapolis after my first truly uneventful Christmas with the Forrests, Abby's father asked me, "Why don't you stay for a few more days?"

I had finally relaxed around him, able to take his loudness in stride. "I have some things I need to take care of down there," I answered.

"Like what?"

"Team things," I said, unable to come up with anything specific.

He squinted at me. He knew that my physical therapy wasn't scheduled to get started for another six weeks. I still wasn't allowed to skate or do anything vigorous.

"With Abby and Derek gone, I figured you'd want the place to yourselves," I continued, getting closer to the truth.

"Not at all. We'd love to have you here. You're like family now."

I could tell that he noticed my reaction to that, so I opened up to explain. "I think Abby would feel like I was infringing."

He laughed. "She doesn't get to make all of the decisions for the whole damned family even if she thinks she should." He put an arm around me. "If it makes you feel better, she and I already talked about this."

"Oh. Great."

He knuckled the top of my head—he had to reach up, since he's about six inches shorter than I am. "She's coming around, at her own pace."

"I think I'll still avoid talking to her about it."

"So you'll stay?" he asked.

"I'd rather not," I said. "Until she does come around, I'd just as soon not do anything to overstep."

He shrugged. "Okay, then. Let's get your stuff in the car."

Before he could pull away, I reached out and embraced him as best I could. "Thank you," I whispered.

"Do you play chess?" Sveta asked me as we sat in the union between classes.

"No. Why?"

"You seem like the sort of person who would, and I'm bored playing everyone else."

"You're too good for them?"

"*Da*. Except Kennedy. She can beat me rarely."

"Sorry. I don't play. I'm not a very interesting person."

She turned and looked at me. "That is not true. You are interesting."

"All I do is study and play hockey. Except when I can only study and mope about not playing hockey."

"You are wrong. It is not what you do that makes you interesting. It is who you are."

"I'm minoring in philosophy," I replied. "Are you sure you want to have this conversation?"

"Fuck philosophy. You are interesting."

"Really? What makes me so interesting?"

"You always tell us you don't understand people, but you do. You figure them out and tell us."

I shook my head. "That's not understanding. That's predicting. To understand them, I'd have to be able to tell you why they do something. I can't tell what motivates people, just what they might do."

"Is same thing."

"No, it isn't," I insisted. "I can't solve problems. I can only see them coming and try to warn people."

"But that is interesting."

"No, it isn't," I repeated. "It's survival. At least it was for me. When you're a foster child, you have to be able to read people. You have to know who is a threat. But sometimes you can't do anything about it. You can see what's coming but have no idea how to avoid it."

"Isn't solving problems for survival, too?"

"It should be." I fell silent, kicking at some gum stuck to the floor.

"I'm sorry, Feba," she said finally, using the Russian form of my name.

"It's okay. Actually, I was just thinking that it took Abby and Caitlyn two years to reach the point where I told them this. For you, it was five months. That means I'm getting better, right?"

"Maybe I am just good listener."

"That, too. The funny thing is, when I was little, like six years old, I was really good at manipulating people. I still didn't understand them, but I could get them to do what I wanted."

"What happened?"

"Mr. Wilson taught me that it was wrong to treat people like that. I listened to him, and now I think it's wrong to do it. I probably couldn't do it anymore. The skills are long gone."

"That is bad?"

"I think he was eventually going to teach me when it was okay, but he died before he could. So here I am, out on this tree branch, unable to go forward or down."

"See, you are interesting."

In October Caitlyn and I had talked almost every day. By late January it was about twice a week. A certain distance developed, which didn't keep me from thinking about her. In my dreams the cords that bound us stretched over the horizon.

Her training got more intense as the Olympics approached.

The European teams didn't centralize until a few weeks before the Games, but Kat was preparing to leave to join Team Slovakia, and Sveta would follow soon to Team Russia. Our bench was going to be even shorter for a month.

I was frustrated, bored, and lonely. It was hard to stay mentally engaged in our season when I wasn't a part of it. All I had to look forward to was daily sessions with a physical therapist as soon as my shoulder was deemed ready.

I missed Caitlyn's physical presence. When I meditated, I had no anchor and floated aimlessly. When I was with teammates, I was fine, but at home I sat around accomplishing little. The mandatory tutoring sessions became important as my grades slipped, at least by my standards. Darkness enveloped me. Kennedy drove it into the background when she pulled me out, but it lurked, ready to return when I was alone.

Then the bomb dropped.

Caitlyn and I had been discussing Team Canada's preparations. The name Steve kept coming up, so I finally asked, "Who's Steve?"

"He's one of the administrative guys. He's actually from the Olympic committee rather than the hockey association. I've ended up spending a lot of time with him."

"What's he like?"

"Oh man, he's fabulous. He's going to law school in the fall."

I felt uneasy. "Where?"

"Western Ontario."

"So what do you two do together?"

She laughed. "Not much, except talk sometimes. Everything is so hectic right now that we don't have time for anything else."

"How well do you know him?" And how many leading questions could I come up with without just coming out and asking whether they were dating?

"Pretty well, I think. As I said, it's really tough right now. We're going to spend some time together when all of this is over. I'll probably take a couple of weeks before I come back to campus, to decompress."

I suddenly wanted the conversation over with. "It sounds like you've got your plans figured out."

"Good God, no. I'm going to be making it up as I go. Nothing past the seventeenth of February exists right now. This is more intense than anything there has been. It's nothing but hockey."

"You sound like you're enjoying it."

"I am, but it's stressful. I miss sleeping with you."

"I do, too."

And after that bit of encouragement, the bottom fell out. "It's not the same with Steve. And we have so few chances with this schedule."

The pain was physical, starting in my gut and spreading. I kept my composure long enough to say good-bye. "Hey, I need to get going. I've got a paper due on Friday I need to work on." Completely true, and suddenly utterly irrelevant.

"Okay. I've got stuff I'm supposed to do, too. It was good to talk to you. Love you, Phoebe."

"I love you, too," I managed before punching my phone off.

The next day Kennedy took one look at me and asked, "Are you all right, Phoebe? You look awful."

I was sitting in the lounge. "I'm okay."

Kennedy sat down next to me. "Are you sure?"

"Not really." I wasn't sure of much of anything. I'd probably gotten a total of three hours of sleep the past two nights. It was bad enough lying there thinking about Caitlyn. When I actually got to sleep, it was horrifying. All of the old nightmares were back, and they'd brought new ones.

"You found out about Caitlyn, didn't you?" I looked up at her sharply. "Erika told me. Apparently she's not being very secretive about it."

I gave a strangled laugh. "Why would she? She just flat out told me."

"She did?" Kennedy sounded startled. "Well, at least she's honest about dumping you."

"No, that's the thing. She didn't dump me." I tried to fold in on myself. "She just brought it up casually, a part of the conversation."

"She what?"

"She said she misses sleeping with me and that it's not the same with him. That's how I found out."

"You're kidding."

I shook my head, tears starting to leak out.

She pulled me into a hug. "Good grief. Is she insane?"

As always, I answered the rhetorical question. "I don't think so. I just think that the two of us means something very different to her than it does to me."

"It would have to, wouldn't it?"

I leaned into her. "I think it's just a friendship for her. A really close friendship. I don't think she even thinks of this as cheating on me. We've never sat down and really discussed what we're doing together. I should have made sure we did."

"Don't start blaming yourself. And don't defend her. She should know better."

"Know better than what?"

"What this means to you."

"She knows that. This is about me not understanding what it means to her."

"Stop it, Phoebe."

"I'm not blaming myself. I'm crying, but I'm not blaming myself."

"Then what are you doing?"

"I'm trying to figure this out. I can't make decisions if I don't understand what she's doing."

"What is there to decide?"

"Everything."

"Even if she comes back, she'll do this again."

"So? That's not the important question." My tears had stopped, and my chin was thrust out.

"What is?"

"What do I mean to her?"

"Isn't that clear?" she asked.

"Stop thinking like you, and start thinking like her."

"I don't think I want to."

"Then you're missing out," I insisted. "She's fascinating."

"That's not how I'd describe it."

"Really, try it. Is she offering me anything less just because she's sleeping with Steve? If she is, is what she's not offering valuable to me?"

My shoulder throbbed as she hugged me tighter. "You're rationalizing," she said.

"Humor me, dammit."

"How can you be thinking logically like this?"

"Because that's who I am. It's how I survived adolescence."

"Okay." She sounded beyond exasperation. "What was the question?"

"Basically, it's why should I care? Think about what Caitlyn really means when she says she misses sleeping with me and that this guy isn't the same. Does that mean that she won't give me what I want?"

"I don't know, because I can't figure out what you want."

"Oh, that part's pretty simple, actually. I want someone who will keep me from being scared. I want someone who will be there at two a.m. Someone who is right there and will keep the nightmares from ever showing up."

"There has to be more to it than that."

"There is. But that's the core. I'm confident that anyone who provides that will provide the rest of it, too."

"That's quite a leap."

"Okay. That's a rational point to discuss."

"And she isn't here at two a.m.," Kennedy pointed out.

"Okay, that's a second rational point, but it needs to be looked at more closely. No one seemed to have a problem with her picking the Olympics over me. If she's not here right now, that has nothing to do with Steve."

"That's not the same thing."

Something clicked inside me. "I think it's exactly the same. Anything that keeps her from being here works out the same as far as I'm concerned."

"Yes, but the Olympics will end."

I gave her my first real smile of the last couple of days, albeit one with a slightly evil edge. "And I'm pretty certain that Steve will, too."

"Wait, what?"

I sat up straight, pulling out of her embrace. "No dipshit lawyer wannabe can give her what I can."

Kennedy looked lost. "Where are you going with this?"

"I mean, she already admitted that. She'd rather sleep with me than with him. Her words."

"I'm not sure I'd rely on what she says."

"Who else should I rely on?"

"I don't know, but—"

"Well, there we are." I was on a roll now. "Thank you, Kennedy. I was feeling really crappy before our talk, but I'm much better now."

"You're delusional."

"What, are you saying that I don't have more to offer than some dipshit lawyer wannabe?"

"You're twisting everything I say."

"No, I'm not. Mostly I'm just ignoring it."

"That still doesn't seem very helpful."

I looked her straight in the eye. "What was your goal when you sat down?"

"I wanted to cheer you up, but—"

"Mission accomplished."

"Yes, but—"

"As for not trashing Caitlyn and just assuming it will work out, honestly, what does it cost me?"

"Your self-respect?"

I stood up and started pacing. "Doubtful. I think that's pretty solid at this point, at least in the ways that matter here."

"I don't know how to explain this."

"That's because I'm not normal. Caitlyn's not normal, either, or she wouldn't have ended up in my bed to begin with."

"You are normal."

"No, I'm not. I'm not sure that anyone is normal, but I'm definitely not. I don't mean in a bad way, necessarily, but I don't look at things the way most people do. This is one of those instances."

"This seems wrong."

"If it makes you feel better, I don't plan to assume anything. Caitlyn and I are going to have a long talk. I think I'd rather wait until we can have it in person rather than over the phone. And I don't really want to do it now anyway, not this close to her accomplishing her dream."

Kennedy sat back and held up her hands in surrender. "I don't know whether you're crazy or a saint."

"Neither. If anything, I'd say that I'm just more ruthless about figuring out my own self-interest than other people are."

"I still don't think this is smart."

"Nothing about this relationship has been smart. And please keep this to yourself. And please ask Erika to do the same."

"I suspect that it's too late for that, based on what she said."

"Wonderful. Could you at least spread it around that I don't want to talk about it? It remains private until March. I will not let this affect this team—or hers. No one is going to be picking sides because there aren't going to be any."

"I don't know if that's possible."

"It is. That was always the deal. That's what Tammy was saying two years ago. She may have been a complete bitch about it, but underneath that, she was right. When we agreed to her conditions, we committed to this not becoming a team thing. And it won't. So far as everyone else knows, we're still together. If we split, it's going to be completely amicable. No talk of cheating. No talk of arguments. That stays between the three of us, and I think it would be better if you don't tell Caitlyn that you know anything about it."

"I'll try. I don't know if I can keep my mouth shut."

"You will. You're going to think about it tonight, and you're going to realize that I'm right. The team is more important." I headed for the door. "I've got a paper I need to write." With that I marched out.

CHAPTER 20

December 2017

"**A**re you sure it's December?" Kennedy asked me as we sat under an awning at a bar near campus.

"That's what they tell me."

The weather wasn't perfect. It was pretty cool by the standards I'd gotten used to, but it wasn't Minnesota

"It's a nice change of pace," she told me. "I couldn't live without winter, but for a couple of weeks a year this has potential."

"You're always welcome to do just that."

"Aren't you done in May?" she asked.

"Yeah, but I'll be staying in the area. I like it here, and the job prospects are good."

"Then this may become a December habit."

She looked up at the fog coming in off the bay. "On a completely different subject, is she serious?"

"Caitlyn is always serious right up until she's completely serious about something else."

"Even for her this is a bit extreme."

"What, getting engaged to someone you've known for six weeks might not be her most considered action ever?"

"You seem to be taking it pretty well."

"I'm putting a brave face on things. Either that or shock. I'm not sure which." I didn't tell her anything about meditating and finding the cords still taut.

"Have you met him?"

"No," I answered, "but she's talked me into going up there in January."

"Erika isn't complimentary about him."

"So I've noticed. I'm trying to remain open-minded."

"How's that going?"

"No comment."

"Keep thinking positive, Phoebe."

I wasn't sure that I wanted to think positive.

My Christmas Eve conversation with Abby from that year is best left unrecorded. She left nothing of her opinion of Caitlyn unexpressed. Even though I didn't feel like defending her, it was still oppressive.

Mom was more sympathetic. As much as anything, it involved pep talks for my upcoming trip to Montreal. They were needed, since I was hoping the State Department wouldn't get me my passport in time. I wasn't that lucky.

It took ten seconds to realize that all of my efforts to be fair minded had been a waste. Brent's looks alone made my skin crawl. I had no idea what Caitlyn saw in him. He seemed like an odd choice for her, even in her less discerning moments. She has a low tolerance for boastfulness and self-promotion, and despite how thoughtless she could be, she isn't mean.

Brent was all of those things. He could be charming in a sleazy kind of way, and he was a completely different person when she wasn't in the room. He fawned on her except when it was time to make a decision; then he gave orders. It was subtle. I don't think she even realized she was obeying him.

The worst moment came when we were sitting in his apartment. They were on the couch, arms around each other. After one notably obsequious exchange he looked at me with an expression of triumph. "Isn't she wonderful?" Caitlyn couldn't see his face. I just mumbled my reply.

The last night I was there Team Canada played an exhibition against McGill. Caitlyn put us on the comp list, so I didn't have any graceful way not to sit with Brent for two hours. The game itself was a hopeless mismatch. Caitlyn played well; she had solidified her place as the second line left wing.

With a yawner on the ice, it was hard to avoid talking to him. Finally, he just came out and asked, "You don't like me, do you?"

"No, I don't." I tried to focus on the Team Canada power play occurring in front of us. "But what really bugs me is that you seem to enjoy the fact that I don't like you."

He laughed. "It means I won."

I sat up abruptly. "This isn't a game."

"Everything is a game," he said, doing nothing to conceal his mirth. "And in the game of Caitlyn, I win."

"What does that even mean?" I asked just as the red light came on for another Team Canada goal.

"It means she doesn't need you anymore."

"Really? Is that what you think?"

"It's what I know. You hold her back. She's going to be something else once we're together."

Suddenly my anger drained away, and only sadness was left. "You know, Brent, I just realized that you're not only loathsome, you're also stupid."

"I was eighth in my class at McGill."

"Uh huh. I know some really stupid software engineers at Stanford, too."

"What's your point?"

"My point? Caitlyn does some really dumb things, but she isn't stupid. She eventually figures out that she's made a mistake, after she's dug herself a really deep hole. So you're going to hurt her badly, but she'll eventually have had enough. I give you guys three years, tops. And when it's over, I'm going to be there, and I'm going to help Caitlyn put herself back together."

"Even if you're right," he said, "it sucks to be you. I'll get all of the good parts."

"Wrong." I smiled at him. "You see, I enjoy fixing her far more than you could possibly enjoy breaking her. I just realized that, and

I'll need to remember to point that out to my sister someday. It is, really, the thing I look forward to most in life. So let that haunt you. No matter what you do to her, I not only will undo it, I'll have a good time. In fact, I'll enjoy it enough that I might not break all of your limbs when it's over. Maybe. And you know what?"

He recovered his belligerent tone. "What?"

"When it's over, I'll have Caitlyn, and you won't."

I told myself I could be patient.

February 2018

Caitlyn played in the Olympics twice after we graduated. The overall arc of her international hockey career was impressive. Canada won the Worlds six times in the nine years Caitlyn appeared in them, and she was named the tournament's most valuable player in 2015 and 2017.

That paled before the Olympics, though. The entire country of Canada lives and dies by how their hockey teams do every four years. Being the goat for their failure the first time haunted her, and her anxiety as the 2018 Games in South Korea neared was palpable, even if she denied it.

I inverted my schedule to watch almost every game despite the time difference. As I didn't own a TV, I had to find a place that stayed open late, and so for two weeks I became a regular at a joint called Barney's. By the second day, I was already known as the crazy hockey lady.

Almost every game featured a couple of girls I'd played with or against, and I rooted for individuals rather than teams. One of the bartenders figured out that I had personal connections when I hissed at Mallory Jackson one too many times. "You know her?" he asked.

I nodded. "We traded punches a couple of times when we were in college."

"Where'd you go?"

"Minnesota. Class of '15."

"You've got a bunch of teammates playing in this. You must have been pretty good."

I shrugged. "I couldn't have been that good, or I'd be over there."

"There's good and there's great." He refilled my soda. "So who are you rooting for?"

"I'm not sure, to be honest. My loyalties are conflicted."

"You don't root for your country, whichever one that is?"

"No. I root by friendships."

Which was true but still left me in a difficult place. I was bitter about Caitlyn's impending marriage, and when the Games started, I couldn't cheer for her. As the periods rolled by, though, I found that I couldn't hate her even if I tried. I'd been telling the truth all of those times I'd told her I couldn't.

So I showed up for the gold medal game between the Americans and the Canadians with a small Maple Leaf flag to wave. It was a great game, with the Americans taking a 3–1 lead in the second and then trying to hold on. The Canadians made it 3–2 halfway through the third. When Caitlyn hit the post with three minutes left, I felt physical pain.

I didn't know whether she'd have another chance. Four years is an eternity for an athlete in her mid-twenties, and while the end of her career was not obviously close, it had begun to take form. She relied upon her blazing speed and frantic pace to overwhelm the other team. If she lost a step of that speed, she'd have nothing to fall back on. Like the mythical shark, if she stopped forechecking, she'd die.

It hurt to watch the medal ceremony. It was the first Canadian team ever to go to consecutive Olympics without winning the gold. The agony on her face was unwatchable. I had to pay my check and leave.

I waited several hours to call her. I could remember tough losses in big games. There comes a point where the pain stops and numbness takes over. I always found that to be the worst time.

"Hi, Caitlyn."

"Hi, Phoebe." Her voice was dull.

"I'm sorry. I thought you had them."

"I did, too. I thought this was the time."

"You'll get 'em in four years."

"Yep." She sounded exhausted and unconvinced.

"Is there anything I can do to help?"

There was a long pause. I didn't breathe. "May I come see you?" she asked in a small voice, giving the answer I was hoping for.

"Of course."

"It will be a few days. We have some things to clean up."

"I'll be waiting for you."

It was sheer folly, but I couldn't tell her no. I wondered what Brent would think about who needed who.

Disconsolate didn't even begin to describe her. She lived the third period over and over again. I suspected that it was still really about four years before, because she was great. She was everywhere on the ice, had an assist, and was +1 in a 3–2 loss. All I had were the TV angles, but I didn't see any mistakes. That she drew iron rather than net on that last attempt hurt, but it was a good play.

Her confusion was overwhelming. She didn't know what to do, and I didn't know what to do about it. I wanted to shake her and ask why she was in my apartment rather than with her fiancé, but I knew the answer to that. I felt too horrible about it to say anything. I enjoyed the fact that she needed me like this. My expressions of commiseration felt hollow because I wanted it that way.

Outside of one phone call, I think the word "Brent" was uttered twice in the three days she stayed with me. Mostly there wasn't any talking at all. I don't have the kind of experience losing huge games by miniscule margins that she does. Except for that Big Ten final my freshman year, we won big games any time it was close. When we lost, we got our asses kicked.

But I could put myself in the position. It isn't hard to imagine a goal here or there going the other way. Caitlyn had often pointed out that I was quite good at that imagining. The two of us just sat quietly on the couch. There wasn't anything for me to say that was going to make her feel better. All I could do was just be there for her.

Unfortunately, someone else wasn't as good at staying quiet. That one call was to him. The volume on Caitlyn's phone was loud enough that I could make out what Brent said to her. That was the point where she cried. I had no idea whether I should say what I thought; by default I said nothing.

The most difficult part was that we didn't sleep together, at my insistence. As badly as I wanted to, I couldn't share a bed with someone else's fiancé.

April 2018

I faced two weddings that spring. Abby's came first. I'm not much for sentimentality, and even I thought it was a majestic ceremony. Abby was beautiful, Scott was Scott, and I didn't screw anything up as the maid of honor.

It was disconcerting that I caught the bouquet. I didn't mean to, and I suspected a conspiracy. Abby threw it right at me, and Kris made an indifferent swipe at it. The damned thing almost hit me in the head. What was I supposed to do? I stood there trying to figure out what message they were sending me.

After the reception, a bunch of us sat around in the hotel bar. When the inevitable comparisons to Caitlyn's impending nuptials started, I felt uncomfortable. Erika knew Brent better than any of the rest of us, and Kris and Tammy managed to egg her into expressing her real opinions.

"I think he'll be fine," I said, lying through my teeth. "Just give it a chance."

This drew stares of surprise from around the table. I probably hadn't managed to force much conviction into my voice. "Really?" Tammy asked. "He seems like a complete loser."

I glared at her even though we completely agreed on the issue at hand. She returned it unabashedly, and I realized that the attendance at the table bore an uncomfortable resemblance to that meeting six years ago. Abby had vanished with Scott, of course, and several others had wandered off. That left just me and the members of Abby's class.

"Maybe we should all just let Caitlyn make her own romantic decisions," I said.

"That's worked out really well for you," Tammy shot back.

Latent resentment bubbled up. "I know you blame us for torpedoing that season, but it's time to get over it."

"You two put your hormones ahead of the team. Is that what's going on now? Are your hormones not up to the job anymore?"

Kris grabbed me even as I stood up. Kenna did the same with Tammy. I shrugged Kris's arms off. "Don't worry. I'm leaving."

I stalked out of the bar. A half hour later there was a knock at my door that I'd known would be coming.

"Can we come in?" Kris asked when I opened it.

"Sure." I sat back on the bed and turned off the TV I'd had on for background noise.

"We'd like to apologize for that." There were several more of them than had been downstairs. Kathy Zimmerman looked irate.

"None of the rest of you have anything to apologize for. I don't like to listen to everyone dump on Caitlyn, but she is acting bizarrely."

"It's more than just that," Kris insisted. "This whole thing has festered long enough, and you're right. It's past time to let the whole thing drop. You did what you did. We did what we did. And two years later you guys proved that it took more than two of us to screw up team chemistry."

I looked around at the group. "I appreciate it. I've been trying to tell Abby ever since that I don't even blame you guys. What we did was selfish, though I'll defend it as being a justifiable bit of selfishness under the circumstances."

"I agree," Kathy broke in. The glare she shot around suggested that she'd knocked some heads together.

"Thanks. I don't blame you all, but I do think that all of the tension back then hasn't helped Caitlyn's tendency to self-destruction. So I'd like you to do me a favor, if at all possible. Just keep quiet with your opinions of Brent. I'm going to be a disaster at their wedding. I don't think I'm going to be able to help it. Could everyone else just offer her their support? Please?"

Several of them obviously bit back their responses. "Yes, we can do that," Kathy said. She looked around at everyone else. They all assented with varying degrees of enthusiasm.

"Thank you. Either it works out, or it doesn't. If it does, then you guys can help me move on with my life."

"I don't think we need to worry about that possibility," someone muttered.

"Sorry," Kathy said. "I'll have a word with them about keeping promises for more than thirty seconds once we get outside."

I stood up. "Thanks. I love all of you."

"I still want to apologize for what Tammy said," Kris continued. "That was unbelievable."

"Some of you are harder to love than others," I admitted.

May 2018

I begged off being Caitlyn's maid of honor, so Amy got stuck with the job. I was still one of her bridesmaids, though at least she didn't make me dress in green.

There were nine other former Gophers in attendance, and I found solace that they all shared my opinion of Brent. It wasn't just us; Caitlyn's mother sat in the first pew, stony faced. At one point she cornered me and said how much she wished we were still together. Apparently, there were worse things than your daughter being in a relationship with another woman.

So I sat at the reception getting quietly blitzed on good bourbon while Kennedy, bless her, made sure that no one decided to celebrate with me. I wasn't fit company, and my plan was to be drunk enough not to look for our bindings.

But how do you stop the bride?

"Come dance with me."

I could still focus. "No, Caitlyn, that's not a good idea." I was not going to call her Kitten, even in my thoughts. Not then.

She pouted. It wasn't endearing. "Come on." She grabbed my hands, but I didn't budge.

"No. I'm not going to get in the middle of this."

"What's that supposed to mean?"

I drained my drink. "It means that you chose him, not me." I didn't mean for it to come out so bitter.

"I want to dance with you, too."

"You can't, Caitlyn," I say softly. "It will kill your marriage if you do." I was still sober enough, barely, to recognize the damage I was doing, but I couldn't stop. I threw the bomb at her anyway. "You can't dance with both of us. Brent's the one who can call on you when he needs you now, not me."

"I can't believe you're saying this."

"Have you told him about us? I mean really told him?" My determination not to say anything negative about him had become an ugly, twisted thing. Six months spent making sure that when their relationship inevitably cratered, my fingerprints were nowhere to be found ended up in a hopeless parody of offering her support.

"He knows we've been together. He says it doesn't bother him."

I bet it didn't. "It's not the sex, Caitlyn. It's the absolute trust. It's the willingness to drop everything to help one another. That's what you and I have been about."

"I'm sure he understands that."

Right. "Well, that's what you need to do with him now. Not me. That's the choice you made." A part of me wanted to punch myself.

She stood there, confused. I suppose that I was glaring at her. At last she walked away without saying anything else.

I surged up and made my way across the room. I dropped two twenties on the bar and reached behind to grab a full bottle of Wild Turkey. The college student working it recognized the wisdom of not getting in the way of a drunken ex-defenseman spoiling for a fight. I found Kennedy right behind me. "I'm going to my room. I'm not helping anything here." I put my arms around her. "Try to have fun."

"Are you sure you don't want me to come with you?"

"Yeah." I couldn't find any more anger inside me, just sorrow.

CHAPTER 21

January 2014

'd meant everything I'd told Kennedy, but I wasn't really that good at keeping emotions out of it.

I went up to the Forrests' for the weekend. It had only been four weeks since I had said I didn't want to infringe, so I felt kind of silly, but they both assured me that it was fine. I spent a lot of time talking with Jerilyn, and she mostly just listened. I suppose that's what I wanted.

I think Tom missed having his kids around. We spent that Sunday afternoon working on the car Abby had sold me when she left, though I just handed him things when he asked for them. He had been in the process of teaching me how to drive a stick when I got injured, and there was no way I could drive it for another couple of months, so it just lived in their driveway. We talked about all sorts of stuff that had nothing at all to do with Caitlyn.

By Monday morning I'd decided to wait and see.

Our next conversation began with Caitlyn apologizing.

"I have no idea what you're apologizing for," I answered.

"Yes, you do. Heck spent a half hour yelling at me over the phone yesterday."

"Still—"

"We need to talk about this."

"No, we don't." I had no intention of talking about it. "If you think that there's something to talk about, it should wait until you're back. I don't like having serious discussions on the phone."

275

"You aren't going to budge on this, are you?"

"No. Go win a gold medal. For the next three and a half weeks, that's all that matters."

"No, it isn't. We matter, too."

"It's not going to get any worse between now and then."

"I'm already worried about it now. Waiting isn't going to do what you are hoping it will."

"It hurts, Caitlyn. It hurts a lot. But it also hurts in a complicated way and maybe not like you think it does. I don't know exactly what I want to say yet."

"I'm sorry."

"I know you are. If I didn't, this conversation would be going differently."

"I'm really sorry."

"You're going to have plenty of opportunities to grovel. I think we can make this work, but there is going to be a long talk and some ground rules. Things we should have talked about a long time ago. It isn't going to get any worse between now and the end of February, and there's nothing irreparable. Is that good enough for now?"

"Yes. Thank you. I stopped seeing him."

I wanted to tell her that that didn't really matter, but that would have sent all the wrong signals. "That's good. Now win. I love you, Caitlyn."

"I love you, too."

I became an assistant assistant coach for a couple of months. I took notes during games and went over them with the coaches on Sundays; then I used them to put together the video presentations we reviewed as a team. I stood on the bench during practices, observing and offering whatever comments I could. I don't know that I added much value, but it gave me a way to stay engaged.

Then, with Illinois in town, I found myself up in the press box checking over the notes I'd taken as the clock counted down the last seconds of the first period.

"You look so serious doing that," Heather Kemp said. She was my current companion among the walking wounded. A hockey team is allowed to dress eighteen skaters and three goalies for each game. With her joining me and Kat and Sveta off in Russia, we were three skaters short of a full roster.

"I am serious doing it."

"Why? You don't want to be a coach later."

"Because I was bored out of my mind. This at least gives me something to focus on."

"So why don't you want to be a coach? You'd be good at it, even just volunteering somewhere."

"When I'm done playing here, that's going to be it for hockey for me." I gathered up the pieces of paper in front of me and began the trek down to the dressing room.

"You aren't even going to play just for fun?"

"I don't think so. I don't think anything else will be able to compare to this. It would seem like chasing a ghost."

"I don't think that's the way it's going to work for me. I want to play forever."

"There's nothing wrong with that. It just doesn't work for me."

"Will you follow it at all?"

"Some. I'm not into watching sports, but I'll certainly keep track of the Gophers from wherever I am. I'll also follow international hockey, at least as long as people I know are playing."

At the end of the month I finally got onto the ice. It was the most thrill I'd had putting on my skates since I'd made the team.

After practice I just skated around for awhile. Kennedy stayed out with me. I didn't pick up a stick, but we played around a bit. My physical therapist wouldn't have been happy to see some of it, but I had a blast. It was probably the first time I'd really relaxed since I'd heard of Steve.

We stayed out there long enough that no one else was in the dressing room when we were done.

"So what are you planning to do?" she asked me.

"I don't know. Honest to God, I think I need her too badly not to forgive her for just about anything."

"That's not healthy."

"I know that, but what are my choices?"

"Find someone else?"

"I have no idea how. I don't know where to begin."

"All right. I'll drop it."

"I'm going to miss you next year."

"I'll still be around. I'll just be in St. Paul more."

"I'm glad you're staying here for grad school."

"Me, too, really. I want to go back to Dauphin, but not yet."

I chuckled. "I can't imagine living there. Minneapolis is as small a place as I want to be."

"I love the quiet. I get out on the prairie, with nothing in any direction, and I feel at peace."

"So why not head back up there, at least part way? There's a vet school in Winnipeg."

"Too soon. I need to have more time away, so that I'm not always expecting Mom or Dad to show up. The family that's left up there . . . I don't think I really know them anymore. It's not that new. Dad moved off the farm when he was my age, and Mom's family had lived in town for generations. It sounds kind of strange to say here, but we were the radical cosmopolitans. If you think I sound backwards sometimes, you should hear my cousins."

"Kennedy, I never thought you were backwards."

"I told my parents about you and Caitlyn. That was a couple of months before they died. That's how different they are than the rest of my relatives. They thought it was sweet."

"It's too bad you're an only child. I would like to have met your brother."

"Me, too. I wish I could introduce you."

We laughed. "God, it's good to be skating again."

A week later things got underway in Russia. Coach told us not to change our sleeping schedules because we had games of our own to play. I suspect that he wasn't the only coach in the country who had a hard time enforcing curfews for those ten days. I didn't have to change my schedule much in order to watch games that started at three thirty in the morning.

There were no surprises on the first day. The US beat Switzerland, and the Canadians destroyed Finland. The biggest excitement was that Jenny scored two goals in the US game.

The US and Canada played their round-robin game the next Monday. There was a lot of good natured betting over it, some of which involved embarrassing payouts. I shuddered to think what the gold medal game was going to bring. I was glad I'd opted out of having a rooting interest.

Heck, Kennedy, Rachel, and Teri, as the resident Canadians, spent the afternoon crowing about their win. I still didn't get the whole nationalism thing, but I decided that it was probably more entertaining than if the outcome had been different and it was the majority enjoying it. Canada spent a lot of time killing penalties, and Caitlyn caused her usual short-handed mayhem. Kennedy watched me watch Caitlyn, but I had no idea if she noticed anything.

To understand what happened next you have to grasp how totally the US and Canada dominated women's hockey. Between them they had lost exactly one significant game at the top international level to anyone else, when the Swedes beat the Americans in the 2006 Olympics. Outside that, the North Americans steamrolled the Europeans and settled things in the gold medal game.

So the mood in the lounge as we watched the end of the Canada-Finland semifinal ranged from stunned to horrified. I fell into the latter category, along with our four Canadians. Canada played sloppy and overconfident all game, and the Finns were inspired. Still, it was 3–3 late in the third.

Then Caitlyn melted. She missed an open net and then, out of frustration, hooked down a Finnish player for no reason. The ref had swallowed her whistle all period, but she couldn't ignore it.

Thirty-four seconds later Caitlyn stepped out of the box, and

Canada was down 4–3. I know that feeling—you want to just disappear on the bench. But I never did it on international TV during the biggest tournament in the world. I tried to curl up in the corner in sympathy.

They put pressure on with the goalie pulled but gave up an empty net goal instead, making the final 5–3. Teri went into hiding until it was time to show up for that night's game. She learned that a freshman shouldn't be so vocal when things are going well.

A quick perusal of a few websites indicated that the typical sports fan was out in full force. The level of vitriol directed at Caitlyn by her countrymen was shocking. I felt sick for her, but I couldn't keep myself from wondering whether or not, from my own selfish perspective, it was a good outcome. It disturbed me that I even thought it.

The conversation came six days later, after the Canadians took their frustrations out on the Russians in the bronze medal game and then returned to Toronto to officially disband.

When I heard the apartment door open, it was hard not to go help Caitlyn with her luggage, but I made myself stay seated in the living room. I dog-eared the page of my book and set it aside.

Caitlyn put her coat away, and then her head peeked around the corner. "I probably shouldn't put my stuff in the bedroom yet, should I?"

"That depends upon where you think this is going." I hoped I kept my fears out of my voice.

"Okay." She sat down in the chair, facing me. "I'm sorry."

"Caitlyn, what do I mean to you?"

"Oh, boy. I don't know what to say."

"Try the truth."

"That's the thing. I'm not sure exactly what that is, and I haven't figured out how to articulate what I have figured out."

"I'm not going to fly off the handle at the first thing you say and hold you to that. I understand that things can come out wrong."

"I'm still not sure where to begin."

"Then I'll go first. You know some of the reasons why I need you. The nightmares. The getting me out of the house and interacting with people. But I'll try to put into words what all of that means.

"Caitlyn, you make me feel safe. I'm not sure it makes much sense, but I feel like no one can hurt me when I'm with you. No matter what they say or do, it doesn't matter. You give me the confidence to ignore them if I need to."

She took a deep breath. "I don't know whether it's the same for me or the exact opposite. You make me safe from myself. You aren't judging me if I fail. You don't have some image of what you want me to be except myself. If I do something stupid, you'll laugh at me, and then it won't matter.

"You're my rock. Whatever happens, you'll be here. I have no idea how I would have made it through the last six months without you. The pressure was unreal. I found myself wishing that 95 percent of the country had never heard of ice hockey, like it is here. Knowing that you didn't really care whether we won or not, at least as far as how you think about me, was the only thing that kept me sane."

I nodded.

"I'm sorry, Phoebe." She was crying. "I got . . . I don't know. Too complacent, maybe. I didn't think about it enough to realize that there was a limit to just how stupid I could be. That I might do something so stupid that you won't take me back. When that goal went in and I had to skate back to the bench, all I could think was that I hoped I hadn't screwed this up as badly as I did that."

I sat there for a few minutes. I didn't exactly intend to leave her twisting there, at least not consciously.

"Phoebe, please say something."

"I'm afraid that you'll leave me. You need me here. I need you here. But you don't need to be here. I can do what you need me to even when we aren't together."

"That's not true."

"Yes, it is. You enjoy being together, but you don't need it. You said it. Just knowing that I'm here keeps you sane."

She hung her head. "I guess."

"I've thought about this a lot over the last few weeks. If I understand myself, the problem may not be quite what you think. Believe it or not, that you were sleeping with someone else is not what bothers me. What bothers me is when you are not sleeping with me. Honestly, the reason why doesn't make that much difference to me. It can be another person. It can be the Olympics. Whatever."

"I—"

"Let me finish that thought. The difference is that I know the Olympics will end. One of the reasons—not the only one, but one of them—why I fundamentally don't care whether you win or not is that that question is overshadowed by the fact that, either way, you're coming back. But if you're sleeping with someone else, I don't know that that's going to end."

"I can't imagine loving someone more than I love you," she said.

"I can imagine it. Since you aren't gay, I can imagine it really easily. You're using me as your fallback position. I'm the person, of the wrong gender, who will be waiting for you if whatever else you try isn't better."

"That's not fair."

"Isn't it?" I was starting to cry, too. "Isn't that exactly what you told me?"

"I didn't mean it like that. You said that you wouldn't get stuck on things that came out wrong."

"Then tell me what it does mean that you know I'll be here no matter what stupid thing you do, when that includes seeing other people."

"It means that, when I'm stupid and just assume that you'll understand what I'm thinking, even though I've never discussed it with you, that you'll give me the benefit of the doubt as I try to explain."

"I'm trying. I really am. I just need to know that I'm more important."

"You are. I just don't think I'm ready to settle down yet. There are so many—wait, that was the wrong thing to say, wasn't it?"

I nodded as my tears got worse.

"I don't know what to say. I don't know how to explain it. I know what I feel. I know that I love you so much that you being a woman doesn't matter. I know nothing could possibly replace you. I just . . ." Her voice tailed off in frustration.

"I'm scared that it will change. I'm scared that you will change."

"I can't promise I won't change. I can't promise that I will always be there for you. But I will promise you this. Whenever you really, really need me, I will be. I will drop anything else that I am doing to come to you, wherever you are."

I thought about that. "Would you? Anything?"

"Yes. If it were the night before the gold medal game, I'd do that."

I sat there, my mind whirling. "What about all the other times? Having you here keeps me from reaching that point."

"I really don't know what I can tell you. I love you, Phoebe, but I don't want to make a promise I'm not sure I can keep."

"So where does that leave us?" I asked.

"I don't know. For the next year, I won't be going anywhere. It's fourteen months until we graduate. I can't promise beyond that, but we won't be interrupted between now and then, except for things like Christmas. I don't know if that's enough for you."

"Can I think about it?"

She laughed quietly. "Of course. I wouldn't blame you if you strung me out for a couple of weeks after this."

"It won't be that long. I need you too badly to . . . Oh, who am I kidding? Of course I'm going to say yes. I'm going to hem and haw. I'm going to agonize about it. Then that's the answer I'm going to give, so let's skip that part."

"I'm not sure I like the sound of that entirely."

"You shouldn't. I can't promise that I won't become some kind of stalker if you leave me."

She looked down. I think she was trying to hide a smile. "If I leave you, really leave you, for good, I'll be happy if you don't kill me right then and there."

I thought of several possible responses to that, but I didn't feel like joking around. "Is that okay, then?"

"Of course it is," she replied.

"Then can we go to bed? I know it's only four in the afternoon, but I'm exhausted."

She exhaled. "I am, too."

CHAPTER 22

To say that I reacted poorly to Caitlyn's marriage is an understatement. When I got back from Montreal, I kept it together long enough to defend my thesis and then collapsed. When I should have been out looking for a job, I fiddled with Dennis's robot problems and sat and watched movies. It was impossible to motivate myself to do anything difficult.

He finally sent me an email that read, "You don't work for me these days so stop sending me things. If you've changed your mind and do want to work for me, come in for an interview at 3:30 Tuesday. Until then, everyone here has instructions not to open anything you send them."

I showed up on Tuesday because it seemed easier than explaining that I wasn't interested. When I arrived, Dennis promptly bid good-bye to the other seven people in the office.

"Where are we going?" I asked him.

"Herbert's. It's been a long day, and I need some food and a couple of beers."

"I thought this was a job interview."

"Why the hell would I need to interview you?" he replied. "I already know I want to hire you."

"Then why did I bother getting dressed up?"

He indicated my khaki slacks and polo shirt. "If you call that dressing up, you've been in this industry too long. I conned you into coming out here because you need to get out and talk to someone. And I'll do that better with some beer, so come on."

I stood there for a moment as he walked to the door before realizing that there was no point in staying there. I intended to walk back to my car and go home but found Dennis blocking the sidewalk. I could have walked around him. Instead I let him shepherd me toward his SUV. I was acutely aware of his hand in the small of my back and resented that I liked the physical contact.

On the way over Dennis talked about his dreams for the company. I'd heard his sales pitch before, so I mostly ignored it. I leaned my head against the window and watched San Jose crawl past me.

Once we sat down and had closed our menus he began in earnest. "Do you want to tell me what's wrong?"

"No."

"All right, that was a stupid question. Are you going to get up and walk out if I start pestering you to tell me what's wrong?"

"My car is at your office so I don't really have that option."

"I'm lucky you're too cheap to call a cab."

"Making fun of me isn't likely to make me want to open up."

"I've tried everything else. You seem immune to straight-up sympathy."

I shrugged and ordered some whiskey. That should have clued me in to where I was headed.

We verbally fenced for awhile, Dennis trying to draw me out and my refusals becoming more strained. Finally he asked the critical question point blank. "Who is Caitlyn?"

"No one you need to know about." I threw back my drink, and the waitress magically appeared to ask me if I wanted another. Of course I said yes.

"Maybe not, but you need to tell someone."

"I do tell someone. Just not you."

"Does someone live within a thousand miles of here?"

"This is the twenty-first century. They don't need to live on the same continent."

"Bullshit. Maybe that works for other people but not for you. You need to have someone present."

"How do you even know that name?" I asked, glaring at him over my glass.

"You mentioned it a couple of times lately."

"No, I haven't," I muttered.

"I'm sure you believe that. I've been surprised how careless you've been recently. It's one of the ways I know how distressed you are."

"So what else have I been saying?"

"Not much or I wouldn't need to keep asking questions. So who is she?"

I found out much later that he already knew the answer to that, because Caitlyn had called and asked him to look after me. Had I known that at the time, I'd have been livid, but it was years before she told me, and by then I saw it differently.

Right then, though, I just said, "She was one of my teammates. Someone I was close to."

"Was?"

I shrugged. "She's moved on without me."

"So move on without her."

That rattled around in my brain, mixed with the alcohol, and prompted me to make a stupid decision. "Take me home."

He looked at me for a moment. "Okay, but call me in the morning. Until you come up with something else, I want you working for me in an official capacity and coming into the office."

"I meant your place. I don't want to sleep alone tonight."

"No."

"Because I'm drunk?"

"I wouldn't sleep with you if you were sober."

"Why not?" I asked belligerently. "I know you think I'm attractive."

"Yes, I do. It doesn't matter."

"I'm lonely."

"I understand that, but it's a terrible reason to sleep with someone. I want to be your friend, and I want to be your boss. I will not be your lover."

"I can't move on without her," I mumbled.

"I think it is time to take you home, though." He caught the waitress' attention to pay the check. "I'm sorry, Phoebe. Getting you drunk was a mistake."

"I don't want to be alone."

As he guided me back to his truck, he said, "If you want, you can sleep in my guest bedroom."

Which is what I started doing a couple of times a month when things got bad.

July 2018

"Wow. Manitoba is flat."

"Yes, it is," Kennedy agreed. She'd graduated in May, and I'd taken the opportunity to visit her for once.

"I think I can see Minneapolis from here."

"Not like that you can't," she said laughing. "You're looking almost due east."

"I'm trying to think if there's any place on earth less like San Francisco than this."

"Yes, but do you like it?" she asked me.

"I'll like it for about four days. Then I'm going home."

"Convenient timing."

I stepped off of her porch to get a better look. The view didn't change much. "I guess the more important thing is that you like it here."

"Yep. I think I've had my fill of city living. I'm glad I did it, but this is home."

"So what's the nightlife like?"

"Quiet," she answered. "Me, three cats, and satellite television if I'm feeling lazy."

"And if not?"

"Then it's me, three cats, and something active."

"Nothing social?" I asked.

"Sure. There are get-togethers in town. Church functions. Markets. Then I come home."

"I never pictured you as the solitary type."

"I didn't, either. I see people when I'm working. I find that that's enough, usually. I like the quiet."

I shook my head. "It's funny. I'm the misanthrope, and I need to live in a crowd. You actually like people, and yet you live out here."

"Yep. It means you'll have nothing to do for a few days except talk to me."

"I've got my computer. I can get work done."

"I hope it's all already on there, because I'm not telling you the password to my router."

"You wouldn't."

"Try me." She sounded serious.

"I guess we're going to have to talk to each other." It would have been cheating to point out that I could have just connected through my phone.

"You really like being alone like this?" I asked.

"I do."

"Can you at least mail-order spices?"

"Yes, and I do."

"Want me to cook dinner?"

"I was hoping you'd offer."

"I think I'm going to enjoy four days up here just cooking and talking. And maybe some running."

"I'm planning on teaching you how to ride a horse." She tried to look innocent as she said it.

"Not a chance."

My last night in Canada, Kennedy got serious. "Phoebe, you need to move on."

"You sound like Abby."

"Great minds think alike."

"I don't want to move on."

She refilled her wine glass. I refused her offer to refill mine. "This is at least the second time she's done this to you, maybe more depending on what you want to count."

"I can wait."

"Hmm. Maybe you can, but you shouldn't. You're wasting away, just letting life punch you."

"I'm not miserable," I said defensively.

"I think you are. You're just so used to it that it seems normal."

"Now you really do sound like Abby."

She swirled her wine in its glass for a moment. "I remember the first time I saw you."

"You mean about a week before that slumber party?"

"No, no. I don't mean the first time we actually met. I mean the first time I saw you. You probably saw me, but I'm sure you don't remember it."

"When?"

"My parents insisted that I make official visits to five schools, even though I knew I wanted to go to Minnesota as soon as Greg offered me a scholarship. So I made them, but I scheduled it so that I went when the Gophers were playing at that school as often as possible. Mom and Dad stopped fighting it after awhile.

"One of the places I went was Ohio State. After the Friday night game, I was out by the bus, chatting with a couple of the freshmen."

I shivered, realizing where this was going.

"I saw you lurking around but didn't think anything about it until Greg came out and you stepped up to talk to him. I heard the whole conversation."

"Why didn't you ever tell me this?"

She sipped her wine. "I didn't have the courage to mention it to you when we first met, and before I could, someone else told the story, and I watched you react. That convinced me to just stay quiet. No one else realized how much you hate people talking about it."

"Abby did. And I don't hate it as much now—the pain has dulled over the years."

"Still. But I have to bring it up now."

"Why?" I asked.

"Because I remember being so impressed by that person. When I arrived in Minneapolis and saw that you had made the team, I was so happy. You knew what you wanted, you overcame ridiculous obstacles, and you made it."

"I got lucky."

"You also worked hard for it. You moved forward and didn't wait for anything to come to you."

"I'm working hard."

"Yes, but toward what? What are your goals?"

I shrugged. "I don't know. Surviving, I guess."

"Stop just surviving. Stop being passive. Figure out a goal, Phoebe. Or several of them. Then start making it happen."

That conversation rattled around in my head for a long time.

October 2018

It took six months to get the first sign that the marriage was going bad.

"Hi, Bear."

"Hello, Caitlyn," I said, not responding to the endearment.

"What are you up to?"

"Working. That's about it." We still talked on the phone but not as often. I'd also figured out that it meant that Brent wasn't around when we did. "Is something wrong?"

"No. I just wanted to chat." She was lying. Unless something is wrong, Caitlyn speaks in run-on sentences.

"How is Brent?"

"Out."

"Out where?"

"I don't know."

"Caitlyn, seriously, is something wrong?"

"I think he's cheating on me."

The irony of this left me flummoxed. "Are you sure?"

"No."

"Caitlyn, is there anything I can do to help?"

"I don't think so. I'm sorry, I need to go."

She hung up before I could say anything else. I immediately dialed Amy.

"I just had a very weird phone conversation with Caitlyn."

"She called you?"

"Yes. Is there something wrong?"

She sighed. "Nothing that would surprise you. She didn't want anyone to tell you."

"And that doesn't surprise me, given my behavior at the wedding. Well, given that she just went ahead and told me herself, it may be worse."

"I'll see what I can find out. I'll be in touch."

"Please."

The dam started to crack the next June. I picked up an increased sense of urgency from Erika but a disturbing lack of specifics. Then Caitlyn called and asked if she could visit for a few days. I said yes without hesitation.

I met Caitlyn at the airport. From the moment I first spotted her she seemed shrunken. My apprehension only increased when she got close.

"What happened to your face?"

"Nothing," she said indifferently.

I took hold of her chin to get a better look. She tried to pull away, but without much effort. "How'd you get that bruise on your cheek?"

"A high stick."

I looked at her dubiously. "And the one fading around your left eye? Were you in a fight?"

"Yeah."

"With whom?"

"Some rec league player. I don't remember his name."

"Is Brent hitting you?" I asked more out of my own prejudices than from any evidence, but I knew immediately from her reaction that I'd hit the mark. I let go of her chin before I started squeezing as my anger rose.

"Occasionally."

Something twisted inside me. I realized that there was nothing inanimate around that I could break, save for her carry-on. "Caitlyn, we—"

"I just want to go to your place. I'm tired."

I picked up her bag, feeling my fingernails digging into my palms. Wrapping my other arm around her shoulders, I directed her to the train station to get to Palo Alto. When we got home, she fell asleep crying without getting undressed.

Three days later I looked at Caitlyn in total frustration. "How can you be going back?"

"I have to get back to my job. I'm out of vacation time." She wasn't looking me in the eye.

"Okay, fine, but you can't go back to that apartment."

"It's where I live."

"You can't. Not with Brent there."

"It'll be fine." She finally looked up, and I could see tears.

"No, it won't. He'll do it again."

"I don't think so. It'll be okay."

I wanted to scream at her. We'd been having this argument for six hours, after having it for another eight before falling asleep the previous night.

So I finally gave up. It had become clear that the entire point of her visit was to let me see the bruises and figure out what she couldn't speak about. Mission accomplished, she was headed back home.

I pulled a cheap phone out of my pocket. "Here. Take this. All you have to do is hit the speed dial. Mine is the only number programmed in there. I've set my phone for a special ring if you call. You don't need to tell me anything. If you call me on that phone, I'll be on the next flight to Montreal. Any time. No matter what."

She nodded at me. I had no idea what the chances of her actually using it were.

As I watched her dwindle into the concourse, I dialed Kennedy's number.

"Phoebe?" I could hear the anxiety in her voice.

"She left. She's on her way back to Montreal."

"You couldn't stop her." I couldn't tell whether it was a question, a declaration, or a commiseration.

"No, I couldn't."

"You did everything you could."

"So far. This isn't going to progress much farther before I do something else."

"Phoebe . . ." There was a warning in her voice.

"I'm not going to do anything stupid. I promise."

"Just be careful."

"I wish Erika still lived around there."

"Amy will be checking in on her."

"I want to help her with that."

"I know you do. Just . . . you getting involved has the potential to really blow up. In all sorts of ways."

"Abby says I need anger management therapy."

Kennedy laughed. "That's a good way to make sure that some therapist gets his lights punched out."

I laughed with her. "We probably shouldn't joke about that."

"Right now, it constitutes stress relief. I'm sure that if it reaches a point where your presence will help, someone will let you know."

"Okay. I give. I just wish she hadn't gone back."

"You and me both. She doesn't want your help yet."

"At least she let me know. That's something."

"It is. Now you have to wait."

"And hope."

"And that, too."

October 2019

Four months to the day after Caitlyn got on that plane my phone rang. "Phoebe, please come help me."

I didn't bother to ask why she hadn't used the phone I gave her.

I rented an SUV at the Montreal airport and drove to her place. I had a hard time finding a place to park it, Montreal not having been designed with large vehicles in mind, but I managed.

Someone was leaving the building as I walked up, and he politely held the door open, thus eliminating any need to call up. So I got to the door and banged on it.

Caitlyn opened it. "Phoebe." There were fresh bruises on her face.

"Get your keys and your purse. Where is he?"

"He's at work. Come in."

"No. We're leaving. I'm going to put you in a hotel and then come back for your stuff."

"But—"

"No arguing. You're done here." She nodded meekly. I didn't like that, but it made it easier. I stepped in long enough to see her pick up her purse, then took her by the elbow. "Come on."

She was silent as I took her to a Holiday Inn on the edge of the city. It took some talking to get her to give me her keys.

"Just stay here in the room." I told her. "I'll be back with your things, and then we can figure out how we're getting to California. Got it?"

She nodded. "Thank you, Phoebe."

"Where do you keep your passport?"

"It's in the center drawer of my desk."

After making sure I knew where to find the desk, I hugged her tightly and left.

When I unlocked the door to the apartment, Brent was standing there. "Where is she?"

"She's leaving. Now get out of my way."

"You can't just come in here."

"Sure I can." I started to brush past him. "Just watch me."

He grabbed my arm. "I said stay out."

I wrenched my arm free and used it to pin him against the wall. I wasn't any larger than he was, but he didn't fight back much.

"Stay out of my way. I'm just getting her things, and then I'm gone. If you touch me, or anything of Caitlyn's, I'll pound you into hamburger. Got it?"

He tried to push me off. "I won't let you—"

"You're going to let me do anything I want."

He awkwardly struck out at me and landed a glancing blow on my other arm. I punched him once in the gut. He tried to double over, but my arm across his chest kept him upright.

"Give it up, Brent." I put my face close to his. "You may be stronger than I am, but I'm a whole lot meaner than you are. Understand?"

"Let me go." He was still trying to catch his wind, so it didn't take much to keep him pinned.

"Not until I'm sure that you're not going to interfere."

"I'll call the police."

"You're not comprehending the situation, Brent. Once I let you go, feel free to do that. For the moment, all I'm trying to do is to get you to stay out of my way."

"Or what?"

I almost laughed at him. "You seem to think the difference between us is that I don't enjoy hurting people, but you're wrong. I really do enjoy hurting people. The difference is that, thanks in large part to Caitlyn, I've learned to control my impulses. I have no idea how you ended up as a bully, but I got here by being worked over by real experts.

"I'm going to let you go. I'm going to start carrying Caitlyn's things out to my car. I'll keep coming in until I have all of them packed. Then I'm going to drive off, and if you're lucky, you won't ever see either of us again. By the way, anything that I decide is Caitlyn's is hers.

"If you touch me, the car, or anything that belongs to her, I will beat you. It's been a long time since I got to indulge this little pleasure, so I don't know exactly where I'll stop if I get started, so the risks of testing me are very high. It might be best if you just sit on the couch and watch me. It's too big for me to take, so I guess you get to keep that.

"Do you understand me?"

He mumbled something that sounded affirmative, so I let him go. The first thing I did was get Caitlyn's passport and put it in my pocket. It was right where she said it was.

Unfortunately, Brent didn't try to interfere.

The next day I belatedly called Amy. "Phoebe?"

"I'm sorry I forgot to call yesterday. I just listened to all of your voice mails. I had my phone turned off so I could just focus on Caitlyn."

"Are you okay?"

"I'm fine. So is she. She's sleeping at the moment."

"Good. Where are you?"

"At a Ramada outside of New York. I decided to just drive us to San Francisco rather than trying to get on an airplane."

"Is that a good idea?"

"I don't have the foggiest notion. Caitlyn seemed to like it, though, so that helped me make the final call." I looked over at her and smiled.

"Where did you bury the body?"

"Oh, ye of little faith. I barely touched him."

"I'm pleased."

"I'm not. I was really disappointed that he didn't give me enough reason to take him apart. But he folded."

"Good. I didn't want to have to bail you out of jail."

"Your kind thoughts are appreciated."

"What are your plans?" she asked me.

"Jesus, I'm supposed to think ahead? Once we get home, I'll make sure some doctors look her over. Hopefully she'll get some therapy and not hate it like I did. Beyond that, I really don't know. I'm sure Abby will offer me plenty of advice, and she'll probably even know what she's talking about."

"Will you listen to her for once?"

"I'm wounded," I answered. "I take Abby's advice all the time, except when she's wrong."

"Oddly, that's not how she describes it."

"I can't help it if she's wrong a lot."

"Mostly she claims that it takes you forever to arrive at the right conclusion."

"You know, I think I'd rather join Caitlyn in bed than discuss my family."

"You should probably do that. I'd tell you to take care of her, but that seems unnecessary."

CHAPTER 23

Once the doctors let me put skates on, I was able to participate fully in practices. Since I wasn't going to play, I tried to make myself useful teaching things. My pet project was turning Sveta into a proper power forward. She far outstripped my skills in transition and playmaking, but there comes a point where you have to discard all of that and just get your nose dirty and push people around.

She had the size for it, certainly, though not necessarily the inclination. "No, no. Don't let me tie up your stick," I told her one evening when we were working by ourselves. "I haven't been a defenseman for two years, so it shouldn't be this easy for me."

"You are too strong for me."

"Not with this shoulder I'm not. You just aren't trying very hard."

"Am trying."

I stood up straight and looked at her. "Okay. You've been out of sorts ever since you got back from Sochi. Do you want to tell me about it?"

"Is complicated."

"Do you want to go sit somewhere and tell me about it?"

She thought about it for a moment and nodded.

We ended up at the same McDonald's where I'd told all of my stories to Abby. I got what I always got. "So what's bothering you?"

She'd at least pulled herself together enough that her grammar was better. "I am worried about when I graduate."

"So am I, but you've at least got three years to figure it out."

     J. Michael Neal

"You do not have to worry about going home."

"Going home? You mean back to Russia?"

"*Da.*"

"I thought you loved Russia."

"I do," she said, "but not always. Right now I don't feel very welcome."

A bunch of pieces suddenly fell into place. "You're gay."

She looked startled. "You know?"

"Not until just now."

"I don't want people to know."

"They won't hear it from me," I assured her.

"Thank you." She ate a few fries in silence. "Do you know why I came to Minnesota?"

"Not really. I know you had scholarship offers from all over the place, but you've been vague about why you picked this one."

"Because of you."

That was not what I had expected. "Me?"

"You and Caitlyn."

"How did you hear about us?"

"Someone at another school told me. I think trying to say something bad about Minnesota, that it's where *those* people go, and I said to myself, 'That's where I want to be.'"

"You haven't told anyone else that?"

"No."

"Just as well. The feelings about it are kind of all over the place."

"I figured that out."

"Thank you for trusting me enough to tell me," I said, trying to channel Abby. "If you want to talk about things, I'm always available. My only advice is not to bring it up with Caitlyn. She's not gay, and while she doesn't mind people knowing about us, she gets kind of defensive talking about the whole thing."

"She's not gay?"

"I'm not even going to try to explain it. It's a complicated mess."

"If you say so."

We packed up to leave. "Now that you've told me what's bothering you, I expect you to work extra hard tomorrow, okay?"

"*Da.*"

We made the field for the NCAA tournament. Barely. It took an upset win over Michigan in the conference semifinals to pull us over the line. I made the trip to Boston with the team for our quarterfinal against Harvard. It was a hectic trip, flying in the night before with a game at two thirty the next afternoon, but I managed to get out to grab a snack and coffee with Abby.

"So how's Harvard?" I asked. I knew what she really wanted to discuss, but I wanted to get a few other things in first.

"Pretty good. It's a lot different than undergrad was." She was bouncing with impatience to tell me what she thought about Caitlyn but managed to play along.

"I'd hope so, given what they're charging you."

"It's a good thing I've got a TA fellowship."

I took a deep breath and bit the bullet. "I know what you want to talk about, but I have something else first. It will probably affect how that next conversation goes."

She sat up and stared at me. "Okay, what?"

The words I'd rehearsed came tumbling out too fast for me to stop them. "I know you made your feelings about this clear, but I've been spending a lot of time at your parents' place, and they said that it's okay if I come and go like I was a member of the family."

I stopped and watched her digest that before continuing. "I tried to say no but then—"

"Stop," she said sharply. I complied nervously. "I'm not angry."

"I didn't want to—"

"Stop. It's my turn to say stop and listen to everything I have to say before you ask questions." She reached across the table and took my hands in hers. "Relax. I'm not mad, and I don't think you'll hate this too much."

She smiled when my hands clenched hers tightly. "I've thought about this a lot over the last year. I'm sorry I brushed you off the way I did. I let the fact that I was angry about other things get in the way of listening to you. You opened up the way I'd always asked you to, and I slapped you down."

I really wanted to say something but remembered the rules just in time.

"I'm still not sure how I feel about this. I said it badly when I told you I wanted a friend and not a sister, but I wasn't lying. But I'm not going to fight about it, either with you or with them. And you'll be happy to know that it's all three of them. I tried talking to Derek about how I feel, and all he could do was gush about you."

She fell silent, and I waited for her to continue. When she didn't, I pulled my hands back into my lap. "That sounds grudging."

"Yeah, I suppose it is," she said with a sigh. "I'll get there, I think. I'm just not ready yet."

"Then I'm going to go cool on spending time at your parents."

"You don't have to do that," she said quickly.

"I'm sure you mean that, but I don't want to put any pressure on you over this. It's too important to me that you—"

"You're putting pressure on me just having this conversation," she snapped.

"I'll do whatever it is you want me to do. Just tell me."

"No. Make up your own mind, and do what you want. Your decisions are not my problem."

"Okay," I said uneasily. "I'm sorry I brought it up."

She pinched the bridge of her nose. "Don't be sorry. We needed to say all of that. Now what is going on with Caitlyn?"

"I don't really want to talk about it."

"You can't seriously be—"

"I said I don't want to talk about it," I said more firmly. "I don't know where we stand. That's why I asked that question. I'm not sure what I'm comfortable saying."

"And you do know where you stand with her?"

I wanted to say yes and be done with it, but I failed. "Sort of. At least in the short term."

"What the hell does that mean?"

"It means that at least for the next year she's helping me make decisions."

She glared at me.

"Okay, I'm sorry I said that. Look, it's complicated, but she isn't promising anything. The short answer is that I'll make it to graduation, and then we'll see what happens, and that's where we reach the boundary of what I don't really want to talk about."

"Oh, come on. Friends can offer advice. They tell each other things."

"Sometimes. And sometimes they don't. Can I be really blunt here, Abby?"

"Sure. Why not?"

"The way you demand information seems a lot more like what a family member would do than a friend."

"I'm like this with everyone. You know that."

"No, you aren't. You want to be, but you push a lot farther with me. I've watched you."

She started to say something and stopped. "Okay. You're right. This isn't a good time to talk about this."

"I'm sorry."

"Don't be. Last night, I promised myself that no matter how the conversation went, we were going to leave here happy with each other. I'm going to make sure that happens, and so we're going to drop that line of conversation altogether."

"You don't get to decide that all by yourself."

"Yes, I do," she said, smiling for the first time in a half hour. "I'm older, so I get to decide things like that."

"Wait. What?"

"I'm going to think about what you asked me. Really think about it. And when I have an answer, then I'm going to ask you about Caitlyn."

"Abby, you're giving me whiplash."

"I know. I'm sorry." She stood up. "I really do need to get some studying done, but thank you for coming."

I pushed my chair back and stood next to her. "I'm confused."

She reached up and put her hands on my shoulders. "We all are. But I think I'm less confused than I was an hour ago."

"That's good."

"May I hug you?"

That startled me. "Of course."

"Good." As she did so, she whispered in my ear, "I'm not sure exactly what this means, but I will always be here for you."

We lost 5–1 to Harvard to end our season and then flew home. The next day Kennedy, Heck, Traci, and Morgan all cleaned out their lockers. Once there had been seven. Then there were three.

All of us, including Caitlyn and Jenny, went out afterward. This was the worst part of every season. It was worse than game losses, even one that crushing.

We wouldn't really say good-bye for a couple of months. Kennedy was staying at the U to become a doctor of veterinary medicine, and Morgan got a job with a bank downtown. So it was only Traci and Amy who would really be leaving town.

It felt like the end, though. No more practices. If they watched the games, it would be from the stands. Amy had hopes of making one of the CWHL teams, but for the others it was time to transition to a post-hockey lifestyle.

It was the first time in my life I can say that I actually got drunk. I decided not to repeat it much. I started talking about things that only Caitlyn, Abby, and Kennedy had known.

I knew that the next year it was going to be me packing everything up.

CHAPTER 24

Seething, I followed Dennis down the hall and into his office. I tried my best to slam the door, but the pneumatic piston defeated my efforts.

"That was some performance," Dennis said as he tried to suppress a smile.

"I wanted to strangle him," I raged.

"No, you didn't. You wanted to punch him."

"Thank you so much for that observation." I paced the eight-foot width of the room.

"You handled it perfectly. Once Doug is done replacing the internal organs you ripped out of him, he'll go back to Monterey and actually do the work we need."

"And start another email chain complaining about what a bitch I am, forwarded to everyone I have to work with except you."

"And the work will get done," he insisted, leaning back with his fingers laced behind his head. "The fact that a woman just cut him off at the knees and handed his head back to him will motivate him."

"You're mixing your metaphors. And I don't like those scenes."

"Maybe not, but you're very good at them. I've enjoyed watching you get better at motivating people over the last year. For someone who claims to be socially inept, you're impressive."

"I think of it more as the wearing away of the thin veneer of my civilized behavior," I said. My motions started to calm down. "If I wanted to spend time dealing with idiots who behave like fourteen-year-olds, I'd go coach a hockey team of actual fourteen-year-olds."

"Look, I agree that Doug is an asshole. He's unreliable, and he's staying a contractor because I don't want him here permanently. But he's also a fucking genius who can solve the problem with the valves. Hence, I need you to ream him out periodically so that he actually solves it."

"I don't like being the bad guy," I said.

"Don't worry—I've got your back."

"That's not what bothers me."

"Well, just take a deep breath, because I have a favor to ask you."

"Why, yes," I said, "I would be happy to speak at a roast in your honor."

"That's actually closer than you realize."

"Uh oh."

"This one is kind of delicate, and I'm still trying to come up with a way to phrase it that you don't take wrong."

"Out with it. This is getting embarrassing."

"I'm trying to figure out a way to ask if you'll be my best man."

My heart sank. "You're kidding."

"No. I figured out that, of all of the people I know, you're the one I like the best."

"Have you discussed this with Jane?" I asked him.

"Briefly. She seemed noncommittal."

I sighed. "Being noncommittal means she doesn't like the idea but won't tell you."

"Are you sure?"

"Yes, Dennis, I'm sure."

"How?"

"Because Jane doesn't like me. She does a very good job of hiding it from you but less so from me."

"Does she feel threatened by you?"

"Probably." I shrugged. "Telling her about the time I made an inept, drunken pass at you wasn't your smartest move."

"So you don't like her?"

"I didn't say that. I said she doesn't like me. I think she's fine, though her hostility makes it hard for me to feel all warm and fuzzy toward her."

"I'm sorry." He scrunched his face up the way he does when he feels embarrassed.

"Don't be. Jane will be great for you, I'll keep working for you, and she and I will get along enough for it not to be a problem."

"Wonderful."

"So I'm going to do you a favor and decline your invitation to be a part of your wedding party."

May 2020

"I'm proud of you, Caitlyn." I hugged her from behind as I said it.

"I hope so. You nagged me enough to get it done."

She sealed the envelope containing her divorce filing. She had taken several weeks to fill it out, but she hadn't ever wavered in her intention, and that was the only thing I cared about.

"You're doing better."

"I think so," she agreed. There was an underlying sadness that was new, but she was much perkier and active than she had been when we first got back. She worked out regularly and had even applied for a US work visa.

"What do you want to do this evening?" I asked.

"In celebration?"

"We'll call it anything you want."

"We haven't danced together in a long time. Can we do that?"

The last time she'd asked me, I'd been drunk and angry, and I'd turned her down. "We'll do anything you want."

"Do you want to?"

"Yes. Yes, I do. You won't have to pester me to do it."

I brought Caitlyn home with me for Christmas that year. Mom and Dad had moved into a smaller house, so Derek stayed with them, but the couples had rooms at a hotel. So rather than a comfortable living room, Abby and I stayed up talking at one of the plastic tables in the lobby.

"I'm glad all of us are together this year," I said over a mug of coffee. Tech culture had won out over my athletic instinct to avoid caffeine.

"You realize it isn't going to last, right?"

"I know that."

"You sound resigned."

"I am. It's going to be hard, but I'm going to kick her out. I don't want her staying with me because she's scared."

"Isn't that why you stay with her?" Abby insisted on pointing out.

"Of course." It cost me nothing to admit that. "But I don't want it happening to her. I'm going to do my best to make sure that the shell never hardens."

"Good."

"I haven't even gotten to the part you'll really like."

"Oh?"

"This trip is the last hurrah. Once she leaves, we're done as a couple."

Her cup stopped halfway to her mouth. "You're serious?"

I nodded, feeling miserable about it.

She took a deep breath. "Have you told her?"

"Not yet."

"I'm sorry."

"It's going to be the hardest thing I've ever done."

"I'm sure it will be. It's also the right decision."

"Don't worry," I said bitterly. "I'm sure you'll have other chances to criticize."

She stared at me for a moment before deciding to treat it as an attempted joke. "I'm not sure why I bother."

I appreciated the effort. "You do it because you love me. And there's that smug sense of superiority that comes from telling me I'm being an idiot."

"Yes, and I wish you would just let me enjoy it."

"So how is your life going?"

"Pretty well, except that I hardly see Scott at all."

"Too busy?"

"Both of us. He still seems to think that if he can just get promoted high enough, he'll start to like his job."

"I take it you disagree."

"If he could just do numerical analysis and never have to deal with the people, he'd love it, but there are too many assholes in finance for him to really enjoy it."

"I mean, look at who from our team went into it."

Abby sighed. "I want to defend her. I just can't."

"It's okay. We all have weaknesses for members of our class."

She narrowed her eyes a bit at that. "I wish he would quit his job and find something else that he wants to do, but I'm not having any luck convincing him of that."

"You need to work on your powers of persuasion. Derek doesn't do what you tell him to, either."

"Someday they'll make me dictator, and then all of you will have to listen to me."

"Abby, we all listen to you now. It's too much fun not to."

"It is a terrible cross that I bear."

"You're a regular Cassandra. It must be tough."

"You have no idea."

Two weeks into the New Year, I finally called a meeting of the two of us in the living room.

"Kitten, are you going to keep playing hockey? I mean seriously, with the goal of making the Olympics again?"

"Of course. Why wouldn't I?"

"Then you can't stay here." I almost bit my tongue saying it. "The people you can play against here just aren't good enough. You'll never make it."

She nodded and replied in a small voice. "You're right. I've been thinking that."

"There's more to it than that, though. I need to get off this roller coaster. If you leave now, no matter how good the reasons, then our relationship needs to change. We need to just be friends. We need to see if we can make that work, because this isn't working."

She looked as if I'd hit her. "Why? I mean, I know I'm not always here, and I've done some awful things, but we're past that."

"I'm sorry. I just can't go back to worrying about whether we're still a couple or whether you're going to find someone else. We've always said that you need the stability of knowing that I'm waiting for you, but I can't provide that any more. I need emotional stability of my own, and I can't have it if you're two thousand miles away getting into trouble."

"I promise I won't."

I shook my head. "I know you mean that, but I don't trust you to remember it. I'm sorry. I just can't."

"I guess I deserve that."

"No, Kitten. No, you don't. This isn't about deserving. It's about what we've been doing being unhealthy. We can stay together and really work on it, or we can split up and see if we can just be friends. We can work on that long distance."

Trying not to cry and failing, she asked, "May I have a couple of days to think about it?"

"Of course. And right now, I want a hug."

We embraced for several minutes, just swaying, before I said, "There's one more thing."

"What?" she asked in a voice muffled by my shirt.

"You're going to laugh at me."

"Not right now, I'm not. I couldn't laugh about anything."

"I did something really stupid the first time we had sex. After you fell asleep, I tied our wrists together with magical, imaginary rope. I did it to make sure you wouldn't ever really leave me."

She looked up at me. "Bear, that's ridiculous."

I felt miserable. "It sounds that way when I say it out loud, but I'm afraid. I'm afraid that it's screwed up every decision we've made since then. That you've wanted to leave but couldn't. Or that it perverted my desire for you to stay. Or something. I don't know. I just think I did something very wrong."

She brushed ineffectually at the tears on my cheeks. "It's okay."

"I need to know that you are making this decision freely. I need to cut the ropes off."

She nodded. "All right. What do you need me to do?"

"Just stand there. They're imaginary, magical ropes, so an imaginary, invisible knife should do the trick, right?"

"Yes, it will," she told me.

I stepped back, and she held her arms out, as if they were tied together. "Thank you for not laughing at me," I said as I drew the knife between her wrists and then over my own.

"You think it's important, Bear, and that's enough for me."

I opened my hands and let all of the nothing drop to the floor. "There. You're free."

"Thank you," she said, hugging me again.

Six days later we said good-bye. It was the first time I'd ever cried while taking her to the airport.

"I'm sorry," she whispered as we stood before the security gate. And she was. I knew that.

I smiled wanly. "It's okay. I'll be okay." I suddenly realized that these occasions were the only scenes in which I ever thought of her standing still.

"I'm going to make it this time. I'm not going to fuck it all up again."

I let my skepticism go unexpressed and just held onto her.

"I mean it," she insisted.

"I know you won't," I said, swallowing my doubts. "You're going to rock the world, Caitlyn."

"Damn straight." She stepped back, giving me a sloppy grin. I let her go.

Caitlyn reached into her pocket and pulled out the gold medal she'd won at the previous year's world championships. "Here. I want you to have this."

I looked at it. "I couldn't. It's yours."

"Phoebe, please. We're a team. I wouldn't have it without you."

I gingerly took hold of the ribbon it hung from. I'd never touched one of her medals. Maybe it was some form of superstition about not touching what you haven't won yourself. It was heavier than I'd imagined. I let it hang there for a moment before saying anything. "Thank you."

"Put it somewhere your coworkers can see it."

"I'll call if I need you, Kitten. And even if I don't."

"You do that." She gave me a quick hug. "I love you, Bear."

CHAPTER 25

June 2014

Caitlyn managed to talk me into a trip to Vancouver that June. It's an astonishingly beautiful city. I have nothing bad to say about Vancouver itself, but it's a terrible place to visit if you're dating Caitlyn Morris.

At lunch the first day with Caitlyn and her mom, I looked down at the plate of food and then up at Caitlyn. She offered a sheepish smile. Returning my gaze to the plate I regarded the watery quiche and the bright red lump of gelatin. I wondered if there was any way I could volunteer to cook dinner.

Ms. Morris launched into a disquisition about how since getting to know me she had become active in the movement to reform foster care in British Columbia. I told Caitlyn later that this movement benefited from her not actually taking in a foster child. I wasn't sure she thought that was funny.

I was hard pressed to think of subjects I wanted to talk about less than the foster care system. The only one I could think of right then was Caitlyn's and my relationship, which is what came up next, albeit obliquely. "So you're planning to go to graduate school next year?"

"Yes. A master's in computer science."

"Where?"

"I've got about four or five places I'm hoping to get accepted into. Stanford. Cal Tech. MIT. A couple of others. My grades are good enough that I should have my pick of at least a couple of them."

"You must be looking forward to meeting new people."

"Not really. The thought terrifies me, actually."

"Nonsense. You're a sensible girl. You should be able to meet lots of nice people."

Caitlyn opted not to meet my gaze. "I suppose."

"I know people in the arts community near all of those places. I can let them know that you're coming."

"You don't need to do that, Ms. Morris."

"Call me Anne. I'm happy to help a friend of Caitlyn's any way I can."

I was hungry enough that eating the quiche wasn't too difficult. I avoided the gelatin. "Well, thank you. I need all the help I can get."

"Would you like some more quiche?"

"Yes, please." Well, I *was* hungry.

"Caitlyn?"

"Sure."

She took our plates to the kitchen.

"Sorry," Caitlyn murmured.

"For what?"

"I'll tell you later."

Her mother returned with full plates. After setting them down, she commenced complaining about IT people she had to interact with. I mostly nodded and offered pro forma defenses where they seemed to be expected. I really just wanted the meal to be over so we could head somewhere without her. It took me about twenty minutes to get my wish.

"What was that earlier?" I asked as we wandered the streets eating ice cream.

"That whole business about helping you meet other people. She means so that you'll date them instead of me."

"I've missed something."

"What you've missed is two years of nagging me about finding some boy to date and getting over my 'experimental' phase."

"Now I'm confused," I said around a mouthful of mint chocolate chip.

"About what?"

"Several things. Wasn't she hinting that San Francisco is the perfect place for me because there are a lot of gay people?"

Caitlyn barked laughter. "Of course she was. She's very, very tolerant as long as it doesn't involve *her* daughter being gay. And before you ask your next question, I refuse to discuss my own sexuality with her even if that would clear up her anxieties."

"Where does that leave me?"

"It leaves you with me being sorry that you're stuck in the middle of my issues with my mother."

It also left me with lots of questions I avoided asking and a new way to fear that Caitlyn resented our relationship.

Every so often Caitlyn made an attempt to appreciate the music I listen to. It never lasted more than two days.

"How do you listen to this stuff?" she said as she took off her earphones.

I shrugged. "Aesthetics isn't a subfield of philosophy I'm really interested in. Ask me about epistemology or metaphysics."

"I'm serious."

"So am I. It's a question I don't know how to answer. I told you once why I started listening to it. I can tell you about the music, though I can't get too technical. But I can't really tell you why I like it."

She was lying on her stomach on the floor and propping her chin in her hands so she could look up at the couch where I was sitting. "I don't believe you. I can tell you why you like it."

"Oh, really?"

"You like the beat. I'm pretty sure that's the only part you really focus on. It's why you keep saying things like, 'Melody is overrated.' Everything else is just a distraction to you."

"Sort of," I admitted. "A good bass line helps, too."

"What I really want to figure out is why you dislike melody so much."

For whatever reason, I decided to take the question seriously. "Melody is easy."

"From anyone else that wouldn't be much of an answer," she responded, "but I think you mean that."

"Not really. It was just what popped into my head." I shifted so my feet were underneath me. "A better answer, I think, is that I want to lose myself in the experience when I listen to music. It's like meditation. Melody is a distraction to that. It's easier just to lose myself in the rhythm."

"You didn't start meditating until long after you were listening to this sort of music. Why did you like it before then?"

"I was doing the same thing. I just didn't realize what it was."

"I think you like it because it was something you wouldn't have to share, because there was no one else you would ever meet who liked it, too."

I laughed. "Probably. If so, it worked. There weren't a lot of industrial music fans in Vicksburg."

"I was the other way. I just wanted to fit in so I liked the same silly love songs everyone else did."

I grimaced. "Those aren't love songs."

"What do you mean? That's all they're about."

"No." I shook my head. "They're about something else. Passion, maybe. Or just silly. They make love sound easy. It's not. Love is hard."

"I'm not sure I like where this is going," Caitlyn said evenly.

I pushed on. "Love isn't the fun stuff. Love is about having a bad day and knowing that you can go home and if the other person has had a good day, that will make your day better. And it's knowing, when you've had a good day, that it's your responsibility to make your partner feel better."

"All right," she replied. "I can buy that, but I'm not sure how that refutes anything I said."

"A love song needs to explain that you need someone so badly that you can't imagine giving them up, even on those days when they're really annoying or when they're doing something destructive."

Caitlyn looked at me for a moment then levered herself to her feet. She took two steps and sat down in my lap, facing me. "Did I do something recently to prompt that, or is it just a general observation?"

I closed my eyes. "I'm sorry. I didn't consciously mean for it to be about us at all, though I'm sure that's what I meant on some level."

"Don't apologize."

"I'm applying to the University of Toronto."

I felt her jerk and heard an intake of breath. "That came out of left field."

My heart sank. "They have a good CSci program, and I figure you'll want to be up there in order to keep playing at a high level."

I opened my eyes and caught her gaze before she dropped her face to my shoulder. "I already gave away my reaction, didn't I?"

"Uh huh."

"I want to say something trite. That I'm not ready for the hard part of love."

I just sat there.

"It's true. I'm not."

"There doesn't have to be a big commitment," I said, struggling on. "It can be like it is now."

She drew a deep breath. "Phoebe, I need to be on my own. I don't know how to explain it. I need to make something of myself."

"I'm never going to understand this, am I?"

I heard a strangled laugh. "Shit, I don't understand it."

"You're not gay." I said it matter-of-factly.

"That's not it."

"Yes, it is."

"Maybe. Sort of. I don't know. I really don't know."

"It's okay." I reached up to stroke her hair. "I understand."

"Are you trying to make me feel guilty, or am I just doing it to myself?"

I didn't answer that question. I held onto her instead.

"This year's assistant captains will be Crosser and Kat," Coach Long said from the middle of our locker room. "The captains are Jenny and Phoebe."

I sat there, stunned.

Everyone clapped me on the shoulder as they filed out. It wasn't a mandatory meeting, but no one would have missed it, so there was plenty of congratulating.

I finally dragged myself to my feet and went up to him. "I'm not sure I'm ready for this."

"I disagree, and I'm the coach. You'll do fine."

"If you say so, but I'm not even sure what I'm supposed to do."

"Everyone has a different leadership style. You'll figure yours out."

I mumbled something on my way out the door.

The last weekend of September I got a call from Amy Heckenthorpe. "How's life as a junior marketing executive?" I asked her.

"Crazy. It makes juggling hockey and school look like a vacation. I'm starting to wish I'd dislocated a shoulder in order to put it off for a year. How are you?"

"I'm all right. I'm excited for this season. I can't say I'm that unhappy that you aren't here, since that would all but eliminate my playing time."

"Do you ever plan to stop pretending that you're just a fringe player with no ability?" she asked. This was a long-standing disagreement between myself and my teammates. They liked propping up my self-image.

"No, but I'm not really interested in getting into that argument right now."

"Fine, but you're on the second line of the number two team in the country for a reason."

"Be that as it may," I replied, trying again to dispatch the subject.

"How's Caitlyn's mood?" she asked.

"The usual. She's bouncy-bouncy most of the time. As long as I keep my fears hidden, her down periods aren't too frequent or too bad."

"You shouldn't have to do that."

"Actually, it's good for me, too. I'm really trying to live in the present and not worry about next spring. There isn't much I can do about it. I've made all the preparations I can, and barring a change of heart on her part, we'll be going our separate ways. So I'm just trying to enjoy the season. After that, what happens happens, and I'd rather deal with a breakdown then than now."

"I'm sorry."

"You don't have to take responsibility for her just because you're both Canadian."

"I know. It's just that talking to her gets so frustrating. She has no idea what she wants, and I just want to throttle her when she comes up with yet another stupid idea."

"We're twenty-two years old. Aren't we supposed to still come up with lots of stupid ideas?"

"I suppose. Unless you're Kennedy. But you should try to listen to your friends when they tell you that they're stupid ideas."

"Uh huh. Remember when we all told you that Alan was a stupid idea?"

"Hey, I was only twenty," Amy objected. "Besides, if that didn't provide enough evidence that you should listen to your friends, what will?"

"Getting burned herself. Besides, Caitlyn has some serious ongoing issues. I don't know if she talks much about her parents with you."

"Not really, no. What's happening?"

"They're fighting over custody of her brother again."

"Isn't he an adult now?"

"Yeah." I sighed. "So it's not a legal battle, really. But he can't take care of himself, and they're fighting over who should be in charge of his therapy. The answer ought to be neither of them, but that doesn't seem to be an option anyone is considering."

"Ugh."

"And her mother keeps suggesting, in tremendously unsubtle attempts to be subtle, that Caitlyn really needs to find a nice boy to settle down with. Emphasis on gender."

"Still?" Amy sounded exasperated. "When is anyone in that family going to come to terms with Caitlyn's sexuality?"

"How's that?"

"She's gay. They need to just accept that."

"I don't think she is."

"Then she's bi."

"No, she isn't bi, either."

There was a long pause. "Phoebe, what the hell are you taking about?"

"I'm pretty sure Caitlyn is straight."

"Um, I'm not even sure how to respond to that."

"Well, if anyone would know, it'd be me, right?"

"I think you need to reexamine the evidence."

"I'm confident about it," I insisted. "Trust me."

"I'm going to remain skeptical. On the whole, though, I must say that you're taking it all pretty well, considering how idiotic she's being."

"Thanks. I'm pretty sure that I'm going to have a complete breakdown next May, but I'll worry about it then."

"That sounds like a plan. I'll help however I can when the time comes. She'll come to her senses eventually. I just hope she doesn't wait until it's too late."

"I'm going to give her all the time she needs. There won't be any 'too late.'"

"Be careful, Phoebe. Take care of yourself first."

"I will." I said it because it was the only way to avoid a lecture on the subject, and I got that enough from Abby. "I do have a different question for you, though. What am I supposed to do as captain?"

She laughed. "I was wondering when you'd ask me that. I called Kathy Zimmermann in July last year asking the same thing. Set the tone you want. Do everything for the team, and they'll follow. They already know you'd run through a wall for them. It won't be as hard as you think."

CHAPTER 26

May 2020

One casualty of Caitlyn's marriage was whatever was left of her relationship with her mother. Anne shared all of her feelings about Brent before Caitlyn agreed with them, and her presentation was worse than her timing. I listened to Caitlyn's end of one telephone screaming match and was filled in on others. They hadn't spoken to each other since the wedding. Her divorce hadn't changed that.

In an uncharacteristic fit of diplomacy, I set aside my own resentments and became the tenuous link between them, albeit without Caitlyn's knowledge. Every three months or so I called her mother to give her an update.

"Phoebe, it's good to hear from you." I could make out the worry in her voice. "How's Caitlyn?"

"She's fine. I talked to her a couple of days ago. She's still living in Chicago."

"Is she in any trouble?"

"Not that she told me about, and she didn't sound like she was trying to hide anything."

"Are you sure?"

"No, but that's my best guess."

"I wish she'd talk to me."

I did too, if only so I didn't feel compelled to do so behind Caitlyn's back. "Give it time."

"Is there anything else you can tell me?" She sounded desperate.

"I'm sorry."

"Are you sure?"

"She'd be angry if she knew I was calling you at all," I told her for the umpteenth time.

There was a moment's silence. "Thank you for the call. I hope she settles down with you soon."

Her timing hadn't improved any.

"So what do you think of the paintings?"

I shrugged. "I don't understand them well enough to have much of an opinion one way or the other."

"That's an interesting way to phrase it. Most people blame the art if they don't understand it."

I ate one of the little snacks being carried around by waiters before answering. "I had a friend who was really into art. I haven't seen him in almost a decade, so what little I once knew about it is long gone, and I just don't have enough interest to bother trying to figure it out myself."

"So why are you here?"

"I know a friend of the artist, and that person is convinced that my life depends on her helping me get out more and meet people. So she talked someone into sending me an invitation. I decided I was bored enough to use it."

The woman laughed. "That's refreshingly honest."

"People say that until they get to know me. Then they stop adding the 'refreshingly' part."

She laughed again. "So who is it that you know?"

"A woman named Anne Morris."

"Really?"

"You've heard of her?"

"I know some of her work. What do you think of it?"

"I never paid the slightest bit of attention to it."

"How do you know her then?"

"I played hockey with her daughter."

"You do look like an athlete." She held out her hand. "Hi. I'm Wendy McCall."

"Phoebe Rose. What brings you here?"

"Interest. I've been trying to get into one of Stein's shows for months."

"I suppose you resent it when people who don't care at all get invitations to events like this."

"Only until I find someone who isn't pretentious about it and doesn't realize when she's name-dropping."

"Is Anne Morris that important?"

"She thinks she is. There are others who agree."

I snorted. "Yeah, that sounds like her."

"Not a fan?"

"I love Caitlyn. Anne just irritates me."

"So what do you do, Phoebe Rose?"

"I program robots to talk to each other."

"Mmmm. Not very artsy."

"I'm not an artsy person."

"Would you like to go get some coffee?"

"I thought you were interested in the paintings."

"I looked at them. They aren't as interesting as I thought they would be."

"And I am?"

"That's what I intend to find out."

August 2020

"Okay, Dennis," I said after we'd placed our orders. "What's up?"

He tried to look innocent. "Why does something have to be up? Maybe I just wanted to have dinner with you."

"When you do, we have lunch at a burger joint. The last time you invited me to a fancy dinner at Carter's it was to celebrate me finally breaking down and agreeing to work for you full-time. That was two years ago. So what is it this time?"

"We're celebrating the fact that I'm giving you a promotion."

My water glass stopped halfway to my mouth. "What?"

"You're the new executive vice president for special projects."

"Oh no," I protested. "I have to accept the position before you get to celebrate."

"Of course you'll accept it. I need you to accept it."

"What's in it for me? More useless stock options?"

"No, no," he insisted. "This comes with a big salary increase. A new office. Increased power within the company. And a lot of stock options that I swear to you will be worth a lot of money someday."

"None of which are things I need. I don't spend the money I have, and the only power I want within the company is the ability to make people leave me alone so I can program."

His face went serious. "I mean it, Phoebe. I need you. The venture capital guys are crawling all over everything, and I only get to name one senior person in the whole place. That means that that one person has to be someone I trust completely, who will tell me the things I need to know." He was jabbing at me with a dinner roll.

"Oh, c'mon," I said, grabbing the roll. "Executive vice whatevers need to have people skills that I lack. And what the hell are special projects?"

"They're whatever I say they are. That's the point. You'll be able to poke your nose into whatever I need you to."

"You make me sound like a wayward puppy."

He ignored that. "And you have vastly more people skills than you admit to. In particular, you have one that I completely lack. No one is scared of me."

I rolled my eyes. "Oh, great. You want to promote me because I frighten people?"

"One of the reasons, among many, that I want you in this position is because you can scare people when you have to. There are still people who wonder whether you killed Doug Goodwin with your bare hands last year even though they saw him a week ago."

"I don't want to be your hatchet man, Dennis. I just want to be a programmer."

"Please?"

Somehow he managed to talk me into it.

September 2020

The first time we actually slept together, Wendy gasped as she pulled off my shirt. "Ow." Her finger traced the scar down the front of my shoulder. "Hockey?"

"Yeah."

She leaned over and kissed it. Then she held up my left hand. "And I'm finally going to ask what this is."

"You mean my finger?"

She nodded.

"I broke it when I was sixteen."

"My brother broke his finger. It doesn't look like that."

I chuckled. "He probably went to a hospital and had it set rather than not telling anyone and continuing to do whatever it was he was doing when he broke it."

"Why didn't you tell anyone?"

"Because my coach was looking for excuses to pull me from the lineup and I didn't intend to give him any."

"That's nuts. Is that it?"

"That's most of the big stuff."

"Most of? Big stuff?"

"Pretty much."

She looked at me skeptically. "I'm going to see what I can find."

The process started with my hands. She found two other, more subtly, misformed fingers. "I broke that one, too, but it got fixed since I was in college. This one the knuckle dislocated."

Wendy checked out my face but didn't find anything. She found the small scar on my lower abdomen. "That had nothing to do with hockey," I said.

"What is it?"

"Just a surgical scar. I had a small growth. It was benign."

Her search was more fruitful when she got to my legs. "I had that knee scoped for a meniscus tear around the time of my shoulder surgery. It wasn't major, and I'd been putting it off, but as long as I was going to be out for the season, I decided it was time."

She commented on my misshapen ankles and feet. "Nothing

major. Just wear and tear from blocking shots and getting slashed. Bruises only, but there were a lot of them."

"Why did you do it?"

"It's the price of playing the game."

"There are hobbies that don't do this to you."

"None of them are hockey."

"It's that important to you?"

"It was."

"Why?"

"I couldn't tell you why it was initially. I just wanted to play as long as I can remember."

"Was it worth it?" she asked dubiously.

"Yes. It's not even close. If the same thing had happened to my other shoulder, too, I'd still say that."

"How can it possibly be worth that much pain?"

"It kept me kind of sane through high school. And thanks to hockey, I have thirty-eight of the closest friends you can imagine. I was on two teams that won national championships, and that's a feeling I can't even begin to describe. My junior year I had a partial scholarship to help pay my tuition and living expenses, and it was a full scholarship my last two years. All of that is before accounting for the hundreds of times I got to play the game between the ages of eight and twenty-three."

"And you just quit?"

"That's not how I think of it, but yes."

"How do you think of it?"

"I reached the finish line. There was nowhere else to go. There's a tiny professional league in the eastern US and Canada, but I'm not good enough to make those teams. The only thing left for me would be to play in adult recreational leagues. I decided that they were too much of a step backward for me. So I hung up my skates."

"If there were a real professional league and you were good enough, would you have played?"

"I have no idea. It really isn't worth thinking about."

"That's it?"

"Yes. I don't worry about things that never happened and don't exist."

The sex was disappointing, but at least I got to sleep with someone.

March 2021

"How are you?"

"I'm tired, Bear."

The endearment hit hard. For three months after she'd left, Caitlyn and I had hardly talked and exchanged only the barest emails and texts. I hadn't appreciated the extent to which just being friends would require building up rather than tearing down. When regular communication did resume, it was banal. Neither of us asked about the things we thought were most important to the other.

So when she called, forgetting the protocols, I had no idea what to make of it. "Physically tired or mentally?"

"Mentally." There was no inflection in her voice. "I'm having trouble just getting out of bed."

"What's wrong?"

"I don't know. It's like I'm some wind-up doll and the spring wore down."

"Are you getting to work?"

"Yeah. Every day. I'm doing what I have to. I used to like this job, but now it's just a chore."

"Make sure you keep going. It's important."

"I know."

"How is hockey?" I asked, trying to find the positive.

"Okay," she replied weakly.

That worried me. "Are you guys going to win the Worlds, or should I put my money on Crosser?"

"I don't know."

Once, that would have been my cue to invite her to come stay with me. "Are you going to make it?"

"I think so."

"Would you like me to call you every morning to make sure you get up?"

"Would you?"

"Sure. What time do you need to be out of bed?"

"About six thirty."

"Okay. I'll do that."

"Thanks." Her voice suddenly perked up. "Wait, what time is that there?"

"It doesn't matter."

"I can ask Amy. She'd do it."

"No, I'll do it. It's no problem."

"Are you not sleeping again?"

"I'm doing okay," I replied. "Not great, but okay."

"Is Wendy helping?"

I let that slide by. "I'm up ridiculously early anyway. Being an executive vice president keeps me busier than I'd expected."

"That wasn't an answer."

"It kind of helps the couple of times a week she stays over, especially now that Dennis is married and his rollaway isn't an option. Besides, I have something new to do that should be good for me."

"Really? What?"

"Kennedy kept pestering me to do some volunteer work. Said I'd meet an entirely different type of person than I do now, ones I liked better."

"So you're going to be a hockey coach?"

I stopped and just looked at the phone in my hand. "I was going to make you guess, and you were supposed to fail."

"Oh, please. We've all known you were going to end up doing it someday. You enjoyed that part of our last couple of seasons too much not to."

"But I gave up hockey."

"Uh huh. So what ages?"

"U18s. The district hasn't had a team at that level, so I'll only get the youngest, plus those who weren't good enough to play in another district when they aged out. At least I'll get the whole summer to work with them and do what I can."

"They have summer leagues out there?"

"Well, it's in-house for the local association, but yeah. I have to finish up my USA Hockey certification, but I'm almost there."

"You were working on that and didn't tell anyone?"

"I didn't tell you."

"Pfft. You didn't tell anyone, or I'd have heard about it."

"Hah. Almost. I told Kennedy, but she kept her mouth shut."

"You're supposed to tell me anything."

I almost reminded her that I was only supposed to tell her things that I told Abby, but I stopped. Instead, cold reality intruded. "I was supposed to tell you everything. That changed."

There was silence at the other end before her defeated voice returned. "I'm sorry."

"I am, too."

The world championships started two weeks later, and one look at the box score told me one source of her misery. At the bottom, it read, "Caitlyn Morris—Healthy scratch."

Wendy picked up on my worry over Caitlyn almost instantly. The next night over dinner, she asked, "What's wrong? Work?"

"No, one of my old teammates."

She waited expectantly until it was clear I wasn't going to elaborate. "What is it?"

"She's struggling with the approaching end of her hockey career."

"I like the way you handled it, just walking away. I really wish you weren't getting back into it."

"I'm just going to be coaching," I offered.

"Still. Which teammate is it?"

"Caitlyn."

"Anne Morris's daughter?"

"Yes."

"If you're so close to them, why do you talk about them so little?"

I shrugged and busied myself with my food.

"Phoebe, please. There's something else going on here."

I took another bite. "Caitlyn and I were lovers for a few years in there. So this is extra personal to me."

"While on the team or after?"

"Mostly just while on it."

"That sounds like unfinished business."

"She got married, and that ended up spoiling things even once she divorced. So I care about her. I'm worried about her. But there's nothing left unfinished."

"Are you sure?"

"Yes. It's over." Fortunately, Wendy never picked up on my body language the way my teammates did.

"That seems like an odd sort of team relationship."

"It's unusual, that's for sure. Its origins had more to do with helping me over my nightmares than sex, to be honest."

"You aren't over your nightmares."

"I now get them five or six times a month rather than three or four times a week. That may not be over them, but it's a lot of the way there." I didn't mention how much less often I had them when Caitlyn was around.

May 2021

I wore the commemorative cap from one of our championships to the first day of practice with my new team, hoping for instant credibility with the parents as much as the players. I stood on the ice, surrounded by nineteen of the latter and watched by a small contingent of the former. It was less reassuring to have parents watching a practice than when it was Mr. Wilson sitting there.

"We're going to start out with some skating drills," I told my assembled charges.

I ran them through the wringer, watching not so much for their performance as their attitude. By the second drill there was muttering about just being here to have fun and play some hockey.

I waited until we were done to respond. I blew my whistle and said, "Gather 'round." Nineteen sweaty young women did so. "Here's the deal. When you signed up for this league, you committed to one to two practices a week. I'm going to be here Tuesday and Thursday evenings. This is what Tuesdays are going to be like. Thursdays are going to be a lot more fun."

I watched to see who reacted how. "Once we start playing games, whether you come on Tuesdays will not affect your playing time. As long as you have fulfilled your commitment to make it to one practice a week, you'll get regular shifts. This isn't a travel league. We will play to have fun, and if you're not having fun, please tell me so that we can figure out how to make sure that you do.

"Tuesdays will be all about improving your skills. Skating. Stick-handling. Passing. You name it. It will be a lot of drills, one-on-one work, and a few things with lines, if we have enough players. I will work you hard on Tuesdays.

"If you intend to play on the travel team come fall, I highly recommend showing up on Tuesdays. I'll be the coach of that team, too, and it won't hurt to go into the tryouts having already impressed me."

By the end, I had five players identified as likely Tuesday participants.

Wendy called my office phone on Saturday afternoon. It was a good guess on her part after she found my cell going direct to voice mail.

"Some of my friends are going down to the Mission to try that new Guatemalan restaurant and then catch a couple of bands. You should come with us."

I pulled my mind half away from the problem I was working on. "I can't. I need to get this procedure working."

"C'mon, Phoebe. They've wanted to meet you for a month."

"I'm sorry. This isn't a good weekend." I edited a line of code as I said it.

"It won't be good during the week, because you'll be coaching. When are you going to be free?"

"I don't know. I'm really busy."

"Even Dennis says you need to get out more. He'll understand."

"Sure, he'll understand. Then he'll load me down with more administrative duties. I hardly ever get to program anymore. I've managed to carve out a project and some time, but it has to be now, or I'll lose it."

"When can you carve out some time for me?"

"I said I don't know. I'll work on it."

"You'll love Guatemalan food if you ever try it."

"I'm sure I will."

"Can I at least come by when we're done?"

"Sure. What time will that be?"

"When we're done. We're not planning it that far ahead."

I looked at the clock. "I'll try to be home by midnight."

She giggled. "We won't be done that early. I'll make sure to wake you up."

I got it dead on. The next Tuesday night, I had five eager participants. It wasn't as grueling as I had implied. Working people to exhaustion is only useful if done sparingly and to send a specific message.

It got tedious, though. That first night there were no pucks, just two hours of skating drills. Some of them are simple, but they all test something. They skated figure eights, because every hockey player has a natural preference to turn to her left or her right. As I watched, I could pick up those tendencies and structure practice time to break the habit, in order that the player goes the best way in play.

It became apparent that I had one player better than all the others. She was fluid and purposeful in drills where the others struggled. Her form wasn't perfect, but the flaws were small, and she picked up on adjustments I suggested.

What I didn't like was the way she stood apart from the others. Each player should be exerting herself a third of the time and resting the other two-thirds, while others skate. That meant the others had time to chat. Eddy remained by herself.

As I blew the whistle marking the end of practice, I skated to her. "There's more to this than just the skating. You should get to know the other players."

"I got nothing to say to them."
"They're your teammates."
"Yep."
She skated off.

CHAPTER 27

When we took the ice for the first game of my last year, it was on a line with Caitlyn as the left wing and Sveta at center. We scored on our first shift, and the coaches didn't tinker with us all year. We had a nice blend of size, speed, skill, and grit and made each other better players, but the connection I felt with Caitlyn made it special.

It was easy to feel special on that team, though. We were deep, and having Caitlyn and Jenny back created a logjam for playing time. We had seven senior forwards, though Sonja didn't dress much. Crosser was the only senior on D, but the rest of the top four were juniors. If you took our top three lines and top four defensemen, thirteen players, we had an aggregate of twenty-nine years of experience at the collegiate level. And four of us had played in the Olympics.

Every year, we set three goals: the Big Ten regular season title, the Big Ten playoff championship, and the NCAA championship. That year, nothing short of all three would constitute success. From the first day of practice we didn't hope to accomplish them; we expected to. Every single night, we went in thinking we would win.

I dreamed of scoring a hat trick, but I never bothered including it on my list of personal goals. Some things are so improbable that it's not worth considering them. So when someone tells you that you need to hold onto your dreams because they'll never come true otherwise, tell them they're full of it.

Monica Guest of Minnesota State went down in history as the goalie who managed to let me slip three pucks past her. If you're looking for an asterisk, it's that it was the first game of her career and she only played because their top two goalies were injured. If you check out my stats page, it won't say that. It will just show three goals on the first Saturday of my senior year.

My connection with Caitlyn played a role. I've watched players who had great chemistry on the ice. Caitlyn talks about the sixth sense she and Heck had about where each other was on the ice, and I watched them execute some amazing plays. I'd never experienced it before I started taking regular shifts with her. It was still an amazing feeling. I would just know when she wanted me to go to the net. If the puck went into the corner, I didn't need to guess whether I should go in there or provide support while she did.

I know that this is just the product of the two of us talking about all of these situations and fooling around after practice. It was the same thing that drove me for all of those years to relentlessly imagine myself in every conceivable situation over and over until the right play was drilled into me so deeply it didn't require thought.

But when it was happening, that's not what it felt like. All of that squeezed into an instant so short that it didn't exist. I hesitate to call it mystical, but I couldn't escape that feeling.

Take my second goal that night, maybe the prettiest I ever scored. Caitlyn had the puck along the half boards, and I broke for the net. Really, it was the wrong play; she was getting pressure, and if she sent it along the wall behind the net, I was supposed to be there to receive it. Something about the way she played it told me not to worry about that, something too small for me to identify. Rather than drop down below the goal line, I slipped out front. Sure enough, her pass got there at the same instant I did. All I had to do was keep my stick on the ice and redirect it through Guest's five hole.

I asked her about it late that night.

"How did you know I'd be right there?"

"I don't know. Honestly. I'm trying to picture it, and it was a dumb pass. I shouldn't have made it."

"Maybe, but I liked it."

"Of course you did. You scored three times."

"That's not what I meant."

"I know. And I *have* felt something out there. I think it may just be the joy of playing together, but time will tell. If we manage to keep pulling plays like that off, then definitely."

"I'll keep my eyes open."

"Mmm. I won't."

With that, she was asleep.

Kennedy weaseled her way into the locker room on Monday. She just looked at me, and I sighed, put on my gear, and went to run my punishment laps.

I hated Michigan State. I really hated losing to them. So it made me extra mad that our first loss that year was against them at Ridder. They weren't even that good; we just didn't get the job done. Overconfident and underprepared, we let them get back into our heads. We got outhustled. I lost physical battles along the boards to players I should have walked over.

Later that night, Jenny wrote twenty-five small signs that said, "October 25, 2014: Michigan State 4, Minnesota 1," and taped them over everyone's lockers after the rest of us had left. They stayed there the rest of the season.

By the official rules of hockey, the only job a captain has is that we're the players who are allowed to talk to the officials for clarification on a call or to express a concern. Unofficially, it's a lot murkier. The coaches make the decisions that really matter.

It's a role full of intangibles. You set a good example for the rest of the team. You get on players who aren't pulling their weight before the coaches step in. You're the conduit for players' concerns to the coaches. It's mostly stuff that played to my insecurities. Fortunately, I was just a co-captain, and Jenny had the vocal parts of the job covered.

I led quietly. While Jenny exhorted them publicly, I talked to the girls privately. That included my own linemates, if necessary. After that series, I pulled Sveta aside.

"Okay, what's wrong?" I asked her.

"Nothing."

"Well, if nothing is wrong, then you need to start pulling your weight. You're coasting. You're not going hard into the corners, and you're not going to the front of the net. You're back to trying to do everything pretty, and you're not even doing a great job of that." My voice wasn't as harsh as my words. "But I'm pretty sure something is wrong, because you're moping off the ice as well as on it."

"What is 'moping'?"

"It means you're going around not talking to anyone and acting like you're in a bad mood. It's a stereotypically Russian thing to do, so maybe this is normal, but you weren't like this last year."

She shrugged. "I'm homesick. I miss my parents. I miss Russian food. I miss hearing Russian all the time."

I tried to suppress my natural inclination to offer advice and instead give sympathy. "I'm sorry. Is there anything I can do to help?"

"You don't speak Russian."

"No, and I probably can't learn it between now and March. But I do cook, and I'd be happy to learn some Russian recipes."

"It's okay."

"No, really. Come over a couple nights a week, and I'll fix some Russian food. Caitlyn and I would be happy to have the company."

"Are you sure?"

"Absolutely. Just get me some recipes."

"Okay."

"In exchange, you need to start playing harder. We need you."

"Okay." She gave a weak smile.

One element of a college athlete's senior season is that every road trip marks the last time you play in that building. Since the Big Ten Final Four was going to be in Ridder that year, it meant that each regular season road trip was the last. Except Madison. The NCAA Frozen Four was going to be held there, and we had every intention of being a part of it.

By the first week of December I was never going back to Iowa or Michigan. I wouldn't miss either place, but there was still an element of sadness as the games ended.

Our last series of the first half of the season was in Columbus. Mentally I had it circled on the calendar. My performances there had gone from disastrous to mediocre. I didn't say anything, but my teammates didn't need talk to know how much it meant to me. They could have guessed even if I hadn't been radiating intensity.

I came through. I kept myself under control, but I was a wrecking ball on the rink. The ice there was always soft and choppy, which hurts the finesse players we had so many of. For me, though, it just meant that everyone else came down toward my level. Brute strength is a great counter to sticky ice.

By halfway through the second period of the Saturday game I'd picked up four assists, two penalties, and a lot of nice plays. What I didn't have was a goal. I wasn't the only one who had noticed that. We'd built a big lead, and everyone else was feeding me the puck, trying to help me get it.

At 10:28 of the period Crosser rifled a shot in from the point. The OSU goalie couldn't control it, and the puck slipped to the ice just outside the crease. I had to turn inside a defenseman to keep her from clearing the rebound and get my stick on it before the goalie could cover it. Rather than just trying to jam it in I pulled it to my forehand. The goalie was on her belly reaching for it. I managed to flip the puck up over her sprawled form.

As her trapper waved at it futilely, I went numb. I watched that rubber disk float into the net. The sensation of dislocation overtook me, and I watched myself from above. A roaring sound filled my ears. The others on the ice started to converge on me, arms raised. I didn't see them. My vision narrowed down to a tunnel.

I see myself drop my stick, and I fling my gloves off as my body skates down the length of the ice. I know he's at the far end of the grandstand, right by the entrance, sitting in the fifth row. My hands tear my helmet off, and my arms finally lift in front of me.

Both middle fingers rise to salute him. There's no one in the arena except the two of us. The players, the officials, the coaches, and the Buckeye fans sitting around him have all vanished.

My body stops in front of his seat, and my fists pound the glass. My mouth screams at him. "I beat you, you fucker. You can't hurt me anymore. Look at me, you bastard. It's over. I win."

My body turns around, and that's when I come down from the sky and flow back into it.

I threw myself into Caitlyn's arms as she skated up to me. All four teammates mobbed me. I let go at last and completed the ritual by skating down the length of the bench before getting a hug from Alice by our net. It was a lot of hoopla for a goal scored when it was already 6–1.

I started to come down about then. I went over to the ref. "You're going to toss me for that, aren't you?"

He nodded.

"That's okay. It was worth it." I collected my gear and skated to the gate, headed for the dressing room. As I went, the team banged their sticks on the boards in salute. That made my night.

I just sat against my locker, still in my uniform and skates. Ellie, Stef, and Kat burst in a couple moments later, having come down from the stands. "He wasn't really here, was he?"

I nodded. "He's always here. Every time we've played."

"Why didn't you tell anyone?"

"The reasons change. But mostly for this. I wanted him to be here when I scored. I wanted him to watch."

"You planned that?"

"Not really . . . I've thought about it a lot. What I was going to do. Then it happened, and I kind of snapped. I didn't do any of the stuff I'd imagined. It's probably just as well, since screaming obscenities at the crowd is enough to get tossed from the game."

We heard the horn sound, ending the second period. I got to

my feet, waiting for the team. As they trooped in, they filed past to bump fists with me. Coach Long was last.

I tried to look contrite, but I think I failed. "Sorry, Coach."

I could tell he was having a difficult time looking angry. "Just don't let it happen again."

I nodded solemnly. "Can do."

"Good. Go take a shower."

I didn't get the shakes until Caitlyn and I were alone in our room, hours later. We said very little. All of the congratulations had been expressed during the postgame meal. Tom and Jerilyn, who had made the trip, weren't there. I didn't find out why until the next day.

Later, when it was just the two of us, all of the emotion slowly leaked out of me. Caitlyn held me, my head resting on her chest. She kept quiet and just let me focus, making sure I could hear her breathe. We eventually fell asleep like that. The next morning we were both stiff, but neither of us cared.

CHAPTER 28

June 2021

"It's nice to finally meet one of Phoebe's mythical teammates," Wendy said as we sat down.

"I hope she's said good things about me."

"She's hardly said anything about you."

Kennedy chuckled. "You should have tried to get information out of her eight years ago. If it makes you feel better, she hasn't told me very much about you, either."

"Maybe she should start now."

"We'll probably be better off talking to each other."

"I talk sometimes." I felt like I had to somehow prove that point.

"Only if you have to," Wendy replied.

We chatted through dinner before Wendy got up. "I need to go to Oswald's and schmooze, so I'll leave Phoebe in your care. She'll be happy she doesn't have to tag along and pretend that she's interested."

As soon as Wendy was out of sight, Kennedy frowned. "What are you doing?"

"Having a relationship. I thought you'd approve, since you told me to get out and do something."

"I meant that you should set goals that you really wanted and strive for them, not find stopgap measures and pretend they're goals."

"What does that mean?" I asked.

"It means that it's pretty obvious that you don't love her or, frankly, respect her. What are you trying to do?"

"I'm just trying to have someone I can sleep with. That's a goal."

"She's your security blanket?"

"What's wrong with that?" I said sharply.

"She doesn't realize that's what you're doing. Have you told her that you don't have any real commitment here?"

"Yes."

She raised an eyebrow. "Really?"

"Okay, not very hard, but it's more complicated than you realize. I can't really tell her things like that because she doesn't really listen. Sleeping with me is a political act. I'm the noble rape survivor she needs to guide to a better life. She knows what I need and doesn't bother with any observations I make. She's a little like Abby, except without an ounce of self-awareness or the ability to learn."

"If you let her think that, you're leading her on. She clearly thinks this is a long-term thing."

"Maybe we are."

"No. This isn't healthy."

"Since when do I do healthy relationships?"

"You could at least try one sometime."

July 2021

I pulled Eddy aside after a game. "This is a summer league. You're supposed to be having fun."

"I *am* having fun."

"Having fun usually means smiling, maybe even laughing."

She gave me the exasperated teenager look. "This is the only hockey around here during the summer. If there were a serious league, I'd be playing in it instead."

"Fine, but this is the league you have, and I expect you to play in a manner that's appropriate to it."

"What does that mean?"

"It means not taunting the other team. It means not arguing with the refs. And most importantly, it means stop showing up your teammates when they make a mistake. They're here to enjoy them-selves, not to have fingers pointed."

"How are we going to get any better that way?"

"*You* are going to get better by coming on Tuesdays. Learning those skills will do more for your game than anything we do on Saturdays. As for your teammates, a lot of them probably won't be getting any better, and there's nothing wrong with that."

"Then why play?"

"Sometimes having fun is its own reward. I can tell you from personal experience that just learning to have fun on the ice will improve the way you play."

"Whatever. Can I go shower now?"

Things changed as summer came to an end. Where the summer was basically a rec league with kids signing up and getting assigned to teams, the winter had what Eddy called "a serious league." In September the twenty-two best girls under the age of nineteen from the local area were selected by tryout. They traveled to play similar teams around California and, occasionally, to tournaments around North America. Elite players might get invites to USA Hockey camps, where they would be evaluated for the national teams and get watched by coaches from various college teams.

Having enough teams in northern California for a full league was a recent development, and it was the first year our association fielded a U19 team, so my whole roster consisted of high school sophomores and older girls who hadn't been good enough to make other teams.

It was a good group of kids, and I was distressed at what was going to happen next. At the end of the last practice before the season I blew the whistle and called them all over.

"Huddle up." I waited until we were all in a circle, arms around each other's shoulders, before continuing. "Our first game is Saturday at eleven a.m. I'm proud of the way you guys have gotten ready, and I'm going to be proud to coach you.

"When I was your age, I was on a team that was terrible. No one had any fun, and we all ended up hating each other. That's not going to happen here. No matter what happens, we're going to play for each other. We're going to love each other, and we're going to back each other up.

"As I told you before the first practice, our motto is, 'Twenty bodies, one soul, one team, one goal.' Everyone understand?"

They replied in the affirmative.

Two weeks later, my fears were coming true. We had lost our first game 3–2, and we were getting shellacked in the second. I sent the fourth line out for a shift and tried to talk to my first-line center.

"When you see them set to trap you like that, you need to pass it across the ice, out of the trap. They want you to try to carry the puck through that. They'll strip it from you every time."

Eddy nodded half-heartedly, but the assent didn't reach her eyes. After she did it again, I sat her on the bench for the third period.

After the game, her father accosted me as I left the rink.

"You can't sit my daughter," he yelled. "She's the best player on your team. Without her, you can't win."

There wasn't any evidence that I could win with her, either, but I didn't say that. "Mr. Howser, they made me the coach, which means I make the decisions about who plays and who sits."

"How old are you?"

"I'm almost thirty. Why?"

"You don't have the experience to know who should be playing and who shouldn't."

I held up my hand for him to look at. "Do you see that ring? Do you know what it is?"

"No. What is it?"

"It's the ring I received for being the captain of the team that won the 2015 NCAA national championship." I didn't normally wear it around, but I'd been anticipating a confrontation like this. "I have another one like it from three years earlier. I've spent a lot of time on the ice with the very best players in the world. I have plenty of experience at figuring out who is and is not helping a team win."

He jabbed his finger at me. "None of that means you're qualified to tell my daughter she can't play."

"I also work for free, and that seemed to be a major consideration of the board."

Eddy walked out of the locker room, freshly showered, and regarded the scene with a look of horror. "C'mon, Dad, we need to go," she said, tugging on his sleeve. "We're supposed to be at Hannah's picnic."

She led him away, though I could hear him continue to complain.

"I'm sorry about my father," she said when she arrived the next Tuesday.

"It's okay. I've stood up to a worse hockey parent than him."

"You haven't seen him enough, then."

"Be that as it may, it's also not your fault. Unless I get the sense that you are putting him up to it, his rants will have zero effect on how I coach, and you don't need to apologize for him."

"Thank you."

"Still, if you want playing time, what you do with it is going to have to change."

She instantly went from contrite to sullen. "I'm the best player on this team."

"If the game was played one-on-one, sure, but you have teammates out there. Use them."

"They'll just screw it up."

"Then teach them how not to. Politely."

"I don't have the time," she said.

"Why not?"

"I'm trying to get a college scholarship. I need to get noticed."

I had an ugly feeling of déjà vu. "No one is going to notice what you do here."

"It worked for you."

"You've looked that up, have you?"

She nodded.

"I got insanely lucky. Besides, no one did notice anything I did in high school. What I did in the games didn't matter, except to the extent that it made me a better player. A better team player."

"So what am I supposed to do?"

"Right now you aren't good enough to play for an NCAA team."

"I've got three years to get better."

"Wrong. You have one year to catch a coach's attention. If you aren't being recruited by early in your junior year, it's not going to happen."

"That's why I don't have time."

"I'll make you a deal," I said. "Because I played, I know some coaches personally. If you play my way and make sure that you are a part of the team, then I will contact them and try to get you the attention. If you play hard and smart, I will use my connections to help you to a level you can succeed at."

She looked at me guardedly for a moment. "Promise?"

"Here's one lesson for you to learn. Never back out on a commitment you've made to one of your teammates. I don't."

"Hey, Phoebe," Caitlyn said through the phone later that month, "I have a favor I want to ask of you."

"Shoot."

"I would like to come and visit. Just for a week or so."

I stopped, not saying anything. We hadn't actually seen each other since we'd broken up. We'd made a lot of progress, but I wasn't sure I wanted to go there.

"I'll be on my best behavior, honest. Actually, that's part of why I want to come. I'm trying to do things differently this time, so I don't make such stupid mistakes during the run up to the Games. I want to make one more attempt to learn how to meditate from you." There was a pause. "And I just want to see you. I miss you."

"I miss you, too. Sure, come on. When would it be?"

"Next week. I hope that's not too little notice. We're off from Wednesday to the next Monday."

"Do you mind if I show you off to my team?"

"That'd be great. I look forward to it."

I picked her up at the airport, restraining myself from reaching out and touching her. That lasted until we got to my apartment, when we hugged for what seemed like forever. I regretted that we'd agreed that she was staying at a hotel. And then I felt uncomfortable with that realization.

When I let her go, she looked around. "So this is the new apartment?"

"Yes. It's not that amazing."

"You said it actually has three bedrooms. By your standards, that's ridiculously extravagant."

"I'm planning on using one of them as a study." I sounded defensive even to myself.

"That used to be called the living room."

"Okay, yes, I upgraded my living arrangements."

"You don't need to sound guilty about it. Lots of people get a better place when they become an executive vice president. Besides, what are you paying in rent?"

"About $6,000 a month. And it's just a job title."

She stopped moving around long enough to stare at me. "Look, I know your self-image is built around being a scrapper that's just barely holding onto whatever position you happen to have at the moment, but you're a success. We weren't ever able to convince you were wrong about your hockey abilities, but Dennis has more tools available to him. You won."

"Fine. Whatever," I mumbled.

"And when do I meet Wendy?"

"We're having dinner tomorrow night after practice."

"I'm really looking forward to that."

"Meeting Wendy or practice?"

"Both, really."

"Mmmm. I was wondering if you could do me a favor at practice."

"Name it."

"If we scrounged up some gear, would you participate?"

"Oh? Why?"

"I've got a player who needs to be taken down a few pegs, and I'd like to let her see what top-notch competition is like."

"That sounds diabolically fun. Of course."

Caitlyn had the effect I was hoping for. I ran a scrimmage and put her on one of the teams and myself on the other. She took Eddy apart, especially on the backcheck. By the time we were done, Eddy was a frustrated wreck. I felt bad about it, in a way, but it was necessary.

Other than that, I just spent time watching Caitlyn play. It had been a long time since I had seen her do anything with such simple joy. She refused to score a goal, instead dishing out assists and playing defense. And she had so much fun it was hard to watch anything else.

Dinner had a related revelation: with Caitlyn there, I found Wendy tedious. It didn't matter the subject, Caitlyn was just more interesting. I wasn't the only one who noticed; by the end of the meal, Wendy was silent and sullen.

When it was over, we dropped Caitlyn off at her hotel. As I pulled away from the door, I said, "We need to talk." I didn't look at Wendy as I said it.

"Yes, we do. You lied to me."

"About what?"

"It's not over between the two of you."

I sighed. "If it makes any difference, I didn't lie. I was mistaken. I thought it was over."

"That doesn't help me any."

"No," I conceded, "it probably doesn't. I'm sorry."

"Just take me to your apartment so I can pick up the stuff I have there."

The rest of the drive was silent. I watched her gather her stuff. "Do you want a ride home?" I asked finally.

"No. I'll take a cab."

When she was gone, I picked up my phone and then was caught, unsure whether I wanted to call Kennedy or Caitlyn. I rationalized calling the latter by arguing to myself that the former was probably already in bed.

"Phoebe?"

"Would you rather sleep here than there?"

"What about . . . oh. You broke up."

"Yeah."

"I'm sorry I got between you."

"Don't be. Kennedy tried months ago to make me look at what was going on, and I didn't listen, so it's not about you."

She paused. "Does this mean that you want us to start sleeping together again?"

"No. I just want company."

"Then I don't think it's a good idea. Not now. I'll come over, or meet you somewhere near here, to talk and be together, but I'm going to sleep here."

"Okay."

I spent the rest of her visit enjoying her company but feeling alone.

She left Monday afternoon, and I was still down when it was time for practice on Tuesday. My mood wasn't helped by the team being 0-4. I'd talked big about the players avoiding frustration if we lost, but I was struggling to take my own orders.

As I sipped a coffee, there was a soft knock on the doorframe of what passed for my office. I looked up, and Eddy was standing there.

"You're early."

"May I come in?"

"Always," I replied. "What's up?"

She didn't sit down. "It wasn't fair, what you did on Thursday."

"It wasn't supposed to be fair, and you weren't supposed to like it," I replied, leaning back in my chair.

"Why?"

"Because if you want to play D1 hockey, that's what you're going to face."

"No, it isn't. She's playing in the Olympics."

"She's also slower than she used to be. You won't face that every night, but you will face it. If you want to play at that level, you'll have to have some answer for dealing with a player like Caitlyn. Maybe that answer will be to get off the ice quickly so that your coach can get a better line match-up out there, but it will have to be something. And if you can't match her, then you won't be good enough to succeed on your own. You'll have to become a part of a unit."

"I'm only a sophomore."

"Which means you have plenty of time to learn. Eddy, I love your work ethic. You bust your ass out there. But working hard isn't enough."

"What is?"

"Use your teammates. Work as hard when you don't have the puck as you do when it's on your stick. Make the smart play, and trust that they will do the same."

"But I'm better than they are. We're a better team if I—"

I cut her off. "Then it's your job to bring them up to your level. You're not as much better than they are as you think you are, but fix that gap." I heard the sound of others heading for the dressing room. "Now go get dressed."

After a skeptical glare, she headed out the door.

"Oh, and Eddy, thank you for coming in to talk to me rather than having your father do it. That counts for a lot."

She left without looking back.

We both held our tongues until we were back in Dennis's car. As soon as the door was closed he let me have it.

"What the hell are you doing? You're going to screw up the deal."

I crossed my arms across my chest and looked out the window. "I thought you brought me along to meetings like this because you trust my ability to judge people." My voice was calm, but Dennis knew me well enough not to judge my mood by that alone.

"Seth Hammersmith has been a friend of mine for fifteen years. That's longer than you have been, you might notice." He slammed the car into drive and launched it out of its parking space.

"Maybe he was your friend, but he isn't any more. He's going to fuck you on this."

"How? All we're doing is buying some patents from him. How is he going to fuck me?"

"I don't know." I turned and saw him bouncing in the driver's seat. At other times I was amused looking at the disparity in our seat adjustments, but right then it just struck me as ridiculous. "I don't understand any of the legal stuff. You know that, and you brought me along anyway. If you didn't want me to express my concerns about him and that sleazy sidekick of his, why am I here?"

"Express them to me. Not to everybody in the room."

"I have been expressing them to you for two months," I said, finally letting my frustration show in my voice. "You haven't listened."

"And so you decided to accuse Seth of lying to us about a subject you admit you don't understand?"

I took a deep breath. "I'll try again. Why did you bring me to this meeting?"

"I just wanted you there. I'm more confident with you in the room."

"Don't use me as a crutch, Dennis. I want a role in which I do things, not just be a security blanket."

"You are doing something. You're helping me negotiate better."

It took a moment for that to sink in. "Do you have any idea how patronizing you're being?"

"It's not patronizing. You shouldn't feel that way."

"I . . . forget it." I lapsed into silence for the rest of the drive.

CHAPTER 29

It turned out Tom punched my former foster father several times once he figured out who it was I'd screamed at. He didn't press charges, but Tom was still held by the campus police for a couple of hours.

I went to the airport with the rest of the team, but I said good-bye at the security checkpoint. Then I drove down to Warren County to file a report with the police. Jerilyn stayed with me to provide support.

The assistant DA I met with had all the right facial expressions. I still shook uncontrollably.

"He raped me."

"When was this?"

I gave him dates.

"Are these exact?"

"Three of them. The rest are within a couple of days."

"Did you tell anyone about them at the time?"

I shook my head.

"No one knew?"

I hesitated. "I . . ."

"Someone did know?"

I struggled to say anything and then looked at Jerilyn. "Please. Help."

"She told her school counselor."

"And what did the counselor do?"

"She told Phoebe's foster father."

The attorney looked up at me sharply. "She told Mr. Jenkins?"

I nodded mutely.

He blinked. "I think you need to get your own representation."

"I don't want to sue. I just want this over with."

"Maybe not. But aside from you changing your mind, there's a good chance someone is going to sue you if you make these accusations."

"I . . ." I nodded again. "I'll do it when I get home."

"You should probably go ahead and do it now."

"I can't afford one. I need to talk to Student Legal Services back home."

"All right. Are you sure you want to continue now?"

"Yes." If I didn't do it now, I never would.

"All right."

"Just—I mean, one thing."

"What's that?"

"I need to finish the season. I don't want to have to deal with this until it's over."

"That could be a problem."

"Please?"

"I'll talk to my boss." He sighed. "I'll see what we can do."

"Thank you."

He started walking me through the facts again.

I was a wreck by the time I was done in Dayton. As soon as exams were done, I went up to the Forrests'. I asked Caitlyn to come with me, but she declined. She preferred not interacting with Abby at all, and I wasn't able to convince her that it was just like the time Derek's girlfriend had spent the weekend.

So I went up by myself. I apologized to Tom for getting him into trouble. He just said that he wished he'd killed him before someone pulled them apart.

Jerilyn and I spent a good deal of time talking about everything that was going on.

"Are you sure you want to go through with this?" she asked me.

"No. I'm pretty sure that I don't, but the ball is rolling now, so I guess I'm rolling with it."

"Make sure that you control events rather than letting them control you. If you want this to stop, you can make it stop."

"Really?" I asked. "How?"

"Stop cooperating. Nothing can go forward if you don't."

"Isn't that surrendering? Letting my fear control me?"

"It depends on how you approach it. All things being equal, it would be good to see him prosecuted, but all things aren't equal."

"Everyone else I talk to is congratulating me for doing this. They tell me that it will bring me closure."

She smiled. "Closure is more complicated than that. Everyone is different and has unique ways of dealing with things. Make sure that what you do doesn't upset those structures."

"If I drop it, won't that just be letting him get away with it?"

"What's more important to you, making sure that he doesn't or being able to live your own life?"

"My own life," I replied without hesitation.

"That's what I thought. A lot of people in your situation need the spectacle of justice to move on, but I don't think that's true of you."

I thought about it for a moment. "I don't want justice. I want it not to have happened."

"So don't let the one thing interfere with the other. Protect yourself."

"I seem to be doing a lot of that these days."

"I know you are. I think you're doing an admirable job of it, too."

"You do? Almost no one else does. Abby keeps telling me I'm being stupid. I had to make her promise she wouldn't mention Caitlyn when she's here."

"Abby doesn't do nuance very well. You know that. It's all black and white for her."

"That's for sure. She's one of the people I'd be scared to tell if I decided not to press charges."

"If you decide not to, I'll tell her and deal with it."

"Thank you."

My Christmas Eve conversation with Abby was a bit stilted, since she really wanted to offer her opinion about Caitlyn and I'd made it clear that I had no intention of listening. Still, we found things to talk about.

"I think we have a real chance to win it all again this year."

"I'd hope so," she replied sharply. "You're 18-1-1 and the number one team in the country. You should think you can win it all."

"You know what I mean. We aren't just winning. It feels like all of the pieces are in place. We can score. We can play defense. This is our year."

"It must feel nice."

"It does. I know you're still mad that it didn't come together your senior year but—"

"I'm not mad. Really. I'm still disappointed, but I'm not mad. You're right. There was a lot more to it. We just didn't have all of those pieces. We couldn't keep the puck out of our own net when it counted. That had nothing to do with the personalities. It just was."

I drank some cocoa, letting that whirl around in my brain.

"No," Abby continued, "I'm really glad it's working out like this. You deserve it. You all deserve it. Just win it."

"Thank you. How are things there?"

"They're going well in kind of an odd way. I'm starting to think that I'm not cut out to be a practicing therapist."

"That's the going well part or the odd way part?"

"Both. I think I'm better off becoming a researcher. That's the part I really enjoy."

"You're also less likely to accuse a patient of being stupid that way."

She glared at me for an instant, but even that was half-hearted. "You're right. That's why I'm not sure I should go into practice. I don't have the patience with people."

Though I agreed with her self-assessment, I said, "You did all right with me before I confused it with Caitlyn and all of the sister stuff."

"That's because you're a strange one. Most patients shouldn't have to learn how to tell their therapist that she's full of shit."

"Can I just take this opportunity to thank you for everything you've done for me over the last five years?"

"I'm glad I could be there."

"Abby, just accept the thanks, and shut up for a moment."

"Okay. You're welcome."

"I think you're right. I think you have a perfect mind for doing research. You do a great job of discarding assumptions in favor of what appears to be true. You have a level of intellectual honesty that I've never seen in anyone else. But you need things to be true or not true, and that wouldn't be so good working with patients."

"You've been talking to Mom."

"Of course. I suspect that she's been telling you the same thing, but she hasn't said so to me. That was my own independent judgment."

"You're right. It just took me a long time to realize it. It's hard—I want to help people. I know that I can do things in the lab that will do so, but it doesn't have that same, immediate reward."

"That," I said with emphasis, "is why I wanted to thank you right now. With me it worked. If nothing else, you have had that direct effect at least once. For me, you had a perfect approach as a therapist."

"It's funny—"

"Abby, you're supposed to laugh when something is funny."

"Quiet, you. It's funny because Mom told me several times that first summer that I needed to remember that I wasn't your therapist. She told me not to try to fill that role with you."

"Whatever. All I can say is that the approach you took worked. I wouldn't have made it without you. So thank you."

"You're welcome."

The next morning, when all of the presents had been unwrapped and the floor beneath the tree was empty, I started to stand up. "Thank you for . . ." That's as far as I got before registering that no one else had moved. They all had an air of anticipation about them.

Jerilyn held out an envelope to me. "Phoebe, you should open this."

I took it and sat back down, wondering why everyone was watching me so carefully. I opened it and unfolded the note inside.

> Dear Phoebe,
>
> We are all proud of the way you have grown over the last five years. The time that we have spent with you has overwhelmingly been a joy. Even when it has been a sadness, we are glad that you have chosen to share it with us.
>
> We hope that you will always be with us to celebrate life. We would be honored if you would join our family as our sister and daughter. Please accept our invitation to become one of us.
>
> Love,
> Tom, Jerilyn, Abigail, and Derek

It was a couple of hours before I was able to read the whole thing without crying too much to finish. I didn't manage to say anything right there—I just nodded. They seemed to accept that as a yes.

CHAPTER 30

January 2022

One problem with coaching players who aren't as good as the ones you got used to playing with is that it's hard to tell whether one of them made a bad decision or whether she just didn't recognize the opening you wanted her to take in the split second it existed.

"Did you see Katie here in the slot?" I asked while I highlighted the player in question with my laser pointer. Around Thanksgiving, I'd paid to have a camera on a tripod stationed high in the bleachers at center ice of our rink. The picture wasn't great, and it couldn't pan or zoom, but the complete lack of video to break down was so frustrating that I'd had to do it in order to save my sanity.

"Yes," Eddy replied. I hadn't made attending the extra video session on Sundays mandatory, but about half of the girls showed up. Unlike with the summer team, attendance at them did affect playing time on the travel team.

"So why didn't you pass it to her? The defense is out of position, and that's a scoring chance."

"I didn't think I could get the pass through their center."

"Then that's a drill we're going to run on Tuesday, because it should get there." I'm sure my skepticism of her claim registered in my body language, but at least she was learning what answers I'd accept even if I didn't believe her.

I looked at the clock, and said, "Okay, that's enough for today. Go home and do whatever it is that teenagers do these days."

They filed out, and I watched the tape some more. We'd had a pretty good game the day before—a rare win. After the bad ones, I watched it at home, where I could pet my cat to relieve the aggravation produced by a bunch of kids failing to live up to the standards set by national champions. I was getting better at not letting that show in practice, but it was still a work in progress.

When I stepped out, I found Eddy sitting in the parking lot by herself. "What are you still doing here?" I asked.

"My parents are both working today. My mother is going to swing by when she's done."

"Would you like a ride?"

"It's okay. I live down in San Mateo."

"I'm not in a hurry. Besides, it will give us a chance to talk."

She looked at me suspiciously. "About what?"

"Don't worry. I don't have anything bad in mind."

She regarded me for a moment and then stood up. "Okay."

"I've started to send out feelers to coaches," I said once we were in my car.

"Really?"

"It's all kind of tentative because I don't have any decent video. I'm trying to arrange a way for them to see you, but that's still really iffy."

"I thought you didn't like the way I play."

"That was the other thing I wanted to talk about. I know I get on you a lot in practice, but I'm pleased with the progress you're making."

"It doesn't usually seem like it."

"Right. Which is why I figured that I needed to come out and say it."

"Are you about to tell me that you get on me the most because I'm the best player on the team and so you make an example of me?"

I laughed. "No. I get on you the most because you're the best player and you have the highest ambitions and so you need to be pushed harder than the others if you want to make it. Serving as an example for the others to watch is just a side benefit."

"Thanks, I guess."

"You'll thank me later, if this works. If it doesn't, you'll just curse me."

"So where are you sending these feelers?"

"Right now, to anyone who will listen. But that brings up another question. How are your academics? And what kind of school do you want to go to?"

"I want to go someplace where I can play hockey."

"That still leaves a lot of choices, hopefully. How are your grades?"

"Good, except for math."

"Do you need a tutor? I used to do that for teammates."

"My parents hired me a tutor already."

"Are they any good?"

"He's terrible. I usually want to punch his lights out."

"Well, my offer remains open."

When we arrived at her home, before getting out, she asked me, "Why are you doing all of this?"

Without really thinking about it, I ventured the truth. "Because being on a team means a lot to me, and it's something I've missed since I graduated."

She opened the door and got out. "I'll have to think about that."

Dennis looked up as I stepped in, and he looked puzzled when I closed the door. "What's up?"

"I'm resigning. Consider this my however long notice. Two weeks would be nice, but anything up to the seventh of February is fine. That's when I have a plane reservation to Helsinki to watch the Olympics."

He looked at me stupidly for almost a minute. "Why?"

"Because I'm not happy. You also don't seem to trust my judgment, but that's just the minor part of it. I'm tired of being an executive vice president. I'm tired of sitting through meetings I don't understand. I'm tired of riding herd on a bunch of people who are doing actual work. I'm tired of reading misogynist emails about my bitchiness. Oh, and about that, I'm tired of your policies on continuing to deal with people who make rape threats so long as they act like it was a joke."

"I can change that."

"No. Well, yes, you should, but I'm not sticking around. I came to work for you because you were involved in some very interesting software creation. I hardly get any time to code anymore, and the problems we're trying to deal with now just aren't that interesting."

"So what are you going to do?" He sounded panicky.

"Consulting. For people with really interesting software problems."

"You're not going to avoid awful meetings by consulting. You'll actually have to market yourself."

"Maybe it will be a flop. Fortunately, with the IPO coming up, all of those stock options will keep me afloat even if I never work again."

"I never should have convinced you those would be valuable."

"If it makes you feel better, I didn't actually believe you until one of the VC guys actually showed me the math on how much they're about to be worth."

"What am I going to do without you?"

"Hire someone who actually wants the job."

"I don't trust anyone who actually wants that job."

"You could resign and set up a consulting business," I offered. "You've got the stock options for it."

"You spent the last five years telling me you hated the thought of going through the job search process to move somewhere else, and now you're going to do it constantly?"

"If you're that worried about me, you could come up with some really interesting programming problems and hire Rebound Software to solve them for you."

"That's what you're calling it? Rebound Software?"

"Hey, I scored a lot of my goals on rebounds."

"You're going to need to hire a consultant for your consultancy. It's never going to work."

I laughed. "Worst-case scenario is I give up and just become a hockey coach full time. I enjoy that."

He sobered up. "This isn't a joke, is it? You're really leaving."

"Do you need it in writing?"

I went to the Olympics to watch Jenny and Caitlyn play for one last time. The difficult part was that I didn't get to watch Caitlyn. It had become clear that, barring an injury somewhere in the lineup, she wasn't going to dress. The end had arrived, and she wasn't taking it well. She was all anger in the lead-up to the Games, putting in ridiculous efforts in practice to show that if someone did break a leg, she'd be ready.

I hadn't known that I had some small measure of fame within the world of women's ice hockey. I'd cut myself off from the game so much that I didn't follow the conversations. When I introduced myself to any of the younger players, they immediately knew who I was.

It had little to do with my game performances. I'm proud of them, but they weren't in any way memorable. They remembered the trial and the stories that came out at it. One of the younger Canadian players told me I was her hero. I didn't have the heart to tell her how I felt about it all.

Caitlyn laughed when I discussed it with her. "We've been trying to tell you this for years."

"That I'm a hero?"

"Yes. And you're incredibly dense about it."

"Some hero. I wilted on the stand." I flinched even mentioning it.

"You only see it from the inside. I guess I can't blame you, but that's not how everyone else sees it." We were sitting in a coffee shop.

"What do they see?"

"They see that you spoke up. Twelve idiots in your hometown didn't believe you, but everyone in the game does. All of the things that make you so bitter, that hurt you so much, don't mean that you weren't heroic. They're exactly the things that mean you were."

"It was still stupid."

"No it wasn't. It was brave. Do you follow the news at all?"

"Not really, no."

"There was a scandal three years ago at a prep school in Ontario. A bunch of girls on the hockey team had been abused by the coach over a decade and a half."

"I vaguely remember something. Someone sent me an email, I think."

"Several people did. I was one of them."

"I trashed them. I don't want to read about things like that."

"Understandable, but that means that you missed the fact that the girl who finally went to the authorities mentioned you as her inspiration."

"She did?"

"Yes. And at least one of the American players who's introduced herself to you was an abuse victim. Jenny had to convince her that she shouldn't tell you that and how she thinks about you."

"Oh."

"I'm not telling you to change," she said. "There is no way I'd pressure you to do that. But you should at least know what gets said out there. You've made as much difference to women's hockey as any of us."

"I'm not sure how to feel about that."

"Let's just say that Tammy has started keeping her mouth shut on the subject."

I laughed at that. "Isn't that too damned bad?"

"I know. But take it all to heart. You'll have to decide whether the pain was worth it, but it wasn't for nothing. Always know that."

Russia played in the bronze medal game the day before the final. It had been impossible to see Sveta before then, but when their tournament was over, the rules loosened, and we were able to have dinner together.

It was the first time I'd seen her since I'd left Minnesota. In the end, the pull of the familiar had overcome worries about being accepted, and she'd gone back to Russia after graduation. We'd exchanged emails but nothing more for seven years.

"You look great," I said when she sat down at our table.

"Thank you. You, too."

"Sorry about the game today."

"Winning is hard," she replied.

"Tell me about it. My team is 4-14."

"I heard that you are coaching. I am glad to see it."

"Your English is a lot better than it was when you were in school."

"I use it every day at work during the off-season."

"So what's it like doing PR work for a gas company?"

"Less glamorous than playing hockey but more shitty."

"That should be 'shittier.'"

"It's more poetic my way. And I'd rather not talk about it."

"Sorry."

"So how do you like coaching?"

"I love it."

"I thought you would. You seemed like a natural for it."

"Everyone says that," I exclaimed. "Why didn't you tell me earlier?"

"We did. You just didn't listen."

"No, you didn't."

"Sure, we did. I know you listened to my Kazmaier acceptance speech, where I told everyone how you'd turned me from a good player to a great one."

"That's not the same thing as saying I'd be a good coach."

"It is. That's just not what you wanted to hear."

"All I ever wanted to hear was the truth."

"Truth is a funny thing, Feba. Take it from someone who works in public relations. We often take what we want to be and turn it into the truth."

They won. Team Canada vented eight years of anger on the Americans in the gold medal game. The final was 6-2, and it wasn't that close.

Caitlyn put on her spotless uniform as the clock wound down and skated onto the ice at the final buzzer. I was sitting in the fourth row behind the bench, so I could see her clearly, and it hurt. The team exorcised its ghosts, but she'd never get rid of hers. If she had played, it might have been different, but she never had the opportunity.

To anyone who doesn't know her, she probably looked happy and gracious as the IOC representative hung the gold medal around her neck. Someone who hadn't seen her scramble over the boards twice when we won national championships could have been fooled. This was not that Caitlyn Morris.

I was there when she came out of the dressing room. Her teammates were all wearing their medals. The ribbon of hers was crushed in her fist, and the disk hung limply. She walked up to me and in a whisper said, "I'm done." She buried herself against my chest.

I took the medal from her. I tried to fit it in my pocket, but it was too big. I just held onto it until I could put it somewhere safe, with the one she'd given me from the Worlds, in the hope that she'd want it someday.

She'd recovered a bit by the time I met her the next morning, so I asked her, "What are you going to do now?"

"We're flying back to Toronto on Monday. Then it's back to the real world—for good this time."

"Back to the same job?"

"Yep." She smiled weakly. "For the very first time, I made it through the Olympics without burning every bridge I'd ever crossed. My boss messaged me right after the game was over and said he was proud of me and that he was looking forward to having me back."

"Caitlyn, I'm proud of you. I know you're disappointed that you didn't play, but you're keeping it all together."

"That's a low bar."

"Maybe, but you understand why I consider even that to be a step forward."

She nodded. "It's much, much better. I have some things I need to tell you, but I'd rather do it somewhere private."

"Should we go back to my hotel room?"

"I'd rather . . . Could you come to Toronto?"

"Not right now. I may be unemployed, but I promised the girls I'd only be abandoning them for two weeks."

"Maybe later? It can wait a couple of months. Hell, maybe I'll figure out exactly what I want to say."

I was extremely curious, but if she could be patient, so could I. "Sure. Actually, I've been thinking about bringing the team up there for a tournament. Not a top-notch one, but at least something."

"Your association would pay for that?"

I laughed at the idea. "No. I'd cover all of the expenses except what the girls and their families can cover."

"That's awfully generous."

"Dennis gave me a severance package I don't need, so I dedicated it to doing whatever I can to give my team chances that the better funded associations take for granted. Besides, I owe it to Eddy. She isn't perfect, but she really has tried to live up to our deal, and I'd like to give her some more exposure."

"Do they realize what an awesome coach they have?"

"No, and I'd like to keep it that way. And by the way, you aren't going to tell them."

"If you insist."

March 2022

Coaching hockey involves all of the stress that playing does, without the ability to get out on the ice and make anything happen.

I didn't have the same problems seeing over my players that some coaches (like, say, Jenny) do, so I'd gotten a perfect view of a gruesome first period that ended with us down 4–0 to an elite team from San Jose. It wasn't a surprise; we were 0–4 against them to that point, and none of the games had been close.

I'd also gotten to see us claw back in the second and third. With a minute to play, we were behind 5–4. We got into the offensive zone and forced their goalie to make a save. She froze the puck for a face-off in that end.

Timeouts give coaches the illusion of controlling the game, so it's always a temptation to make sure you don't go home without having used the only one you get each game. Fortunately, this was a moment when calling it was the right thing to do.

I pulled out my dry erase board and drew up a play designed to spring a forward loose in the slot. I told Eddy to try to win the draw to her wing rather than pulling it back to the defenseman, and then rub the opposing center out of the play, hopefully giving the wing a free lane to the net. A purist might have said that it was based on an illegal pick, but no ref in that league would call it, not late in the third period of a close game. When you're the underdog, you have to use whatever openings you get.

The goalie stayed on the bench, and I sent out an extra forward. Hopefully the extra bodies would create a mismatch. I knew I was kidding myself about the play; there was no way it would survive first contact with the ice, but we all felt better thinking that we had a real plan.

I could tell that Eddy was disappointed that I had directed all the action to the direction away from her, but she sucked it up. As the huddle broke, I tapped her shoulder, and she looked at me as the others skated out.

"You know everything I've told you about playing within the system and not being selfish?"

She nodded.

"There comes a point where great players take over, and they make things happen. This is one of those moments you need to seize."

She grinned and went to her spot along the edge of the face-off circle. We promptly lost the draw, and the other team cleared the puck. All I could do was chew on the marker as we collected it and brought it back into the zone with less than thirty seconds to play. I had no power left to affect the outcome; I couldn't even order a line change.

Eddy carried it down the left half boards and rifled a pass to a wing in the high slot. In a better world, or at least on a better team, she one-times it as the goalie slides across. In this case, she fanned on it. It looked like San Jose would get it and kill the rest of the clock, but Eddy, thirty feet out of position, got to it first, wove around a defenseman, and then, in traffic, put a shot into the top corner to tie the game.

We lost in overtime, but I was thrilled with our competition level and how we'd fought back. I could start to see the beginnings of a decent team.

April 2022

Dennis had been right: marketing sucks, and it was very tempting to just avoid it. That would have left me with an unbearable amount of free time, though, so I made an effort. Dennis glowingly recommended me to whomever he could, and I picked up a number of projects, most short but a few longer. I still had a lot of time on my hands, though.

It was an entirely new experience. I read a lot, including a bunch of philosophy papers. It was fun to read pieces unlike anything I'd seen for a decade.

I also found that there were times I just sat in my living room, letting the fog roll in off the bay and through my brain.

That May was a reunion of sorts, when I brought my team to a tournament in Toronto. Jenny came up to watch some games. She was an assistant coach at a D3 college in upstate New York and could claim it was a recruiting visit. Amy and Caitlyn lived there. So we had a majority of the class in the same place, and we even set up a conference call that Kennedy, Morgan, and Traci joined. It almost felt like old times.

Still, there were two main reasons to be there. For the first, Jenny expressed skepticism that Eddy would make it even at one of the weaker small programs. She did promise to look at any videos I put together and to keep an open mind. It was all I could ask for.

The second took place at Caitlyn's apartment. I smiled when I saw it. It was homey in a way mine never looked, by which I mean that it was a mess. At least she'd washed all the dishes.

As requested, I sat on the couch. Caitlyn stood before me. Her fidgety mannerisms ought to have seemed perfectly normal, but it was only when I saw them that I realized how absent they had been when I saw her in Finland.

"So," I asked, "what's up?"

"Two things, mainly. The first is that I have a partial explanation for why I've always behaved so strangely."

"Oh?"

"I'm bipolar," she blurted out.

"Since when?"

"Probably since before I met you. It's not severe, but it gets worse under stress."

"That would explain a lot."

"Uh huh. I got diagnosed last fall. One of the team doctors saw me starting to stress out and sent me to a psychologist. I know how you feel about them, but he's really helped me."

"Good."

"I mean, I know you don't believe in therapists, but—"

"I've never been against therapy. I've just said that it doesn't work for me. If it works for you, I'm glad. Keep going."

"That's the small part." I could see her tensing up even more but didn't know what to do about it. "I could have told you that anywhere. It's one of the things I realized in therapy."

I started to get up to hug her, but she motioned me back down.

"I can do this. Phoebe, I'm gay." Her words were running together. "I know you like to think that I'm not, and it's my fault for insisting that I wasn't, but I am."

"I don't like to think one thing or the other. You are what you are."

"Yes, you do. You like to think that I'm straight because you love the idea of being so awesome that a straight girl fell for you anyway, and that means a lot to you, and I'm sorry to take it away, but it's true, even though you are that awesome. I'm sorry. I'm really gay."

"It's okay," I said when she paused to take a breath. "I love you no matter what you are."

"I know you do, but that's not enough. It's important to me that you really accept and acknowledge that I'm gay. It's who I am, and I can tell from your face that you don't really believe me, and it hurts."

"I accept this, Caitlyn. I mean it. I know you're gay." I wanted to punch myself when I felt my shoulder drop. I couldn't even figure out why it was hard.

"No, you don't. A long time ago you told me about how being black was important to the Wilsons, and this is like that. I'm a lesbian, and it's as much who I am as being African American was to them."

That hurt me in a way that was almost physical, and I didn't let any protests keep me from standing and embracing her. "I'm sorry. I'll try. I really will. I didn't think what I thought you were was important to me, but I guess it is. Can you give me some time?"

"Uh huh," she mumbled into my chest. "Please try."

We stood there for awhile before she pushed me away gently. "I'm not done yet."

"There's more?" I asked. I released her but didn't sit down.

"I really should have realized a long time ago. If I weren't trying to be who my mother wanted me to be, I might have. I wanted you from the very first time I saw you. I know you struggled with your body, but I thought it was fantastic from the very beginning. God, you're gorgeous."

I didn't argue with her.

"Amy realized it long before I did. She thought us rooming together was a terrible idea and argued against it, but no one listened." Her words started to slow down. "And one more thing. This is really important to me. I have never, and I mean never, slept with another woman. I don't know why, but that was the line I wouldn't cross. For all of the other stupid shit I've done, that is what being unfaithful to you would have meant. So I've never done it, and I never will."

I flinched. "You don't need to say that. You can't be unfaithful to me because we aren't together anymore."

She smiled for the first time in two hours. "Uh huh."

CHAPTER 31

January 2015

'd long suspected that some information about the rapes had leaked out into the women's hockey world. Once I'd told my teammates, and they'd told their parents, it's too small a world for it not to have. No one ever said anything directly; apparently there are some topics even the nastiest chirpers won't touch. But facial expressions, gestures, and half-completed sentences over the previous three years had suggested it wasn't entirely a secret.

Now that the story was out in the open, the lid came off. A couple of Indiana players approached during warm-ups to express support, and more did so in the handshake line after the game. It made me uncomfortable. I didn't want sympathy from opponents or to have friendly conversations with them.

I mostly just grunted acknowledgment. My teammates often made reassuring noises back to them to the effect that I appreciated their concern. They knew it was mostly bullshit, but I didn't interfere. Even if I don't understand some social niceties, I try not to interfere with other people exercising them on my behalf.

More importantly, we came out flying and won both games that weekend by identical 6–2 scores. My contributions were greater than the single assist I picked up indicated. I caused mayhem in front of the net, screening the goalie and distracting defensemen.

It was hard to improve on how we did against Indiana over my career. In those five seasons we played them twenty-four times and won all of them. I dressed for sixteen of those games and totaled six goals, seven assists, and forty-two penalty minutes. There were seven more league teams I'd get to complete my tally against.

Sveta and I spent a lot of early mornings working out together. We ran, and we worked on those parts of the game where she wasn't already miles better than I could hope to be. That meant I spent a lot of time acting as a defenseman. That it now seemed a bit alien bothered me.

One day in mid-January, though, my heart wasn't in it, and she sensed that. "You seem unhappy, Feba."

I captured a puck with my stick and sent it down the length of the ice. "That's because I *am* unhappy."

"Caitlyn?"

I forced a smile. "Yes, Caitlyn."

"Does she refuse to make a decision?"

"Oh, no. She's made a decision." I skated to the corner and sat down along the boards. It had been awhile since I just sat, on a rink, and thought.

Sveta joined me but remained on her feet. "Do not be too sure. Caitlyn avoids decisions."

"Usually," I agreed morosely. "This time she said she doesn't want me."

"Are you sure that is what she really said?"

"I offered to go to Toronto with her. She said no."

"You have chosen a hard one, Feba. I do not envy you this choice."

I looked up at her. "I have no idea what you mean."

"The advantage of speaking in foreign language is easy to be vague and mysterious."

"Gee, thanks."

"You're welcome." She sat down next to me. "Truth is I do not know what advice to give. I do not understand Caitlyn."

"Caitlyn doesn't understand Caitlyn," I complained.

"That is why you shouldn't overreact to what she says and does now. She wants you, but she doesn't know how."

"I thought you didn't like her."

"I don't like or dislike her. She is too . . ." Her voice trailed off as she searched for a word.

"Flaky?" I offered, echoing Abby.

"Is that proper word?"

"Yeah, probably."

"Then she is too flaky for me to have opinion on. But that is not relevant, Feba, because you do like her."

"Sometimes. Sometimes I just want to kill her."

"Different sides of same coin."

"Do you deliberately drop the articles when you talk in order to sound more Russian and enigmatic? I know you know how to use them."

"I do not understand this word 'enigmatic.'"

"Yes, you . . . never mind. I'll take that as an answer."

"Stand up, Feba. I wish to play more hockey."

For the first three months of 2015 I lived hockey with an intensity I hadn't since I'd made the team. In anticipation I was taking the minimum class load necessary to stay eligible; one was on coaching hockey. I was determined not to let anything distract me as my career came to an end.

My idea of an evening's entertainment was watching video of our next opponent, trying to figure out tendencies. At least that's what I told myself I was doing. Mostly I was just wallowing in being on the team, reminding myself at every opportunity that I was a hockey player.

Even Caitlyn thought it was too much. "I'm going home," she finally declared one evening when we were the only ones left at Ridder.

"I'll be there in awhile," I responded.

"Phoebe," she said with exasperation, "relax."

I looked up at her. "I am relaxed." I leaned back and put my hands behind my head. "Really. Have I been showing any of my usual signs of being stressed out?"

"No," she admitted.

"I'm just enjoying it. I have two more months of being a hockey player, and right now that's all I want to do. You've got the national team to look forward to, and the CWHL, for years still. I don't."

"You don't have to quit playing. Even if it's just beer leagues. You're having fun. I don't understand why you're insisting that it's over."

"You've spoiled me, Caitlyn."

"I have?"

"All of you have. Wherever I go, it won't be like this. It isn't really the game I love. It's great, and it's part of it, but what I love is being a part of the team. It's hard to explain."

"Try," she said quietly.

"Even if I could stomach the thought of starting over, of trying to build new relationships on a new team, it wouldn't work. The level of commitment would never be there. I'd be back on a team where no one works as hard as I do. You know me well enough to understand that I couldn't approach it with anything less than full intensity, and it would piss me off that my teammates didn't."

"I can see that, but—"

"That's not the worst of it. I could live with that, and if it was just commitment to the game, I probably would. But it wouldn't. It's the commitment to the people. I just have a different definition of what a team is."

"You keep saying that. It's bullshit. The rest of us are as committed as you are."

"To this team, yes." I could feel myself starting to become agitated. "I don't doubt that it means as much to all of you as it does to me, but it isn't something necessary for you to think of it as a team. You have a broader concept of it than I do. It works for you even without that commitment.

"If I started playing rec league hockey, it would be just a bunch of people playing hockey. That's what I can't be a part of again. If I tried, I'd just be chasing the past and hate what I actually had."

I clicked off the TV and the video equipment.

"You're upset," Caitlyn said.

I just shrugged.

"I'm sorry. I didn't mean to make you upset."

"It's okay," I offered. "There was nothing wrong with asking. I just . . . let it overwhelm me."

"If you want, we can stay. I'll probably fall asleep, but you can keep watching."

"No." I tried to slow my breathing down. "I'd rather go home. It's easier there."

"Are you sure?"

"Yes. I keep forgetting that that's part of being on the team, too."

The one truly low moment that winter was a three-day trip to Ohio to testify before the grand jury. I left at noon on a Tuesday in order to appear on Wednesday. Thanks to a snowstorm I didn't get back until almost midnight on Thursday. All in order to provide ninety minutes of testimony.

The DA was as gentle as possible. He even apologized for bringing me down, but he was obviously correct that there was no way to secure an indictment without me being there. I was just no longer sure it was worth it.

My new mother offered to travel down with me. I chose that moment to act tough and say that I'd be fine. She clearly, and correctly, thought I was making a mistake, but she didn't insist. I appreciated that she didn't say, "I told you so," when she picked me up at the airport.

Caitlyn was waiting for me when I got back to the apartment. She didn't say anything. Instead, she just put me to bed and joined me. For once I may have gotten to sleep before she did.

Other than that, I kept it together until the second week of February. It helped that we kept winning. Everything is easier when you're winning every night.

The festivities connected with the last regular season home series of the year burst the bubble I had around myself. It started with the banquet that Thursday.

There was an uneven demarcation in the room during the cocktail hour that preceded the meal. The team gathered in one corner, and for the most part the fans stayed out of it. Players' parents mingled, and some of the girls wandered to talk to people they had gotten to know. As always I remained a fixture in our little corner.

I never became comfortable with our fans. I don't even understand the idea of fans or watching sports as entertainment. I watched lots of hockey video, but it was all with the idea of getting better. Once I stopped playing, I stopped watching, too.

I never fed off of their presence the way the others did. They were performers, and the people watching were a piece of their motivation. When the building got loud with cheers, their energy level increased. When we were on the road, getting the other team's fans to shut up accomplished the same thing.

It never worked that way for me. I would have preferred to play in front of a bunch of empty seats, sharing the successes and failures with only the people I knew. I found it creepy that people I didn't know were nevertheless invested in my life and curious about who I was.

None of that was the fans' fault. Word got out in the wake of that disastrous reception my freshman year that I really didn't want to meet any of them. A couple of minor, almost accidental, incidents aside, they never violated those boundaries.

It was with all of that running through my mind that I ate dinner. Afterward Coach Long introduced each of the seniors in turn, and we gave a brief speech summing up our thoughts on the whole college hockey experience. I had plenty of time to think about it because we went in alphabetical order, so I was last. Going by jersey number would have accomplished the same.

I squirmed through eight speeches. Fortunately Mom and Dad attended in lieu of any biological parents of my own. I was still getting used to calling them that.

However badly I wanted to avoid it, my turn came up eventually. Coach stood at the podium, talking about me. I know this is what he said because I keep a recording of that night and watch it occasionally.

"Our last senior is Phoebe Rose. She has scored 31 goals and 38 assists while playing in 138 games.

"I have never had a player work so hard just to get onto the team. That spring five years ago, she kept showing up. Sometimes she'd ask if we'd give her a tryout. Sometimes she just watched. A couple of the players mentioned this girl to me that they couldn't seem to get rid of.

"I had no idea then how much it cost her every single time she talked to me, how very scared she was to even open her mouth. I thought she was just confident in herself. I finally had no choice but to give her that tryout.

"By that time I knew a little bit about her. I confessed to her awhile back that I only let her onto the team because I couldn't bear to say no to someone with her story and who worked so hard. All I saw at first was a big, slow kid who didn't fit the kind of team we are.

"I spent the next eight months thinking I'd made a mistake. None of us understood all of the things about our own lives that we took for granted every day. There were days I wished we'd never taken on the burden of learning. There were times it was frustrating, when it felt like dealing with her was a distraction from the job of building a winning hockey team.

"I'm glad she had the patience and the stubbornness to put up with the rest of us. It turned out that she was important to building a winning team, that she taught us as much as we taught her. I'm not just a better coach for having had her on my team. I'm also a better parent and a better friend.

"If she hadn't pushed her way onto the team, I would have missed out on more joy and rewards than I can describe. Far from being a mistake, giving her that tryout was one of the best decisions I've ever made.

"Phoebe, come on up here."

I got up from my table and walked to the stage. I hugged Coach Long when I got there—harder than any of the others, I think. I got to the podium and looked out.

"I'm nervous. Some of you may remember that I don't really like public speaking." A few people chuckled. "But I'm going to get through this.

"When I arrived here five years ago, I had about four changes of clothes, a few books, one complete set of used hockey gear, a home-made computer, and a stuffed cat. I'm leaving here with a family.

"Dreaming of being on this team kept me going through some bad times, and it didn't disappoint. So many people talk about how, when they get what they really want, they find out that it wasn't what they thought it would be. I can't say that.

"Everyone has said that the most important thing about their experience here has been their teammates. That's true for me, too. I can't describe how important. This is my family. These are the people I can lean on. The ones I can trust.

"It's hard to think about not being a part of this every day. Thank you, Coach Long, for taking that chance on me. Thank you for finding a place for that big, awkward girl who had played for a high school that didn't even have a girls' team and who had never been to a real hockey camp. Thank you."

I was crying. I stepped back and looked around. All of the emotion finally hit, borne up by the applause. And there was suddenly no escaping that it was almost over.

CHAPTER 32

August 2022

Summer was a time of more relaxed hockey. No outside leagues, just internal teams, and everyone was supposed to have fun. Some had a harder time of it than others. I made sure I kept Eddy on my team, even if others complained that I was stacking things in my favor.

That wasn't my intention. I just tried to do things to make sure that she was challenged while still enjoying herself. Twice I told her before a game that she wasn't allowed to shoot the puck, only pass it. Other times I had her play defense.

I took her out for lunch a couple of weeks before the tryouts for the winter travel team. It was a shoo-in that she'd make it. After some small talk, she beat me to the punch on the important stuff.

"I'm not going to make it to D1, am I?" she asked.

"I'm the last one who should tell someone that it can't happen, but, no, you aren't. I've been sending out the videos, and there isn't any interest."

"Thank you for trying."

"Hey, we're not done yet," I answered. "Division 1 is out, but there's still Division 3. Have you considered that?"

"I'm not sure I want to go to a school that small."

"That's good thinking. Always keep in mind the academics and what kind of place you want to attend. But I bring it up because you're about to be a junior, and now is the time to start contacting coaches. By the end of the year, the places will start filling up."

"I'll think about it."

"I wish I could offer more. You've taken what I told you last year to heart and done all I asked."

"You were right. I had more fun playing your way. If nothing else, I'll always have that."

"It's a good thing to have."

"I'm going to play for the club team wherever I end up going. I probably wouldn't have said that a year ago."

"Where are you considering?"

"Michigan is high on my list, because of the academics. Why are you making that face?"

"Old rivalries die really hard."

"Oh?"

"That was where I got my shoulder dislocated. There was a lot of bad blood."

"I'll tell them they were wrong."

November 2022

"Do you ever reach the point that you don't miss playing?" Caitlyn asked me in one of our phone conversations.

"No, you don't."

"I don't know if I'm going to manage giving it up completely like you did."

"Why are you trying to?"

"Because I thought that everything you said sounded sensible."

"Well, stop it. Join a beer league or something."

"Okay, okay. I will."

"How's your job?"

"It's okay," she said. "I mean, it's a job. It pays the bills. I go to it every day."

"Good."

"I think it's better than if I loved it, to be honest. Everything on an even keel. That's the way I'm trying to take things."

"Keep plugging. I'm proud of you."

She sighed. "I suppose. One thing I'll say about my life before I got diagnosed is that it was rarely tedious."

"Boredom is underrated, Kitten."

"Hey," she said, "I never said I had the slightest desire to stop taking my meds. I just never realized that life is so long."

"Are you finding anything that provides satisfaction?"

"You sound like my therapist."

"Sorry."

"It's okay. Besides, I need a pep talk."

"For what?"

"I think it's time I started talking to my mother again."

"If you want to, I think it's a good idea."

"I didn't say that I want to. I said that I should."

"Before you do, I should warn you that I stayed in touch with her. I've reassured her every few months that you're still alive and given her brief updates on how you were doing."

There was a long pause. "I suppose that's a good thing. You didn't tell her I figured out my sexuality, did you?"

"Good Lord, no. I wouldn't have touched that conversation."

"I guess I'm thankful for that, except that it means that I'll have to do it."

"Good luck."

"It's my year for reconciliations, I guess."

"What does that mean?"

"It means that Abby and I are on better terms now."

"Really?"

"Yeah. She came up to Toronto back in July with some bullshit excuse about attending a third-rate academic symposium. We sat down and had a long heart-to-heart talk and cleared a lot of air."

"Good, I guess. Did anything in particular prompt this?"

"Not that I could tell. I just got an email from her one day that she'd be in town and could we have dinner."

"So what did you talk about?"

"Stuff."

"You're being evasive, so I assume that I was the subject."

"Not entirely."

"There's no point in my pursuing this, is there?"

"None. I brought it up just so you knew that you don't have to indelicately avoid the topic of me when you talk to her."

"What makes you think I avoid the subject of you when I talk to Abby?"

"Because you always avoid difficult topics when you can. Besides, she told me you do."

"Hey!"

"Hey, yourself. You're the one who always said you wanted a sister, not a therapist. So you should be used to being treated like a little sister."

I didn't have a good answer for that.

December 2022

"What do you actually do?" Eddy asked me as I drove her home after a film session. Giving her a ride had become a regular occurrence.

"For a living?"

"Yeah. I mean, it seems anytime one of us has a problem, you always have time to help. That's not like anyone else I know in tech."

"I'm an independent software consultant."

She made a rude noise. "That could mean anything from unemployment to a secret government contract."

I laughed. "In my case it means I made a lot of money by being in the right place at the right time. Then I decided that I didn't like what I was doing and quit. I still work, but I'm really selective about who I'll work for. I won't work for people I don't like, and I won't take jobs that threaten to take over my life."

"That's cool. I knew about the company you helped launch. My father investigated who you are way back at the beginning. He shut up about you after he did."

"I'm glad."

"You don't like him, do you?"

"I don't know that I should say that."

"You know one of the things I like about you?" she asked. "You talk to us like we're adults. You say what you think, and you don't make things out to be simpler than they are."

I took the hint. "No, I don't like him."

"That's okay. I don't like him, either."

"Don't become too set in that thought. Sometimes parents look different once you're older."

"That sounded forced."

"Sorry. That's what people tell me, at any rate. I don't really have any experience with it."

"What was it like, growing up like you did?"

I pondered the question for almost a minute. "Lonely," I finally said. "Very lonely."

"I feel that way sometimes, too. I mean, it's nothing like it was for you, but my parents are gone all the time. Sorry. That probably sounds . . ." Her voice trailed off.

"It's okay," I said. "I long ago realized that there isn't some competition for the most awful childhood. What happened to me has nothing at all to do with whether you feel lonely."

"Thanks."

I spent much of that Christmas chasing my eleven-month-old nephew. "I don't think I've ever seen you tired on Christmas Eve before," I told Abby.

"It's constant. Thank you for watching him this afternoon."

"No problem. He took a nap, and then I taught him how to cross-check."

She laughed.

"You shouldn't assume I'm joking about that. I don't relate well to kids."

"Yet you coach a bunch of them."

"It's different once they're seventeen. Besides, I've been told that I don't treat them like kids, so I'm not sure how well I really relate."

"You do fine," she said. "You're better at it than you think."

"People keep telling me that about all sorts of things."

"That's because it's true."

"To change the subject, I heard that you had a long talk with Caitlyn last summer."

"I assume you heard that from her, so yes, we did."

"About what?"

She drummed her fingers on the end table. "About you, about her, and I guess a bit about me."

"That's not very specific."

"No, it isn't." She exhaled heavily. "I'd like to tell you more, I really would, but I promised her that I wouldn't."

"Why did she have to have her heart-to-heart with someone who actually keeps promises?"

"What I will tell you is that we've buried the hatchet. I still have issues with how she has behaved, but no more sniping. And I can see why you've always said that she can be a hell of a lot of fun when she's in the right mood."

"Okay, now I'm as curious about what you did to have fun as I am to know what you said about me."

"Sorry."

"You don't sound the slightest bit sorry."

"More seriously," she continued, "don't let her being bipolar be an excuse for the way she's treated you. I still wouldn't count on her to be reliable."

"It's okay. We're just friends."

"Still, keep it in mind."

CHAPTER 33

The Friday night game after the banquet was almost an afterthought, and we played like it. It was the only blemish on our record against Ohio State during my career. I was as guilty of taking them lightly that night as anyone on the team, so I can't complain about it.

The next night was Senior Night, when those soon to depart and their parents are introduced to the crowd. Given the size of the graduating class, they had to roll out an extra-large red carpet for the parents to stand on at center ice.

I never liked being announced as a part of the starting lineup before a game. It interfered with my attempts to remain anonymous. Maybe it would have been different if the first time it happened, way back in Columbus, hadn't been such a catastrophe, but I always felt I played worse when my name was called. The numbers don't bear that out, but hockey players are superstitious folks. At least I didn't feel compelled to eat my pregame meal with my left hand, the way Kennedy did.

Senior Night was like that, but a thousand times worse. As I stood in the tunnel ready to come out, the fact that it was the last regular season game I'd ever play at Ridder almost overwhelmed me. I'd always thought it was a nice little ceremony until the year when I had to participate. What was worse was that I was going to be standing out there by myself. I'd asked to have Mom and Dad out there with me, but Coach told me it was for parents only.

As with the speeches I was the last one to get called. The rest of the girls had bouquets to give to their mothers, even Caitlyn. For fifteen minutes, her family was going to pretend that they liked each other. I was empty handed, having no one to give flowers to. It was rare for me to be bothered by not having parents anymore, but it hit home on this occasion.

When I stepped out onto the ice, it took a second for the sight to register. Then my knees went weak. A crowd waited for me. Kathy looked like she was going to die from laughter. "Surprise!" she cried as I reach them.

We embraced. "What are you doing here?"

"We're representing your family. Did you think no one would be here?"

Kathy let go, and I moved to Linda Barron. "There were too many who wanted to come out, so we had to limit it to just the captains."

I was at a loss for words, so I just hugged all eight in turn. For a moment I was even pleased to see Tammy. Jenny skated over from her parents as well. I suppose the crowd was deafening at this point, but I'd forgotten about them entirely. We posed for photos, both official and personal. Kathy cackled like a loon through the whole thing.

It would have been easy for the game to be anticlimactic after that, but we'd gotten it out of our system the night before. We rolled 8–2 and in the process clinched the regular season title that had eluded us in all of my previous seasons.

There was still one weekend left in the regular season. Just as we'd never won the regular season crown, we'd never come home from East Lansing with two wins. We spent a lot of time at practice that week making sure we remembered that fact.

The best word to describe the mood on the flight was "focused." On the way back it was "raucous." The games weren't even dramatic. The 3–0 and 4–1 final scores failed to do justice to how thoroughly we dominated. We scored early both nights and never let them get established.

It was a series full of good omens. We had the league title clinched before going there. We'd only lost twice all year, and the number one overall seed for the NCAA tournament was ours, so all we had to play for was pride and the satisfaction of putting Michigan State's season on the brink. By beating them twice we left them in a position where they had to win the Big Ten playoff title and its automatic berth if they wanted to make the field for the NCAA tournament.

The team I compared us to was Wisconsin from when I was a freshman. Like them, we got two star forwards back from the Olympics who just destroyed everything in their path. I didn't have fourteen goals and thirteen assists because of my own talent; it's because I skated through the wreckage my linemates left behind.

Even the little things broke the right way. We played a lot of poker that year on the bus trips. Penny ante. I was up almost thirty dollars on the season. A fair chunk of that money was Caitlyn's. I made her earn it back around the apartment.

Two weeks later we were in Madison for the Big Ten Final Four. On the first night we played Michigan for the last time in my career. It was the typical bruising affair. My main contribution was eight minutes in penalties, but I didn't get anything worse than a coincidental double minor for roughing after the game got out of hand in the third. Fortunately, the national rankings indicated that they were going to be Wisconsin's problem the next week in the first round of the NCAA tournament. I was happy to be done with them.

Later that night Caitlyn and I talked with Jenny. We found ourselves doing that more often as the season wound down. There were six other seniors, but the bond wasn't the same. The three of us came in together, and we were the only ones left who remembered how that first year ended: the worst game we played as a team in five years. The two of them played against each other in the Olympics. Caitlyn and I were . . . whatever we were, and Jenny stuck by us.

So we found ourselves together a lot late at night in the hotel room Caitlyn and I shared on the road, pounding bottled water. I still led the team in ice bags; I had four of them that night.

"This is it, guys," I said. "I'm going to play at most four more hockey games in my life, and I want them all."

"We all do," Jenny answered.

Caitlyn scooted behind me and put her arms around my waist. We're kind of funny to talk to that way, because she either peeks out under my arm or just over my shoulder. "We won't let this end for you until the schedule makers won't let us play anymore."

Jenny looked at me. "What I said about always being available for you doesn't end with the season. That's for life."

"I don't know how to thank you guys. I think about what would have happened if I hadn't made the team and—"

"Don't," said Caitlyn. "It didn't happen."

"But it could have." I don't know what had happened to my mood. "I got lucky."

"No, you didn't," Jenny said. She'd seen my moods before. "You worked hard for it."

"Yes, and I got lucky, too." I shuddered.

"Shhh," Caitlyn whispered as close to my ear as she could get.

"What am I going to do? I'll be in California all by myself."

"Any of us will only be a phone call away."

"It's not the same."

Jenny looked questioningly over my shoulder. In response to something Caitlyn did, she moved to the bed we were sitting on. She didn't quite sit in my lap, but she joined the hug.

"Breathe easily," Caitlyn said softly. "Don't talk." I'm not sure which of us she was talking to.

I closed my eyes and focused on the sounds. There was only breathing—the three of us and the ventilation system. I let everything else slide out of my mind. I noticed as each of us adjusted our breathing until we were in sync.

I was surrounded but in no way trapped. Slowly, the tension drifted away. I realized I was crying, but it was as much relief as anything.

Eventually Caitlyn relaxed her grip. "We're good."

Jenny let go and moved back to the other bed, the one we wouldn't be using. "That was amazing."

My head slumped. Somewhere the terror still lurked, but it was at bay, and I could at least ignore it.

"I'm glad you got to see that, Jenny," Caitlyn said. "That you got to be a part of it. That's what we do for each other."

"I never really imagined." I listened to the two of them, unwilling to do anything that would disrupt my fragile balance. "And this works for you, too?"

"This? No. I start giggling, and it all falls apart. It's completely different for me, but similar. That sounds stupid, but it's the closest I can come to describing it. I just draw strength from Phoebe. I calm her down when she's scared. She pushes me forward when I am."

"It was like I could feel something shift between us."

"She says that, too. I don't. You'd think it would be the other way around. That I'd be the one with the flaky New Age feelings, but it's not. Don't tell anyone, though. Phoebe gets embarrassed even thinking about telling anyone else."

"I won't. God, I can't imagine doing anything to wreck this. Did you notice that we all started to breathe together?"

"No. Did we?" Caitlyn sounded surprised, though I've told her that, too.

"What were you paying attention to?"

"I listen to her heartbeat. But she does the breathing thing, too. You seem to have a lot in common."

"Thank you. Do you think you could teach me more?"

"You'd have to ask Phoebe. She's the teacher. But not tonight. She's not all back yet, and we shouldn't bother her."

"Should I leave?"

I managed to shake my head.

"No," Caitlyn translated. "She likes you being here. We can talk, but just don't expect her to answer. She's listening, though, so you can tell her things."

Their conversation drifted toward other things. Small talk.

I stopped listening to the words and just registered the sounds—those and the feel of Caitlyn's arms around me.

My reverie was broken by the sound of the door. Caitlyn said softly, "She's gone. It's just us."

I exhaled deeply, a rattling sound. "Thank you."

"You don't mind that I invited her in, do you?"

"No. I'm glad. I'm glad she liked it."

"I don't think 'liked it' begins to describe it."

I pulled myself to my feet and started to undress. "Caitlyn, I'm scared. Not right now, but I will be. I really don't know what I'm going to do."

"I know. I'm sorry. I'll visit often."

I nodded. With the fear lurking in the far corners of my mind rather than pressing down on me, I didn't say anything else. I just went to bed and focused on her breath.

As hard as it got to keep from panicking in the rest of my life, I never lost the ability to focus when game time rolled around. If anything, I played the best hockey of my life the last three weeks of my career. Against Michigan it was just being a physical presence. The next night it was more tangible.

It would have been nice if Wisconsin had finished off Michigan State for us, but they lost their semifinal. No matter how much I disliked them there was no denying that the Spartans had decided that they weren't going to go quietly.

They took us right down to the wire in the league final and beyond. We had them down 3–2 with a minute to play, but they tied it up with their goalie pulled.

There's nothing in sports like overtime in a hockey game that could end a team's season with a loss. It's sudden death in the truest sense: the play that ends the game looks just like another shot on goal until it goes in.

This one took just over twelve minutes to settle. As teams get tired, there always seems to be one part of the game that slips away from them. That night it was the ability to hold the puck in the zone. Each team would bring it down the ice and get maybe one chance before the other could clear it.

So it wasn't a surprise that the winning goal was scored in transition, just that I was the player who put it in. Speed never matters as much as it does in transition, and my lack of it meant that I wasn't usually much of a factor until we got set up in the offensive zone.

My workout regime was less extreme than it had been four years earlier, but I was still the best conditioned athlete on the ice. That meant that everyone else had slowed down toward my level, making me look faster than I was. The play started with Crosser forcing a turnover in our end and passing it to Sveta, who took off wide down the left side. I busted up the middle to the net, hoping to draw the defense with me and allowing Caitlyn extra space as she trailed behind me.

Sveta shot the puck, which arrived at the crease at the same instant I did. It bounced off the goalie's pads. The defenseman tried to tackle me, but she was trying to hold onto a bull. In the ensuing scramble the puck bounced off my skate and into the net. The ref signaled a goal.

Two things happened simultaneously: all of my teammates jumped off the bench to celebrate the win, and the entire State team started yelling that I'd kicked it in. It's okay for a goal to go in off your skate, but it doesn't count if you direct it in with, as the rules state, "a distinct kicking motion."

As we continued our celebration, the refs went to the scorer's booth to watch a replay to make sure that it was a legal goal. They spent six minutes in there trying to sort it out. As the time passed, everyone on both sides got increasingly jittery about the outcome. It's tough to stand there waiting after you thought you'd won.

Eventually they emerged and pointed to center ice. In regulation time that means that that's where the next face-off will take place. In overtime it just means that the game's over. In terms of winning and losing, it was the most important goal of my career, the only time I ever scored in overtime or even to put us ahead or into a tie in the last five minutes of regulation.

At that moment I knew that I'd played Michigan State for the last time. We went 14-12 against them in my time, which was the lowest winning percentage we had against anyone in the league, but we beat them when it really counted. We had a losing record in the regular season but went 5-1 in the Big Ten and NCAA tournaments. In three of the five years, their season ended with a loss to us, and the reverse never happened.

It meant that we'd accomplished two goals with only one to go. Only the NCAAs were left.

And yeah, I kicked the puck in.

CHAPTER 34

July 2023

"**I**t was good to see you." I hugged Caitlyn, something I could almost do without feeling sad for what was lost. I didn't want to walk through security in the Toronto airport and leave her.

"It was good to see you too. Next time, we'll do it in San Francisco." She pulled back and looked at me. "Say it again."

"You're a lesbian. I admit it."

She bounced on her feet. "I believe you mean it. Thank you."

"For what?"

"For doing what I asked and really thinking about it. For not pulling one of your stubborns and refusing to admit the obvious."

"You're welcome. Caitlyn, you're doing so well. Two years at the same job. You seem happy. You look great. I'm proud of you."

"Thank you. I'm marvelous, just like we all knew I could be. There's just one problem."

"What's that?"

"You. Are you okay? You seem, I don't know, just kind of off. You have all week."

"I found out who I am."

"Who you are?"

"When I was born. Where. My biological parents' names."

She stepped back. "You're just telling me this now? As you're leaving?"

"I don't want to talk about it. I don't want to hide anything from you, like you asked, but I don't want to talk about it."

"Why not? Wait, forget I asked that." She hugged me again.

As we broke apart and I picked up my bag, she said, "Phoebe, if you need me, please call me. I don't have a special phone for it, but just call me."

I felt a miserable loneliness as I left.

September 2023

At the first practice after tryouts for the travel team, I gathered everyone around. "First of all, I'd like to welcome those of you who are new to the team. I'm sure you recognize me from all the times I showed up at your practices. The purpose of that was to make sure that Coach Henry and I were on the same page in terms of what we taught and what systems we run. So the transition shouldn't be too hard.

"As for a formal introduction, my name is Phoebe Rose. When we are inside this building, call me Coach or Coach Rose. Elsewhere, feel free to call me Phoebe if you prefer. This is my third year coaching this team. Before that, I played four years of varsity hockey at the University of Minnesota, during which time we won two national championships. So while I'm always open to learning and finding out I'm wrong about something, I do have some idea of what I'm doing. So make sure you have good arguments before you come complain about something.

"While I run the same basic game plan as Coach Henry, you will find that I do so less rigidly than he does. I don't mind you stepping out of the system; in fact, I encourage it as long as you have a good reason to do so. You'll find that a lot of our practice time is devoted to learning when and how to do something different, and how to react when you see one of your teammates do so.

"There are only two rules I won't compromise on. The first is to work hard. If you work hard and don't win, that's okay. I won't lie; winning is important, and I expect to do more of it this year than the last two, but it isn't all important. Just make sure that you couldn't have done more to keep from losing.

"The second rule is that this is a team. Support your teammates. Don't solve things by yourself; involve them. If your teammate needs

395

help, give it. If you need help from a teammate, ask for it. You don't have to be best friends with all of your teammates, but you do have to respect them all. All of that applies off the ice as well as on the ice.

"I take that very seriously. It's the product of having played on a team that didn't follow those rules when I was your age. I don't care how many points you've put up or how good you are, ignoring that rule is the quickest path into my doghouse. If you ask the players who were here last year, I'm sure they'll be happy to tell you about the time I suspended myself for not following it.

"Along those lines, I'd like to introduce this year's captain, Eddy Howser." She hadn't known that until I said it. "Eddy is the example that proves you can learn all of this. The teammates who just voted for her to be captain provide a testament to how she has grown into a leadership role. If you follow her, you're probably going places."

With that, we started another season.

A week later, in my office after practice, I asked Eddy where she had applied for college.

"Wesleyan. Hamilton. Kalamazoo College. I particularly like the last one."

"Hah. There aren't very many coaches out there for whom my recommendation would be a negative, but you picked one."

"Coach Jackson told me you'd say that the first time I talked to her."

"Our relations were a bit contentious back when we played against each other."

"So I gathered. She also said that you knew what you were doing and that she'd respect your opinion about a player."

"She's not as good at carrying a grudge as I am, I guess." I saw apprehension on her face. "Don't worry. I won't let any of that affect what I tell her about you."

"Thank you." She started to head for the door, then stopped. "Coach Rose, are we friends?"

"Sure. Why?"

"Well, I want to ask you something I can't imagine asking any other coach."

"What's wrong?"

"That's just it. That's what I want to ask you. Is there something wrong?"

That pulled me up short. "Why do you ask?"

"Well, you've seemed kind of . . . I don't know. I've heard your preseason speech three times, and it came out kind of flat this year."

"Maybe it's just getting stale," I offered.

"Maybe." She sounded skeptical. "But now that I'm the team captain, it's my responsibility to deal with potential problems."

I leaned back in my chair. "And I'm a potential problem."

She chewed her lip. "That didn't come out right. I . . . You mean so much to me. I'm a better player and a better person than I was two years ago. That's because of you. You're not like any other coach I've ever had. You say you're a part of the team and that we're supposed to help teammates."

I blinked away tears. "Thank you. I'm grateful you asked. I don't think you can help right now, not directly anyway. I'm dealing with some very personal things that either I can't share or that it wouldn't be appropriate for me to share. But coaching you, both you personally and the whole team, is the bright spot. I'm sorry the enthusiasm isn't showing, because it should."

"Then I guess . . . maybe I can help by making hockey fun for you."

December 2023

Christmas Eve started out with Abby talking about her research. She realized she was mostly talking to herself. The fact that I was drinking bourbon instead of cocoa had clued her in that something was up. So she made noise, waiting for me to open up about what was eating me.

"Patterson," I said at last, interrupting something about how children form neural connections.

She stopped in mid-sentence. "Hmm?"

"That's my real name. Phoebe Patterson."

I wasn't really looking at her, but I heard her suck in her breath and sit up straight. "Go on."

"I was born on November 23, 1992, in Dearborn, Michigan, so I'm almost a year younger than we thought. I don't know how I came up with the idea that I was four when they found me, but I was wrong."

I paused to take another swallow of whiskey. Abby did nothing to fill the silence. "I got a letter from a nurse. She read a profile of me in some tech magazine, one that mentioned my AIS. I don't know how they found that out. Dennis swears it wasn't him.

"The letter said that a little girl named Phoebe had been admitted to the hospital in Toledo where she worked in July 1996 with a brain infection. She told me that it could have caused some memory loss, which would explain a lot. When the doctors did blood work, they found that her testosterone levels were off the charts. So they ordered more tests. Naturally, they figured out that the girl didn't have all of the right pieces and, in addition to dealing with the infection, they diagnosed her with Androgen Insensitivity Syndrome."

Now that I was talking, the booze had done its job, and I tried to set my glass on the end table. I was looking at my lap and missed. I winced as I heard it hit the floor and the ice scattered. Abby didn't move.

"They released her two weeks before I was found on the streets of Dayton. I guess my parents couldn't deal with the diagnosis. Why they didn't turn me over to an agency of some sort, I have no idea. Maybe they were too embarrassed even for that.

"Their names were Katherine and Edward. I don't know much about them other than that they were both nineteen when I was born. That's on my birth certificate. I don't know anything more about them. I don't know if they're alive or dead. My mother signed the forms discharging me from the hospital, and that's the last thing I can tell you about either of them.

"I don't want to know more than that. I don't want to know even that much." My voice was cracking. "I won't say that I was happy not knowing anything about where I came from, but I was content. I hardly ever thought about it. None of it really mattered to me once I had you guys. You're family. What happened before didn't matter.

"Besides, I wouldn't have known where to look even if I'd wanted to. The authorities exhausted all of the leads back at the beginning. So it really didn't matter. It wasn't worth worrying about.

"Then this nurse contacts me, and now I do know where to look. I could track them down, alive or dead. It picks at me. I don't do anything about it because it couldn't lead to anything good. If I talked to them, the anger would overwhelm me. I don't want to do that. I just want to move on with the life I had."

I stopped. Abby waited a couple of minutes before saying anything. "How long have you known?"

"About nine months."

"Why did you wait this long to tell anyone?"

At least I got a chuckle out of that. "I didn't. I told Caitlyn not long after it happened. She made me promise that I wouldn't keep things from her when she found out I had AIS eighteen months after we started sleeping together."

"Okay. So why did you wait so long to tell me?"

I could feel her fuming from across the room, but she had at least learned how not to vent certain kinds of her frustrations with me. "I thought I was done. I thought there were no painful secrets left that I'd have to tell. Every time I thought about telling you, it seemed like all of the old, bad times were coming back. I wanted it to go away. I'm sorry. I know it was stupid to keep it bottled up. I couldn't get it out. I mean, I'm plastered enough right now to be dropping glassware, and I could barely do it."

She inhaled deeply. "Don't be sorry. I understand how hard it must be."

"But there it is," I replied. "I'm not a mystery anymore."

"What are you going to do about it?" she asked.

"Hopefully nothing. I hope that by telling you I can put it to rest and stop worrying about it. I'd like to be able to pretend that I don't know any of it. The lawyer said that I could change my legal name and birthday if I wanted to, but that I don't have to. So I won't. I don't want to be Phoebe Patterson. If I wanted to be something other than Phoebe Rose, I'd change my name to Forrest."

"And if it doesn't stop eating at you?"

"I don't know," I mumbled.

"You're going to have to think about that."

I felt a surge of anger and snapped, "I have been thinking about it. I'm just not coming up with any answers that I like."

"Phoebe, look at me." Reluctantly I did so. There was worry on her face. "Thank you for telling me these things."

"You're welcome," I said bitterly.

Then, when hockey season was over, the bottom fell out.

CHAPTER 35

I **woke early** on the morning of March 20. I lay in bed feeling Caitlyn snuggled in behind me. I listened to her breathe. We were in Madison, and my attempts at meditating went poorly. Those warm, humid breaths provoked thoughts rather than relaxation.

I couldn't see the clock, but I guessed that it was ten hours until we would take the ice to play Boston College in the first of the day's two NCAA semifinals. If we won, I could put off for two more days facing that my hockey career was over. If we lost, Jenny, Caitlyn, and I would go instantly from being Gophers to being former Gophers. Even with a win it would all be over Sunday afternoon, but maybe the thrill of winning a championship could ease that hurt, at least a bit.

I'd be twenty-three years old and just entering an athletic prime I'd been working toward my entire life, and it would be over. Caitlyn and Jenny could move on, playing for national teams until someone younger pushed them out of the way. This was the moment it really sank in that hockey was going to be over. I'd been scared of losing my teammates but not hockey itself. It was the moment I questioned my determination to quit the game.

None of the reasons for it had changed. Everything I'd told Caitlyn was true. I couldn't imagine starting over with a new team. But suddenly I couldn't imagine filling the hole in my life that would be left behind. Between training, official practices, and all of the extra work I put in, I spent upward of thirty-five hours a week being a hockey player. College athletes sometimes complain about not having any free time. I was scared of the opposite.

I tensed up and lost whatever focus I had on Caitlyn's breathing. She sensed something was wrong and tightened her hold on me, mumbling something to the effect that it would be all right. I don't think she really woke up.

It mostly served to remind me that in two months, we'd head our separate ways.

Properly applied, fear can be a tremendous motivator. If that was the difference, we applied it more properly than BC did. The game wasn't a blowout, but we were in control the whole way. Our line didn't do any of the damage, but we didn't get scored on, either.

Fittingly our last game was against Wisconsin. The winner would get to claim to have been the best women's college hockey team of the last five years. If it was them, they'd have three national titles. If it was us, we'd tie them with two and be the only team in the country to have a winning record against them over that stretch.

Caitlyn says that I spent the entire last weekend of my career in a trance, and I suppose that's possible, as improbable as it seems.

I remember the game, though. It was all-out war. Not in the sense of being dirty, because it wasn't. But it was the most intense, physical hockey game I ever played in. After two periods they were ahead 4–2. It was almost a mirror image of the Big Ten final we'd played my freshman year, except that they refused to collapse the way we had. Alice played the finest period of her life in the third as we tried to claw back into the game. We cut the lead to 1 with about eight minutes left. Five minutes later she stoned Courtenay Havelock on a clean breakaway to keep us in it.

This time we were the ones who had to score in the last minute to tie the game up. Jenny came out as the extra attacker with our line. She scored with eighteen seconds left on a wrist shot from the bottom of the circle. I got a good view because I provided the screen that kept their goalie from seeing it.

The overtime was anticlimactic. I never even got to take a shift because Kat scored twenty-seven seconds in.

Given a second chance I proved that I could celebrate. And I was right. Winning did take the sting out of my career's end, at least for a few days. Time enough to ease into my future.

Thirty-five schools play Division I women's ice hockey. Only one of them can win the championship each season. Every team starts official practices in the middle of September, and then it's six months of blood, sweat, toil, and tears. Since every college hockey team makes their conference playoffs, thirty-four teams go through all of that and lose their last game. Only one hoists a banner the next year.

We did it twice. It was only the second time I really absorbed what an accomplishment it was. Three years before, winning had mostly been a relief, both for me personally and for a team that had been disappointing at the end of previous seasons.

This time, it was a raucous and euphoric celebration. It lasted from that puck hitting the back of the net and the dog pile on the ice until we bussed home the next day and carried the trophy into our own arena in front of our fans. I didn't just sit in a room and feel quietly satisfied.

This time I'd made far more direct contributions to success. I didn't spend any time wondering whether I deserved it. I'd scored eighteen goals skating on the second line, and I was one of two captains. It was my team—not just in a sense of belonging but also in a sense of ownership.

The intervening years had taught me a lot. Some of it was just the fact that being one of the thirty-four after tasting victory gave me perspective. Learning how to enjoy hockey was another big part. I played to win, not just to survive. It makes a difference.

CHAPTER 36

April 2023

"Phoebe?"

"Hi, Caitlyn."

"Holy . . . what's wrong?"

"I don't know."

"Phoebe, are you okay?"

"Not really, no."

"Do you need me?"

"I don't—"

"Shit. I'll catch the first flight."

"But you'll—."

"'It's the willingness to drop everything to help one another,' someone once said."

"I'm sorry about that. Really—"

"Screw that. You were right."

"I love you, Caitlyn."

"I love you, too. Bear, promise me you won't do anything stupid."

"I promise."

"Good. I should be there tonight. Love you. I'll call back in a few minutes, once I make my reservation."

When she arrived the next day, Caitlyn looked haggard. I'm sure I looked worse.

"I'm sorry, Phoebe."

"It's okay," I mumbled. "I watched the Delta website."

"Oh God, I bet you did." She knelt in front of me and gently pulled me off the couch. "Come here."

I let her envelop me. I've never felt anything as powerful as that first time she saved me, but her touch never fails to feel mystical when pitted against my distress.

I let her guide me. She pulled me down, into her embrace.

We lay on the floor. Almost. My favorite rug provided a thin cover over the hardwood, but it was really just the floor.

I didn't care. She was soft. The floor didn't matter.

"Thank you, Kitten." I tried to fold up. "Thank you for saving me. Thank you for being the goddess. I've never told you. I've never told you what it feels like. I'm sorry I've never told you."

"Shh. It's okay, Bear. You've told me. You tell me every time. You told me that first night. You just never remember. Just go to sleep. Just go to sleep."

I slept. Sleep that was just sleep.

The next morning I sat at the kitchen table, slumped in my chair. Caitlyn put a plate of toast in front of me. "I burned the eggs," she said sheepishly. "I'll try again in a few minutes." That explained the smell.

I got my first good look at her. There were dark circles under her eyes, but the wrinkled clothes she wore were smart and professional looking. "That's okay." My voice was flat.

She took one of the other chairs, spun it around, and sat. "When was the last time you ate?"

"Tuesday, I think."

"I guess I need to get the eggs right on the second try." She rested her chin on the chair back. "Phoebe, what's wrong?"

I looked down at the toast.

"Talk to me, Bear. This isn't like you. Not anymore. Not with me."

I sat there, silence stretching between us. Then, "He's dead."

"Who's dead?"

"He is. I won. I won for good." I pulled the obituary from my pocket and handed it to her. I'd printed it off of the website.

"He's dead? Really?" Then confusion set in. "What's the problem? I would think you'd celebrate. You certainly have the right to."

I looked up at her. "I beat him, and then realized I don't have anything else. That's all it's ever been. Just trying to beat him."

She looked hurt for a second, but it vanished. "That's not true. It isn't true that beating him was everything. The most important things were never about him."

"They were."

"Phoebe, when did you start to want to be a Gopher?"

I looked back at the toast.

"Look at me." It cracked out, hard and insistent. "Look at me and tell me when you started wanting to be a Gopher."

It drew my gaze to her. "When I was nine."

"Right. And that was six years before you ever met him. Six years in which you busted your ass every day because you wanted to be one of us. That wasn't about beating him. It couldn't have been about beating him. That was you."

I shrugged and examined the toast some more.

"You wanted to be a Gopher so bad. You worked so hard. I watched you, and dammit if I didn't try to keep up. I was never the hardest worker on the team, but you had me running those stairs. There was something about you that I didn't want to let beat me. So I ran them like you did, until the second day it was ten below and I decided that you'd won."

"You've told me that story before," I muttered.

"Yes, I have, but it doesn't seem to have taken. Here's something I haven't ever told you. About six years ago, I went to see Mrs. Wilson. I'm sure her first name was mentioned when we met her that one time, but I couldn't remember, so it was a pain in the ass to find her, but I did it. I told her about you. I told her about the things you had done. And I told her about the person you had become. The person I not only loved but admired more than anyone else. Do you know what she told me?"

I shook my head, still not looking up.

"She said that she wasn't surprised. That you had always been that determined. That you had always cared about people. That you worked hard every day for what you wanted. That didn't come from him. That is you.

"What I said then is still true. I admire you more than anyone in the world. I admire you so much that you scare me sometimes. The feeling that I'm not going to live up to your standard is . . . it's frightening. I want you to admire me as much as I admire you. And that's because of you. Not him. You."

I turned and saw tears running down her face. "I—"

"Shh. I know you don't. You love me, but you don't admire me. Let's face it, there has been a lot about me over the last twelve years that you really can't admire. But I keep trying. Because you're worth it."

"I'm not."

She swung her legs off the chair and stood over me. She pulled my head against her chest. "I didn't expect you to believe me right away. But you will. You will." She rocked me slightly. "I'm going to go cook some more eggs, and I'm going to do it right this time. Then I'm going to watch you eat them. Then we can go lie down again. We can do that all day, if you want."

She burned the eggs again. She settled for making me eat a couple of English muffins and some raspberries I had in the fridge.

We tried again the next day. "Are you feeling better this morning?" she asked me.

"I think so, yeah."

"Well enough to cook?"

"Yes."

"Thank God. I'm starving."

"I'll make omelettes. I'm not up to pancakes, though."

"I'll live."

I was sitting at the table, eating my first good meal in five days, when she prompted me:

"There's something you want to ask me. I think you've wanted to ask it for two years now, and I'm getting really tired of waiting."

"I don't know what you mean."

She just looked at me.

Eventually I continued. "You don't need me anymore. Look at you. You're a success now, without me."

"I . . ." Her face lit up. "Is that what's really been bothering you? You're afraid that I don't need you?"

"I don't know," I mumbled.

"It is. Oh God, it is."

"You were wrong, yesterday. I do admire you, Caitlyn. The way you got up from everything and started again, still cheerful. And now look at you. It all worked. You've got a great job, and you're happy. But even before that. I've always admired you."

"Really?"

"Well, except for the wedding. Brent was a tool."

"Okay, you got me there."

"You sacrificed so much for me. Your life has been a mess because of me. And now you want to throw away the success because I need you more than you need me."

"Phoebe," she said crossly, "I love you dearly, but you have always had an annoying habit of thinking everything is about you."

"But—"

"My fuckups were my own, thank you. You didn't make me do any of those things. I could have been really smart and just stayed with you in the first place. Or the second or the third. But I didn't. Do you know what I really wish? The one thing I wish I could change more than any other?"

"No. What?"

"I wish I'd given up hockey when you did. I wish I'd stopped playing and built a life right then."

"No, you don't," I said.

"I—no, you're right. I don't wish that. It was great, and I made them pry my stick from my cold, over-the-hill fingers. I do wish I'd done something more right then. The hockey is what came between us, you know."

"No, it didn't."

"Yeah, it did. You resented that I was still playing."

"I did not!"

"You didn't realize that you did, but I could tell. I never understood why you quit it cold turkey like that."

"It was over. I'd had my team, and I was never going to play on it again. I told you a long time ago that it was the team I played for, not the game. I couldn't transfer my loyalties. Not until I found a way to make a team my own again."

"You know, that makes sense. Maybe I am starting to understand you."

"Great."

"But that was the smaller part. When I was done playing, hell, even while I still was, I looked up, and you had gone on and become really good at something completely different. You'd left me behind."

"That wasn't what I did."

"You aren't the only one who gets to have irrational insecurities."

"I should be."

She laughed. "Okay, but you have it backward. I don't want you to ask me that question despite being a success. I want you to ask it because I'm a success. Do you think I said that only because of the last few days?"

"I—"

"Never mind. I'm not sure why I bothered to ask. Of course you do. I'll try again. Bear, this isn't about you."

"Okay, what are you getting at?" I was genuinely curious.

"No. You're not getting anything else until you commit."

I was seized by fear, inexplicable because she'd telegraphed her answer. At last, I said, very quietly, "Kitten, can we get back together? For real this time?"

"Of course we can." She giggled. "It crossed my mind to say no, as a gag, but you wouldn't have found it funny right now. But remember that I could have." She leaned over and kissed me.

"So what were you getting at? About it not being about me?"

"If you'd asked me two years ago, really asked me, that time you wanted me to come here from my hotel, I wouldn't have been ready. I needed to be a success first. I won't say that I needed to be a success without you, because I don't think I ever have been without you. But I needed to do it there. If I had come back then, I'd have fucked it up again."

"I'm sorry."

"I don't know exactly what you're apologizing for, but I accept it. You're forgiven."

"So what are we going to do?"

"I'm moving in with you."

"Just like that?"

She stuck her tongue out at me. "It's not just like that. FlorTech has a facility up in Santa Rosa. The commute from here will be ghastly, but I can just work up there."

"How do you know they have an opening?"

"I think it's really important that you are the one who asked if we could get back together, even if I had to twist your arm, because you were the one who said we needed to split up in the first place. But I was running out of patience. I worked it all out with my boss six months ago, and if none of this had happened, I was going to force something soon."

"You did?"

"So I'm going to stay here for a few more days. Then I'm going back to pack my things. I talked to my boss while you were sleeping yesterday, and he said to take a couple of weeks of vacation while he got the paperwork filed. It helps that I won a gold medal."

I looked at her, noticing for the first time the crow's feet that were forming in the corners of her eyes. She was more beautiful than ever, and she was going to be mine.

"Welcome home, Kitten."

EPILOGUE

June 2025

Lies! **Lies!** It's all lies, I tells ya!

Okay, most of it is true.

Would you believe that she wrote all of this down? I guess if you're reading this, it means that you read the rest of it first, so you probably do believe it. Still, that's a lot of work, especially for something she initially had no interest in publishing. If the rest of the story didn't convince you that she's really stubborn once she gets an idea in her head, that should do the trick.

I demanded, whether this thing stays between the two of us, or she does decide to publish it, that I get the last word. And I got away with it. Wrapped around my little finger, she is.

I'm not the airhead she sometimes portrays me as. I'm just exuberant. I'll let it pass, though. That's the kind of generous person I am. That and there were times she would have been justified in throttling me, so I guess we're even.

There's plenty in here I disagree with. Maybe I'll write my own memoir some day in order to tell my side of the story. There's one thing, though, that I simply can't let stand, and that's this idea that Phoebe wasn't a great hockey player.

Reading her words you'd think Greg Long gave her a place on the team as a gift and that we kept her around as some sort of mascot. It's bullshit. No one turned her into a forward because they thought it would make her happy; that was a side benefit. Greg did it because we had an injury crisis our second year, and he threw her into the lineup at wing, and she was really good—better than she ever was on defense. She scored eighteen goals as a senior for a team that won the national title. You don't do that if you're not really good.

She isn't lying about it. She really does think she was a marginal player at our level. She's not the only athlete I've met with a self-image of not being as good as she is, but she takes it to a whole different level. It's important to her that we befriended her for reasons that had nothing to do with hockey, and we did, but she's wrong about her ability.

If she had gotten the kind of coaching the rest of us did growing up she would have been amazing. As it was, she never did turn into a very good skater, but the rest of her game more than made up for it. In a way it's just as well she didn't get that coaching, because if she had, I'd be the second best hockey player in the household, and I don't know if the relationship would have survived her being better than I am at everything.

Speaking of the relationship surviving, getting to write the postscript means I get to pass along the good news. We're engaged.

It didn't work out well when I tried to be a wife, so I get to be the husband this time. Yes, I'm going to make her wear a wedding dress. I think I'll look fabulous in a tux. And I know she'll enjoy getting to act all girly. Forget the rest of it; her real dirty little secret is just how femme she really is.

Starting this fall, Phoebe is back in college hockey, as an assistant coach. At Michigan, of all places, so I guess some bygones actually can be bygones. She can still hate the color green, though.

It's not living happily ever after. I'm not perfect, and Lord knows she isn't either. We fight sometimes. Occasionally, we scream at each other. But you know what? It's better than all of those times we stared sullenly at anything except each other, not talking. It means that, whatever our problems are, we aren't scared of each other anymore. It's amazing how big a difference that makes.

And I am not going to screw it up this time. It took me thirty-five years, but I got my life to a place where I want to be with plenty of time left to enjoy it.

—Kitten

October 1997

For the very first time I am going to play hockey. I skate onto the ice with all the dignity a five-year-old can muster while on skates. The other kids aren't taking this as seriously as I am, and it irritates me. It's my baptism.

The game lasts ten minutes at most. I'm frustrated because what we are doing doesn't resemble real hockey. We're supposed to be passing and skating and scoring, but instead we just swarm around the puck and fall over a lot.

I push and shove and get my stick on the puck some. I fall fewer times than most. The highlight is when I actually guide the puck into one of the nets, which have been pulled to the bluelines.

It is the first day of the rest of my life.

ACKNOWLEDGMENTS

Becoming Phoebe came into existence the night of January 30, 2011, as I was driving home to Minneapolis from Madison, Wisconsin. Eight months prior, I'd switched my most intense sports loyalty from the University of Minnesota men's hockey team to the women's team. It was apparent that this was one of the best decisions of my life almost from the moment the puck dropped to start that season. As I returned from the first road trip I'd made with a sports team in twenty-five years, Phoebe and her story began to take form.

In the spring of 2012, that narrative I'd created became so compelling that I had to start writing it down. It's said that, to be a professional writer, you can't want to write; you have to need to write. This was the moment when I crossed that threshold. I originally intended to produce just a twenty-page character study so I could stop obsessing about the character. A hundred thousand words later, I had to figure out what to do with it, which led eventually to this book.

There are many, many people I need to thank for their help along the way. Perhaps the most important from the standpoint of bringing the story into existence are those who volunteered to read it and provide feedback along the way. The first of those was Lynda Jacobs, who read the scenes as I created them, completely out of order, and said that she wanted more. Sharon Danes read those hundred thousand words, still not in anything resembling chronological order, and said the same. Mark Gibbons overcame his reluctance to read the next draft of a novel a friend pushed on him. Paula Rice Biever provided invaluable beta feedback when I was a bit further along. Finally, based on a small number of conversations at 4th Street Fantasy, a shared love of hockey, and a shared dislike of a certain popular fantasy author, Marissa Lingen agreed to read the final product and, if she liked it, to provide a blog review and blurb for the cover; I guess she liked it, because I have the blurb.

I've had the pleasure of working with three different editors on this project, all of them immensely helpful. Keri Knutson read and edited the second and third drafts. Kellie Hultgren of KMH Editing did the same with the fourth and fifth. And Beth Wright of Trio Bookworks provided the copyediting and critical information on women's fashion. *Becoming Phoebe* would never have taken flight without them.

I am rarely productive at home, as I have three cats who strongly and falsely believe that their input would improve things. I do most of my writing at bars and restaurants, and there are several in Roseville, Minnesota, that deserve special thanks for their tolerance of someone taking up a booth and an electrical outlet and only ordering food intermittently: Stephanie and the rest of the crew at Buffalo Wild Wings; Panera; Chili's; the sadly defunct Don Pablo's; as well as the Zantigo's in Fridley.

I owe thanks to the folks who backed the Kickstarter that funded the process of turning Phoebe's story into an actual book, including, but not limited to Matthew Minton, Jonah Kaitz, Michael Carnow, Massimo Voci, Dave Murphy, and Myron Peabody of the Montgomery Ward Baseball League; Andrew Christian, Jolene Danner, and Keith Apperson of the Mpls/St. Paul Pathfinder Society; Wendy Istvanick, Lindsey Huntoon, John Edwards, and Paula Rice Biever from the old days of hockey-l; Dave Malerich, Linda and Will Kenny, Bob Milligan and Sharon Danes, Barb Hoese, and Mark and Paula Gibbons of the Power Play Club; Mary Green, Nancy Mickenbecker, Richard Graham, Gene, and Roger Moore from the community at Balloon Juice; Sydney Sweitzer, Leslie Wolfe, Phyllis

Overstreet, Scott Slemmons, William Whyte, Julian Neal, Michael Corcoran, Dan Dolan, and Douglas Katzer.

There are several people I need to single out for contributions that extend far beyond just backing the Kickstarter: David Burton, who has been a reliable friend and then some for twenty-five years; Charles Franklin and Liann Kosaki, who share some responsibility as the people who host me in Madison every year; Annabelle Shepard, who provides all the support that grandmothers are capable of; Kathy Terry, who did as much as anyone to make me feel welcome in the world of Gopher women's hockey; Marianne Jackson, who provided thought-provoking feedback on other stories at critical times; and Carrie Neal Jackson, who has tolerated a brother's teasing, with varying degrees of forbearance, for longer than she can actually remember.

None of this would have happened without my parents, John and Gretchen Jackson. While there is a lot of myself in Phoebe, our families couldn't be more different, and I am eternally grateful for their love and support all along the way. My father in particular has been a part of my hockey fandom, and I never would have appreciated it the way I do without him.

Lastly, I owe thanks to the women who have played varsity hockey at the University of Minnesota and around the WCHA for providing the inspiration for Phoebe's very existence and the framework in which she could grow and thrive. I look forward to being a fan for many years to come.